To Make Matters *Worse*

A novel by: Elle Rivers

Copyright © 2022 by Elle Rivers

All rights reserved.

No portion of this book may be reproduced in any form without written permission from the publisher or author, except as permitted by U.S. copyright law.

Editing by: Kasey Kubica

Cover Design by: Elle Rivers

Contents

	To...	V
1.	A Note from Elle	1
2.	Chapter One	2
3.	Chapter Two	15
4.	Chapter Three	26
5.	Chapter Four	43
6.	Chapter Five	65
7.	Chapter Six	80
8.	Chapter Seven	91
9.	Chapter Eight	99
10.	Chapter Nine	109
11.	Chapter Ten	122
12.	Chapter Eleven	142
13.	Chapter Twelve	152
14.	Chapter Thirteen	170
15.	Chapter Fourteen	193
16.	Chapter Fifteen	205

17.	Chapter Sixteen	216
18.	Chapter Seventeen	229
19.	Chapter Eighteen	243
20.	Chapter Nineteen	263
21.	Chapter Twenty	284
22.	Chapter Twenty-One	298
23.	Chapter Twenty-Two	313
24.	Chapter Twenty-Three	326
25.	Chapter Twenty-Four	331
26.	Acknowledgments	345
27.	If You Liked This...	346
28.	About the Author	349

To . . .

For my found family.
You mean everything to me.

A Note from Elle

Please be advised that this novel contains topics readers may be sensitive to. There is an on-page collapse of an apartment, emotional manipulation, and arguments between characters that some may find toxic.

I want every reader to take care of themselves, so if you find any of these topics to be too much for you, feel free to skip scenes or this novel. If you find any topics I have not mentioned, please reach out to me on Instagram at @elleswrites, and I will rectify the situation.

Chapter One

Violet

Contrary to popular belief, Violet didn't intend to be the one at the engagement party to have a drink thrown on her.

Things just happened that way.

The party was in full swing. The venue was filled with people—some Violet knew, others she didn't. It was after seven, which was when the party was supposed to begin.

And *he* was late.

Violet took another sip of her drink. This wasn't like him, but she wasn't worried.

She was hopeful.

This was actually the best-case scenario. She wanted a good night. If *he* came then it wasn't going to be anything close to good. It was going to end in a bloodbath.

And since this was her best friend's engagement party, *bloodbath* was not the goal.

Violet turned to the bride-to-be, who was in the center of the occupied room. Her curly hair was piled onto her head into a gorgeous bun, and her brown skin was shimmering against the soft light.

Liv was going to be an amazing bride. Her skin glowed, her smile dazzled, and it wasn't even the big day.

Her fiancé, Lewis, looked just as happy. His light, curly hair was styled today, sitting a bit more organized than usual. He was wearing a white button-down shirt to match Liv's form-fitting white dress, and his hand hadn't left hers all night. They looked perfect.

"You look fantastic!" Violet said the moment Liv saw her. She pulled her friend into a tight hug.

"Thank you!" Liv said. "I can't believe any of this is real."

"You're perfect together," Violet reminded them. "So, I can. I can't wait to help with the wedding."

Violet wouldn't be sleeping for the next few weeks in order to get everything done, but she would manage.

"Are you sure you're not too busy?" Liv asked. "I know you've got your job to deal with . . ."

And she did. Violet's job as a middle school teacher barely paid her bills and took up all of her time, but she loved it—just like she loved Liv. She would make it work.

"Your family is spread out across the country," Violet replied. "I know how hard it was getting them here for the party, and they have to fly back in for the wedding. I can help. I promise."

"Are you sure?" Liv repeated.

"Of course I am," she replied.

Liv smiled and hugged Violet again, obviously grateful. These moments were worth the stress.

When Liv pulled away, she glanced at Lewis, who was looking at his phone with a frown. Violet instantly knew who he was texting, and by the nervous look on Liv's face, so did she.

"Come on. Let's go get something to drink," Liv said, her voice tight.

"I have something," Violet replied, showing her friend the half-full cup she was holding.

"Well, you need another."

"It's fine," Lewis said, putting his phone away. "We want Violet to be able to drive home, right?"

Violet wanted to ask what was going on, and she knew who it was about.

Why wasn't *he* here? He never missed an event like this, especially not when Lewis was involved. They were best friends.

But if Violet asked, she wouldn't get an answer, and maybe it was for the best. Liv and Lewis knew Violet shouldn't be around *him* at any cost.

It was obvious Lewis had some information, though. And judging by the way Liv was glancing at him, her best friend was curious.

"You know what? I think I want some of those little cupcakes I saw," Violet said, ignoring the rotten feeling in her chest. She hated stepping away, especially when it was for *him*. "I'll catch you guys later?"

Violet wished Liv would have stopped her, but when the other woman's smile turned grateful, she knew she was doing the right thing.

Pushing down her bitterness, Violet walked away. She went to the cupcake table, sighing as she got a dessert she didn't actually want.

This sucked. Why didn't *he* cancel and get it over with? Why make things worse by holding Lewis and Liv hostage?

Violet's thoughts were turning dark, and it didn't help that her other friends were busy chatting with the happy couple. Violet hated being alone with her thoughts. She always liked having someone to talk to.

But then, as if her body knew what was happening, *Charlie Davis* walked in.

Violet didn't know how she could tell when he arrived. Maybe it was Lewis turning around suddenly. Maybe it was the fact the venue got quiet for half a second. Maybe Violet knew Charlie better than she wanted to.

He was taller than her, with an angled face that would be attractive to some. He had brown hair that used to be lighter when he was younger, and bright blue eyes.

He was smiling when he entered, carrying a huge bouquet of the prettiest flowers Violet had ever seen.

She rolled her eyes. Of course—he was late because he was picking up flowers.

And to make matters worse, his devastatingly beautiful girlfriend, Lauren, was right next to him. Her red hair glistened in the low light, and her eyes were confident, as if she owned the place.

Violet put the cupcake back and went for another drink instead.

It was going to be a long night.

Charlie

Charlie was pointedly ignoring Violet Moore's presence. He had seen her the moment he walked in. She was in the corner with the same sour expression on her face whenever she saw him. He wanted to go to her and start a fight he probably shouldn't, but Lewis had begged him over text to avoid her, and that's what he was going to do.

"You can't help it if she bothers you." Lauren noticed where his eyes lingered. "Lewis has no right to ask you to hold back your emotions."

"I know," Charlie replied. He was already irritated, despite the night being young. "But it's my friend's engagement party, so I'm going to try."

Lauren sighed the same way she did whenever Lewis asked for him to keep the peace. Sometimes Charlie wondered if Lauren even liked peace, or if she would rather watch him argue with the five-foot-three schoolteacher who despised him.

Either way he looked at it, the sparring had earned him a reputation.

Everyone knew Violet and Charlie hated each other. And Charlie didn't like to be *that* guy. He may not be perfect, but he never wanted to be known for petty fights, but he couldn't help it when it came to her.

She was always under his skin, ever since she woke up one day and decided their friendship was over. And try as he might, he could never let her get the last word.

Charlie planned to talk to Lewis but snuck one more glance at Violet. She was wearing a light blue dress, which was tight and hugged her figure. She was a slight woman, but he had only seen her in her looser A-line dresses for school.

Tonight, she looked... different. She looked less like she belonged at the front of the class and more like she was heading to an evening dinner. Her shoulder-length dark brown hair was curled, spiraling against her face. Her deep brown eyes looked to anywhere but him.

"Come on." Lauren grabbed his arm tightly. "Let's not think about her. We should go greet the guests of honor."

Charlie swallowed dryly and nodded. Their fights had earned them a reputation. Just like everyone else at the party who knew their history, he was nervous. Neither he nor Violet knew how tonight was going to go. They could easily ruin the party by simply speaking to each other.

Liv and Lewis had been keeping them apart for years, after all.

"Hey, man," Charlie greeted Lewis, pulling him into a hug. Lewis looked on edge, and yet, he looked perfect next to Liv, his fiancé. Charlie truly hoped their marriage lasted. "I brought these for you two."

"Oh wow," Liv said, smiling. "These are beautiful." She gingerly took them from him and set them on the table next to her. They added a stunning pop of color to the scenery. Charlie hated to be late, but he hated not bringing anything to an engagement party more.

"And Lauren," Liv started, turning to her, "good to see you too."

"You as well," Lauren said, a slight smile on her face.

His on-and-off girlfriend had never been invested in his friendships. Lauren, Charlie, and Lewis grew up together, but she and Lewis never truly got along. She mostly saw them when she was with Charlie, and half of that time Charlie figured he didn't even need to invite her.

Their turbulent relationship was hard, but it was all they could manage. Tonight, they were off, and Lauren was only here as a friend. But he knew how this went. They were heading back into relationship territory.

"I'm glad you could make it," Lewis told him. "When you said you'd be late, I didn't think it would be for flowers."

"Only the best for you two."

"And about the other thing..."

Charlie held his hands up. "I've got it. I won't bother her."

He snuck a glance and found Violet talking to Micah, another of their college friends. Micah wore a long dress, similarly colored to Violet's.

Violet was possibly one of the most giving people he had ever met. She would drop everything for others, and when she smiled, Charlie could have sworn the room grew brighter.

And she was smiling at Micah. Her prominent upper lip was curved in a beautifully captivating smile, one he was never the recipient of these days, in recent years, even. As much as Charlie could appreciate her from afar, he could never stop the large twinge of bitterness that tightened his body whenever he saw her.

She could be a ray of sunshine for nearly anyone, and yet to him, she was cold, cruel.

Lewis cleared his throat, and Charlie turned quickly, trying to push her out of his thoughts.

His friends knew they hated each other. Most hangouts were planned around when the other wouldn't be there. They were gracious about it, but this was Lewis and Liv's engagement party—their celebration of the joining of their lives.

It shouldn't be about Charlie and Violet.

So, *why* couldn't he stop looking at her?

"Sorry," Charlie said, shaking his head. "We're going to be fine."

Both Liv and Lewis glanced at each other. It was clear they didn't believe him. Next to him, he could feel Lauren's annoyance rolling off her in waves.

Charlie wanted to spend more time with them, but he also didn't want to piss off Lauren. He said, "We've taken enough of your time. I can tell your family is wanting to talk to you guys. We'll be around."

He smiled and led Lauren to the refreshments table, the farthest place away from Violet.

"Ugh, they're so on your ass about Violet," Lauren muttered. "She always starts it."

"They want to have a good party," Charlie defended his friends.

"They could have a great one if they didn't invite her."

That was never going to happen. Liv and Violet loved each other. At this point, they were basically sisters. They roomed together for years in college, and their friendship had only grown stronger with the challenges of adulthood. Liv wasn't going to drop Violet for any reason.

But Lauren hated it when Charlie would tell her that.

After a few moments of silence, Lauren announced, "I'm thirsty."

Violet was intermingling in the middle of the room again, talking to someone he doubted she knew. There was *that* smile again.

"You should go get a drink," Charlie told her.

Lauren shook her head, muttering something under her breath before leaving. Charlie could only sigh. Lauren was always in a bad mood when they were with his friends, and he didn't understand why.

Her bad attitude was already rubbing off on him. And instead of taking a moment away from the crowd of people, his eyes drifted over to Violet again—the usual bane of his existence. She was on the move, and his heart stopped when he figured out she was heading toward the food table, right where he was. It was like she was drawn to negativity.

Drawn to him.

Charlie didn't think Violet had noticed him yet, and by the time he got his wits about him, she was standing next to him, her eyes meeting his.

Shit. There was no going back.

Charlie bit his tongue. He needed to leave, yet his feet rooted him to the spot. Defensiveness and anger, years in the making, simmered under his skin.

Violet rolled her eyes and moved past him. She smelled like jasmine and sugar. A person like her shouldn't smell so addictive.

"You know, I thought of you today," she said, turning to him. Charlie blinked for a moment, his skin warm. Why the fuck would she be thinking of him? "And it reminded me I needed to take my trash to the dumpster."

And there it was.

"At least I'm getting taken out more than you are."

God, he hated how he was when he was around her. He didn't talk like this to anyone else. But once it started, there was no going back.

Neither of them *ever* backed down.

"It should probably be by a hitman," she replied. "Do you know any?"

"If I did then you wouldn't be bothering me right now."

"If I'm bothering you, there's an easy solution. You could leave. Maybe you should have canceled entirely. It would have spared me some grief."

"Maybe if you hadn't walked over here, you could have spared it yourself."

"I didn't see you until I was here," she snapped. "Besides, you've been looking over at me the whole time you've been here. Don't think I didn't notice."

"The only thing I was noticing is what you were wearing to your best friend's engagement party."

"What's wrong with what I'm wearing?"

"It's a little rude to try to upstage the bride by wearing the tightest dress you could find."

Violet's cheeks turned red, and Charlie enjoyed the fact he had stunned her into silence—even if it was only for a moment.

She always had something smart to say. When he had seen her last, months ago, he said he was jealous of all the people who hadn't met her.

Violet responded only a second later and told him he was human version of menstrual cramps.

It was a never-ending cycle.

"I would never try to upstage Liv!" Violet cried out.

"Did you get that thing at Walmart in the little girl's section?"

"Target, actually. And it was the *adult* section. Not that you'd know anything about being an adult with the level of immaturity you have."

It was a multi-layered burn. He *hated* it when she did that. He always spent too long coming up with a response, and by the time he had something to say, she was firing off again.

"And by the way," she continued, "if you're going to be late to your best friend's engagement party because you wanted to suck up with flowers, try picking out a bouquet that doesn't look like it's from the clearance section of a dollar store."

"That bouquet was forty dollars."

"Honestly, you probably should have brought your winning personality instead. Oh wait, that's shit too."

"Moore, give your parents my condolences," he said, gritting his teeth. "They need it."

"Careful, Davis, don't tire yourself out. That's the most syllables you can use in one word. Don't push it."

"I wish we were better strangers."

"We could be."

"You talked to *me*. You did this to yourself."

"And you keep answering me. It takes two to have a conversation. How about you use your ridiculous height to take the high road for once?"

"I can't when all you do is use your tiny stature to get under my fucking skin. The bar is in hell, and somehow you are playing limbo with it."

They were standing close now. Violet's cheeks were a light pink, glittering like little diamonds in the dim light. He *hated* that she was so annoying and so pretty.

"The only thing I'm playing limbo with is your ability to find a good comeback."

"Do you even have a soul?"

"Yes, and it's confident enough not to be late for shitty flowers."

"You couldn't *afford* shitty flowers."

"Oh, okay. Since you're so fucking well off, how about you buy a ticket to a deserted island and stay there? You can take your stupid girlfriend and get the fuck out of my hair."

They were chest to chest at this point, and Charlie breathed heavily. He wanted to shut her up. He wanted to shock her with a response so mind-blowing she would finally, *finally*, be beaten for once.

Then a drink was thrown on Violet's back.

The other partygoers gasped, and Charlie swore he saw a camera flash. Violet turned, looking like she wanted to *stab* whoever had done that.

Lauren held an empty cup in her hand.

"Get the fuck off my boyfriend, Moore." Lauren's tone was ice.

Violet took a moment to seethe, and when she looked back at Charlie, he wondered if she was about to pay it forward by dumping something on him too.

"Next time you think about talking to me, remember that you're incapable of finishing what you start—your girlfriend has to do it for you."

Charlie wanted to answer, to say something as mean and conniving, but Violet turned and walked away before he could, which was somehow more insulting than her staying.

"Good riddance," Lauren muttered.

Now that Violet was out of his sight, he could think clearly. The haze over his mind loosened, and he felt bad—like he usually did after she was gone.

"Why did you do that?" he asked Lauren.

"Oh, come on." Lauren sounded proud of herself. "She insulted you."

"That was between us."

Lauren rolled her eyes. "And? You were causing a scene and she was getting *way* too close. Shouldn't you be happy I stuck up for you?"

"I don't think the drink was the way to do it," Charlie said.

"Whatever. She had it coming," Lauren nonchalantly replied. "Let's go dance. It's starting to get interesting with her out of the picture."

Lauren dragged him to the corner of the venue where people were dancing. He went willingly, but he caught Lewis's eyes while doing so.

Lewis looked disappointed, but not surprised.

Liv shook her head and went after Violet, who had left the main hall in a rush.

Charlie looked away, feeling like shit for doing this at their party. He needed to be better. He wanted to be better.

But there was something about Violet Moore that always stopped him.

Violet

Her dress was ruined.

Luckily it was cheap, but that didn't make her like it any less. She hoped to wear it on a date if she ever got one.

But now it was going into the trash the minute she got home, which was going to have to be soon, considering she was cold, wet, and looked halfway feral with the red stain all over her.

Violet leaned against the counter of the venue's bathroom, running her hands through her hair. She felt like she always did whenever she saw Charlie—annoyed, embarrassed, and stupid.

She shouldn't have talked to him. But he had looked so smug, so full of himself, like he always did. He arrived late to their friends' celebration and he didn't even feel bad. His only goal was to look nice by bringing flowers, nothing else.

Only she knew what he was *really* like.

Violet knew she was still fuming. Whether it was the drink, or the comments about her dress, or his general existence, she didn't know.

But it was an uncomfortable feeling.

The door to the bathroom crept open, and when Violet saw Liv, her anger turned into guilt. Her friend didn't look mad, but she didn't look happy, either.

Violet felt terrible. She should have been able to keep it together, and now that she was looking back, it would have been easier if she had walked away.

"I'm sorry," Violet said immediately. "I didn't think . . . the drink . . ."

"It's fine," Liv said, coming in fully. "I figured this would happen when we invited you two."

Violet looked away, face aflame.

Liv was never mad about their fights. But Violet was terrified that one day Liv would get tired of it and wash her hands of them. She already made the effort to plan different social events to keep them apart; it couldn't get much worse.

Liv sighed. "Hey, don't be upset. At least it wasn't Charlie who threw a drink on you."

"I hate her," Violet muttered.

"I'm with you there. It's one thing to have you and Charlie in each other's faces, but she made it physical. I don't know why he still sees her."

"Because they both suck."

Liv winced and Violet let go of some of her anger. To her, it was so obvious why Charlie liked Lauren. Fake people loved other fake people. Violet was simply the only one who had seen Charlie's other side.

"I'm sorry about the stain." Liv changed the subject and Violet let her. "What started it?"

"He said I looked bad."

"Did he?" Liv asked, looking skeptical.

"He implied it."

Liv sighed and shook her head. "I'm sure some version of that happened. Let me guess, you gave it as good as you got?"

"Yeah . . ."

Liv was quiet for a moment, but then she sighed. "Lewis asked Charlie to stay away from you tonight. He was trying to avoid a fight."

Violet cringed. "Then I'm at fault. I started the conversation."

"You didn't know," Liv said. "And I know better than to think you guys aren't going to fight. We've managed to keep you apart in the past, but we can't have two separate weddings to continue that."

"I know," Violet said. "I would never ask that."

"But I guess fighting with him is in your DNA. So, I'm not going to ask you *not* to fight with him. Just . . . do it outside? Away from people? Think of it as a wedding gift."

Violet sighed. She hated herself for even making Liv feel the need to ask this of her.

"Of course. Consider it done."

"And for planning, how about you come over Tuesday night?"

Violet almost jumped at the chance to hang out with her friend, but she paused.

"Isn't that Charlie and Lewis's game night?" she asked.

"It is, but we can't let you guys avoid each other only to then fight at events. I'm sure Lewis would rather keep you two in different rooms, but I'm tired of it. Let's do it at our apartment for practice."

"What, like practice fighting?"

"Practice fighting *outside*."

"I don't know if that will work."

"It'll be fine."

"Liv, I don't want to ruin your night."

"You won't. I know what I'm getting into. Besides, if you're not busy fighting, then you can help address wedding invitations."

Damn. Liv was going right where it hurt. Her friend knew Violet would never say no if she was needed.

"Okay," Violet said. "I'll give it a shot."

Liv smiled. "Perfect. Now get home. You need a hot shower."

Chapter Two

Charlie

Tuesday night was one of Charlie's favorite times of the week. Game nights meant he got one-on-one time with Lewis; since Charlie lived alone, rarely saw Lauren, and didn't have many other friends, it was nice to hang out with someone who truly enjoyed his company.

With the wedding so soon, Lewis asked that they postpone game night until after it was over. This Tuesday was the last one for the time being, and he wanted to enjoy it.

Charlie and Lewis had a routine. They would meet up at Lewis's place and scroll through the unlimited food options in walking distance of the apartment. Then they would pick a game to play for a few hours, settling in to catch up on everything going on in each other's lives.

His friend's home was tiny, at only five hundred square feet. It was a one-bedroom unit on the third floor of a modern-living apartment complex. Sometimes it was a tight fit, but Liv was usually out, so they made it work.

When Charlie arrived at Lewis's at five, he saw a car parked in his usual spot. It wasn't one he recognized, but it still irked him. His routine was slightly off but he chalked it up to a guest of a neighbor and thought nothing of it.

After a busy day, he was more than ready to relax. Unfortunately, he quickly figured out relaxing wasn't an option when the door opened and Violet was on the other side of it.

"Sorry, man," Lewis said, coming from behind Violet. "Liv insisted."

Violet stepped away and Charlie fought not to glare at her. Why was she *here*? Wasn't it an unspoken rule to keep Violet as far away from him as possible?

"Insisted on what?" Charlie asked.

"A practice run," Liv said from the dining room. "On taking your fights *outside*."

Lewis looked at Charlie's expression for all of one second, and then said, "This isn't going to work."

"No one thought to ask me if I was okay with Violet being here?" Charlie asked. Violet looked at Liv questioningly, but Liv only shrugged.

No one else answered.

"We could . . . reschedule?" Lewis offered.

Violet looked at him with raised eyebrows. He knew her. She wasn't going to back down, and if he did, she would never let him live it down.

"It'll be fine," Charlie muttered.

"All right," Liv said. "If either of you get a whiff of each other's blood, go outside."

"I'm fine," Violet replied. Her stance loosened, and for a moment, Charlie thought she was *actually* fine. Then she glared at him in her strange, relaxed form, which looked so unnatural that Charlie thought maybe she was a witch.

Violet returned to Liv at the dining room table. She tried to act as if Charlie wasn't even there.

He was kind of offended.

"Come on," Lewis urged. "Let's play a game."

"Shouldn't we find dinner?"

"Violet brought fried chicken," Lewis said. "But if you wanted . . . I could eat again."

"If she brought it, I doubt she meant for it to be for me."

Lewis rolled his eyes, but Charlie was sticking with that theory.

"You can have some," Violet cut in. "I brought it for everyone."

Charlie wasn't sure he heard that right.

Maybe this was a test to see if he would lose his mind. Maybe she had already thrown the rest away and was gearing up to watch him look for food that wasn't there.

Surely, Violet wasn't being nice to him. He didn't think that was even possible.

"Fine," he said, not sure which was worse. Turning her down or taking her up on the offer. "I think I'll have some. Thank you, Violet."

For a moment, Violet tensed, as if the words were mean. Then her shoulders slowly relaxed and she looked halfway normal.

Liv looked impressed.

Lewis still looked worried.

Charlie spared one last glance at Violet before he served up a plate of food. He didn't imagine Violet made much money with her job, but at least she had gotten chicken from one of the best places in Nashville. It was still hot too.

He ate quickly, and chatted with Lewis, carefully avoiding topics Violet could interject on. His best option was the bachelor party. Charlie had been asked to arrange it since he was Lewis's best man. The current plan was a relaxing Saturday night with their friends. Elijah, another groomsman, had been insisting Lewis have one since it was his last "single" night.

Charlie didn't know whether or not he wanted this responsibility.

"I don't want any strippers," Lewis said. It was not the first time he had said it. It wouldn't be the last. Charlie knew Elijah disagreed with him *strongly* there. "N-not that I don't respect the profession, but I'm not wanting to look at other women."

"Amen," Liv called.

Elijah wanted to hire them as a goodbye to Lewis's single days. It wasn't going to be fun telling the guy no, but at least being best man meant he got the final say one way or another.

"Don't worry," he said, despite his own worries. "I'll make sure of it."

"I mean this whole bachelor party business isn't my thing anyway. We could always cancel and not have it."

"Nope, you need a day off," Liv called from the other room. Charlie dared a glance over at the table and found Violet quietly watching. "You've been working overtime to pay for the honeymoon and the decorations. Take some time for you and the guys to relax."

Lewis didn't look happy about it, but he let it go. Charlie tore his eyes from Violet and looked at his friend.

"About that video game . . . you need a distraction," Lewis said, seeing where Charlie's eyes had been lingering.

Gaming with Lewis was one of his favorite things to do. But this time, he could feel Violet's presence in the room like a jasmine-and-sugar candle left burning for too long.

He couldn't focus, and Lewis could tell. When Charlie was staring at the TV, he couldn't see Violet. What if she hurled a stapler at his head?

She had never made it physical before, but that was before the drink incident at the engagement party. He was waiting for the consequences of Lauren's actions to come back to bite him in the ass.

"I know this is weird," Lewis said after a few minutes of distracted gameplay. His voice was low, as if he didn't want Violet or Liv to hear them. Charlie glanced at Violet again, and she seemed focused.

"Yeah, it is," Charlie replied under his breath. "Did you check her for weapons? I'm afraid she's waiting to throw a knife at me."

Lewis sighed.

"It was a joke," Charlie said.

"You are so different with her. I don't get it." Lewis shook his head. "But it doesn't matter. Listen, Charlie . . . Liv asked for a specific wedding gift."

"And?"

"Liv asked for Violet not to publicly fight with you at the wedding. That's it. That's the gift."

"She only agreed *as a gift*?" Charlie asked. How low could Violet be?

"I'm asking the same of you."

"I mean, of course I'll do it. I'll try. But it doesn't have to be a gift. I'll just do it."

"Will you?" Lewis asked. "It's important to us. We want to have a decent wedding without the public fights. Liv thinks it being outside is enough, but I genuinely want no fights. At all."

Charlie wished he could say yes. He wished he could promise it. But he didn't know if Violet would keep up her end of the deal.

"I'll do it if she does."

Lewis sighed. "I guess that's all I can ask."

Charlie nodded, feeling sick to his stomach. This should be something he could promise. It should be easy, compared to the other things they could ask. So why wasn't it? What about Violet sent him spiraling into anger every time?

A clearing of a throat interrupted his thoughts. Charlie was surprised to find Violet standing in front of him, looking nervous but also firm.

He couldn't help but take note of her solar system dress. She looked like Ms. Frizzle but with tamed, brown hair. He wanted to make a comment, but swallowed it.

Hard.

"Davis," she said forcefully. She hadn't used his first name in years. "Can I talk to you?"

"Me?" he asked.

"Yes, you." She said it like she wanted to say more, as if she had a biting comment behind it.

Lewis glanced between them, worry on his face. But Charlie couldn't get past what his friend had asked, and how hopeful he had looked while doing so.

Charlie had to try.

"Yeah, fine."

"Let's step out on the balcony," she suggested. Without a word, Violet turned and went outside, her dress flowing with her.

"Is this a good idea?" Lewis asked.

"I did say to take it outside," Liv reminded him.

Without another word, Charlie followed Violet, unsure of what was about to happen. She wouldn't go so far as to push him off the balcony, right?

Violet

"I heard Lewis ask you not to fight with me," Violet said, ignoring her racing heart. It had been killing her to sit at the table and work without saying anything to him. But she did it. And now she wanted to be sure Charlie was going to do the same.

"How?" Charlie asked. "We were across the room."

Violet crossed her arms. "You have two brain cells and they're both fighting for third place. I teach middle schoolers. I have good ears."

"And they still don't pay you more than fifty thousand a year?"

That hurt, and Violet had no doubt he had meant for it to. The reason she was in a teaching job instead of going to grad school was his fault anyway. Of course he'd rub it in.

Violet wanted to make a scathing, mean remark. Technically, she could—they *were* outside.

"What did you say to Lewis?" she asked instead.

Charlie paused. That was obviously not the reaction he was expecting from her, and she didn't even blame him. Usually she would have blown up, but she was focused.

"I said I'd do it if you did," he replied.

Violet paused. She could do this. She had to. This was her best friend's *wedding*.

"Of course I can. I can get along with anyone."

Charlie shook his head, his forehead creased in a way that should have been unattractive.

"We have six years of experience telling us you can't," Charlie reminded her.

"I can. I'm an English teacher in the public school system, remember? I get along with people I dislike all the time."

"Please. You couldn't be friends with me if someone paid you."

Violet glared at him, letting the challenge wash over her. *He* was the one who had started all of this six years ago. Was he expecting her to let it go, without so much as an apology? *He* had gone from being kind to cruel in an afternoon—not her.

But this was Liv. And Charlie was challenging her. She had put a lot of pain in a lot of boxes before. She could do it again.

"I can be friends with you," Violet said. She forced her voice to go to its normal tone, almost as if she were talking to a sixth grader who had thrown gum at her.

Charlie stared at her like she was growing a second head.

It was almost enough to make Violet break, but she didn't.

"That's . . . weird," he said.

"I'm pretending you're one of my students."

"I don't like it."

"Are we doing this?" Violet asked. "Because you said I couldn't be friends with you, and I know I can. Can *you* be friends with me?"

"I'm friends with everyone."

"Even me?"

Charlie's smugness turned into something that almost looked pained. "Of . . . course."

"Here's the deal." Violet's voice was serious. "We're not going to like this. But we do this until the wedding, got it?"

"So, we're friends until the wedding?"

"As soon as the reception is over, we can meet in an alleyway and let each other have it. Sound good?" Violet said, holding out her hand.

"Can I make a list of all the things you're inevitably going to do in the next few weeks that piss me off?"

"Only if I can too. We can even hurl insults at each other like in-laws at Thanksgiving. The point is, we bury this feud in the darkest depths of the ocean until after the wedding. Got it?"

"Fine." Charlie didn't look happy about it. Violet wanted to laugh at his pained, annoyed expression, but she would save that for the moment the wedding was over.

Violet nodded, forcing herself to smile.

"I preferred it when you glared at me," Charlie said uneasily.

Oh. Maybe there was an upside to this. Seeing Charlie squirm was *fun*.

"Come on, *friend*," Violet said, smiling wider. "We've got this."

"God, this is terrible." Charlie groaned, but his hand met hers. It was warm and solid, and it made all of this real. "But I'll do it. Only so I can rub it in your face that I *can* do it."

"I'm the only one smiling right now," Violet told him.

"That's not a smile."

"What are you talking about? This is definitely a smile."

"It's unnatural."

"I'm just being sweet."

"Stop!"

Violet laughed and Charlie stared at her, displeasure on his face.

"You need a better poker face if this is going to work," Violet said. "I've got years of practice with my students."

"Go inside, Moore."

As always, Charlie's use of her last name made her want to stomp on his dreams and make him cry, but she buried the feeling in the darkest pits of hell and turned to walk inside.

"Wait, are you actually going inside? Are you listening to me?"

"Only to give our friends the *good news*."

Charlie glared at her, but she only smiled. It was so easy to piss him off. If anyone was going to break, it wouldn't be her.

"Oh good, you're still alive," Liv called from the dining room table. "I win ten bucks."

"You only win it if the cops weren't called," Lewis said. "They weren't, right?"

"He's still standing," Violet told them. "He's coming in soon. He needed some air."

"You seem . . . oddly elated," Liv said. "What happened?"

"Oh, nothing," Violet replied. "Nothing bad anyway. Charlie and I had a good conversation and—"

"We decided to be friends."

Violet turned to glare. Not only had he interrupted her, but he stole her thunder too.

He was such a *dick*.

And he knew he was pissing her off. He was all smiles now that she was scowling at him. The worst part about it was that he had a decent smile. It was like the Antichrist came down with the face of Chris Pine.

"What?" both Liv and Lewis asked.

"Right," Violet said, turning back to them. All she had to do was think of Charlie as one of her students and she'd be fine. She'd never wanted to run over one of her students with a monster truck loaded with explosives no matter how irritating they could be, so she could stop herself with Charlie too. "Friends."

"Yep. We're letting bygones be bygones and trying out friendship for your wedding."

There was a long moment of silence. Liv started laughing.

"No," she said between cackles. "There's no way!"

"Guys, you don't have to do this," Lewis added.

Violet knew her friends wouldn't believe her, but Liv's laughter combined with Lewis's immediate dismissal felt like a challenge. She glanced at Charlie and saw he had the same expression she felt.

After all, they did have one thing in common.

They didn't like to lose.

"We're trying to move forward. It'll be good for everyone!"

"No more thinking about the past," Charlie added. "It's all about the future. And in the future, we may be *best* friends."

Ugh. Too far. Now they sounded like they were used car salespeople trying to offload a lemon.

"This is . . ." Lewis began.

"Perfect!" Liv said. Violet blinked, knowing there was no way Liv was convinced that quickly. She was playing along.

Lewis wasn't.

"Don't you see, Lewis? Now we get the best of both worlds. They can dance together at the wedding. We were trying to find a good partner for Violet anyway."

Oh God. Anything but that.

Violet and Charlie were in the wedding party. For months now, Violet had assumed she would be dancing with Damon, which was the best out of the three groomsmen Lewis had. The other groomsman, Elijah, was a guy Violet dated briefly, and it ended with many tears. She and Damon had barely ever talked, but even so, he was the best option; she had the least amount of bad history with him.

Of course, if she and Charlie could manage it, Liv was going to let Violet stand next to her at the altar. Liv's sister, Bree, was too busy to be maid of honor, and Violet had been bestowed that spot. Charlie was Lewis's best man, which meant they would be standing in the first spot behind Liv and Lewis. They not only had to make it down the aisle at the end of the wedding, but pose together for photos.

Liv sheepishly admitted they were thinking about not having one or both of them in those positions because of the possibility of disaster, but in the end, no one knew Liv and Lewis better than Violet and Charlie.

"Of . . . course we can," Charlie said. His voice sound strangled, but at least he was still smiling. His arm came to rest around Violet's shoulders, and she had to fight every cell in her body to stay still. She wanted to *run*. "That's what friends do!"

"Oh yeah, they do . . . dance together," Violet added.

"Oh my God," Lewis muttered, rubbing his palm over his face.

"You two should take lessons. I have a few places in mind. I'll text them to you," Liv said, her face set into a smirk.

Ugh. She'd rather be tied to a chair than take a dancing class with Charlie.

"Sure!" Violet said, somehow forcing her fake smile back onto her face. Charlie was *still* touching her. He was too warm, he smelled too good, and it had been far too long since Violet had been on a date with anyone.

Somehow, Charlie felt sort of *nice*.

"And I will get the details from Violet . . . you know, since we're friends," Charlie said.

"Of course," Violet said, trying not to pass out from the heat radiating off of him. It was like being far too close to a fire. "This is all going to be perfect."

It was *so* not going to be perfect. It was probably going to end in murder, and she wasn't sure which one of them would be left alive.

Chapter Three

Charlie

Charlie had a routine. He woke up at six and went for a jog. Then, he would make coffee, eat a bowl of oatmeal, and go to work.

To some, his routine might have been boring, but to him, it was everything. His work was mentally taxing, and the regular exercise and healthy food made sure he was prepared for the day ahead.

He worked for a large IT company. He had his master's degree in computer science, and now held a high-level position in coding for website design. He was busy nearly every day from the moment he walked in to the moment he left.

After this morning's routine, Charlie drove to work in a decent mood. He got in, brewed more coffee in the break room, and turned to find one of the directors of the company waiting for him.

"Hi, Paula," Charlie said. She was looking at him expectantly. "How are you today?"

"My computer is frozen again."

Charlie nodded. Technically, this wasn't his job. Paula needed to call IT and deal with the problem through the proper channels. But no one was going to tell the director of the company no.

He assumed the director of an *information technology* company would know something about *technology*, but Paula was over sales. Computers somehow weren't a part of her daily life, so she didn't understand even the most basic things about technology.

Paula liked to feel important and getting Charlie to do her IT work for her probably made her feel just that. He went along with it; there was no point in making a fuss. He gestured to her office and followed her in.

As he worked on her computer, Paula sat across from him, trying and failing to look innocent.

"How is that girl you're seeing?"

Charlie grimaced. He hated when people asked about Lauren at work, especially Paula.

"She's fine," Charlie replied.

"Any plans to move in soon and start a family?"

"No, not yet."

"Well, there's got to be something wrong with her, then. Why make you wait?"

Charlie paused. If he was being honest with himself, he knew it wasn't Lauren making him wait. It was mutual. For one, he and Lauren couldn't stay together for more than a few months at a time. Two, Lauren hated where he lived and preferred her apartment.

And three, Charlie could never see himself loving someone enough to move in with them. He didn't know if he believed in love in the first place. His parents had failed at it. He knew millions of others did too.

Ultimately, people couldn't be trusted to stay. They relied on feelings, and those faded. There were times he wanted nothing more than to drop Lauren out of his life, but then there were times where he wanted to keep her close. When that loneliness set in, he almost wanted to keep *anyone* close.

He knew he loved her. He had to after dating her nearly all of his adult life, but love was futile. It was a feeling and nothing more.

Settling down wasn't an option. Charlie was going to spend his days alone in his house, probably with Lauren coming in and out of his life. And he was okay with that.

"We like taking it slowly," Charlie said instead. There was no need to have a debate with Paula over love in the office.

"When I was your age, I had a kid already. You young people do nothing but move slow."

"If I had a kid, I wouldn't be able to help you with your IT issues. And then you'd have to put in a ticket."

Paula's lips twisted, and he knew he had won this round.

"Anyway." Charlie straightened up. "It's all fixed. It needed a reboot."

"Oh, wow. You sure are quick with these things. I guess that's why you make the big bucks."

"Us young people know how to do *some* things fast."

Paula scoffed. "Only with technology and driving. Not the real stuff."

He made a graceful exit before Paula could ask anything else about his personal life. When he was gone, he couldn't help that his mind flickered to Violet. If he could make it work with his weird director, he could make it work with her too. Even if it made him want to vomit a little.

Although, seeing her face when he played along almost made it worth it.

Charlie shouldn't be petty. He was too old for it, but being around Violet made him feel like a college kid again, like not a day had passed since their feud had started.

They *had* been friends. Maybe they could have been more, but Violet ruined that when she turned on him after she asked for help. And ever since then, he didn't understand how someone could take constructive criticism so personally.

It never made sense to him. She could handle insults and mean comments. Half the time, she threw them right back. But when she asked for help with an essay for her personal statement to apply to grad school, that was the last straw. Apparently, his questioning of her overarching theme for the paper ruined their friendship.

Violet vexed him sometimes.

Charlie forced her out of his mind. He needed to get to work.

A few hours later, he finished fine-tuning a website, pushed out software updates, and completed more lines of code for several more projects.

It was past lunchtime, which meant he needed to eat. He planned on walking to the grocery store a block away to grab food, but those flew out the window when he ran into Lauren at the front desk.

She looked beautiful, but annoyed. She was dressed up, as if they had a date Charlie had forgotten about.

"You didn't answer my texts," she said as a greeting.

He hadn't even noticed them. "I was working."

She sighed. "You're always working."

"That's what a job is."

"Whatever. I want lunch, so let's go get something."

Charlie knew he couldn't get out of it.

He'd wanted a quiet break so his brain could rest before he finished his work for the day, but since Lauren was here, he knew that wasn't happening. Besides, they were so close to getting their relationship back. It was the least he could do.

They went to a pizza place on the ground floor of the building. It was packed to the brim with people on their own lunches. Charlie cringed at how loud it was, but Lauren seemed to be right at home.

When they sat down, she immediately ordered salads for both of them. Charlie wanted something more filling, but didn't argue. The last thing he needed was to start a fight if he disagreed with her.

"So, how has your day been?" he asked once they were alone.

"Oh, you know, the usual. I've been busy with this case from hell. Something about a dog being let loose and biting a kid."

"Which side are you defending?"

"The dog owner, of course," Lauren said. "The family is rich. I'm getting *such* a huge bonus when I win their case."

"Right," Charlie said. He figured that was enough of talking about Lauren's work.

Things were easier when they were kids and all they had was school. Lauren was smart and got the best grades. It made sense she became a lawyer when she graduated, but her actual cases were . . . wrong.

Charlie sometimes couldn't stomach it.

"I bet your day was the usual. Computers and stuff, right?" she asked.

"Yep," Charlie said. "Nothing new there."

"Hm. Maybe we need to mix it up."

Charlie almost wanted to tell her about his deal with Violet. But he stopped himself before he could. Lauren despised Violet and wouldn't take kindly to any sort of truce with her.

He needed to avoid fights with Lauren, not start them.

"Maybe," Charlie said, his voice quiet.

"We should travel. Maybe we can go to Fiji or something when I win this case."

"I don't think I have time for that," Charlie said. Besides, a vacation with Lauren sounded like hell. She would push him to do things he didn't want to do, and he found he began to hate her if he spent more than a few days in her presence.

But she was the best he had. She was successful and smart as hell—far more so than he was. He couldn't even stop fighting with Violet, much less handle the massive cases Lauren did, even if they were morally gray ones.

Lauren pouted. "Not even for a vacation? With me?"

"I have a lot of projects I can't step away from."

"God, where's your adventurous spirit? You're so tame these days."

Maybe Charlie was. But where Lauren thrived with chaos, he liked routine. Where she wanted to travel, he wanted to root to the spot. Opposites may attract, but sometimes Charlie wasn't so sure.

"I have a house and a job, Lauren. I have responsibilities."

"Your house is more of a shack still standing."

"It was my great-grandmother's," Charlie corrected, feeling more than a little offended.

"Yeah, but she's dead now."

"She left it to me," he added. "It's been in the family since it was built in the 1800s."

"And you can definitely tell."

Charlie gritted his teeth but didn't say anything. Lauren never changed her mind when she thought she was right, but neither did he. This was his family's home, one of the last pieces of his great-grandmother. She had left it to *him*, asking he take care of it.

And despite its flaws, he loved the place.

That just meant Lauren would never move in with him.

Some days he was fine with that.

Lauren sighed, but it came out like a scoff.

"I'm sorry for insulting your shack of a house," Lauren said. "I'm sure to some it's charming."

Well, it was an apology at least.

"It's fine. Let's enjoy our food. I have to be back soon."

"Seriously? You're already thinking about work again?"

Charlie sighed. "I'm only on my lunch. I have a lot to get back to."

Lauren shook her head. "You know what? I'm glad we're on a break, Charlie. You never make time for me."

This was how their fights would start, and that was *not* something he wanted. "I'm trying. I came to lunch with you, didn't I?"

"You're not trying hard enough."

He didn't have anything to say to that. He didn't have anything else to give.

"You know what? Fine. If you're not going to put in the effort, then I don't have to stay. Enjoy your lunch, Charlie. I'll enjoy mine elsewhere." She stood and walked away. When she got near the door, she paused, waiting for him to come after her.

But Charlie didn't have it in him to stop her. He was tired from only one lunch with her.

When he didn't move, Lauren rolled her eyes and left the building.

She wasn't always like this. She used to make him feel like the best boyfriend in the world, but ever since college, and the subsequent stress of being a lawyer set in, she had lost a bit of herself. Now, more often than not, Charlie didn't even want to be around her.

But they had been together since high school. He loved her, or at least in the way he knew how to. That was why he stayed, right?

This wouldn't last forever anyway. She would be mad for a while, stay away for a few weeks, and then reach back out when she was ready.

He could apologize then.

Charlie quickly finished his food and got back to his desk to continue work. He was trying not to let Lauren's attitude get to him, but when he almost cursed out loud at one of his coworker's terrible coding, he knew he was going to have a long, frustrating day.

Damn it. Lauren could have picked *any* other day to be mad at him.

Violet

Violet always began her morning with coffee and yoga. She woke up early to get her daily practice in. Then she ate her usual breakfast with coffee, put on a tiny bit of makeup and whatever dress she laid out the night before, and rushed out the door for work.

Her routine, if you could call it that, was the one thing keeping her sane. Her students sometimes pushed her to her limits, and her little exercise regimen helped keep her head on straight throughout the day.

Violet worked at a middle school on the south side of the city. She didn't get paid much, but it was enough for her to have her apartment, her car note, and a little bit of savings. Her job was hard work, and she often put in more than forty hours a week. She loved working with students, though, and seeing them grow almost made it all worth it.

This particular morning, however, was off to a bad start. Violet woke up to a text from her mother, sent at 5 a.m., linking an article about teachers and how they developed depression.

It was no secret Nancy Moore hated Violet's job. Originally, her mother wanted Violet to attend grad school, but she'd kept her potential application secret from her friends in case she didn't get in. When she had to write her personal statement for her application, it was torn apart by none other than Charlie himself, back when she had any semblance of trust with him. His cruel rebuttal to every part of her work made her question her decision, and she took a few extra credit hours to become a teacher rather than pursue the career she really wanted.

Her mom never forgot.

These days, Violet heard how beneath her teaching was. It didn't help that every other person Violet knew made way more than she did and could afford life inside Nashville's expensive city limits.

Violet barely scraped by, but she lived in a terrible neighborhood no one wanted to visit, and her apartment was barely habitable. She had the oldest car with the most miles, the smallest amount of savings for an emergency, and rarely had extra money to go out with friends.

And yet she put in as many hours as everyone else did, if not more.

Violet was also good at her job. She loved her students, the summers off were nice, and she was grateful the school allowed a twelve-month plan for her salary, making the summer months when she wasn't in the classroom easier to manage with a steady paycheck. It meant smaller bank deposits, but it beat going through June and August with no money at all.

All she wanted was to work a job she loved and make a decent living. Sometimes it seemed impossible.

Violet ignored her mother's text and continued with her routine. Her mom would certainly reach out again in the next few days, but Violet would be prepared for it, and she would be able to ignore the crushing weight of her mother's disappointment.

She worked at a medium-sized school, where kids from the community would filter in and out as they moved through their grades. It was the nicer side of town, with older houses she'd never be able to afford. Some mornings when Violet drove in, she imagined what it would be like to live in one of the beautiful homes in the neighborhood.

Violet always parked on the side of the school building and walked to her small classroom. It was well decorated because she wanted to at least give her students something interesting to look at, even if she spent all her money doing it.

Right as she walked through the doors, she ran into the principal and her boss, Dr. Jones. He was an old man with thin, white hair. He always wore thick mittens in the winter, and he had on his trademark gray windbreaker.

Dr. Jones had been doing this so long that no one dared say anything to him about looking more professional. Violet was still a newbie by most teachers' standards, even though she had lasted longer than any of the other hires brought on in her year. She didn't get the dressing-down privileges until at least year ten.

"Hey, Dr. Jones."

"Ms. Moore!" he said happily. "Good to see you. I like your Shakespeare dress."

"Oh, thanks," Violet said. Her dresses were nerdy, and everyone knew it, but they were always cheap on Amazon. They made some of the students laugh, which made it worth it. "Tomorrow is going to be a book dress."

"That's fantastic. If only your students could see your wit."

"Some of them do," she replied. "When they're not mad at me for assigning reading."

"They all love you," he said. "Your track record speaks for itself."

Violet couldn't help but blush at the praise. She liked teaching and liked spending extra time helping kids actually learn the material. While she hated standardized tests, her class's scores were high. But the greatest satisfaction came at the end of the year, when she would look back and see how far they had come.

"Speaking of your record, I wanted to ask if you were available to do work on the winter festival this year."

Violet nodded, thinking of the after-the-holidays event that happened every year. It was a time when the school put on a fun learning festival for the students and their parents to attend. There was free food and lots of activities that needed a lot of planning.

Technically, the event wasn't until *after* Liv and Lewis's wedding, and it *was* a fun event.

"I can help," she said. "Send me an email of what you need me on."

"Thank you. It's good to know we can always count on you."

Yes, they could. Maybe then she would get a decent raise or something to account for how much she worked her ass off.

But that wasn't up to Dr. Jones anyway. He submitted his recommendations, but the school board was in charge of offering raises and promotions, not him. Her anger couldn't be directed at her good-natured boss.

She walked away from the conversation focusing on how she would manage to get everything done. It was going to be tight, but she could still do it.

From there, her day didn't get any better. Her students were all in a bad mood, and when sixth graders were angry, they were annoying.

A headache was beginning to form behind her eyes after lunch rolled around. One of the teachers had an emergency, and there were no substitutes available, so she had double the classes to ensure the kids had a place to study.

One of her students, Jason, decided to act out, and she almost had to send him to Dr. Jones's office. She hated doing that because it never got anything accomplished. It only made the child leave where the learning happened.

By the time the day was over, all Violet wanted to do was drink an entire bottle of wine. She couldn't shake her headache, but she also couldn't go to sleep because she had papers to grade.

It was such a bad day that she drove home in total silence.

Her apartment complex was old. It hadn't been maintained in thirty years, and she kept pepper spray on her anytime she was outside.

The lock barely worked, and she had to put her entire weight on the door to get in. And when she finally managed it, she was greeted with the familiar smell of old lady and mold. But she had a roof over her head, so she couldn't complain.

Her upstairs neighbors were being loud, and their footsteps echoed through her pounding head. Violet sighed and tried not to grab the broom to hit against the ceiling. Her day couldn't have gone worse.

Violet rubbed her temples and headed to the fridge. She poured a glass of wine and flopped on the couch, glad she was alone and that the day was over.

That was when the ceiling started creaking.

Violet glanced up, hoping it was all in her imagination, but then she saw a crack form, right in the middle of the plaster.

For a second, she blinked dumbly. Was that real? Or was her mind playing tricks on her?

Still, her chest tightened. Cracks shouldn't be forming in ceilings, at least not *that* fast.

She stood and watched as the crack grew, and her ceiling bowed downward. She walked backwards to her door as the ceiling got lower and lower. She threw her weight on the door and had just made it out into the hallway as the building let out a loud groan. Water began spewing out of the crack, and Violet watched as the ceiling fell in.

Violet covered her face and felt water splash her from head to toe. She heard screams that might have been her own, and she helplessly curled in on herself as things crashed around her. She was powerless in the wake of the destruction, and she could only wait for it to be over.

When the building stopped falling, there was a moment of eerie silence. Violet stayed rooted to her spot, huddled over, not truly believing it was finished.

After the silence stretched on, she peeked around, surveying the devastating damage in front of her.

Furniture that wasn't hers was strewn all over the floor. The noisy neighbors were running down the stairs, cursing and panicking.

"Oh my God, are you all right?" one of them asked. "Was that your apartment?"

"Yeah," Violet said numbly.

"I'm calling 9-1-1. Stay here!"

Violet glanced down at herself. She was covered in building dust and gross, old water. Nothing hurt, other than the sinking feeling in her chest that everything she knew had changed.

She looked over at what used to be her kitchen and found only ruins. Tiny bits of her cabinets lay soaking wet on the ground. Furniture from the apartment above her sat where she once stood.

There was no doubt in her mind: if she hadn't moved, she would have been crushed.

Violet could only stare at the mess of her home until an EMT pulled her away, insisting that he check her over. When he offered to take her to the hospital to check for further injuries, she declined—she couldn't afford the ambulance ride.

Luckily, she was uninjured by their guess, but not everyone made it out unscathed. When the ambulance drove away, one of her neighbors was in it.

It easily could have been her.

Charlie

Charlie was at the end of his workday when he got a call from Liv.

He was tired, and more than ready to go home. He was riding in a silent car, hoping to be alone for the night.

He answered the call anyway. Liv was never the one to reach out, so if it was her, something was up.

"Hey," he said. "Is everything okay?"

"Everything is fine. With me at least."

"That's cryptic."

"Listen, you'd do anything to help a friend, right?"

"Uh . . . yeah, of course. Just name it," he said. He could feel himself growing worried. Was Lewis okay? What about Micah?

"Can you come by our apartment? Someone needs help."

"I'll be there in ten minutes," Charlie said, hanging up the phone and changing his trajectory. Screw going home. If someone needed him, he'd be there.

He arrived at Liv and Lewis's apartment in record time. When he pulled in, he couldn't help but notice someone was parked in the guest spot again. It was the same car from Tuesday.

Violet.

Charlie climbed out, the panic turning into annoyance. This had to be a prank for them both. Nothing was wrong, and if it was, he would be the last person they'd call to help.

This wasn't something he wanted to deal with, and he debated leaving.

Charlie sighed. He was too curious to go home. He walked to Lewis and Liv's apartment and opened the door.

He expected laughter when he walked in. He expected Violet to be perfectly fine, either as shocked as he was or in on the joke.

What he didn't expect was Liv to be at the door, her brown eyes wide and nervous. Charlie's panic returned tenfold, and then he heard crying from the direction of the living room.

"The whole place," Violet sobbed. He saw her sitting on the couch. She looked *awful*. Her dress was soaked and her hair was covered with dust and grime. She looked like she had been in a war—nothing like the person he knew. "It *fell in*. Right where I was standing. If I hadn't moved, I would have died."

"Jesus Christ," Lewis muttered from where he stood next to her. He rubbed his forehead, while his other hand messed with the hem of his shirt. Charlie knew

Lewis couldn't sit still when he was nervous and seeing both hands moving told him something bad had happened.

"And I can't even get a hotel because of some stupid hockey game," Violet said. "Everywhere is packed."

Something terrible had happened *to her*. Something dangerous. His feelings for her didn't matter. What once was annoyance turned into protectiveness. Who had done this?

And to Violet Moore no less?

Charlie could easily find them and make them regret it.

Liv cleared her throat, causing Violet and Lewis to look at them still standing in the entryway. Violet's eyes found his instantly.

"What the hell?" Lewis asked.

"Oh my God," Violet added, hiding her face. Charlie knew he should look away but couldn't.

"Who did this to you?" he asked lowly. Feelings he hadn't had since middle school, since he stood up to Lewis's bullies, were bubbling in his chest, making him ready to hunt down whoever had hurt her.

"What are you doing here?" Violet asked.

"I told him to come," Liv explained.

"Why?" Lewis asked.

"Violet needs a place to stay."

"Liv," Lewis said, his voice tight. "This is a bad idea."

"It's the only idea."

"Hang on, what happened?" Charlie asked, his voice hard as he looked at Violet in tears. "No one's explained that to me yet."

If he could think a little clearer, maybe he could have put the pieces together, but his mind was running too fast to even attempt to. His fists were clenched, and he was ready to fight.

Violet heaved a long sigh, then answered, "My apartment collapsed."

Charlie took a moment to process. Her apartment *collapsed*? Did that even happen these days?

"What the fuck?" Charlie blurted. "How does that even happen?"

"It was an old building," Violet said, not looking him in the eye. "And besides, *I'm* not hurt or anything. At least as far as I can tell."

"You didn't go to the hospital?" Charlie asked.

"An EMT checked me out."

"That's not the same thing."

"Do I look like I can afford a hospital bill?"

Charlie sighed. She had him there. His eyes trailed her body, and he could only find a tiny bit of comfort that she wasn't bleeding anywhere.

Lewis cleared his throat.

"Was anyone else hurt?" Lewis asked.

"When I left, the EMTs took one of my neighbors. They were awake and talking, but I think they broke something in the fall."

Holy shit.

"Anyway," Violet said, shaking her head. "Davis obviously doesn't want me staying with him, so he can go."

"Hang on," Liv said. "We can't have you here because all the wedding gifts arrived early, and Bree is flying in and out over the next three weeks for the wedding. Micah is moving right now. So, your options are Charlie or your mom."

Violet stared at her best friend. "I have my car."

"Wait," Charlie said incredulously. "Between me and your mother, your best option is your *car*?"

"Violet," Liv said firmly, "you said you were friends. After the wedding, you can stay here, but I'm trying to prevent you from sleeping in your car."

"It doesn't matter what I think. It's obvious he isn't going to let me."

Lewis shook his head, looking frustrated. He knew how Charlie felt about his house. He didn't let people come over. He didn't even let Lauren stay.

Most people didn't like his home. It was old, original, and a family heirloom. Lauren had spent years picking it apart and telling him to sell it. Over time, he simply stopped talking about it.

"I'll do it," Charlie said suddenly.

Everyone in the room turned to him.

"What?" Lewis asked.

"I said I'll do it."

Lewis only stared.

"I-it's fine," Violet stuttered. "A hotel will open up eventually, I can—"

"I have a whole floor you can stay on," Charlie said. "We don't even have to see each other."

"I can't ask this—"

"You didn't ask," Liv interrupted, "I did. It's the best and safest option. You'll lose your mind if you stay with your mom, and someone could hurt you if you're in your car. I promise you can stay here when the wedding is over."

Charlie didn't love the prospect, but he also didn't love the idea that anyone could hurt Violet; that wasn't an option.

Violet looked torn between crying and yelling, but she turned to him. Her expression was nervous, yet hopeful.

Charlie would regret this decision in two days when they were back to fighting, but at that moment, it was the best decision of his life.

"Okay," she said quietly. "Thank you. Text me the address."

"I . . . don't have your phone number," Charlie said.

"Right," Violet said. She pulled her phone out of a pocket of her dress and tried to unlock it.

Nothing happened. That was when Charlie noticed the shattered screen. She must have dropped it at some point.

"What a great fucking time for this to break!" she snapped. Her eyes were still watery and her face went beet red.

"Just . . . follow me back," Charlie said, her anger feeling off when it wasn't directed at him. "I'll lead you there."

"Fine," she replied. "I'll need to shower."

"Yeah, I know."

Violet glared at him, as if she took what he said as an insult. He didn't mean it as one. She *did* look objectively awful, or as close as she could get to it anyway.

He doubted she could truly look bad, even if she tried.

"Okay, guys," Liv said. "Charlie, thank you for doing this. But seriously, don't kill each other."

"It's going to be fine," he reassured them, not feeling so sure about the situation himself.

Neither Liv nor Lewis looked convinced. In fact, Liv looked worried, which wasn't normal for her.

"I'll call you if I need anything," Violet said.

"Your phone isn't working," Liv reminded her friend.

"I'll call if we fight," Charlie said. "Okay?"

Liv nodded. "Okay, but before you go, I need you to know I wouldn't have suggested this if it wasn't the only option."

"Yeah, I get it," Violet said.

"Okay. Be safe, guys."

Judging by the way Liv and Lewis looked at them when they left the room, neither of them expected this to go well.

And Charlie didn't either.

Chapter Four

Violet

Charlie, of course, lived in a beautiful, historical neighborhood. The very beautiful, historical neighborhood right near her school, the one she wished she could live in every time she passed it.

Goddamnit.

It had huge, old trees with well-lit, paved roads and pristine grass-lined sidewalks.

His house was on a corner, nestled behind two ancient oak trees that still had a few red leaves hanging on from the end of fall. There was a small driveway that led to a large, gated backyard. The house was an American foursquare, with old, white siding and original windows. It was truly a house preserved in history.

Fucking hell. How did he get a perfect house like this?

She parked behind Charlie's Mercedes and tried not to lose her mind.

All she had to her name right now was her laptop and a basket of old laundry she kept meaning to take to a laundromat. That gave her a few changes of clothes for work while she waited on her renter's insurance to pay for the damage. Her mind was a mess of things she needed to do, including replacing her entire life, but most importantly, new clothes and toiletries.

And she was going to have to do it all in Charlie's house.

For the foreseeable future, Violet was going to be horribly uncomfortable. She was staying with her enemy, had barely any possessions, and no phone. She would be able to at least get her phone replaced the next day, but everything else was going to take time.

To top it all off, Violet's landlord was going to drag his feet. He never cared to answer repair requests, and she found herself doing a lot of the dirty work when she had the time. Her landlord hadn't even shown up when his own building fell in.

It was going to take a long time to fix this, but she only had to survive in Charlie's house for two weeks. That was it. Then she could be with people who didn't hate her.

She could do it. She literally had no other choice.

Charlie got out of his car, looking tense. "Here we are."

"It's nice," Violet muttered.

"You don't have to compliment it because I'm letting you stay." His voice was closed off and rough. Violet blushed and decided to keep her mouth shut. "This house was my great-grandmother's. Every generation of my family was raised here."

Violet could have easily had a killer comeback. *Oh, were all of them as evil as you?*

But her mouth stayed shut. She didn't dare piss him off now—not when he was giving her a place to live.

Besides, she didn't even know Charlie's family. Obviously, this home had history she could only begin to imagine. When she was a kid, her mom had moved them around once a year. Until she moved out on her own, she had never stayed in one place long enough to grow roots.

Not like Charlie's family had.

Charlie gestured for her to follow him, and he opened the faded red front door, revealing the most elegant foyer she had ever seen. There was a grand staircase going to the second floor and beautiful oak trim panels that rose to her waist. The house smelled old, but clean—not moldy like her apartment.

He didn't give her long to look around. He was moving to the left, and she scrambled to keep up with him.

"This is the dining room," he said. Floral wallpaper lined the walls from chair height up. Above her, a golden chandelier dangled over a red oak dining room table meant for at least ten people. "I know the table is scratched."

Violet hadn't even noticed. The table caught her eye, but only because it was magnificent.

"Through here is the kitchen," Charlie said, walking under an ornate archway.

Violet silently followed him and saw the original kitchen.

The cabinets were a mossy green, which shouldn't have looked good, but it somehow worked. The floors were an intricate white and black tile. They showed their age, but only spoke to the history of the home.

Violet was entranced.

"The cabinets are metal. They're original."

Violet didn't have anything to say. She was too busy imagining how the space could be used and lived in by a family.

It was a shame it was only Charlie living here.

"My room is on this floor. Don't go in there," he added, gesturing to the door opposite them. "It's connected to the kitchen. It was an addition some time ago."

He walked away again, and Violet followed him back into the hallway and up the huge set of stairs.

"The guest room is here." Charlie opened the door to a small room with a desk and a bed. "There is an extra bedroom furnished as an office right next to it. You can do whatever you need to there. The bathroom is the door across from the stairs, and the door next to the bathroom is for another bedroom, but it stays closed. Don't go in there. As for everything else, you should be able to live mostly up here. No need to come down to the living room."

Violet nodded. According to Charlie, she needed to stay up here and out of sight. Seemed easy enough.

She knew she couldn't screw this up. She had been putting on a brave face earlier. Sleeping in her car would be the lowest of the low, especially in the winter. She wanted to avoid it if she could.

She turned to go into the bathroom to finally get the grit off her, but she froze when she saw the doorhandles.

They were the original iron doorhandles, with intricate designs molded to them. They were *so* perfect and seeing the beauty of something so historical amid a shitty night made her unable to move.

"What?" Charlie asked, his voice hard. "Are you worried they don't work or something?"

"N-no."

"The house is old, but everything here is in working condition—"

"This house is beautiful," Violet admitted before she could stop herself. "I mean the original tile, the doorhandles. The archways! There's so much detail in this house that builders don't do anymore. Wait . . . is the bathroom original? Is it only a clawfoot tub?"

"Uh, my great-grandmother added a shower, but the tub is still in there, yeah."

Unable to help herself, Violet ran to the door and poked her head inside. "It's fantastic! I bet the paint could probably still give you lead poisoning."

"We've repainted it since then."

"Damn. A good poisoning sounds great right now."

Charlie was looking at her with a confused expression. "You like it?"

"Of course I do. This entire house is perfection," she said. "I'm honestly jealous."

"I thought you'd hate it."

"Me? No, I love historical stuff like this. I was a history minor in college."

"That's . . . right. You were."

Violet's excitement waned as she remembered *who* she was talking to. Charlie . . . right.

"Um, is Lauren here?" she asked after a moment of awkward silence.

"What?" Charlie's voice came out harsh.

"You're dating her. You've been dating her forever. Doesn't she live here?"

"No. She's not a fan of old homes."

"She's got bad taste then," Violet said under her breath. Charlie looked at her, eyes narrowed, and she clamped her mouth shut immediately. *Shit*, she was about to ruin it.

"You can use the tub if you want," Charlie eventually said. "But the hot and cold knobs are flipped. My great-grandmother had bad plumbers."

"Oh, I'm sure I can figure it out," she said. "I should probably clean up now. I feel terrible and I probably look it too."

Charlie nodded, his face scrunching up.

"You know, you could tell me I look fine," Violet added.

"I don't want to lie."

"Or maybe I'm justified to feel and look like shit because of the night I've had?"

Violet stared at him, wondering if she had pushed her luck. The Charlie she knew would easily fight her, and make some cruel, biting remark.

"Just get clean. It *is* justified that you feel the way you do, but you don't look bad. You're safe, which matters more."

Violet only stared at him.

Charlie cleared his throat. "But you're also probably covered in asbestos."

"Oh, God." Violet realized he was right. "Get out. I need to get this off immediately."

"Do you need clothes?" Charlie asked.

"I have some dirty ones in my car." Violet was peeling off her sweater. Charlie looked at her arms warily, as if she would attack him at any given moment.

"Clean clothes, Violet. I don't want you wearing dirty clothes in my guest bed."

"I don't know what I'm supposed to do, considering all I have to my name right now is dirty."

Charlie let out a long, painful sigh. "I'm asking if you need to borrow some."

Violet paused. She didn't *want* to borrow anything from him.

But she needed to.

"Fine. That would be . . . great. Thank you."

Ugh. That hurt to get out.

"I'll set them outside. The door lock works. Just . . . wait for me to get downstairs before you open it. I don't want to see you naked."

"Please, as if I'd give you any ammunition for later by letting you see me naked."

Charlie opened his mouth to say something, but then quickly shut it. Violet ignored him. He was gone before she could slide out of her shoes.

Taking a deep breath, she locked the door and slowly took off the rest of her clothes. She felt awkward and exposed, but at least she could get clean.

She stared at the tub longingly. It was sitting in the corner, angled to fit in the smaller space. It was painted white, but the claw feet were a brushed gold.

As much as Violet wanted to use it, the shower would be better in order to get clean. It would be easier to wash away the events of the night if it all flowed down the drain instead of stewing in it. She stepped over to the white tile of the stall shower and turned on the water.

It took a while to get warm, but Violet climbed in the moment it was hot enough for her. As she showered, she heard Charlie come up the stairs and then leave again. Despite wanting to stay under the pounding stream of water, she felt the need to check to be sure he hadn't tried to come in. He probably wouldn't, considering he seemed very adamant he didn't want to see her naked, but she was paranoid; this could all still be an elaborate prank.

The door was still shut and locked. Violet let out a long breath of air and stepped back into the now-warm spray of water.

Even though he lived alone, he had a bar of soap and shampoo in the guest bathroom. Violet eyed them, wondering if he'd care if she used them. But as the reality of how gross she was set in, she conceded and decided she would buy him more if he got mad.

The pounding water eased her tense muscles slightly, and the bathroom was a humid oasis by the time she was done. Violet stepped from the shower and peeked out into the hallway to make sure she was alone, and quickly swiped the clothes Charlie left her.

It felt weird to be putting on his things. He hadn't given her anything but a basic set of pants and a shirt. They were comfy, but they weren't hers.

Violet cleaned up after herself, making sure there was no trace of her having been there. When she got to the guest room, she slowly sat on the bed, which groaned in protest. She winced at the sound, knowing she needed to stay out of Charlie's way while she was here.

The quilt on the bed was warm and inviting in the chilly air of the house. She settled under it, unable to fully relax, but happy to be warm.

She tried to mentally prepare herself for staying with Charlie for the next two weeks. He was being amicable, but she knew he hated this. She hated it just as much as she did.

But Violet was no stranger to being unwanted somewhere. She could leave no trace, and she was good at not pissing people off. They already had a deal to not fight until the wedding. That would have to extend to this weird situation too. But she could do it. She was good at pushing down her feelings and making herself invisible.

She would simply have to do it with Charlie too.

It was going to fucking *suck*. He had already hurt her six years ago, and she sometimes thought it would be easier to be invisible around him, but doing so would let him get away with what he did. Now she had to make herself invisible inside of his home. She had dealt with worse things, but it was hard to remember those once her current reality set in.

In the silence of the darkened room, a single tear slid from her eye.

Maybe her apartment hadn't fallen on her, but it felt like something else did.

Charlie

Violet was quiet that night. Almost as if she wasn't there.

Charlie would have to be in the living room to even hear her, but he expected her presence to be . . . larger. Everywhere else she seemed to take up all the space she could, even in his own mind.

But now she was almost invisible.

When he woke up, he thought for a moment it had all been a dream, but then he saw her car from the kitchen window and knew she was around.

Just not loud about it.

Charlie wasn't used to guests, but it wasn't supposed to be like this, right? Shouldn't she make a mess, or maybe annoy him by shutting a door too loudly?

He found it impossible to focus. He kept wondering if Violet was up to something, or if she was looking for him.

This was why he hated having guests over. They always broke his rhythm.

He left for his run on time, barely. He didn't feel great about leaving Violet alone, but he knew his day would be ruined if he didn't at least attempt to exercise. He could only hope his house was in one piece when he got back.

However, after his run was over, the house remained silent, and she was still not making herself known. Charlie frowned. Her silence was worse than her snark.

Charlie climbed the stairs, wondering if she was alive. He peered into the bathroom, but not one thing was out of place. She hadn't even left a trace of water.

Did she shower? Was she in the guest bed still asbestos covered? God, he'd have to get a whole new mattress if so. He walked to the guest room and gently knocked on the door. It opened at his touch, and he was surprised to find it wasn't latched.

"Yes?"

Charlie looked up. Violet was in the clothes he gave her the night before. Her hair was messy but clean, and her face scrubbed free of any dirt. She was sitting on the floor in front of the bed, which was already made up. A laptop was in front of her, with a paused video of a woman doing what must have been yoga.

"I was checking on you," Charlie said.

He expected her to snap at him, to mention how cold the house got at night, or how sparse the furniture was. He could feel his chest tighten as it always did with someone in his home.

"I was . . ." Violet closed her laptop and pushed herself off the floor. "Never mind. I wasn't making too much noise, was I?"

Charlie blinked. "What?"

"I was doing yoga, but if you're here then you must have heard me."

"I'm here because I didn't hear you at all."

"I was trying not to bother you."

Charlie could only stare at her. She was being considerate? He thought she was planning his murder.

The kindness was so off, so wild to him that he could only turn and walk away. Violet didn't follow, and when he was back downstairs, he tried to gather his wits about him.

Violet was being nice. Since when did she do that? Yes, he was letting her stay in his house, but she didn't owe him anything. The Violet he knew wouldn't show him kindness no matter what he did. Why was she doing it now?

And yet . . . here she was.

She looked so odd to him. Charlie had never seen her in anything other than the dorky dresses she wore for school. But this time, she looked like someone else. Someone who was in his house casually. Someone who *fit* in his house. And no one ever did that.

He had to shake this off. Whatever weird funk Violet was in would pass and she'd be looking for the perfect moment to strike. He had to be ready.

It didn't matter that she was staying in his house and wearing his clothes. It *didn't*.

Charlie made his oatmeal and sat at the dining room table. His mind was a mess of emotions, but he had a long day in front of him. He needed to put her out of his mind and ignore her.

Violet came down the stairs in his clothes. His sweatpants, something old and never worn, looked so good on her that he couldn't look away. They mostly fit her, but they were rolled at both the waistband and legs. His shirt draped over her and hung off one shoulder, obviously much too large for her.

Violet had always been such a large, imposing figure in his mind that he forgot she was actually much smaller than him.

Suddenly he was back in college, meeting her for the first time. He used to think she was the prettiest woman he had ever seen. She was smart and funny, and there was nothing he could do to get her out of his head.

"Don't make fun of me," Violet said, crossing her arms.

And then the spell was broken. Charlie blinked back into the present. Violet was looking at him with narrowed, annoyed eyes. She was his enemy. She hated him.

He needed to remember that.

"I wasn't going to," he replied. He sounded breathless, even to his own ears. He expected Violet to call him out on it, but instead she looked away.

"Yeah, right," she muttered. "Usually when you stare is when insults start flying. But you won't see much of me. I'm going to the laundromat to clean what few clothes I have in my car."

"Why are you going to a laundromat?"

"Did I not just say I needed clean clothes?"

Charlie rolled his eyes. "Yes, but why go somewhere? I have a washer and dryer here."

"You told me to stay upstairs."

"I . . . I didn't mean to say—"

"I know what you meant. I need to stay out of your hair, which I can do."

"You can use my washer and dryer," he said. "You don't have the money to waste."

Violet glared at him. "My apartment never had a washer and dryer. I'll be fine."

"Seriously, is it always this impossible to get you to listen?"

"I am not in the mood to fight with you about this. I'm staying out of your way and doing my own thing. Shouldn't you want this? Besides, I don't even know where your washer and dryer are."

Charlie opened his mouth, but then shut it. She was snapping at him, but the image of her scared gaze from the night before flashed through his mind, and his anger vanished.

"It's in the basement. I honestly forgot to show it to you."

"You don't have to." Violet seemed put off by his sudden calmness.

"It's fine. Use the one here. But the basement is, uh . . . weird, to say the least."

Violet blinked at him. "Weird?"

"Just . . . spooky. Here, let me show you."

Charlie got up and walked to the kitchen. He opened the door to the basement and gestured for her to head downstairs. Violet went for only a moment, and promptly came back up.

"Okay. It's definitely a dungeon. Is this where you take all the women you bring home?"

"Only the ones who irritate me." His response was immediate, and Violet attempted to say something snappy back, but paused before any words left her, and the moment died.

Instead of the verbal sparring he was used to, she cleared her throat. "It feels like someone died down there."

"I don't *think* anyone did, but who knows? Maybe my great-grandmother wanted to be buried there."

Violet shook her head. "Under the concrete? No way. Not unless she wanted her bones stuffed into the cinderblocks."

"Maybe she did. Would it weird you out?"

Violet shook her head. "I'd take a catacomb basement over my desecrated apartment any day."

He had to keep himself from smiling. This was the kind of thing he'd loved in college. She never backed down. He could make a weird joke that would have everyone else cringing, and she'd play along. That had been so fun back in the day when they got along, but these days it only turned into an argument.

They stood in silence for a moment.

"Do you want me to pay you for the usage?" Violet eventually asked him.

"No? Why would I ask that?"

"Well, one, you hate me and kind of got roped into all of this. Two, if your bill goes up then it's my fault, so I should pay you."

"Don't worry about it." Charlie shrugged "I don't care. It's a high-efficiency unit."

"What? You don't care?"

"I don't."

"Yeah, right you don't. Let me pay you. I don't want this biting me in the ass later."

"What do you mean?"

"I mean . . . when all of this is over, and this weird kindness you got suckered into fades . . . you're going to use this against me. So, I'm trying to get ahead of the curve."

"I wouldn't do that."

"Big words coming from the guy who said I looked like a hooker at Liv's engagement party."

Charlie frowned, trying to remember their last few conversations. "I didn't actually call you a hooker."

"Not in so many words, but you said I was upstaging the bride."

"In what world does that mean I called you a hooker?"

"Maybe it didn't, but you definitely would have gone there if Lauren hadn't thrown her drink on me."

Charlie sighed. "I didn't need a reminder of that."

"Why? I thought from your perspective it would have been hilarious."

"No," Charlie replied firmly. "It was too far. And made it more of a scene than it already was. You and I have fought for six years and I've never made it physical. Why would I start now?"

"Huh," Violet said. "That's oddly mature of you. I thought you and Lauren would have cackled about it the moment I left."

"There was no cackling. The lecture I got from Lewis would have killed any joy I had."

"Well, I guess that makes me feel a little better knowing you didn't enjoy me getting drenched in fruit punch. Thanks for telling me that."

"I'm . . . I'm sorry she did that. I know it doesn't mean much coming from me and not her but . . ." Charlie paused when he saw the flabbergasted look on Violet's face. "What?"

"I never thought I'd hear the word 'sorry' come out of your mouth, Davis. It's a good look."

"I'm trying," he said, a little irritated at her teasing.

The Violet he knew would have smirked and threw an insult at him, but this Violet looked a little alarmed at his tone. She glanced down, blinking as if she remembered something. When she looked up, her face was blank.

"Thank you for all you're doing." Her voice sounded shaky. "I'll . . . I'll use the washer, but if your water bill goes up, I'll pay the difference."

Then she was gone.

Charlie blinked, as if he had imagined her leaving. He had *never* seen her disappear from a fight like that. She had . . . given up and gone silent, like she was a shell of herself.

It was absolutely terrifying.

Charlie didn't like the complete 180 she had done. Fighting with her wasn't pleasant, but it was familiar, almost like a comfort of sorts. Watching her fold everything into a box and run away felt . . . wrong.

He stared at the space Violet used to occupy for a long time. He realized he needed to get to work. He didn't see her when he left, but a part of him wanted to. He wanted to figure out why she had walked away—why she had given up a fight rather than go all in.

It didn't match the woman he knew.

His workday was busy, but his mind kept drifting to her. He wondered if she was getting revenge by trashing the house, which made him leave work early to check on his belongings. But when he got home, nothing was out of place. It still looked like she never existed.

He could hear the washer running downstairs, and her car wasn't in the exact position it had been in this morning, so she had left at some point, but was still completely invisible upstairs. He wanted to go to her and demand to know her problem. He wanted to know why she was giving up, why she didn't think it was worth her time to argue with him.

But then his phone rang, and he thankfully had a distraction.

"Hey, Damon," Charlie said, walking to his room. He locked the door behind him. "What's up?"

"On a scale of one to ten," his friend said, "how mad would Lewis be if someone *did* hire strippers for his bachelor party?"

Charlie's mood plummeted. "You didn't."

"You're right, I didn't. Elijah did."

Charlie held back a wave of insults he wanted to direct at Elijah. *Goddammit.* Why didn't the guy ever listen?

"Lewis specifically said he didn't want strippers. He doesn't want to do anything that Liv wouldn't approve of."

"Trust me, I know." Damon sounded sincere. "I was fine with a night of Mario Kart, but Elijah already hired them. He says it's his right as a member of the party."

"No, Lewis is going to be furious." Charlie groaned. "This is the last thing I need right now. I'll talk to him."

Charlie ended the call, trying and failing to calm himself down before he dialed Elijah. He *hated* talking to him, but he was also Lewis's friend.

"Yo, Charlie." Elijah sounded relaxed, like he wasn't even bothered about going against the one thing Lewis wanted. "What's up?"

"You hired strippers? Really?"

"Of course, man. He needs it before he's stuck with one woman for the rest of his life."

Charlie wanted to hit something.

"Lewis doesn't want anything that would upset Liv at his bachelor party. You *have* to cancel the strippers."

"What, you have a thing against good-looking women?"

"It's not about that. It's that Lewis doesn't want to look at other women the same week he's getting married to Liv. You *heard* him say it."

"Listen, I know my friend, and he needs to sample the menu before he orders, if you know what I'm saying."

"Dude, do you want to stay friends with him or not?" Charlie asked, his voice tight.

"I know him as well as you do. He'll like it. Chill out."

Charlie pinched the bridge of his nose. Lewis would *freak*. There was one time he went to a strip club in college, and he called Liv *crying* thinking he had cheated on her. She hadn't been happy about his whereabouts, but she forgave him.

It was one thing when it had happened while they were dating. But the same week of his wedding? Lewis would lose his mind. His poor friend was already working overtime to pay for the wedding and their honeymoon. He was worried that something was going to ruin his big day, and Elijah's idiotic plan could easily do it.

Nope. Not on Charlie's watch.

Maybe if he hadn't been so unnerved by Violet's attitude, or her refusal to accept any help, he could have found a way to talk Elijah down, or at least warn Lewis.

But fuck it. He was done.

"Actually, the whole thing is canceled. Congratulations, Elijah, you blew it."

"What?" Elijah said sharply. "You can't cancel it."

"I can. Lewis wants to work overtime anyway, and I'll take it off his calendar."

"Dude, have you lost your mind?"

"Maybe I have."

"What crawled up your ass?"

"Oh, I don't know. Maybe it's you trying to ruin your friend's bachelor party. Maybe it's Violet *fucking* Moore in my house because she has nowhere else to go. But the point is, Elijah, I don't have time for this."

"Wait, Violet is at your house? Why?"

"It doesn't matter. Party's off. Goodbye, Elijah."

"You can't ruin my plans—"

Charlie hung up the phone, rolling his eyes. Elijah called him back, but Charlie sent him to voicemail. He instead sent Lewis a text.

Charlie: Sorry, something came up with me at work. I have to cancel the bachelor party.

Lewis didn't take long to answer.

Lewis: That's cool. Honestly, I wasn't looking forward to it anyway. Too much to do.

Charlie nodded, feeling confident in his decision. Lewis didn't seem to see Elijah for what he was, but Charlie always had. He didn't want to make his friend's life any worse before his wedding, so no bachelor party was the best option.

Elijah texted a few minutes later.

Elijah: Fuck you, man. Don't take out your issues with that bitch Violet on me.

Charlie rolled his eyes again and blocked the number. He'd unblock it eventually. *Maybe.*

The guy was such a loose cannon and wasn't worth his time. Besides, it wasn't like Elijah could *do* anything about canceling the bachelor party. It would be fine.

Violet

The day after the accident at her apartment was busy. She contacted Dr. Jones to explain her predicament and requested the day off to ger her life together. She replaced her phone, bought a few new dresses with more on the way, washed and dried a small load of laundry, and filed a claim for her things at the apartment.

While she was folding clothes in the guest room, Violet heard Charlie arrive home from work around three. She knew she needed to stay out of his way and only ventured downstairs to get a glass of water.

They didn't see each other, but Violet still felt jumpy. He said he wouldn't hold it against her, but he had gone back on his word before. Regardless of who it was, she hated being a burden on anyone. She had already felt bad going to Liv and Lewis.

The next day back at school was much easier than she anticipated. Everyone at work had heard, and they surprised her with a pile of gift cards to various restaurants around the area. She almost cried because she knew she wasn't touching Charlie's kitchen with a ten-foot pole.

The teachers she worked with were amazing. They all made the same shit salary as she did, but they were some of the most giving people she knew. There were always going to be rude, mean teachers, but the vast majority were great. It was part of the reason she stayed in the job.

And even the sixth graders seemed to take pity on her. All of her students were well-mannered that day. It was a welcome break from the chaos she was used to.

When the day was over, she finally checked her phone to see she had a missed call from Liv, which she immediately called back. She was sure Liv was checking in to see if there had been bloodshed.

"Hey," Liv said. "You're alive."

"Mostly," Violet said. "It's been weird. But I got my phone fixed."

"I can tell. Plus, you don't sound like you've recently murdered Charlie."

"Oh, no. I'd sound way happier," Violet said.

"How is it going?"

"Um . . ." Violet paused. "It's been okay. He has a huge house."

"I've never been. Lewis has seen it, but Charlie isn't big on having guests over."

"Yeah, I could tell. He was super defensive when I walked in."

"But he let you stay," Liv reminded her. "That's important. Just don't mess up anything."

"I'd never," Violet said honestly. Hurting that house would be like burning history. "I'm the one at a disadvantage here."

"I mean, yeah, a little. But I do know Charlie isn't a terrible person. He wouldn't do anything."

Violet frowned. Liv thought Charlie wasn't a bad person, but Violet knew who he really was.

"He *does* insult me," Violet tried to remind her.

"Yeah, but you guys said you were turning over a new leaf."

Violet sighed. They did say that, but it had been fake. Things were so tense, it didn't feel like they were turning over anything.

"But if it does get bad," Liv continued, "Lewis gets discounts on hotels through his job. Once the city isn't so busy, we can help you pay for a place."

"I can't ask that of you." Even if being alone in a hotel sounded amazing.

"It's fine," Liv said. "Seriously. Ask for anything."

Violet most certainly wouldn't. She already felt bad enough.

"It's fine for now. How is wedding stuff going?" Violet asked, desperate to change the subject. "Do you need any help with anything?"

"Aren't you busy?"

"I'm off work now. I can swing it."

It would beat going back to Charlie's place.

"Um, yeah now that I think about it. Lewis and I are going to a cake tasting. Wanna join?"

Violet's stomach growled. "I'd love nothing more."

When Violet pulled into the parking lot of the venue, she watched as Liv climbed out of her own car with a bulging paper bag.

***

Violet put her car in park and scrambled out to meet her friend.

"What is this?" Violet asked her as she handed over the bag.

"Oh, just all of your favorite bath things."

Violet stared. Half of her hated her friend spending money on her. The other was so grateful for the gift she wanted to cry.

"I know you're going through it," Liv said. "Please take it. It's the least I could do."

Violet nodded quietly and put the bag in her car. Liv hugged her tightly, telling her it would be okay. Violet accepted the hug and tried not to sob. The days had worn on her, and for the first time, even for a moment, she felt safe.

Lewis pulled up, and the moment was over. Liv didn't mention she had helped Violet, and she was glad she hadn't. It was hard for Violet to accept help, and the less people knew, the better.

When they went inside, though, things changed. Liv and Lewis talked about their wedding and what they wanted, and Violet was barely able to get a word in. They tried to include her with each cake, but she could tell she was a third wheel.

Violet tried not to let it get to her, but deep down, she wanted what Liv and Lewis had. She wanted someone to talk to about cake while planning for a wedding. She wanted someone who liked her weird taste and her odd toppings.

Liv and Lewis wanted a regular white cake, which was fine. But Violet wanted someone to try the strawberry with. Someone who'd get it for her even if no one else liked it.

It was nothing against them or their happiness, but being with them in this moment was souring her and the experience. She wanted nothing more than for it to be her turn, and she was tired of waiting.

She had been unlucky in love. Violet wanted someone serious and stable, but there was never a guy who fit the bill. Most were either looking for hookups, or simply weren't ready for commitment.

Violet fell in love hard and fast. And then it would explode when the two of them wound up on different pages. She had been through longer relationships, but her dating history was mostly short and sour.

Only a few of the men she dated ever met her friends, and her friends hadn't liked any of them. Liv and Lewis tried to set her up, but that had also ended in disaster. Elijah was the last one she dared to try it with, and him leaving after sleeping with her was the last straw.

These days, Violet had given up. She hadn't been on a date since she was with Elijah.

Seeing Lewis and Liv together was sometimes like a punch to the gut. They were *so* right for each other it hurt. Liv was always happy with Lewis, and their lives melded together perfectly. They shared everything.

Violet wanted that too.

***

Violet headed back to Charlie's after the cake tasting. She hoped he would be out with Lauren or something so she could go up to the guest room and be alone for the night. Maybe she'd try dating apps again. Or maybe she'd fall asleep lonely.

Of course, when she got there, Charlie was home and the lights were on. Violet planned on making a break for upstairs. Maybe he was in a good enough mood to simply leave her alone.

When she walked in, Charlie was at the dining room table. He had on thick-rimmed black glasses and was squinting at his computer. He wore sweatpants and a band T-shirt, looking more casual than Violet ever thought he could be.

Violet stared for all of two seconds before he noticed her.

"I thought you'd be home hours ago," he said, his eyes not leaving his computer.

She winced at his words. She was hoping he wouldn't say anything to her. Violet could only hope this wouldn't end in disaster.

"I went to a cake tasting with Liv and Lewis after work."

"Oh," Charlie said. He finally looked away from his computer. "Did they choose something?"

Violet was surprised he wasn't jealous. "They did. They got the plain white."

"Seems about right," Charlie said, then returned to typing.

"Why?"

"White is the usual wedding cake flavor."

"I'd want something weird." Violet didn't know why she said it. "Like strawberry."

"For a wedding cake?"

Violet shrugged. "It's my wedding."

There was a long pause, then Charlie leaned back in his chair and looked at her with a sardonic smile on his face.

"Why do I get the vibe you would do everything backwards at a wedding?"

"Because I would. Traditions are boring."

Violet waited for the other shoe to drop. He could easily turn this into a thinly veiled insult where he called her too strange for marriage. Or maybe he could go after how long she had been single. That would have been right up his alley.

"Strawberry *is* an underrated cake flavor," Charlie replied.

Thank God he hadn't gone for an insult. She didn't think she could take it.

"The vendor they chose made an amazing strawberry. It was easily the best one there."

He only nodded, leaving them in a dull silence. Violet felt disappointed, but she didn't know why. She hated this guy. Why would she care if he didn't want to talk to her? She certainly shouldn't want to talk to him.

"Anyway," Violet said. "I'll let you get back to your hacking."

"Hacking?"

"Your typing. You're focused so hard you've gotta be getting into the . . . I don't know, US Treasury or something."

Charlie rolled his eyes. "I'm coding."

"Ah, yes. Nice code word," Violet replied. "I won't tell. Unless the cops ask, of course."

Charlie rolled his eyes and looked back at his computer screen. Violet only stayed for half a second longer, and then she climbed the stairs to the guest room. She muddled in her disappointment for a moment before she decided she could grade papers and not worry about it. Charlie wasn't worth her time. She needed to remember that.

Chapter Five

Violet

There was scratching at her window.

Violet thought maybe she was imagining it, but when she kept hearing it, she begrudgingly got up.

The winter chill was setting in right in time for Liv and Lewis's wedding. The upper floors of Charlie's house were freezing, and the simple quilt barely did enough to keep Violet warm. She hated getting out of bed in the morning.

But the scratching was also annoying, so she glanced over to see what it was.

She came face-to-face with a white cat outside the window. It stared at her for a long moment before it darted, jumping off the sill into the darkness below.

Violet loved animals. She couldn't have any because of her apartment, but she always dreamed of having a cat. Seeing one jump from the second story made her yelp.

She darted to the window and was glad to see the cat was fine, but was now on the long part of the roof of the first floor. Charlie's extra office would have a better view of the cat; she left her room in a rush.

"What's going on?" Charlie demanded from downstairs.

Violet cursed. She hadn't meant for him to hear.

"There's a cat," Violet simply said.

"In the house?" he asked, coming up the stairs.

"No! On the roof!"

"The *roof*?" Charlie said, looking out the window.

"It was outside of the guest room."

"How did it get there?"

"No clue," Violet said. "Does the window open?"

"Yes, but . . ." Charlie paused as she pulled up on the window, letting the cool air in. She hiked a leg up and was about to duck to get outside. "What the hell are you doing, Moore?" he added, his voice urgent, almost like he was worried about her.

"I'm getting the cat. We can't leave it out there."

"You can't go on my roof!"

"Do you want to go do it?" Violet asked.

"No, it's dangerous to—"

Violet rolled her eyes and ducked out of the window. The roof was barely sloped, and her feet didn't slip at all.

"I need cat food or something. Do you have any?" she called back.

Charlie stared at her, wide-eyed. She could understand his shock. Most people wouldn't climb on the roof of someone else's house, but she had never feared heights, and she wanted to get the cat.

"Chicken?" Violet asked.

"Wha—have you lost your mind?"

"I think you know the answer," Violet replied. "Either get me something to give the cat to eat or don't. I'll be off your roof faster if you do, though."

Charlie groaned but turned and left. Violet rubbed her arms and looked for the cat. It was a frigid morning, and the poor, tiny thing had to be cold.. It peeked around the corner at her with curious eyes.

"Hey, kitty," she called, holding out her hand. "I'm not gonna hurt you." The cat didn't run away, but also didn't move toward her. "Come on, there's a nice warm house right here."

She hoped Charlie would return soon because the last thing she wanted was for the cat to try jumping onto the ground. She heard Charlie stomping up the stairs, and the sound of a can opening. The cat darted past her and in through the window. She turned to find Charlie glaring at her.

"What?" Violet asked.

"You could have gotten food. You didn't need to go on my roof."

He was probably right, but it was before coffee, so she obviously wasn't in her proper state of mind. Her face warmed as she made her way to the window and ducked back inside.

"Well, that turned out well," she said, eying the happily eating cat on the other side of the room.

"You got on my roof."

"I know, but there was a cat."

"That was dangerous!" he snapped.

"What? I wasn't near the edge. I've been on a roof before."

"What?" Charlie asked.

"I used to sneak to the roof of my apartment all the time. I loved it there."

"You could have gotten hurt."

"Careful, Davis. I might begin to think you actually care."

Charlie glared at her, his gaze feeling it could pierce her skin. *Yikes.* Maybe she shouldn't have said that.

"Food would have worked," he said with a clenched jaw.

"Well, I know *now*," Violet said.

"Were you raised in a barn?" Charlie asked. "This isn't your house. You can't climb on my roof and possibly damage something because you saw a cat."

Violet knew he was right, and her face burned in shame.

"I just . . ."

But Charlie wasn't done. "And what would have happened if you fell? I'd be on the line. Jesus Christ, didn't your parents teach you anything about etiquette?"

"Did yours?" Violet snapped back. "Yeah, I fucked up, but it's early in the morning and I panicked, okay? I'm sorry I was on your roof, but nothing is damaged and I'm fine."

Charlie glared at her. "You can't go onto roofs and do dangerous shit, Moore."

"It wasn't that bad. Are you telling me you've never been on your own roof?"

"No. If I need anything, I hire someone."

"Well, I don't have the money for that."

Charlie pinched his nose. "You don't have to have money for it. Your landlord should fix it."

"He doesn't fix anything I ask him to. I do it myself."

"That's against any lease agreement."

"I'd love to sue him with my massive amounts of money. But I'd rather use that for something, I don't know, like food."

"If you fell," Charlie said slowly, "I'd be held liable."

"I wouldn't sue you if I'm the idiot that went out to the roof."

"I'm supposed to take your word for it?"

"Well . . . *yeah*."

Charlie shook his head. "You're impossible. Just stay off the roof from now on."

Violet gritted her teeth but nodded. It wasn't an unfair request, but she felt like she had been chastised like a child.

The cat she had done it all for made a happy noise. Both Charlie and Violet turned. In the midst of their fighting, they had forgotten it was there.

"What about the cat?"

"I'll deal with it," Charlie said.

What did that mean? Was he taking it to the shelter? Was he letting it back outside in the cold?

He wouldn't kill it, would he? Charlie was cruel, but not *that* that cruel.

"No, I can deal with it," Violet said. At least if she did, she would know the cat was safe. "I . . . caused all of this anyway."

She turned, intending to get ready for her day. She hated leaving it at this, but she was in the wrong and she knew it. Normally, she would want to have the last word. But here? Now? She couldn't. She was in his territory, not her own.

"That's it?" Charlie asked. "You're not going to fight back?"

"On what?" Violet asked. "The cat? It's your house."

"On anything!" Charlie said. "You're going quiet and agreeing with me, which you *never* do."

"I don't see how that's going to help anything."

"What does that mean?"

"I can't exactly fight back, Charlie. I'm staying here for free. If you kick me out, I'm homeless, in case you didn't remember. I'm not gonna annoy you or get in your way anymore than I have to."

"I told you I wouldn't hold it over you."

"It doesn't matter!" Violet cried out. "You hold the cards here. This is your house. You can do what you want, and I have no say in it. You don't like me, and I'm staying in your home, so I know I'm already on thin ice. My only other option is my *car* and if I push you too far then I'll be sleeping in it."

"I wouldn't . . . I wouldn't do that to you."

"What evidence do I have that says otherwise? When are we *ever* nice to each other?"

"Is it not enough that I'm helping you?" Charlie asked.

Violet could only stare. Why would he help her if not to hold something over her head? After all, he started all of this. He was the two-faced liar. Why the hell would she ever trust something he said?

"Okay." Charlie sighed. "So, you *can't* believe I would help you without some sort of personal gain. Great. Do you ever try and trust people?"

"I do, and then they hurt me."

Violet wondered if Charlie would get it. Maybe he would remember the comments on her work that started all of this. Would he finally admit he was wrong? Would he finally say that maybe he had been way too harsh?

Charlie only shook his head. "I don't know how to get you to trust me, so how about we make it even?"

"What does that mean?"

"You do things for me in exchange for staying here."

"Things?" Violet asked. "Like . . . sex things?"

Violet would be lying if she said she *hadn't* thought about hot, angry sex with him, especially when they were in each other's faces, but the last thing she wanted was to give him more ammunition by sleeping with him.

And besides, what would Lauren think about that?

Charlie's face turned dark red. "No! God. No, not that."

"Then what?"

Charlie cleared his throat. "You want the score to be even, right? You want to hold some power over me?"

Violet wouldn't put it in those words, but he was somewhat right.

When she didn't disagree, Charlie sighed. "Fine. I need some help with things around the house."

"What?" Violet asked.

"There's some stuff I'm not good at doing. House stuff. You said you fixed up your apartment yourself?"

"Yeah, I did."

"Then, I need a few things done. My bathroom has some issues, and some of the steps to the basement are loose. Can you fix it?"

"Um . . . yeah, I probably can."

"Then do it. I need the help, and you need it to be even. So, we'll make it even."

It was a pretty good idea. She would feel less awful about her situation if she was doing *something* for Charlie besides taking up space.

"Okay, I'll take a look then."

Charlie nodded, and then turned to look at the small cat. It had finished eating and was busy sniffing around the house. "I'll take a day off work to deal with the cat."

"What are you going to do?"

"I'm . . . not sure. Maybe a shelter. Maybe it can stay here. Just . . . give me a minute to think, Moore. I can't do that when you're around." Charlie walked away, and Violet was left staring.

The cat followed him downstairs, as if it knew its fate was tied to Charlie. Violet sighed. She should have handled that better, and she knew Charlie was both pissed about the cat and having to offer her something to make her feel better about staying at his house.

He was obviously protective over this place, and Violet couldn't even blame him. She would be too.

It did need work, though. The stairs he had mentioned had almost caused her to fall a few times and fixing it would take her less than an hour.

Charlie probably didn't trust her to do it, so she wasn't sure why he had offered it in the first place.

But she also was desperate to prove her worth; she decided not to question it.

Charlie

Charlie was losing his mind.

For one thing, there was a cat in his house.

An adorable cat.

And Charlie was maybe thinking this should be *his* cat.

All of this was Violet's fault. He had gotten back from his run and then heard her scream. Then she jumped on his roof and yelled at him for worrying about her. Then she told him he could easily kick her out.

As if he ever would.

But Violet didn't believe that. She thought he was an awful person. And he didn't know *why* she'd started thinking of him as such. He hadn't done anything to her, at least until she went at him first.

He didn't understand why she didn't let him help her. He hadn't once tried to make her feel bad for staying with him, and she had gone above and beyond to ensure she wasn't making a mess. Why did she need to do more?

Charlie sighed as the cat came bounding down the stairs after him. It rubbed against his leg kindly, looking up at him with innocent blue eyes.

There was no way he was going to be able to take this cat to the shelter. Not when he had a home he could offer.

Charlie called out of work, knowing he needed to get the cat settled before going back. If anything good was coming out of this, he was going to have a pet.

Lauren was going to kill him. She hated animals, but then again, she never came to his house anyway. He needed someone to fill the space. And one had conveniently been found on his roof.

But Charlie didn't even want to think of Lauren, not since he hadn't told her yet about Violet staying with him. Technically, Lauren was avoiding him. Even if he tried to tell her, she wouldn't answer his calls. He couldn't tell her if he wanted to. Besides, Lauren would lose it if she knew, and demand he kick Violet out.

That wasn't an option.

So, just like the cat, he'd tell her about Violet . . . eventually.

All she would do is run off and not talk to him for a few months. She'd probably find a new guy to sleep with for a bit and then return when she inevitably missed Charlie.

This was how they had worked the last few years.

But he didn't want to think about that. What Lauren did on their breaks never failed to ruin his mood. He didn't have the time for that. He had a cat to deal with.

He took a quick shower and got ready for a long day.

Charlie's first stop was to a vet to make sure the cat wasn't microchipped. That was where he found out the cat was a girl and was only a few months old. He had no idea what to name her or what to get her, but the vet made him a list of everything he needed. From there, he dropped off the cat at the house and bought everything he would need for her.

When he finished and everything was set up, he sat on his couch and let the day run through his mind. Luckily, the cat still liked him after checking out her litter box and food, so she jumped up to get attention.

"Well, now I'm in trouble," he told the cat. "My girlfriend is going to kill me, if Violet doesn't."

The cat didn't answer, only pushed her tiny head into his hand. He hadn't called Violet by her first name, at least to her face, in years. Now he was using it in private.

Charlie knew he was losing his grip. When had letting her work on the house become an option? He spent years being too nervous about breaking something to even start. And how easily he offered it up to Violet because it was the *only* thing he could do to make it even.

Suddenly, his fears were less important than making her realize he wasn't going to fuck her over.

"You know," Charlie said as he rubbed the cat's ears, "I think I'm going to call you Roo, after Violet's attempt to get you down."

The cat purred.

"You like that name?" Charlie asked, smiling.

He didn't regret the choice to keep her.

The front door opened. Charlie frowned and saw it was already after five.

Violet walked in quietly, holding a reusable bag filled to the brim. Planks of wood were in her other hand.

She froze when she saw him.

Violet was in her usual teaching outfit, but she was frowning, as if she was in a terrible mood.

Great. That always went well for them.

"Is that the cat from earlier?" Violet asked.

"What other cat would it be?"

Violet rolled her eyes. He saw her shoulders tense, and he wondered if they were about to slip into a familiar fight. She took a deep breath, and the tight line of her shoulders loosened.

"You didn't take her to an animal shelter?"

"No," Charlie said. "I'm going to keep her."

Violet blinked, followed by a smile. Charlie felt his stomach do a strange flip. She was looking at the cat, but it was still odd to see her smile in his general direction, even if it wasn't for him.

"That's sweet. So, she's a girl?"

"Yeah. The vet confirmed it."

"Are you going to name her?

"I named her Roo after your stunt on the roof."

"That's perfect." Violet walked over and scratched the cat gently. "Listen, I'm sorry for getting upset earlier."

Charlie felt like the floor fell out from under him. "Um, what?"

"I'm sorry for getting upset. And yes, some of what I said is true. You do hold all the cards and I am worried if I upset you, you'll kick me out. But I shouldn't have lost it on you. I've lived alone for a long time, so someone telling me not to do something makes me defensive."

Charlie only gaped. She waited for him to say something, and her expression dropped when he didn't.

"Good talk," she muttered and then turned to walk away.

"No, wait," Charlie said. "I'm sorry. I'm not used to you apologizing."

"I'm trying, okay?" Violet said, repeating his words from yesterday. "Constantly fighting isn't going to work while I stay here. So, I'm trying to keep the peace."

"But you don't have to because you're afraid I'll make you leave. I know I've not been great to you, but I wouldn't do that. Not to anyone."

Violet stared at him for a long moment, and he wondered what was going through her mind. Obviously, there was something that had started all of this, and he had been dying to know what it was for years.

She'd yelled at him over a few comments on her work. Something more happened. Something she wasn't telling him.

He could ask her. Technically he *did* hold all of the cards. Maybe she would finally be honest with him now that he had given her a place to stay.

But it seemed wrong. Charlie didn't like manipulating people into getting what he wanted. That had always been Lauren's thing.

No, he couldn't take advantage of her now.

"I'm trying to believe you," Violet said, grabbing Charlie from his thoughts. "But letting me work on the house helps me feel like I'm pulling my own weight. So, thank you for that."

Charlie nodded slowly. He added, "Then I'm glad I told you to. But . . . be careful. This house means a lot to me."

"I can tell. I promise I know what I'm doing, but you can watch over me if it would make you feel better."

He was nervous about her starting work already, and he knew he wanted to see her in action before she tackled the more difficult parts of his home.

A few minutes later, she came downstairs in jeans and a T-shirt. She set up shop in his basement, including the saw she rented from the local hardware store. He watched as she measured and cut the wood, her arms flexing as she slid the saw through the board.

Those arms made his heart skip a beat. He had no idea she was so *muscular*.

The strange feeling only grew when he saw her lean over the stair, pulling off the old wood and replacing it with a new plank, screwing it securely into place.

They fit perfectly.

He decided he didn't like this feeling.

He'd always wondered why Violet seemed so strong, like she could take him out if she came at him. Now he saw why.

It made her look . . . hot, but he needed to get that out of his head immediately. The last thing he needed was to look too hard at Violet when they were sharing the same house. And yet, heat stirred in him while he looked at her. He had to tear his eyes away.

It was a betrayal to Lauren, but more so to himself. If he looked at Violet for too long, he'd inevitably find himself hurt.

"It's done." When Charlie looked at her again, she was packing the rental tools away. "Come check it out."

Charlie pushed off the washer and inspected it. The final stair held his weight with ease.

"Wow," he said. "How did you learn to do all of this?"

"You figure things out when you live in shitty apartments. It was easy."

Charlie couldn't take his eyes off the stair. He had been struggling to get parts of the house fixed up, partially because contractors were expensive, and because he didn't know if he could trust them.

He didn't know if he could trust Violet either, and yet her repair looked amazing in the dim light of his basement.

His great-grandmother would have been proud of it herself.

"It looks good," he said.

"You don't have to sound surprised. I may only be a schoolteacher, but I like things to be perfect."

He stared at the stair, a thought hitting him. Maybe she was such a perfectionist that she couldn't take criticism. Maybe it was her downfall. He had been the one who told her that her college paper wasn't solid, after all.

"Do you see something wrong with it?" she asked when he didn't look at her.

"No, I . . . It's a different color."

"It's new wood," she said, her voice not angry. "But I can stain it tomorrow."

Huh. Well, she didn't seem mad about *that* critique. What the fuck had happened with her statement of intent then? It had to be something else.

"Don't worry about staining it," he told her. "It's fine the way it is."

"Only if you're sure."

"This is a basement step, not something upstairs. It looks fine. Function over fashion."

"Okay, well, the wood is pretreated so it will hold up to moisture. I'm going to put this in my car and then head to bed." She walked past him, and Charlie only let himself look at her as she walked up the stairs.

He wondered if there would be a day he understood Violet Moore.

Probably not.

Charlie went to his own room after she was upstairs, needing time to think. His mind tried to put together pieces about his temporary roommate, and they simply didn't fit. She was so mature, yet sensitive enough to drop their friendship over a few comments, none of which were cruel.

Thinking about it made his head hurt. He needed a distraction, and he went through his phone, wondering who would be decent to talk to. All of his friends were going to ask about Violet.

But there was one person who didn't know any of this was going on—one person he trusted, that is.

His mother.

Charlie hadn't heard from her in a while. Maybe it was time to catch up.

Mara Davis was his favorite person in the world. She had been both a mother and a father to him when his dad left, and she had done it with grace. She lived on the outskirts of town, and Charlie found himself so busy he didn't get to see her as much as he would have liked.

His mother answered on the third ring. "Hello, Charlie," she said, her voice light. "It's late. Is everything okay?"

"No, I . . . finally got some work done on the house. I thought you might like to know."

"Oh, good. What did you get done?"

"The basement stair."

"Good! It was a hazard anyway. What made you finally make the change?"

I had Violet Moore here, and we needed to make it even.

"Oh, you know. I figured it was time." He needed to change the subject before he brought up Violet. He was already feeling far too conflicted about her. "Hey, are you still coming to Lewis's wedding in two weeks?"

"Two weeks? Shoot, is it that soon?"

"Yep," he said. "There's also the rehearsal dinner."

His mother was silent for a while. "Honey, I'm so sorry. I had a . . . work trip come up."

Charlie tried and failed to not feel disappointed, but his mother's work as a real estate agent *did* have her traveling sometimes, even if it was right around Christmas, and Lewis's wedding.

"It's okay. I can tell them you're not coming. I'll miss you though."

"Oh, you know I'll miss you too. I'm so sorry I didn't manage my time right."

"Don't be. You're busy. I get it." And he truly did. When he was a kid, his mother had to pull long hours to ensure she could pay the bills, but he never made her feel bad for not being home a lot. "Can we meet up sometime after?"

"Of course. I'll come by the house."

"Uh, maybe we should do a work lunch." The last thing he needed was for his mother to meet Violet. "Would that work?"

"I think I could make it happen," she said. "I do need to go. I have a long day tomorrow. Are you sure you're okay, honey?"

"Yeah," he said, still grappling with his disappointment. "Never better."

He said his goodbyes and then set down his phone. His mother was busy for the wedding. *Damn.*

But maybe it was a good thing. Charlie had no idea if Lauren was going to be there since she had been giving him the cold shoulder after their awkward lunch. His mom and Lauren didn't get along. That would be one less thing to worry about.

Plus, Violet would also be there. If his mother didn't like Lauren, who he loved, then she certainly wouldn't like Violet, who he despised.

Maybe this was meant to be. He needed to avoid an awkward situation as best as he could. Things were already bad enough.

Chapter Six

Violet

It was early in the morning. Violet arrived back from grabbing breakfast and was going to work on Charlie's shower. Charlie was usually out of the house at this time, so she figured it would be a good time to get it over with.

In the last few days, she received a list from Charlie on what needed to be fixed. The shower handle in his master bathroom was high on it.

She walked into Charlie's bedroom, feeling a little odd in the space. Roo diligently followed her.

"I don't know if he lets you in here," she told the small white cat, "so don't scratch anything."

Charlie knew she would be coming in here eventually, but she hadn't caught him before he left to tell him her plan.

Working on the house was giving her something to do. She felt better about staying with him if she had a purpose. And he wouldn't kick her out if she was *helping* him, right? He already didn't seem happy he had to let her work on his house. Maybe now he could see that she knew what she was doing . . . mostly.

His room was an addition, but it had bright windows and a fireplace on the wall.

Charlie's bed was made, and he had a basic gray comforter. Roo jumped on it immediately and made herself at home. Violet didn't have the heart to kick her off.

His room was organized, with old, oak furniture lining the walls. Violet couldn't help but trace the intricate designs on the dresser as she walked into the room.

But she was in here to look at the shower, so after one more moment of admiring the antique pieces, she went to the bathroom.

Violet immediately found the problem. The hot water handle was loose, and when she tried to turn it, it fell off. She frowned, looking up a few resources on how to replace it. Thirty minutes later, she picked up a new handle from Home Depot and was working on fixing it.

It was probably something a plumber should have done, but it wasn't too hard. Once the handle was installed, she tested it, finding the hot water running much better. She didn't know how Charlie had even used it before. Maybe he was only taking cold showers, and that was why he was so cranky all the time.

Violet checked the time and knew Charlie should be getting back soon. She cleaned up after herself and turned to leave.

However, she must not have known his schedule as well as she thought she did because she walked out of the bathroom and straight into Charlie.

It shouldn't have been a huge deal, but he was obviously walking into the bathroom to shower. And he was naked.

So very naked.

Violet's jaw dropped. He was tall, lean, and muscled. She was realizing how much bigger he was than her, and how . . . manly he was.

"Wha—Vi . . . ?" Charlie stuttered. He reached around her and ripped a towel off the rack, trying to cover himself. "Why are you in here?"

"I'm . . . The shower. Handles!" Violet said, her face feeling like it was so hot it could fry an egg.

"But . . . I thought you were at work!"

"No, I'm apparently looking at you naked!" Violet said. "And now I'm leaving. It's fixed, by the way. Enjoy your hot shower."

"Wait!" Charlie said, and Violet gave him a moment, but she didn't look him in the eyes. She couldn't, not after seeing his cock in full daylight.

And realizing it was very impressive.

The problem was, Charlie wasn't bad looking. It was the opposite. He was *too* good looking, but he was also taken, and he was Charlie fucking Davis. She didn't need to be looking at him like *that*.

Violet had always done a good job of ignoring Charlie's looks and focusing solely on his bad personality, but there was only so much one could do.

It had been far too long since Violet had gotten laid.

"Let's pretend this never happened," Violet muttered when she realized Charlie was at as much of a loss for words as she was.

"Okay," Charlie said. "Thank you for fixing the shower."

"Yeah, um. You're welcome," she said, before darting out of the room, face still aflame.

Her day didn't get better after that.

Violet struggled to keep her head on her shoulders after the incident with Charlie. Her mind slipped back to it at the worst time, right when she needed to be answering her students' questions.

And that was when, naturally, one of her kids acted out.

"Jason," Violet said, irritated with both herself and the noise in her room. "Please stop tapping your pencil."

"Ugh," Jason said, his voice loud against her sensitive ears. "You're not my mom. You don't get to tell me what to do!"

The silence in the classroom was deafening.

Violet only stared for a moment. Jason had been acting out more and more lately, but had never been the type of kid to yell in class.

She willed away her instinctive reaction. She had wanted to yell back, or to send him to Dr. Jones for punishment, but that would treat the symptom, not the cause.

In that time, Jason shrank away, obviously regretting his words.

"See me after class," Violet instructed, her voice flat, and continued as if nothing happened. A few kids snickered, but she glared at them. No need to make this worse than it already was.

When class ended, Violet thought maybe Jason would try to run. Most kids would, but Jason waited at his desk until everyone left the room, and then walked to her.

"Hi, Ms. Moore," Jason said miserably.

Violet sighed. She couldn't be mad at the kid, not when he looked so sad about it.

"Is something going on at home?" she asked. "What happened today wasn't right, but it also wasn't like you."

"Everything's fine," he muttered.

"I'm not going to use it against you. I want to make sure you're okay."

There was a long pause as the boy considered it. Then he said, "My dad isn't home anymore. Mom says he's not coming back."

Violet didn't know what to say. She could feel Jason's pain, because something similar had happened to her.

When she was five, her dad walked out the door and never came back. She hadn't seen him since.

Violet knew that Jason was hurting, so she decided to be kind instead of punishing him.

"I'm so sorry, Jason," Violet said. "I know that's hard."

"No, you don't. You're a teacher. You can't understand."

Violet sighed, trying her best not to get defensive. Jason's aggression faded.

"I'm-I'm sorry," Jason replied. "I shouldn't talk to you like that."

"You're right, but I also know you've got to be feeling a lot about all of this. And feeling a lot of things is hard."

Jason didn't answer. He glared at the floor.

Violet gave him a moment before continuing. "It's a big change, and I've . . . I've been there. My dad did the same thing, and it's so hard when it happens. But we can't treat others terribly because of our emotions, okay? We can feel them, experience them, whatever you need, but it starts being wrong once you take it out on others."

"I know . . . It's hard right now. My mom's doing it all. She has to work, cook, and clean. And she's always late picking me up. It sucks. I go and wait at the park, but it's cold."

"Why don't you stay in my classroom instead? I can stay late if you want me to."

"Really?"

"Yeah, I'll even throw some extra credit in."

For the first time, Jason smiled, and that made it all worth it.

"You're a good kid, Jason," Violet told him. "We just have to work on some stuff."

"Thank you. Can I stay now? I think my mom is gonna be a few minutes late."

"Sure. I'll be here for a while."

Jason nodded and went back to his desk. He pulled out homework and quietly worked. He seemed to be in much better spirits than before, and Violet was proud. She had given good advice and made his mood a little brighter. It was perfect.

Emotions are okay and we all need to feel what we feel, but not take them out on other people. It was great advice.

But are you living it?

Violet paused in her thoughts. She never wanted to give advice and not take it herself. Was she taking out her emotions on others?

The first person that came to mind was Charlie.

Was she taking out other emotions on him?

She looked at her laptop and thought about the grad school application she had asked him for help with. She could remember the comments like scars on her skin.

You'll waste everyone's time with this.

I thought you were better than this.

She shook herself out of the painful memories before they could overtake her. He had been downright cruel when she asked him to look at her work. She had asked him if he meant what he said—if he thought what he commented was okay.

And Charlie had said yes. He had even looked her in the eyes as he did so. Since that day, she knew he meant what he said.

Ultimately, he had hurt her. This wasn't her taking out her pain of Elijah on him. This wasn't her being mad about school and yelling at him. She was mad at *him*. Maybe a part of her always would be.

Violet knew that all she wanted was a genuine apology, and that would have smoothed things over. But he never said he was sorry. He always said he meant what he wrote.

That was how they got here.

Of course, Violet knew she wasn't right in fighting with him around their friends. She already planned to put an end to that. This wedding was going to go well, whether Charlie stuck to it or not.

But she was still hurt, and she didn't know how to move forward.

Jason stood up, bringing Violet out of her thoughts. He was looking out the window. "My mom is here. Thank you for letting me stay."

"No problem. Thank you for letting me help."

Jason left the classroom in a rush, obviously ready to go home. Violet smiled at him before packing away her things. The last thing she wanted to do was go home and see Charlie, but she also didn't want to stay in her classroom, either.

As she was grabbing her laptop, her phone rang. She groaned when she saw the caller ID.

It was her mother.

She *hated* it when her mother called.

"Hello?" Violet answered. Her day had already been hard. She didn't need anything more.

"Why haven't you responded to the message I sent you? Did you not see it?"

"I've been busy," was all Violet could reply.

"Not too busy for me. I'm your mother. And I'm worried about you being stuck in a dead-end job."

"It's not a dead-end job," Violet said. "There're plenty of avenues I can go—"

"Teaching middle school is for young girls and old wives. You can do more."

No, she couldn't—not that she'd even want to.

"I like my job."

"And yet you can barely pay your bills. What if an emergency happens? Then where will you be?"

Living with Charlie, apparently. But she'd never let her mom know that. She was grateful that her mom was far too busy with work to care to watch the news, otherwise she would have heard about it. Violet could only imagine how unbearable her mother would be if she knew about her near death by falling couch. The woman would insist she move out of town and back in with her. Her mom wanted control, and she wanted Violet to be like her.

Violet couldn't let her in.

"I'm fine, mom," Violet said. "Everything is all good here, and I like my job."

"You will regret this one day, and I won't bail you out."

The words hurt. They always did. But Violet was used to hearing them.

"I know," Violet said. "I'll talk to you later," she added, and then hung up the phone. She put her head on her desk, feeling a mixture of uncomfortable emotions churning in her chest.

Her phone pinged with a text, and Violet was sure it was her mom, but instead, it was her landlord.

Turdlord: Lot of damage. Foundation problems.

Violet groaned out loud. *Great*, more bad news. Just what she needed.

Charlie

Charlie didn't want to see Violet.

Not after her being in his bathroom while he was *naked*.

Ugh. She was never going to let him live it down. All he was going to hear was comments about his body the very minute she got home, and he got enough of those from Lauren.

Violet pulled in after five, and Charlie debated leaving the house entirely. She walked in with her laptop bag in hand, not even looking at him.

He closed his laptop and waited for a moment. Roo, who had been asleep next to him, perked up when she heard Violet walk in.

She bounded over to Violet, unaware of Charlie's worries. Violet smiled and leaned down to pet the cat for a moment, then she saw him looking at her.

"What?" she asked.

"Let's get this over with."

"What do you mean?"

"You saw me naked this morning, and I know you have something to say."

Violet's face turned a light pink. "Um, I don't. I'd honestly rather never speak of it again."

"Come on, nothing about how I wasn't flexing my abs, or how much hair I have?"

Violet looked genuinely confused. "You expect me to say something like that?"

"Kind of, yeah."

Violet shook her head. "I may hate you, but that's cruel. I'm not going there."

"But you could."

"Yeah, and then I would be more of an asshole than I already am. I'm not going to comment on your naked body. No thank you."

"Why not? You have plenty of ammunition."

"Actually, I don't." Violet shook her head. "And I don't want to go there, so don't ask me to explain."

This sounded too good to be true. "What about when we fight later? Will you bring it up then?"

"No. That's a line I'm not crossing. There's not much you could say that would make me go there with you . . . unless maybe you decided to go after how I look first."

Charlie was confused. Even Lauren had made comments on his body, and she was his girlfriend. The rare times he and Lauren were together, she would say how she wanted him to cut back on what he ate, or how she didn't like that he had body hair.

"O . . . okay," he said. "Thank you for not body shaming me."

"I don't think that's something I need to be thanked for."

Maybe not, but he was relieved anyway. "Why did you decide to fix my shower today anyway? You could have waited until the weekend when you had more time."

Violet's cheeks turned red. "I wanted to get that repair done because it was the one that affected you the most."

"Hang on, what? Why would that matter?"

"If I'm useful, then I have a place here," she said. Charlie opened his mouth to answer, but she kept going. "And you're literally saving my ass by letting me stay here for free, so I wanted to help you as a peace offering."

Charlie stared. A peace offering and Violet didn't compute.

"And I made it weird." Violet sighed. "Okay, I'll leave you alone now."

"Wait."

Violet paused and looked at him expectantly.

"It was nice to have the handle working. I appreciate it. And I do actually need the help, but I don't understand why you feel like you have to make yourself useful. What have I done since you've stayed here to make you think like this?"

"You don't like me—"

"That doesn't matter right now. Whether I like you or not, it doesn't mean I'm going to kick you out. Have I somehow made you feel like I was going to? Or is it just that we're enemies?"

Violet cleared her throat. "There is a part of me that knows I'm on thin ice because we're enemies and we always fight. But it's not just you that I'm like this with. I have a hard time accepting help from anyone."

"Really?"

"Yeah. I can barely accept it from Liv. It wouldn't be any better if I was staying there, either. I'd have to find a way to help to make it even."

His chest loosened when he realized it wasn't about him. This was about something to do with her—something he didn't have a part in.

Charlie was curious about her past, but as he opened his mouth to ask, he realized she wouldn't tell him anything about it. Not only did she not like getting help, but she also didn't like him. She hadn't in six years.

Violet had always stared at him like a kicked puppy when she thought he wasn't looking. Her eyes were dull and sad, and he didn't know why. She was always lost in thought, always remembering the thing that had caused this.

Something he had done.

More than anything he wanted to know what that was. He wanted to know why she went off on him after he sent her the first draft of her work back. Why was she so mad, and was it really the critique?

But he had tried to ask her about it a few times in the beginning, and she had looked at him with a confused expression on her face.

"You should know, Charlie," was how it started, and nowadays, it was, *"Fuck off, Davis."*

Eventually, he stopped trying. Lauren always said she wasn't worth his time anyway.

"I'm going to go to bed," Violet said softly. "And don't worry. I'll forget what I saw."

She disappeared up the stairs and Charlie sighed. Maybe he would eventually work up the courage to ask where it all went wrong. Maybe once she had another place to go and felt less trapped.

Maybe then they could move forward.

Chapter Seven

Violet

The next morning when Violet was ready for the day, she came down the stairs preparing to help Liv with decorating the wedding venue. Charlie was getting back from his run, and when they met in the foyer on her way out, they both paused, remembering what happened the day before.

And it wasn't about the repairs anymore. No, what was burned into her mind was seeing Charlie naked in his bathroom.

She needed to put it out of her mind. She said she was going to forget about it, but he looked so good. He was so much taller than her, with wide shoulders and a lithe, muscular build.

The worst part of hating him was that he was *exactly* her type. She loved tall men. She loved guys with strong jawlines and a touch of hair on their chests. She liked how in shape Charlie was, and her only regret was not turning to see his ass as she escaped. She knew from how he looked in jeans that it would have been worth it.

But *nope*. She was going to push it out of her mind.

Violet cleared her throat. "I'm heading out to see Liv for wedding decorating."

Charlie nodded; his mouth set in a frown.

"You know," she started before thinking. "Maybe I should let you see my boobs to make it even." Violet regretted it the moment it left her mouth. Charlie looked startled then turned red. "That was a poorly timed joke. Sorry." She laughed awkwardly and moved to leave.

"It's fine." Charlie shook his head. "You were right. We shouldn't talk about it."

"Fair enough. Boobs and dicks are off-limits."

Charlie looked at her, and then his eyes went down, right to her chest. His gaze snapped back up quickly.

Violet crossed her arms over her chest. She was sure she didn't compare to Lauren. Violet was 90% certain Lauren had gotten a boob job at some point, and Violet's natural pair, which were holstered in an old bra, couldn't compare.

"I'm going to go before I say anything else stupid. I'll see you later, Davis."

Violet made her escape in record time. She blasted music on the way to the wedding venue, trying to drown out all thoughts about Charlie and their last few conversations.

It didn't work.

"Hey," Liv greeted Violet when she got there. Her friend had garland hanging around her neck and tape on her fingers. "What's up? You look . . . weird."

"I'm fine," Violet reassured her.

"Is everything okay with Charlie?"

"Yeah, it's fine," she said quickly.

"You guys fought, didn't you?" Liv asked. "Do we need to reconsider a hotel?"

"You're not paying for a hotel for me." Violet shook her head. "You have enough going on with the wedding."

"But I'm worried."

"It wasn't a fight. It was only an embarrassing moment I'm going to repress forever."

Liv only raised her eyebrows.

"No," Violet said, knowing her friend was trying to get her to spill the beans. "You're going to laugh if I tell you."

"Now you have to tell me."

"I don't! It's not a huge deal."

"It obviously is. If you don't tell me, I'm going to guess."

"Liv, no—"

"Okay, maybe he found a picture of you from when you had braces. Oh! You were picking your nose in front of him, or he was picking his nose in front of you—"

"I saw him naked." It came out pained. Violet didn't even want to answer, but she didn't want to hear Liv guess all the other things that could have gone wrong.

Liv froze, and then she burst into laughter. "Naked? You saw him naked! How?"

"I was in the bathroom for something, and he walked in naked," Violet said miserably.

Liv laughed harder.

"It's so awkward!" Violet complained. "I then said this morning he should see my boobs to make it even."

"You didn't!"

Violet hid her face behind her hands while Liv continued to laugh.

"And you know what's worse? He even expected me to make fun of him, like I would go there."

"To be fair, you do yell at him a lot," Liv said.

"But not about how he *looks*! He can't control how he looks, only how he acts, and besides . . . it's not like there's much to go after anyway."

"I'm sorry, what? Say that again."

"Ugh, you know what I'm saying."

"No, because the Violet I know would rather *die* than admit Charlie is attractive."

"It's been in my face since I've been staying with him, okay? And it was really in my face when he was naked after he got back from a run."

"I mean, don't tell Lewis this, but I *have* looked."

"At his dick?"

"No! In general. He's hot, just not my type." Liv looked like she wanted to say more but didn't. "Anyway, did it cause a huge fight?"

"No, we're barely able to speak to each other. It's terrible."

"But progress. Whatever you're doing is working. Even if it is being 'friends' for the wedding."

Violet shrugged. "The wedding deal never included me living with him."

"But you're trying, and it seems to be going well. This makes us so hopeful for the wedding, so thank you."

"You're welcome. I want your day to go well." And it was going to. Violet would make sure of it.

Liv hugged her tightly. "Thank you. And when your wedding comes around, I'm doing all of this for you. Even if you'll probably never find someone as hot as Charlie is."

"Liv!" Violet admonished, going red in the face.

"Sorry, I couldn't resist!" Liv said, laughing. "Anyway, let's get to decorating. Do you think a twelve-foot-tall tree would fit over here?"

Charlie

Charlie spent the day bored. Weekends were usually the time that he had to try and take care of the house, and now Violet had taken over that task. He wasn't sure what to do with himself.

In the morning, he played with Roo and cleaned her litter, a chore he knew he was going to hate. Luckily it wasn't too bad, but having to clean up in the haunted basement where the litter box was at wasn't high on his list of fun things to do.

He then played an online video game with Lewis, who had been forced into taking a break by Liv. Lewis was throwing himself into working overtime to make sure they had enough money for their honeymoon, and he was so busy that Charlie had barely talked to him.

For a bit, all they did was play their game and chat about day-to-day stuff. As Charlie felt himself grow tired of the game, Lewis suggested they talk.

"Are you busy tomorrow?" Lewis asked.

"No, why?"

"I'm going into work tomorrow. I had requested it off for the wedding setup, but I want to work one last shift before we leave."

"Liv isn't going to be happy."

"I took today off, which was the best compromise we could come to since we're not having a bachelor party. Besides, she's going in too to make sure things are organized at her job before we leave. But I need someone to drop off the music setlist before the rehearsal. Can you do it?"

"Yeah, man."

"Violet will be there."

"Okay."

"Charlie, I want to be sure everything is going to be okay without anyone else there."

"No one's been at the house, and neither of us are dead. She's staying here, remember?"

"Right... which you've been oddly tight-lipped about."

"It's not great, but we're fine. I can handle running into her at the wedding venue. It's practice for the big day, right?"

"Okay, but you need to promise me to walk away if she sets you off."

"And go where? Home? She's here too. She's everywhere."

In both his home and mind.

"Go on a walk or something. Come on, man. You agreed to do this."

Charlie sighed. It was true—he had been the one to get himself into this situation.

"We'll be fine. I'm just dropping something off."

"Okay." Lewis paused for a moment, and Charlie heard talking. "Liv is back. I'll talk to you later, okay?"

"Yeah, man. Talk to you later." Charlie hung up the phone right as Roo jumped up for attention. Charlie sighed. He had forgotten to mention the new cat to Lewis. Then again, his friend was so stressed, maybe it was best that he waited.

Around that time, Violet pulled into the driveway.

He turned off the TV, wondering what kind of mood she would be in.

"Hey," he said when she walked in.

"Hey yourself." She shrugged off her jacket, holding it in her hands. There was a coatrack next to the door, but she had yet to use it, content to keep her stuff in the guest room.

"How is the venue looking?" Charlie asked as Roo climbed on him to get attention.

Violet smiled at Roo's antics, and Charlie felt himself look away.

"Almost done," she said. Her smile fell as she looked from Roo to him. "I have to start setting out chairs tomorrow, but the decorations are there."

"Lewis wanted me to come and drop off the setlist tomorrow."

"Then I'll see you there." She turned to go upstairs.

"Was it fun?"

Violet paused. "Why are you asking?"

"I'm kind of left out of this part of the wedding because of . . . you know, us fighting all the time. I haven't even seen it."

"It's looking good. Or at least I hope it is with how many pieces of garland I hung today. And anyway, isn't the bachelor party tonight? Aren't you busy with that?"

"I canceled it last week," Charlie said.

"Why?" Violet asked with a frown.

"We have a member of the wedding not being cooperative. You know how Lewis is, he doesn't want some wild rager of a party with strippers or anything like that. He's entirely committed to Liv."

"Which is how all men should be."

"I agree, but *someone* said he was inviting strippers anyway because it's his right to as a member of the wedding. So, I canceled it. Lewis would rather not have one than deal with that. The last thing he needs is to feel like he's not fully committed a few days before his wedding."

"Did the person who caused all of this happen to be Elijah?"

"How did you know?"

Violet shrugged. "A good guess. He's the only one who's stupid enough to do it anyway."

Charlie bit down, not wanting to let insults fly about Elijah. He had plenty, but if he started, he wouldn't stop, and maybe it would get back to Lewis that he fucking hated the guy.

"I think you probably did the right thing. Besides, bachelor parties are dumb. Not even Liv is having a bachelorette party."

"Elijah insisted. He said Lewis needed to mourn the end of his single life."

"Ugh," Violet groaned.

"It's dumb. This whole wedding planning is dumb."

"Why?"

"I've seen how much they're paying for this. Weddings are overpriced as hell. Plus, I think a lot of marriage is useless tradition."

"Really?" Violet asked. "Useless?"

"Yeah, you can be with someone without getting the government involved. I don't think I could feel so strongly about anyone to do that."

"Not even for Lauren?"

"No," he said. "Love doesn't work out for most people."

"What about Liv and Lewis? Do you think they won't work out?"

"No, they're happy. And this is what they want. I don't know." Charlie huffed. "I don't even know why I'm saying all of this. I think I'm stressed about canceling the party. Elijah was *mad*. I'm a little worried he'll invite strippers to the wedding."

Violet made a face. "I'd hope he wouldn't be that stupid."

Charlie only shook his head in response.

"Well, it's been a long day." Violet turned again to go to up the stairs. "I'll talk to you tomorrow."

"Have a good night," he said quietly. Roo jumped from him to follow Violet to the guest room. Charlie sighed. Roo had yet to sleep with him, somehow preferring the upper floor of the house. He didn't know if it was the room or Violet herself, but something up there always caught Roo's attention.

Charlie was a little jealous.

Chapter Eight

Violet

The next day, Violet went to the venue in an old shirt salvaged from her car and cheap leggings. They were not her best look, and the leggings were covered in cat hair from Roo constantly sleeping in her room. But she figured she wasn't seeing anyone important anyway.

Of course, she should have known she had cursed herself the moment she chose to look like a trash goblin.

This was the worst time to run into an ex. Her hair was greasy and piled high on her head, and she hadn't bothered to put on makeup.

She didn't expect to see Elijah until the wedding, but when she was putting out chairs, she could practically feel it when he walked in. He was the only ex in her friend circle, but since he had shown no interest in helping plan the wedding, she was able to dodge him altogether.

She should have learned to always expect the unexpected.

When she saw him, she immediately remembered the morning after their one night together. She was nervous to sleep with him, but he badgered her about it daily since their third date. She should have known sex was all he was after.

"You can't have expected me to actually want to be with you, right?"

It might have been two years ago, but the pain was still fresh. He wanted sex. She wanted a relationship. The miscommunication would have been fine if he hadn't berated her for it.

A part of her was still angry about it, but she didn't have time to deal with it. The last thing she needed was to start shit with *two* of Lewis's friends.

Ugh. Why had she ever agreed to go out with him in the first place? She never should have dated someone in their friend circle. It was asking for trouble. Even though she knew it was a bad idea, she hadn't trusted her gut. She'd ignored every red flag, waltzing right past them without a second thought.

Violet shook her head, trying to clear out the self-deprecating thoughts. Things had already been bad enough lately. She still saw her apartment crumbling when she closed her eyes at night. Being around Charlie was weird and painful. She didn't need anything else.

"Well, well, well," he said. Violet paused in her work, cursing every god she knew that he had decided to talk to her.

"What are you doing here?"

"Lewis is worried you and Charlie will blow up the joint, so I offered to keep an eye on things."

He was the last person she wanted keeping an eye on *anything*.

His eyes tracked up and down her body, and he smirked, as if he knew he had made the right choice leaving her. It made Violet want to crawl in a hole and die.

"Oh, come on," Elijah said. "Not happy to see me? Where's that fiery spirit? Or is it only for Charlie?"

"I'm here to put out the chairs," Violet muttered.

"You can't still be salty about what happened years ago. It wasn't a big deal. Aren't you past it already?"

Her whole body tensed. She *hated* the way he talked down to her, like she was less than him because she slept with him.

"Just leave me alone," Violet said. "I don't want to fight with you."

"That's right because you fight with Charlie enough. Be careful or you'll get a reputation."

Violet shook her head and didn't say anything.

"You know, when a girl has problems with multiple guys, it usually means *she's* the problem."

"We don't have a problem," Violet replied, turning to him. "Leave me alone."

"Look, I can't help it if you got the wrong idea from me. You don't have to be mad."

"I'm not mad," she said hotly.

"Yeah, it sure seems like you are," Elijah said. "Are you on your period or something?"

"No," she snapped. "Why are you talking to me? You've successfully avoided me for these last two years, so why now?"

Elijah shrugged. "I have to babysit you. Just like we all do."

"You don't have to do shit. If you were really here to keep an eye on things, you could easily stay in a corner and not talk to me."

"No, I do need to talk to you. No one will say it but me."

"Say what?"

"You make everyone miserable, Violet. You have Charlie so pissed off that he called off the whole bachelor thing. Lewis is panicking on his own wedding day because you delight in arguing with a guy you don't like instead of keeping your damn mouth shut."

"I'm—Charlie and I are going to be *fine*, Elijah," she snapped. "Not that you actually care."

"I care that you can't handle men. One look at the other sex and you're frothing at the mouth. You're a crazy bitch, Violet."

"Okay, enough," she snapped. "The bachelor party was your fucking fault. You didn't listen to Lewis's wishes."

"No, Charlie's been in a shit mood for weeks. You've been bringing him down."

"Oh, fuck off. You know what brings Charlie down? Not being listened to, which you conveniently never do."

"I don't need to listen to some ugly bitch like you. How about you stay away from the candy and run a little bit? Don't you want to be able to fit into your dress?"

Something in Violet broke. When it was her and Charlie, there was a line. She never went after Charlie's looks, and he never went after hers. Maybe they'd comment on clothes, but never someone's *body*.

And she refused to let Elijah do it and get away with it.

She was hurt but would feel it later. Violet had a feeling he had broken women with words like this, but she refused to let it be her too. Not this time.

"You talk mean game for someone with ears the size of his face."

Elijah went beet red. He gaped for a moment before staying, "D-don't mention my ears! Y-you're the one that liked me!"

"Do you really want to do this, Elijah? You think I'm mean with Charlie? That's nothing compared to what I'd have for you. Elijah, I've seen your dick, and let me tell you, it's not impressive."

Elijah's face turned a new shade of red. "How dare you—"

"You started this," she reminded him. "And you *don't* want me to finish, which seemed to be the case for our one-night stand, you selfish asshole. So, leave me the fuck alone. Are we clear?"

"You . . . are such a bitch."

"Thank you. It's an honor coming from a man so perfect as yourself," she said sarcastically and even gave a small bow to accentuate just how ridiculous this situation was.

"How are you ever going to find the love you so desperately want if you shame men like that?"

"I have a better question," Violet said. "Do you even know where the clit is? Try a diagram, or maybe getting your head out of your ass so you can learn how to go down on a woman."

Elijah's jaw dropped, and Violet kept going.

"Listen, I have yelled at a man and won those fights for six years. And Charlie is way better at fighting than you. Do *not* fuck with me."

God. That felt good. Was it going to bite her in the ass later? For sure. Elijah was the type of guy to seek revenge. He was going to either do something at the wedding, or pop back in later and go off.

That was what she didn't like about him. He'd run to lick his wounds like a child and then bite back after the argument was over. He had done it with other members of the friend group. Micah hated him for that exact reason. At least Charlie was quick enough to do it in the moment.

But for now, Elijah was darting away from her with a red face. She leaned back and watched him go, ignoring her shaky hands. She'd been building up the idea of this unwelcome reunion with him for a long time, but getting to finally say what she wanted to felt incredible.

Charlie walked in, obviously shocked to see Elijah running out of the venue, and her mood dropped.

Fuck. Charlie was Elijah's friend, and even though he was mad about the bachelor party, she didn't doubt he would defend Elijah if he found out what she said.

Especially after Violet had admitted she wouldn't body shame someone for something they couldn't help. Sure, Elijah had done it first, but she doubted Charlie would see it that way.

But Violet didn't have it in her to feel remorseful. She did, however, worry that Charlie was going to ask her what happened, and when he started walking to her, she sighed.

This wasn't going to be a pleasant conversation.

Charlie

When Charlie walked into the wedding venue, he wondered if maybe Violet had chosen the wrong career path. The basic room had been completely transformed into a winter wonderland, complete with shimmering lights and beautiful Christmas trees.

All Charlie could do was stare. It looked amazing.

His thoughts were interrupted by a red-faced Elijah stalking around the corner. Charlie froze, wondering if he was about to get yelled at for the damn bachelor party, but Elijah didn't seem to notice him. He nearly ran for the exit and slammed the door behind him.

He found Violet staring at the back of Elijah, looking pissed.

"Were you the reason Elijah stormed out of here?" Charlie asked.

"Nope." Violet turned without another word to him.

"You're lying."

"Maybe, but I'm not doing this with you. I am not telling you about Elijah because you two are friends, and I don't want to get told how wrong I was."

"Hey, no need for insults. I'm not friends with Elijah."

Violet paused, then slowly turned to him. "How do I know you're not lying to me?"

"Come on, Moore. He's an asshole. I canceled a party because he can't respect anyone's opinions other than his own."

"But you hang out with him."

"Only because Lewis does. I don't like him. I think he's self-centered."

"Well . . . I guess we found one thing to agree on."

"I keep my mouth shut because Lewis likes him for some reason and wanted him in the wedding, but he sucks. Anything that makes him suffer is good in my books."

"What if I told you I went off on him?"

Charlie paused. That *shouldn't* have been a problem. He'd love to hear about Elijah getting what he deserved, but for some inexplicable, ridiculous reason, hearing it was *Violet's* doing made him feel defensive, like she should have been fighting only with him. Was this jealousy that it wasn't aimed at him?

"I would say he deserved it." At least *that* wasn't a lie.

This side of Violet, the angry, spiteful side of her, was always so intoxicating.

Violet gestured to one of the chairs and sat down. Charlie followed, feeling an odd mix of curiosity and envy.

"For context, I slept with Elijah two years ago."

"Excuse me?" he said it harshly. Hearing Violet slept with Elijah, of all people, made him lose the battle with his anger for a moment.

"I don't need your judgment."

"Sorry," Charlie said, getting a handle on his dark emotions. "Continue."

"Lewis set it up. We went on a few dates, and he said he wanted a relationship. Then after we slept together, he made it very rudely clear he wasn't interested. I remember what he said," Violet added. "It was along the lines of '*I can't believe you'd think I'd settle for you.*'"

"Him settling for you? I didn't know he had a sense of humor."

Violet paused and smiled at him. "I'd almost consider that a compliment."

"Maybe one in the distance. Go on."

"Today, he blamed me for you canceling the party."

"How?"

"He said I had you in a bad mood since I was staying with you."

"That might be my fault. I did mention you," Charlie admitted. "But I would have canceled it whether you were staying in my house or not. I have a feeling I couldn't have stopped him, so canceling was the best option."

Violet pursed her lips. "Then it kind of makes sense why he blamed me."

"Not really. It's still his fault for inviting strippers to the party. Just because I was already in a bad mood doesn't mean that wouldn't have made me lose it either. I fucking *hate* when people don't listen."

She thought about it.

"And if it was me who was the problem, wouldn't you be *looking* for a way to get out of the house?"

"You're not wrong."

"Anyway, he was here because Lewis sent him because he was worried we would fight."

"I told Lewis we would be fine."

"I guess he didn't believe you."

"So, Elijah was who he sent?"

"I'm not saying it was a good idea, but I'm sure Elijah jumped at the opportunity the moment he heard I would be here. He confronted me about the party. I told him he was wrong, and he went on to call me a crazy bitch who needed to lose a few pounds."

"He *what*?" Charlie asked. "Please tell me you didn't take the high road."

"Oh, I took a low one."

"How low?"

Violet winced. "I threw it right back. He insulted how I look so I gave him a taste of his own medicine." She looked away from him. "I told him his ears were the size of his face, his dick was small, and he needed a diagram to find the clitoris."

Charlie was shocked for a moment before he burst into laughter. He couldn't help it, he'd *never* heard Violet talk like that, but he knew she wouldn't lie. And judging by how embarrassed Elijah was, she'd done exactly what she said.

"That's perfect. He deserved it."

"Yeah, maybe. But I feel bad for bringing his body into it. I was so mad at what he said. None of those things truly matter to me when it comes to dating, but I'm not one to take insults lying down."

"Don't feel bad. You've always been like this. If someone hurts you then you pay it back. You don't take shit."

"I'm surprised you're not offended that I insulted his looks."

"No, if I made a comment like that, I would have had you insulting me in the same way coming. First rule of having an enemy, you don't dish out what you can't take."

"At least someone gets it. This is why you're my favorite person to argue with. And besides, there's nothing much I could say about you anyway. I *have* seen you naked."

"I thought we were erasing that from our memories."

"Hey, I'm just saying, you're working with better parts."

If he thought seeing Violet angry did something to him, nothing compared to her being *pleasant* to him. Heat coursed through his body, and if he didn't have Lauren, and if she was *anyone* else, he'd ask her to dinner.

But he couldn't. He did have Lauren, and Violet wouldn't want him anyway.

"Um, sorry." Violet's face was pink. "We won't talk about it. I'm glad you didn't take his side."

"No, fuck Elijah."

"That's how I got in this situation."

"You can do better."

"According to him, I'm gaining too much weight."

"Weight doesn't matter. You're you."

"I can't tell if this is a compliment or an insult."

It was a compliment, but he couldn't exactly call her the most gorgeous woman he'd ever seen without making it weird.

"Don't worry about him. He's not worth your time."

"Well, at least you and I are getting along. We're not fighting, so I guess I have to release that anger somewhere."

"He's not even on the same playing field as us." Charlie felt bitterness creep back into him. He didn't want to be put in a box anywhere near Elijah.

"Don't get jealous," Violet said, smirking at him and standing. "Our fights will always have a dear place in my heart."

She walked away then, seeming to be in a better mood, and returned to setting out chairs. Charlie sat for a moment longer, wondering why his heart was racing. He shouldn't care about Elijah being an ass any more than he did before. But now, he wanted to punch him in the face.

He shouldn't care that Violet looked at him with her gorgeous smirk, because they hated each other. She was immature and couldn't handle basic critique.

And yet . . . it all mattered. It all felt exactly how it shouldn't, and he didn't know how to get it to stop.

Chapter Nine

Violet

When the day of the rehearsal dinner arrived, Violet was nervous about seeing Elijah again, and didn't know whether or not he would want revenge. Luckily for her, she received a text from Liv saying he was busy that night. He'd still be in the wedding, but she would be so busy that she could avoid him.

Violet spent her night getting ready, putting on an emerald green floor-length dress, similar to the one she'd wear the next day. Her hair was pinned up with delicate curls hanging around her face. She walked down the stairs, still feeling antsy. The last time she had been this dressed up around Charlie, he said she was so overdressed she was trying to upstage the bride.

Charlie was coming out from his room, messing with the cuff of his navy blue dress shirt. He was so focused he nearly ran into her. He jumped, almost like he'd forgotten she was there, and then he took in her appearance. Violet felt like melting into the floor at his gaze.

"If you make a comment about me looking overdressed, I will shove my heel into your eye," Violet said. She couldn't look at him, so she bent down to pick up Roo and pet her. Cats were a great distraction.

"No, I wasn't going to say anything. You look . . . fine."

Roo wiggled out of her arms, and Violet brushed her hands on the soft material of the dress, making sure Roo hadn't left fur behind. She adjusted her heel and grabbed her small black purse. When she turned to say goodbye to Charlie, he was staring at her again, his eyes intense with an emotion that she couldn't name.

If it were anyone else, she'd say he was checking her out.

But she knew that wasn't the case. Besides, Charlie had Lauren, even if he barely mentioned her.

Even if he probably would never marry her.

But nothing good would come of her mentioning his odd staring, so she ignored it. This was a road neither of them needed to go down.

She needed to get to the venue anyway. All of Liv's family would be at the rehearsal and she wanted to make a good impression. Everyone Lewis had invited, minus Elijah, was going to be there tonight too. This was the real deal.

The bridal party was going to run through the motions of walking down the aisle. Luckily, Violet managed to dodge the dancing class but was still paired with Charlie for a part of the first dance and when they left the aisle. Lewis wasn't sure about letting Charlie and Violet dance together, but with their fake friendship deal still in place, he had gone along with it.

Plus, it meant Violet got to stand next to Liv.

They would make it work.

"I'm going to head out," Violet said, grabbing her peacoat. "I have to help Liv with bringing in the food."

Charlie adjusted his tie. "Okay. I'll see you there."

She drove to the venue on the west side of Nashville. As she drove through residential areas, houses were decked out in strings of white and multi-colored Christmas lights. Garlands adorned the streetlamps near the more commercial areas, giving even their bland surfaces a winter-esque feel.

When she arrived, Liv was in a white dress looking stressed. Violet jumped into action to help. The caterers hadn't set up the dinner tables, so she had to do it. Several strings of the lights didn't work, so she fixed that too.

By the time Charlie got there, Violet was busy making everything perfect ahead of the start of the rehearsal. She suddenly realized he had Lauren with him, and it made her stress worse.

She hadn't heard about Lauren at all—other than the fact Charlie didn't see himself marrying her. Violet didn't know what Lauren thought about the situation, but it couldn't be good. Lauren had never liked her.

But Charlie didn't talk or even look at Violet. She expected maybe a *hello* or a wave, but he was so focused on his girlfriend that they didn't even get one word in. It was a little worrying, and she knew all eyes were on them since they fought at every event they attended. The last thing she wanted was to have any issues when Liv looked as worried as she did.

The actual wedding rehearsal was one of the first things they did. They all got into position with Liv, Violet, Micah, and Bree walking down the aisle to meet Lewis, Charlie, Damon, and eventually, Elijah.

Since Elijah had canceled, another friend stepped in.

Violet went through the motions, but when they were standing at the altar, she could see Charlie looked nervous. She raised an eyebrow at him, but he wouldn't meet her eyes. She wondered if she had somehow pissed him off in the last hour, but they hadn't talked.

Not that lack of communication had ever stopped them from fighting before.

When they walked down the aisle, Violet's arm linked with his, the whole venue watched them closely. "Jesus," she muttered. "You'd think I was the bride."

At least that got a smile out of Charlie. It didn't last long; it faded the second he saw Lauren, and the look on her face screamed *murder*.

Violet's eyes darted to the floor.

At dinner when the bridal party had separated, Lauren made a beeline for Charlie. Violet couldn't walk away fast enough. She felt like the whole situation was a ticking time bomb.

Except when she managed to escape, she ran right into Liv, who grabbed Violet.

"Hey," Liv said, her voice so sharp it almost hurt. "What's wrong with Lauren?"

"I-I don't know," Violet said.

"I don't want any drama here. My family's already caused enough and I don't need them talking."

"You want me to go try to fix it?"

"No! You'll make it worse!" Liv snapped, but then she blinked. "I mean . . . maybe you should? Did you do anything?"

Violet shook her head.

"Oh, God. I don't know what to do. Why would he bring her if she's mad?"

"I don't know. He didn't even tell me she was coming."

Liv rubbed her temples. "Okay, I don't think you going over there is going to help, but keep her from making a scene, okay? If you all are going to fight—"

"WHAT DO YOU MEAN SHE'S LIVING WITH YOU?"

The entire venue went silent.

"Oh no," Violet said.

Liv went pale. She glanced at Violet with wide eyes. "Is she talking about you?"

"I don't know!" Violet hissed.

Lauren turned then, and her eyes found Violet's in an instant. And Violet could feel the pure rage in it.

"Oh, she definitely is."

"Take it outside!" Liv snapped. "We had a fucking deal!"

For a split-second, Violet felt the pain of Liv's tone. But she didn't get to sit in that feeling long. Liv turned her around and pushed her toward Lauren and Charlie, the last two people she wanted to see.

"You!" Lauren yelled at Violet.

"Outside. Now," Violet snapped right back.

Thankfully, instead of arguing, Charlie grabbed Lauren and headed for the door. She ripped her arm out of his grasp and glared.

"Lauren," Violet said, losing the battle of staying calm. "Whatever the fuck crawled up your ass will have to wait until we get outside, or I will drag you out like a fucking toddler."

Lauren looked to Charlie, who pointed at the door as well. Lauren looked like she wanted to stab them both, but she turned on her heel and stormed outside. Violet followed, feeling the cool air hit her as they all stepped from the venue where Lauren was waiting.

Her face was red and angry. She looked between the two of them with narrow, furious eyes.

"You're living together?" she accused.

"You didn't tell her?" Violet asked Charlie.

"She hasn't talked to me in weeks," he replied.

Before Violet could digest that, Lauren spoke again, "You should have told me before you decided to let her stay in your house like some half-baked prostitute!"

"Hey!" Violet barked. It was a voice she rarely used. "I understand you're mad at your boyfriend, but—"

"Oh, he is *not* my boyfriend."

"Then problem solved. You have no reason to be jealous."

"He's still *mine*," Lauren said. "Besides I was invited weeks ago by Liv and Lewis."

"First of all, you can't own a person!" Violet said, voice high in irritation. "And you were invited as a *date*. Not as a jealous ex who can't keep her cool. What the *fuck* is your problem?"

"Watch your tone."

"I'll watch my tone when you stop going after Charlie and me for doing nothing wrong."

"Oh, you're sticking up for him? You. *Really*? Are you two sleeping together?"

"No!" Charlie and Violet yelled at the same time.

"I don't believe you."

"Jesus Christ, Lauren!" Violet cried out. "Why would you think that?"

"Because I don't trust either of you."

"Then why are you here? Go home and be insecure there! You don't have to ruin someone else's wedding rehearsal because you're acting like a child."

"You're going to let her talk to me like that?" Lauren asked Charlie angrily.

Violet looked at him, wondering if he was about to turn on her in favor of Lauren. She wouldn't be surprised.

"You're in the wrong, Lauren." Charlie sounded as annoyed as Violet felt.

"Oh, come on! I came here to be your date so you wouldn't have to be alone, and this is how you treat me?"

"I would have been fine to come alone!" Charlie snapped. "You showed up here out of nowhere."

"Wait, seriously?" Violet asked.

"Watch what you say, bitch."

"Lauren, enough!" Charlie's voice was loud. Violet tensed, as if it was directed at her. But for once, it wasn't. "Go home. You're obviously too upset to be here."

"*Me*? I'm in the wrong here?"

"Yes!"

"I can't believe this," she muttered. "Okay, fine. I'm done. Goodbye, Charlie."

Lauren stormed away but slowed after a few feet, giving Charlie the chance to follow her.

He didn't.

When Lauren was out of sight, Violet could only stare. Tonight, she had pissed off her best friend, been the subject of a blowout fight, and been called a bitch by Charlie's girlfriend.

She felt terrible.

But for once, it wasn't Charlie's fault.

She was angry, hurt, and irritated, but *he* didn't have anything to do with it.

She needed to not treat him like he did.

They stood in silence, for once not against each other. Something in the cold darkness of the night shifted. Violet wasn't sure what, but she saw Charlie as a little less of an enemy.

Charlie

"Liv looked mad," Charlie said.

He knew Violet was going to fucking *kill* him.

His heart was racing, and he'd never been angrier at Lauren in his life. Not only did she show up unexpectedly to meet him at the rehearsal, but she ruined it too.

Violet was staring in the direction Lauren had gone, lips pursed. He readied himself for her to turn it on him.

"She was," Violet replied.

"I'm sorry," he apologized. "I didn't know Liv and Lewis had invited her directly, and I seriously didn't think she'd show only to cause a scene like that."

"You really didn't know?"

"No. She met me in the parking lot and acted like we were fine, despite us fighting the last time I saw her."

"Okay."

"Okay?" he asked, his heart racing. "Shouldn't you be mad?"

"I am mad, but not at you. I hate that this happened at their rehearsal dinner. Usually, it's us causing the problem."

He could only stare at her in shock.

"What?" she asked, confused. "You said she came here unannounced, and after what I just saw, I'm more inclined to believe you rather than her."

"We've fought for six years."

"She makes a striking impression."

"I don't understand why you're not mad at me. I should have told her, I—"

"Stop." Violet held up her hand. "It's like I said, I'm not mad at *you*. But I am mad at Lauren, and a bunch of other things we don't have time to go into, but I'm not interested in taking out my feelings on you. I'm not a toddler."

Charlie stared at her. That was . . . oddly mature of her. Not even Lauren could manage being with him for more than a few days before she was snapping at him—even when he hadn't done anything.

"I know I have no business asking this . . . but why are you with her?"

"We've been together since high school."

"And? Is she secretly kind when no one is around? Do you only care about her because she's hot? There must be something."

"I . . . There's . . . We have a history." It was all Charlie could think of.

"Okay, I'm pushing my luck here," Violet muttered. "She sounds like a shit girlfriend."

Charlie wanted to be offended, but he couldn't find it in him to defend Lauren—not after tonight.

"This is how love ends up," Charlie said. "It starts out great, and then at some point, it goes to shit. It happened with my parents, and it happened with Lauren too."

"This is how you think love is?"

"Yes."

Violet stared at him for a long moment. "Wow, you're the cynic."

"I prefer realist."

"Davis." Violet crossed her arms. "I'm not all that experienced in love, so maybe I'm wrong. But I don't think love is what you're thinking it is."

"It's a feeling, and feelings fade."

"It's more like a choice," Violet said. "You work at it and love them even when you're feeling angry or when you're tired and they won't stop rambling about something. Feelings fade, sure, but there's always something more at the end of the day. Sometimes instead of happy feelings, it's work and it's hard. That's why sometimes it doesn't last. Some people storm off and never come back. Some people make it about themselves and no one else. That's when love ends, because that kind of love isn't good and—" She paused, noting his lack of reply. "And I'm rambling, sorry."

"N-no," he said. "It's fine. I don't mind. Go on."

"What I'm trying to say is there's a line to be drawn between what is a mistake and what is a person continuously hurting you because they can. Some people are willing to grow, and when they are, love can last."

"I don't think that is real," he said.

Violet looked disappointed.

"I'd like to think that either one of us could do it," she said, after a long moment. "Maybe not with *love*, but with friendship. *We* could grow." She stared at him, and with his absolute silence again, she looked disappointed. "But maybe that's just me."

She turned to go inside, but Charlie grabbed her arm.

"What are you saying?" he asked. He hadn't dared to hope for another chance at friendship with her, but hearing her bring it up had him ready to beg for it.

"We've changed, right? We're out here in the cold having a civil conversation. We've had multiple, actually. And if we can change, why not anyone else?"

He stared at her. "Violet," he said. "That's all I want."

She blinked, shock crossing her face. "What did you call me?"

Shit. He had been calling her by her last name for *years*. But he had been thinking of her first name for longer. Her first name was what he dreamed of.

"I called you Violet."

"Am I Violet to you now?"

"You . . ." He paused, giving himself a moment to feel how much he wanted this. "You mentioned people could change, right?"

"Yeah, if they want to." She gave him a small smile. "Charlie."

He barely heard it past the hammering of his heart, but it was tattooed on him the moment she uttered it.

"I'm freezing," she said. "Can we go in? We have to face the music sometime."

"Yeah," Charlie said, nodding. "You need to warm up."

He let go of her arm, even though he ached to touch her for longer, and followed her inside.

They could hear people mingling, and no one seemed to notice them slip in. Charlie saw Violet glance over at Liv, looking ashamed.

"This was my fault," he said.

Violet rolled her eyes. "No, it wasn't. It was Lauren's. Liv's just mad that it happened."

Charlie opened his mouth to ask what he could do to fix it, but they were interrupted.

"That was literally the opposite of what we asked you to do," a male voice said. Simultaneously, Charlie and Violet turned to see Lewis.

He didn't look enraged, but he didn't look happy. His face was contorted with disappointment, which was the worst emotion of all.

"This one is my fault. Don't take it out on Violet," Charlie explained.

Lewis's eyebrows furrowed, and Violet sighed.

"No, that's not true. It's *Lauren's* fault."

"Hang on, what?" Lewis asked looking between them.

"Charlie didn't know Lauren was going to show up. I know you and Liv invited her a while ago because she was close with Charlie, but she never made plans with him to be here."

"Hold on," Lewis said, shaking his head. "You're not the ones who fought? You're defending each other?"

"Yes," Violet said. "For once, we weren't the drama. I think we're all surprised."

"I was *kind of* the drama," Charlie said, wincing.

"No, Lauren was all of it."

"Just Lauren?" Lewis asked.

Charlie sighed. "She found out I'm letting Violet stay with me."

"You didn't tell her before?"

"Lauren hasn't talked to me since we had a fight two weeks ago. We weren't even together."

"Which is why she had *no* reason to go off like she did," Violet added.

"Hang on, I'm so confused. So, Lauren was the one who yelled, right?"

"Yes."

"And you two *both* were outside with her, and you didn't pick a fight with each other?" Lewis asked.

"Yes," both replied.

Lewis stared, a look of shock on his face. He slowly shook his head. "Liv told me there was drama between you two and you were outside with Lauren."

"No, Liv sent me to break up the fight," Violet explained. "Forcefully."

"Which she immediately regretted, since she figured you would egg it on."

Violet opened her mouth, but then closed it. The offense on her face faded and was replaced by guilt.

"She didn't," Charlie said. He didn't like seeing her look so guilty. "We were serious when we told you we were trying to be friends for the wedding."

"Yeah, no one believed that," Lewis said.

"Maybe you should."

"Okay, okay. Maybe you were serious about keeping it all in for the wedding, which is . . . oddly working. Is Lauren gone?"

"Yes," Charlie said.

"She left in epic meltdown fashion," Violet said. "She looked like a toddler running to their room when they're told to go to bed."

Lewis sighed. "Violet, don't. You guys made it through tonight without a fight. Don't insult Lauren now."

"To be fair," Charlie interjected, "Lauren called Violet both a prostitute and a bitch tonight. I-I think she's earned a little more than being called a child."

"She said *what*?" Lewis's eyes went wide. "She was this mad about Charlie making sure you weren't homeless?"

"She's got issues, Lewis," Violet answered. "I don't know what you want me to say. I think everyone here is lucky I didn't return the drink from the engagement party."

"You'd be in the right to," Charlie muttered.

"Am I . . . am I in an alternate universe right now?" Lewis asked.

"Maybe you are," Violet replied with a shrug. "I feel like I am. I mean I stood up for *Charlie* against his ex-girlfriend."

"I mean . . . I wouldn't call her an ex," Charlie said. In all the time he had been on and off with Lauren, he never called her that.

"I can, and I will," Violet said, rolling her eyes. "You shouldn't go back to her after this. She's insufferable."

"Okay," Lewis said, laughing uncomfortably. "Let's not ruin your track record here."

Charlie didn't feel like they were going to break it, but he let it go, only for his mind to circle back to what Violet had said.

Lauren was his ex-girlfriend.

When had that happened? Was that always what she was? They had dated through college but broke up for a while right when they were all graduating. Ever since then, ever since his rivalry with Violet started, nothing had been the same.

Had they always been exes? Were they ever truly a couple?

"Anyway," Lewis said, pulling Charlie out of his thoughts. "Liv wanted to say sorry for snapping at you. She'd tell you herself, but her grandma has had her trapped for fifteen minutes talking about 'wifely duties.'"

Violet replied, "It's okay. She was stressed."

Charlie wasn't sure he heard that right. Violet was letting someone yell at her? She never did that with him, and she certainly hadn't done that for Lauren just now. Did Liv get a free pass because they were friends?

"Well, she's not mad at you. She regretted it as soon as it happened."

"Okay," Violet said, nodding. Charlie realized she wasn't mad, she was *hurt*. And it had been by Liv, of all people. He had seen her angry, but she never showed her emotions beyond the anger that came first.

"I've got to go try to rescue her," Lewis said softly. Charlie waved him off, turning to Violet fully.

"You okay?" he asked.

"Yeah, I'll be fine. It's not been my best night, though."

"This thing will be over soon. If you're still feeling weird . . . we can talk about what happened."

Violet gave him a bewildered look.

"You said we were changing. I figured I'd offer."

Violet stared at him, unsure. Then she said, "Okay. I'll-I'll think about it."

Something loosened in his chest. "Pull me aside if you need me."

Chapter Ten

Violet

That night, the plan was for Violet to stay in the hotel suite Liv reserved for them near the venue while Lewis stayed in the apartment. But as the rehearsal dinner ended, Violet wasn't sure if she was still invited.

"If you're not, come back to my house," Charlie said, shrugging.

As much as it pained her, Violet needed to talk to *someone* about what happened. Charlie was the only one who wasn't busy or too close with Liv to talk about it.

Violet told him exactly what she said, and he had listened with oddly rapt attention. He was surprisingly good to vent to.

"I still feel bad for everything," Violet said, taking another sip of her drink. "Liv is different. She's never snapped at me like this."

"Yeah? I mean what if it wasn't Liv?"

"I'd have snapped right back."

"That probably wouldn't have helped. But you do deserve an apology."

Violet looked out into the reception area, where Liv was wrapping up dinner.

"I should say something, shouldn't I?" she asked.

"Probably. This would be the best time to before you head to the hotel."

Violet and Charlie were hanging out near the bathrooms, not wanting to draw more attention to themselves. Dinner had been an awkward affair. Liv was busy with her family, and she and Charlie were seated as far away from one another as was possible. Both of them ate alone.

Violet downed the rest of her drink and handed the cup to Charlie. She took a deep breath and walked out of their hiding corner and into the reception area.

Liv looked up, eyes falling on Violet immediately.

"Violet!" Liv said. "Hey."

Violet wanted to run, but she ignored the feeling. She needed to face this.

"Hey," Violet said. "I know you were stressed earlier, and I know in the past Charlie and I have made things difficult, but this time, it wasn't me who was in the wrong. I did exactly what you asked of me, and I don't think I deserved to be snapped at."

Liv nodded immediately. "You're right. You're totally right. I took it out on you when Lauren was the one causing problems, because I thought . . . I don't know. I don't think I was thinking at all. And that was wrong of me, so I'm sorry."

Violet nodded. "Thank you for the apology."

"And I totally get if you don't want to help tonight. You don't have to come to the hotel or anything, I—"

"No, I'll go to the hotel," Violet said. "I wanted to make sure you still wanted me there."

"Of course I do!" Liv said. "You're helping so much, and I need my best friend there to make sure I don't lose it tonight." Liv blinked away the tears in her eyes. "I feel so bad for snapping at you."

Violet opened her mouth, ready to brush it off as nothing, but then she closed it. This wasn't nothing. It had *hurt*.

"I recently had a conversation with one of my students about how he was taking out his frustrations on people around him instead of dealing with his emotions, and I think that's what happened tonight," Violet explained. "We can't help but have strong feelings about things in our lives, but we can control how we treat others because of them. I ask if this ever happens again, you try to remember that."

Liv nodded. "I will. And that's exactly what happened tonight. God, Violet, you are so much smarter than the rest of us."

Violet laughed humorlessly. "I don't think I would be a schoolteacher if I was."

"No, seriously. It takes a special kind of person to do what you do and like it."

Violet didn't think it took much of anything to teach kids, but the sentiment was nice anyway. Liv hugged her tightly, and the worry Violet had been carrying for hours lightened.

"Do you need any help cleaning up?" She asked.

"Yes, please," Liv said, and Violet turned to get to work.

They tidied the venue quickly before they drove to the hotel.

Violet tried to be happy and cheerful the night before Liv's wedding. They painted their nails, did facials, and watched movies together. The hotel was fancy and beautiful, but Violet couldn't fully enjoy it all.

She was stressed.

Violet and Micah slept on the floor, while Liv and Bree got the bed. She had a fitful, nervous sleep. She couldn't stop thinking about Lauren's accusations, her audacity. She couldn't stop thinking about how sad Charlie looked when he talked about love.

But she had a full day ahead of her. She was supposed to be at the venue early in the morning to be sure everything was set. She had drinks to make and dresses to pick up. She needed her rest.

Her mind was agitated, and it took her a long time to fall asleep. The last thing she remembered was how her name sounded coming out of Charlie's mouth.

When she woke up only a few hours later at dawn, she wasn't fully recovered, but she had too much to do for sleeping in.

Micah, Liv, and Bree were all still asleep and weren't set to wake up for a few hours. But Violet had volunteered to retrieve the dresses for everyone and do the last touches on the wedding venue.

She drove there in a daze, barely remembering the cashier in the Dunkin' drive-through handing over the coffee. At the venue, she sipped on it gingerly, still waking up, while making sure everything looked good. Eventually, Bree arrived with Micah and Liv to help get them ready, which signaled Violet to leave to get the dresses.

She was interrupted by a call from Charlie.

"What's up?" she asked, feeling her heart skip at his name on the caller ID. Never in her wildest dreams did she think Charlie would have a reason to call her—other than to yell at her—and that still never happened before.

"The cake."

"The cake? Is there something wrong with it?"

"Yes, I . . . I'm FaceTiming you."

Violet barely had time to move her phone to see when the call changed. For a second, it was Charlie's face, and then the screen flipped to the cake.

It was supposed to be a three-tiered white cake with the couple at the top. It was traditional and beautiful. But when she looked at the figurines, it wasn't the actual couple. It was two men.

"Wha—Did they think they're a gay couple?" Violet asked.

The screen flipped back around. "They said they were out of women."

"Women in general?"

"Yes, women in general. Well, kind of. They had a woman who was dragging the groom with a ball and chain attached to his ankle. I think the two men was a better choice."

"Yeah, good call," Violet said.

"I need to find an appropriate topper for this thing. But I'm also supposed to take Lewis to get his hair cut."

"So . . . you need me to come get it?" Violet asked. "I still have to pick up the dresses."

"I know you're busy, but I don't want them to know. Lewis is already freaking out."

"About marrying Liv?"

"About being in front of hundreds of people. I don't want him to worry."

Violet groaned. "Fine. That's a fair point. I can try to swing it. I have to get the dresses and then get them to Liv before noon."

"Where would they have cake toppers? Walmart?"

"I don't know. This isn't something you shop for."

"What about a Barbie?"

"That's way too tall."

"Isn't Liv a bit taller than Lewis?"

"I mean, not Barbie versus a cake topper tall."

Charlie sighed, which turned into a groan. He had an impressive lung capacity. While Charlie mourned his losses, Violet looked up where a cake topper would be.

"Oh! The party store has some. And their website says they have one with her skin tone and curly hair."

"Oh, thank God."

"Fuck, it's on the wrong side of town."

"What side?"

"East."

"Hm . . . I can get it. But we have to meet in like fifteen minutes."

"Okay, okay," Violet said. "Meet me at the coffee shop where Liv and Lewis go to all the time."

"The one in the middle of town?"

"Yeah."

"Don't tell Lewis how many laws I'm breaking," he said before he hung up the phone.

Violet took a moment to smile as she darted out the door.

They arrived at the same time. Their cars stopped parallel to each other, and Charlie flew out of his car in a rush.

"Are you still okay to take the cake?" he asked as she climbed out of her car to meet him. "I was supposed to have it at the venue already."

Violet nodded. "Yes, it's fine. I can head there next before picking up the dresses."

Charlie nodded, grabbing the giant cake box. He positioned it in the backseat and buckled it in. It looked ridiculous and Violet almost laughed.

"Thank you. You're the best," Charlie told her before he drove off.

Violet's brain shut off for a moment while she processed his words. It had to have been said only in the heat of the moment because there was no way he meant it.

But she almost wanted him to.

She shook the thought out of her head. She didn't have time to think about this. She needed to get things done.

She sped back to the venue and dropped off the cake. Then she made the fastest fruit punch of her life and raced to the dress shop to pick up all the gowns. She was running behind, but when she pulled back up to the venue, she knew the worst of it was over.

Liv's makeup had been done for a while, and Violet was sure everyone else was ready. Violet ran in and hung up each of the dresses.

"Sorry I'm late!" she told everyone as she ran in. "I, uh, got stuck in traffic."

"Thank God!" Bree said. Liv grabbed her gown and said a more genuine thank you before Micah helped her get into her dress. Violet was about to throw hers on when Bree grabbed her by the arm.

"Hold up," she said, "You look terrible. I'm doing your makeup."

Violet didn't have time to answer, and she knew Bree didn't take no for an answer. She was a makeup artist and hairdresser, so if she said Violet looked a mess, she was probably right.

After rushing around for so long, it was nice to sit still for a bit to get her makeup done. Violet's eyes were painted with a shimmering gold and her hair was curled to frame her face. She looked like a new person.

"There you go," Bree said. "Now you look like a member of this bridal party."

"Thank you," Violet said gratefully.

"No, thank *you*. You're here for my little sister when I'm not. You've run this wedding. You deserved to be maid of honor."

"I only picked up a few things."

"Yeah, right. You're important, Violet. Don't forget it."

Violet nodded, the compliment hitting her hard. She didn't feel all that important, but she wanted to.

From there, it was all a blur until the ceremony.

The venue was a large ballroom with a reception area and bridal suite, but Violet and Liv had made it beautiful. Curtains hung down from the walls with fairy lights behind them, giving the room an ethereal glow. Benches lined each wall of the large room with a perfect arch in the middle. It was adorned with charming greenery and poinsettias, and a huge Christmas tree in the background.

Liv looked amazing. Her dress was a delicate, intricate lace. Her curly hair spilled around her face, which was elegantly made up.

Violet was first in line to go down the aisle. She turned to Liv and flashed her a big smile. She was so happy for her friend. Liv smiled back, her eyes a little misty.

She gripped her bouquet a little tighter as the door opened. "Carol of the Bells" played in the background as they began the procession.

Everyone's eyes were on Liv, and Violet couldn't blame them. Liv was enchanting. But as Violet caught Lewis's eyes, filled with love as he looked at his soon-to-be wife, Violet felt the familiar feeling of jealousy bubble in her gut.

She didn't want to feel this way. She wanted to be nothing but happy for her friends. She *should* be nothing but happy. It wasn't like she was in love with either of them. It wasn't like she didn't trust either of them. They were great together. They hardly ever fought. They respected one another. There shouldn't be one negative emotion in the entire room.

And yet, Violet still felt it.

Lewis was openly crying when Liv met up with him, and she heard him tell Liv she was gorgeous. Violet wished someone would say that to her.

And that was the entire problem. It was hard to be lonely and watch someone else be in love. And Liv and Lewis were *so* in love.

They were lucky to have met each other and it culminated into an amazing marriage. Violet had always wanted this, and while she was happy for her friends, she was sad for herself.

The vows began, and Violet could hear photos being snapped; she hoped her emotions weren't on her face. Then again, maybe it wouldn't matter because Liv stood so magnificently that she lit up the whole room.

As Liv and Lewis spoke to one another, Violet's eyes slid over to the wedding party. Damon looked good, and Elijah looked a little like a rat in fancy dinner wear. His eyes were on Lewis, and it appeared he was busy playing the part of a supportive friend.

She expected to feel a little more anger when seeing him, but her eyes were too busy being pulled to Charlie, who looked right at her.

They rarely looked each other in the eyes without yelling, but this moment felt different than all the rest. Declarations of love were their soundtrack, and Violet was hit with a bit of curiosity. What if Charlie hadn't been so cruel about her work for her grad school application? What if he had been kinder, and they had avoided all this fighting?

Maybe they'd be in a different situation. When Violet met Charlie, they hadn't just gotten along, they *liked* each other. They hung out all the time after Charlie and Lauren went on one of their breaks and could have easily been more if it hadn't been for that one paper.

Violet wanted to let it go so badly, but if she did, wouldn't she be ignoring something that hurt her? Could she trust him?

And did she want to let it go because she truly wanted to move past it, or did she want to do it because he was single and she was lonely?

A million years could have passed while they looked at each other, and Violet couldn't have said what was happening in the ceremony.

Charlie was the one who broke eye contact when he handed Lewis the rings, and the moment faded away, leaving Violet feeling off-kilter.

Once the ceremony was done, as practiced, Violet walked back down the aisle on Charlie's arm. She felt a little lightheaded from all the running around, lack of sleep, and lack of food, but Charlie was a steady weight next to her.

As they left the ceremony to loud cheers and lots of photos, Violet was supposed to go with Liv to help her change dresses for the reception. Before she left, Charlie's grip on her arm tightened and he said softly, "You look nice. Just in case no one told you."

Violet blinked, shocked. She needed to get to the bridal suite, but she also couldn't work through the swirl of emotions that churned when he said that. All she could do was mutter a "Thanks."

Then she was whisked away.

Charlie

Charlie didn't have time to think too hard about what he said to Violet. He had to go be sure guests were getting to the reception.

Lewis didn't leave Liv's side, and both of them were emotional after their vow exchange. Charlie felt bad, but he had zoned out for most of it. He couldn't stop glancing over at Violet.

She looked amazing, as she always did. Emerald was a lovely color on her, and the makeup added to her beauty. But it was never about her looks. This time, it was about her dependability.

During the ceremony, Charlie realized he had called Violet to help him with the cake on autopilot, and he had done it because he knew Violet would make it work. Violet didn't play petty games or give the silent treatment. When she hated him, she hated him earnestly. When she had liked him, she had done that earnestly too.

He was going to ask what had happened back in college after the wedding tonight. Maybe it would be a disaster. Maybe she'd yell, but he had to do it. Their truce was over as of tonight anyway. If it ended in a fight, she could go to Lewis and Liv's apartment as planned, and he would be able to think.

He had to know why they ended up like they did. Was it truly because he given his honest opinion about her personal essay for grad school? Or was it something else?

If she didn't run, if she actually talked to him, he would be willing to work it out. And if they worked it out, then maybe they could fix this. Maybe they could be real friends again.

Liv and Lewis's first dance was perfection. At the end, the wedding parties joined in. Violet and Charlie were technically paired up, but Lewis had told them they could skip.

Charlie walked over to her anyway.

"I'm a terrible dancer," Violet muttered. She held out a hand for him to take, and he placed his other one on her hip. They stood awkwardly apart, not used to touching.

As they moved together, Charlie said, "Maybe we should have taken those lessons."

"I doubt I'll ever dance again."

"You never know. Don't they do middle school dances or something?"

"Who am I supposed to dance with, a student?"

"What about a friendly teacher?"

"There are not a lot of male teachers," Violet said, shaking her head. "And I don't know. I like to keep work and personal life separate."

"Seems like a good rule."

"Don't they do corporate dances or something in the rich people world?"

Charlie huffed out a laugh. "I'm not rich, and no, not my company. Some private companies do big events, but they feel cheap and flashy."

"That's because they *are* cheap and flashy."

"And a school dance isn't?"

"School dances aren't flashy. They're just cheap," Violet said. "And they're probably the most boring event I chaperone."

"Are there ever any fun ones?"

"Hm, the winter festival is fun. It's at the beginning of the post-holidays semester before burnout sets in."

"That's coming up soon then."

"It is. I got roped into planning it, so that's where the rest of my break is going."

"Sounds fun."

"It can be. As long as I can get the inflatables I usually do. It makes the kids look forward to coming back to school, so I think it's great."

"You like kids, don't you?" Charlie asked, unable to help himself.

"I do, surprisingly. Don't get me wrong, there are days I want to pull my hair out, but I do like teaching. It's not a glamorous job. Or high paying."

"Not everything has to be high paying."

"In some ways it does. There *are* bills to pay. At least if you live in Nashville."

Charlie knew she was right. She may have a passion for her job, but even he knew she had never been well-off.

"Nashville has gotten expensive," he told her. "I'd probably be priced out of my neighborhood if I didn't inherit the house."

"Really? Don't you have a good job?"

"I do, but people keep moving here. Apartments are ridiculously high. I think Lewis says they pay almost three grand for theirs."

"It's literally a closet," Violet said, shaking her head. "This city is too much. I mean, don't get me wrong, it's nice, but people who've lived here for years can barely stay."

"If they raise my taxes one more time, I'm screwed." And he was being honest. His salary was decent, but he didn't make as much as Lauren did. He'd already had to deal with plumbing issues and electrical work when he first moved in so the house would be up to code. While he didn't have a house note, the repairs it needed quickly took up that room in his budget. Sooner or later, he was going to be stuck with a big-ticket expense, and he didn't have the savings for that.

"If my apartment doesn't get fixed, I'm not sure what I'll do." Violet looked concerned, as if it was a possibility she could never go back. "But I have a few weeks until I need to worry about it."

"You guys good?"

Charlie and Violet jumped. Micah was standing on the dance floor, without Damon, looking at them both with a curious expression.

"Uh, yeah." Violet said. "Why?"

"The rest of us got done dancing a few minutes ago." Micah crossed her arms. She didn't look mad. She looked almost . . . smug. "Either you guys were having an actual conversation, or you were about to kill each other."

Violet instantly stopped and stepped away from him. He already missed her warmth.

"It's nothing."

"Sure," Micah said, but it didn't sound like she believed them. "They're about to cut the cake soon. Do you want to be in the photos for that?"

"Oh, yeah. Of course I do."

"Plus, Liv needs to give you the key to her place."

The reminder she would be leaving his house that night gave him all the more reason to try and work this out.

"We'll talk later," Violet said to Charlie and they headed toward the cake. They posed for pictures with the rest of the bridal party, before he was whisked away to do his behind-the-scenes work that Lewis had assigned him.

Which he was pretty sure was purposefully as far from Violet as he could get.

But it didn't matter. They could talk at his house, and he was set on asking about their past.

When the wedding was over, Liv and Lewis did a charming walk under sparklers to their car, which would take them to the airport to their honeymoon. They had a late-night flight and would be in Mexico for three weeks. Charlie was glad, after how hard both of them worked for this night—they both needed it.

Charlie was among the few who stayed to clean up. He noticed Violet did the same. He kept an eye on her and left at the same time she did.

When he got to his house, Violet was leaning against the wall in the foyer, waiting for him. She stood straight when he walked in.

"So, the deal is over," she said. "You can say anything you want now."

When they first made the deal, he couldn't wait for this moment. Now, he dreaded it.

"I have one thing," he said. "And it's probably not what you think."

Violet nodded; her arms crossed tightly over her chest.

"What happened between us?" he asked. "Why did you go off on me that day in the dining hall?"

Violet looked shocked, then frowned. "Come on, you have to know."

"I genuinely don't. Was it what I said on your personal statement?"

Violet stared at him for a moment before answering. "Obviously."

He wondered if she was being sarcastic. How could it have been that? She said it like it was the only option.

"The feedback? I only said it needed work. I don't think I deserved what you said that day."

He could see her tense, and he instantly felt like he was missing something. There was no way she was this mad about simple feedback, right? She had to be used to getting constructive criticism in her career, and not all of it could be good.

"Don't worry about it," she said instead. "It's not worth it."

"No, I want to know. This ruined our friendship. I don't get how you can be the most mature person in the room and get upset that I told you your statement needed a little bit of work."

"That's not what you said." Violet turned to him, an old hurt on her face. "And if it's what you meant, then you had a bad way of going about it."

Charlie sighed and pinched the bridge of his nose. "I said you didn't sound proud of your accomplishments. You had so much going for you academically, but you barely touched on it. Maybe that's not exactly how I worded it—"

"No, it's not how you worded it at all." Violet shook her head. "That's really what you think you said?"

"I'm not lying. I genuinely want to get to the bottom of this."

"There's nothing to get to the bottom of. I asked you for help with something important to me and you told me I was a waste of time, that I could do nothing more than be a teacher and make a shit salary."

"How did you get to that conclusion from what I said? I would never say that to you!"

"Oh my God. Fine, I'll show you." Violet stormed up the stairs and came back down with her old, beat-up laptop in hand. Charlie dimly remembered the thing. She walked to the dining room and set it on the table, a tense silence over them both.

"What are you doing?" Charlie asked.

"I'm fucking showing you what you sent me. The computer is old as hell, so it takes a minute to open up the file."

Charlie shook his head but waited. He was anxious to look at this document line by line and show her he never said any of those things.

Violet gestured to the computer screen and moved out of the way. He leaned down to look at what was written.

And immediately noticed something was wrong.

He remembered having only two things to say about what she had written. In front of him were at least a dozen comments.

I'm not going to lie, your life's story is pathetic. Either make it more interesting, or don't submit it. I thought you were an English major.

He scrolled down, shocked.

Yikes. It's their, not they're.

This paragraph is boring.

This whole thing makes no sense.

Do you have dyslexia? Spell-check this nonsense.

This is going to waste anyone's time who reads it. It's worthless.

This is so beyond disappointing. I thought you would be better than this.

Anyway, if you want to save face, then delete it. Don't submit it. Go be a teacher at some middle school because from what I see it's all you'll be good at.

There were more, but he couldn't read them.

He leaned back, covering his mouth.

"See? I know you think I'm crazy, but this is what you sent me. I even have the email with the file attached if you want to be sure I'm not lying." She leaned over and navigated to her email, pulling up the file she had forwarded to herself. It had been starred, as if she wanted to save it to come back to at a later date. "I don't know if you were drunk or what, Charlie, but this was not okay."

"I didn't write this."

"Oh, come on, don't suddenly change your tune now that I've shown you."

"Violet, I didn't write this," he repeated firmly. "Even if I hated your work, you explicitly told me it wasn't spell-checked. Half of these comments are things I knew you hadn't gotten to yet."

"It came from *your* email. You sent it."

"Yes, I remember sending it, but this isn't what I wrote. This is bullying, Violet."

"Yes! It is!" Her voice was high and tight with hurt. "And you did this to me with no fucking warning, Davis. You sent this to me when you were the only one who knew about grad school. I didn't go because of this!"

Shit, shit, *shit*. It all made sense. This was why she never trusted him, why she always had to be even, *all of it*.

"But this wasn't me."

"How am I supposed to believe that?"

"Do you have version history enabled?"

She blinked at him. "What?"

"It's a feature that you enable so you can pull up past versions of the document."

It was a long shot. Most people didn't even know it existed.

But he sagged in relief when her eyes widened. "Oh, I think I know what you're talking about. Yeah, I enabled it after the school's IT department told me about it when I lost a whole paper."

"Mind if I pull up the old version then?"

"Do you think this will prove something?"

"I know what I said, Violet."

She bit her lip, eyes narrowed at him. "Fine. Just do it."

It took forever, but that had more to do with Violet's old computer than anything else.

When it did finally open, he picked one of the oldest dates, and let out a long breath when he saw his own words in front of him.

"Look," he told her. "This is what I said."

This is a really good start, but you don't sound proud of your academic accomplishments. Is there a way for you to do that?

"What?" Violet asked. "There are only two comments here."

"I only made two."

"When was it changed?"

"I can't tell you. I only see the version histories."

"But the changes couldn't have been made by anyone else, right? Did anyone have access to your laptop?"

"Only . . ." He trailed off, realizing who else would have had access.

"What?" Violet said, voice sharp. "Who had access?"

"Lauren did."

"Are you serious?"

"She borrowed it for presentations because it was a nicer model. She did it a lot more often right before graduation."

"So . . . Lauren did it."

"I-I don't know for sure."

"It was either you or her."

"I can't tell you if she did it or not. I mean, I would hope not, but she's never been your biggest fan."

"I can tell."

"She didn't act suspicious at the time. We were on a break and fighting, but we made up after you and I fell out. The only thing I remember her mentioning is you weren't cut out for grad school."

"How the fuck did she know about me going to grad school? Did you tell her?"

"I—" *Fuck.* Now that he thought about it, he hadn't ever mentioned it to Lauren. He thought it had been common knowledge. "No, I didn't."

Violet's eyes were ablaze. He wasn't sure if she was about to kill him or Lauren.

He tried to remember anything else, anything that would have explained it more.

"She's always started everything with you. She's at fault for all of this," Lauren had said.

"I don't get why she's so obsessed with you."

"She's so weird. She's got nothing going for her."

"Charlie?" Violet asked, bringing him out of his thoughts. "So, you're sticking with the fact it was Lauren?"

"Yes," Charlie said, feeling everything shift around him. "It was her. It had to be her."

Suddenly, Violet wasn't the one going off on him randomly that day, it was her retaliating on what she thought he'd said. But it had never been him.

And it shouldn't have made sense because he didn't want to believe Lauren was this cruel.

And yet, the evidence was in front of him.

"Fuck," Charlie muttered. "Violet, I'm so sorry this got sent to you. This is wrong."

Violet blinked at him, her face unsure. "You're . . . sorry?"

"Of course I am."

"You didn't even send it."

"I'm sorry you read it. I'm sorry my girlfriend was so insecure that she sent it to you."

Violet stared at him for a long time.

"I . . . can't believe this."

"I know. I'm sorry it's—"

"Stop," Violet said. She dragged her hands through her hair, tugging loose the curls from the wedding. "You've apologized *three* times within minutes of finding out."

"It's-it's the right thing to do."

"I've waited *years* for you to acknowledge what you did. *Years*. Every time I saw you, I wondered if it would be the time you finally mentioned the comments."

"I didn't know, I swear. When you cornered me in the dining hall that day, I thought you were mad about me saying you needed to add more feeling to the paper. That's it."

"Then I looked like a fucking idiot, Charlie!" She was yelling, and Charlie didn't know if they were about to fight, or if she was about to start crying. "I was waiting for the other shoe to drop for six years, and it never did. Because it wasn't you. *Fuck!* Why didn't you ask me?"

"I . . . I wanted to, but Lauren said you weren't worth my time. She said it was all on you."

Violet looked livid, but she only nodded and turned away from him.

"Violet, I'm sorry. I—"

"Did you ever look at the file?"

Charlie sighed. She was going to hate his answer. "Lauren told me to delete it."

"You know, it's starting to make sense why she's a lawyer. She's great at controlling the narrative to fit whatever she needs. She walked all over both of us." Violet shook her head and crossed her arms so tightly around herself it looked painful.

And Charlie knew she was right. Lauren was smart, but when she became a lawyer, she used it only to her benefit, and no one else's.

"Did you ever tell Liv what I said? Maybe she could have..."

"I never told Liv I was applying for grad school. I was too ashamed about how bad my personal statement was."

"Goddammit," Charlie muttered.

"I took those comments personally. I didn't want to admit that I wasn't good enough for something everyone else was already doing."

"That was... we both..."

"We both let Lauren play us like a fiddle," Violet finished for him, "for six fucking years."

Charlie didn't have anything to say to that. He still didn't know where this would end up. Would they yell at each other? Were they finally on the road to recovery? It could go either way.

But he knew he was pissed. At Lauren. At himself. That dull gaze he had seen every time she spoke with him was her thinking of this exact essay, thinking of words he hadn't even said. Because of Lauren, Violet thought he had called her a waste of time, a disappointment, and it stuck with her all these years later.

It made him angrier than he had ever been.

But as he looked at Violet, whose wet eyes complemented the murderous expression on her face, he realized he wasn't angry at her. Not at all.

Maybe she didn't feel the same way. Hell, she probably didn't, but her character suddenly made so much more sense now. She'd never been immature. She'd been torn down by comments made under his name, by someone she trusted. It wasn't that she couldn't handle criticism. She couldn't handle being ripped apart.

No one could.

He saw her for who she was. Someone who trusted him, and then someone who had been hurt. She kept her misery secret and her pain even closer. She always had.

And him? He had been letting Lauren control his life. What once had been a smart, talented girl in his class who always sat next to him and helped tutor him was now a woman who had manipulated him into fighting with a former friend. She'd molded him into a worse version of himself, and he listened instead of trusting his gut that told him it was wrong—that it didn't make sense.

The haze in his mind had never been Violet. It was Lauren. It had been all along. She had been putting poison into his head for years, all to keep Violet out of the picture, all in desperation to keep them apart.

And it worked.

As he stared at his former friend turned enemy, he promised himself no more. It ended here. That promise turned into something harder than diamond within him, and he knew he was no longer Violet Moore's enemy.

Chapter Eleven

Violet

Violet was spiraling. She had gotten the apology she needed, but it felt wrong.
It wasn't even his to give.

She felt like an idiot. She had been waiting for six years to get confirmation Charlie was two-faced. She waited for him to rub her work in her face, to repeat the evil comments that had cut her to her soul.

And it never came.

Of course, it never came because he didn't make the fucking comments. It was *Lauren*.

Lauren, who had thrown her drink on Violet at the engagement party. Lauren, who Liv hated and didn't trust. Lauren, who was a morally questionable lawyer who made a lot of money by ruining others' lives.

Liv had said Lauren was a terrible person many years ago, and Violet thought she and Charlie were perfect for one another. But now she was seeing Lauren was the one egging it on. And if she had hurt Violet with simple comments on her work, what had she done to Charlie in the last six years? That kind of meanness didn't end on paper.

No, it spread.

There was a knock at the door—a loud, insistent sound. Charlie glanced at it but made no move to answer it. Violet put her pain into a box and walked toward the noise.

Only for it to come back tenfold when she opened it.

Lauren stood in the doorway, leaning against the frame like she owned the place. Violet resisted the urge to attack because all the anger she had felt for six years had shifted, settling right into the person in front of her.

She thought she had maybe hated Charlie or Elijah, but this was different.

"What the fuck are you doing here?" Violet asked, crossing her arms. Instead of Charlie's perfectly beautiful girlfriend, Lauren was one of the ugliest people she'd ever seen. Her narrowed gaze was calculating—dangerously so. The slight tilt of her head was a tell that she was figuring out how to manipulate rather than a sign she was interested in anything being said.

"God, are you always here?" Lauren said and rolled her eyes. "You'd think you'd be more excited about getting out of here considering you hate him so much."

"Lauren," Charlie said in such a sharp voice it made the hairs on Violet's skin raise. She hadn't even realized Charlie had walked over. He stood behind her, his form tall and intimidating. "We need to talk."

Lauren was unperturbed by Charlie's tone. "Sure, but can the middle-school teacher leave? This should be an adults-only conversation."

"No, actually, I want to have a talk with you too," Violet said. "So, I think I'm staying."

Charlie *nodded*, of all things.

Wow, it was weird being on his side.

Violet was not only mad, but curious. Was Charlie going to hold Lauren accountable? She remembered Liv telling her Lauren was able to get away with whatever she wanted. There was a part of Violet that knew she wouldn't let it. She wanted Lauren to *burn*.

But after everything, Violet wasn't going to fool herself into thinking she was important to Charlie—not enough to dump Lauren. Those two had years of being together. Violet and Charlie only had years of pain.

And yet, Charlie was still glaring at her. Anger simmered on the surface of his skin, but Violet could see the hurt boiling underneath.

For the first time, Lauren seemed to realize Charlie was mad. Her haughty attitude faded slightly, and she narrowed her eyes at him.

"What's your deal?" Lauren asked.

"I know about what you did to Violet right before we finished undergrad," Charlie said. "I know you saw her essay for grad school, got on my laptop, changed all the comments, and then let me send it to her with them attached."

There was a long pause before Lauren answered. Violet wondered if she was even going to try to deny it.

"I'm guessing that's something *she* told you?" Lauren asked, pointing at Violet.

"I showed it to him, Lauren. I still had it."

"With all the comments, ones I know I didn't make," Charlie added.

Lauren paused for a moment. "So, you're blaming me for all of this?"

"You're admitting it," Charlie said.

"Maybe I did it as a prank," Lauren said. Violet had to stop herself from punching Lauren in the face. "But you kept it going. You two had plenty of chances to talk about it. I'd hardly say that was my fault."

Charlie didn't say anything, and Violet risked a glance at him. His anger dissolved, and he looked like he was actually considering what Lauren was saying.

"Hang on," Violet said. "When did you ever let us talk? Whenever we were at a party together, *you* were always there. If I remember correctly, you usually egged it on."

Lauren rolled her eyes. "Of course you would try to blame me for your lack of communication."

"You know what? Yeah, we suck at communicating, but you also did something wrong. You don't get to absolve responsibility because we also made a mistake. Yes, we should have talked it out, but that's on *us* and isn't a part of this conversation. We wouldn't have been in this mess if you hadn't taken Charlie's laptop, edited the comments, and then lied about it for six years. My middle-school students have a better understanding of ethics than you do."

Charlie looked at Violet again, listening to her with rapt attention.

Was this how Lauren got away with everything? Would she twist words until Charlie questioned himself and why he was even angry?

Violet turned to Lauren. "You're an abuser, Lauren. You're manipulative, a liar, and a fucking monster."

"You don't get to call me that with the things you've said to him."

Violet didn't need the reminder that she had been a bad person to Charlie. It hurt to hear it, but there was no doubt pain was exactly what Lauren wanted.

"I'm not perfect, but I'm the only one admitting that, aren't I?" Violet shook her head. "You did a bad thing. What I've done is none of your business, and it's between me and the person I screwed up with, and that's Charlie."

"Lauren, you still haven't apologized for your comments on Violet's work," Charlie said, finally finding his voice. "You've always talked down about Violet to me. You blamed her for everything that went sideways. You tried to stop me from apologizing, for asking what went wrong. And I let you."

"Charlie, can't you see she's manipulating you?" Lauren asked.

"Wow," Violet said. "I am a lot of things, but I am not a manipulator. I don't need to throw blame because I can easily say what I've fucked up on. Obviously, you can't."

"Fine, then. I'm *sorry* for you two fighting all the time. I guess I'll take all the blame!"

"Oh, shut up," Violet said. "You're not taking any of it. Try a real apology, Lauren."

"I obviously already apologized. Nothing is good enough for you."

"Because you're saying it now that you're caught. You made us look like fools for six years, but I'm done with it. You can leave."

Lauren looked at Charlie.

Violet wondered if Charlie would back her up. Maybe he would fall for Lauren's tricks and let her in to work things out.

Thankfully, Violet had another place to stay now. If he did forgive Lauren, she would leave. Easy enough.

"Yeah, you should go, Lauren," he said, his voice hard.

Oh, thank *God*.

"What?" Lauren said sharply.

"I think we're done here."

"Oh, whatever." Lauren rolled her eyes. "When you two are fighting again you'll come crawling back."

"No," Charlie said. "Not this time. We're done with everything. This relationship, this conversation. Don't call me again. Lose my number. Lose my address. I don't even want to think about you again."

Violet smirked. *Finally!*

"You'll be alone once *she's* gone," Lauren hissed.

"Not really. I have a cat now."

"*What*?" Lauren screeched, as if this was the most shocking thing said tonight. "You let a wild animal into your home?"

"A wild animal?" Violet said incredulously. "Well, Charlie is letting *you* stand here, so I guess it's true."

"No, I'm the only sane one here," Lauren replied. "You're making a huge mistake, Charlie."

"I don't think I am," he said firmly.

"Fine, then I'll leave," Lauren said before adding, "but everything I did, I did for us. I did it so we had a fighting chance. Obviously you don't care about that."

"I care about not being lied to. If this is how you show love, then I don't want any part of it."

"You're going off what she told you. What, are you jumping from her to me? Are you going to let her make all the rules?"

"Oh, no," Violet said. "I don't want control over anyone else. Not my cup of tea. And I'm not on his side because I want him for myself. I'm on his side because he's right. This is all on you. It's your actions that got you here. Maybe try taking responsibility rather than blaming it on me."

Lauren stared at them before she shook her head, as if she didn't believe it. "Whatever. Have fun ruining your life, Charlie. Don't say I didn't try."

Lauren turned to leave, but paused, as if waiting for Charlie to call out to her. He didn't.

"Bye now!" Violet called. "Be sure to bundle up. It's cold out there! And fuck you!"

Violet slammed the door on Lauren, and then locked it. For a moment, there was only silence, and Violet could feel the dangerous swirl of emotion within her. She took a deep breath, knowing she wasn't the only one hurting.

Charlie was too.

She didn't know what their future held, but for a moment, she saw it a little bit brighter than before.

Charlie

Charlie stared at the space where Lauren had just been. The door was shut, and Violet was in front of it, fists clenched, posture tense.

He had done it. He had finally broken up with Lauren.

Charlie didn't think he ever could. She had always found a way to make it sound like his fault. She never took the blame when they argued, only skirted around the truth. Usually he fell for it, but tonight, Violet kept him grounded enough to see through it.

He felt the haze he usually associated with the woman standing next to him dissipate.

All he felt was relief. Maybe he should have felt sad, or lonely. Maybe he should still be clinging onto his anger; but seeing Lauren walk away, having someone else listen to her and tell her she was wrong, had him feeling like he was free.

He used his last bit of conviction to block her on every social media platform he followed her on, and finally, her phone number.

Meanwhile, Violet turned to lean against the door, eying him with a curious expression.

Charlie didn't even know what to say to her.

He needed to apologize for dragging her into this. Or maybe beg for her forgiveness. He wasn't sure which should come first.

He'd let this thing with Lauren go on for too long. He let her twist his words to make herself seem like a better person than she was, breaking himself in the process. Over time, it had slowly killed him, and he wished it hadn't taken this long for him to end it.

A part of him felt like he needed to keep her around since he'd known her for so long, because she was familiar, and yet he had been trading away pieces of himself to do so.

Their friendship couldn't matter when she had grown into a terrible person.

Everyone had tried to tell him. Liv and Lewis mentioned he needed to find someone new. His own mother hated Lauren for years.

Why didn't he listen? Why didn't he move on?

He didn't know why. But he was free now.

"Are you okay?" Violet asked. He was surprised she even cared.

She was the one that got screwed over. Lauren had been cruel to her, and Violet thought it was Charlie the whole time. Hurt like that didn't fade overnight.

Anyway, if you want to save face, then delete it. Don't submit it. Go be a teacher at some middle school because from what I see it's all you'll be good at.

Jesus. How could Lauren have ever said that?

"Charlie?" Violet repeated. "Are you okay?"

"S-sorry," Charlie stuttered. "I'm thinking."

"Hopefully not that you made a mistake by breaking up with her. Because that's the best thing you've ever done."

"I don't think I've made a mistake. I feel free."

"Oh," Violet said.

Charlie didn't want to think how terrible it had truly been. He didn't want to think of the many times Lauren walked out on him, and the times he kept following her. How could he have been so stupid?

"Charlie, I'm sorry this happened to you," Violet said.

Charlie's eyes flew to hers. "*You're* apologizing?"

"Should I not?" Violet asked.

"You were the one who got screwed over."

"Yeah, maybe in a way. But I didn't date her. I imagine there was other stuff she did that was as bad. The whole relationship had to take a lot out of you."

"It wasn't all bad." Charlie sighed. "Whenever we would fight, she would give me time and then come back by doing something nice, and it usually worked. It felt like how a relationship should work. But this time I blocked her number, and I plan on keeping it that way."

"If she shows up here again, I can always run her over with my car."

"She won't," Charlie replied. "For one thing, getting talked down to by someone else is the thing she hates the most. So, she's going to stew on it a bit, just like she always does. We have a few weeks before she comes back. Besides, she'll want to meet up somewhere other than here—at least for date purposes. She hates this house."

"What? Why? This is the coolest house I've ever seen."

Charlie laughed softly. "Try telling her that."

"I don't plan on ever talking to her again," Violet said. "No offense, but she's got the moral backbone of a gummy worm."

"Wh-where did you get that analogy?"

Violet shrugged. "A student said it once."

Charlie laughed, but it quickly died out as the memory of what happened played back in his mind.

"Thanks for sticking up for me," he said. "After everything that's happened, I would have understood if you didn't."

"You don't have to thank me. I'd do it even if I still hated you."

"You don't still hate me?" His throat felt thick with emotion.

"I don't think it would be right to," Violet said. "I think it's going to take some time for me to fully come to terms with everything. I've thought about this for six years, wondering why things happened the way they did. And now that I know, I have no clue where I'll end up. We were still terrible to each other, after all."

Charlie nodded. He didn't want to continue as they were, but they needed to work on every terrible thing said in the aftermath.

"I'm supposed to go stay at Liv and Lewis's apartment tonight," she added.

He knew she was leaving and he had wanted to ask her what happened as their last conversation before things went back to the way they had been before her apartment collapsed.

But *he didn't want* things like they were before. He wanted to work on this. He now knew exactly what happened, and he needed to see the bigger picture now that they had all the pieces of the puzzle.

Charlie didn't want to wait months to see her again.

"But I'm worried if I do, we'll never move on from this." She looked up at him, expression unreadable.

"What?" he asked, daring to be hopeful.

"Being apart makes everything worse. I know how I am. I never work through something until I have to. Work keeps me busy, and a great distraction from everything else—even if I don't mean for it to be. But being here, it's forced us to deal with how shitty we've been. I know you probably want your house back to yourself, but—"

"I don't. Violet, I want to work on this. You're right, being together makes us actually try. We need to do that. You can stay as long as you need to."

"I want to be clear, if I piss you off, I'll—"

"Violet, stop. The same still applies now. I won't kick you out and you can still work on things around the house. We can see where we're at when your apartment gets fixed."

"Okay," Violet said quietly. "But this isn't going to be easy. I'm not good at moving on, and pain sticks with me. I can't be your friend instantly."

"I don't expect you to. You're doing more than most by even giving me a chance."

"It still wasn't you that sent those comments," Violet said with a shake of her head. "You can't put all of this on you."

"She was my girlfriend."

"That's not how this works. You didn't know what she had done."

Charlie didn't know if he believed her. Violet stared at him for a moment before she took a deep breath.

"We'll give this a shot. Friendship. A real one. Deal?"

She held out her hand. He remembered the last time he shook her hand, and how he dreaded touching her. Now it felt like hope.

Their hands met and he promised himself he was going to do better. He was going to be how he was in college. He wasn't repeating the same mistakes again.

As she pulled away, the conflicted feelings in his chest settled on a quiet, delicate hope.

Chapter Twelve

Violet

The next day dawned vibrantly. The sun's rays woke Violet up from her fitful sleep. It was as if the sky decided to brighten in response to her and Charlie's feud finally being put to an end.

Violet rubbed her eyes. Roo noticed she was awake and came to get attention. She pet the cat absentmindedly as she tried to make sense of everything. It had taken her a long time to fall asleep. She kept turning over everything in her mind, trying to make sense of it all.

But, in the end, she finally dozed off with no more understanding than before.

She washed her face, trying to remove any traces of the more stubborn parts of her makeup from the wedding. Then she checked to make sure Liv was okay in Mexico for the honeymoon. Once she received confirmation the couple was happily settled in, she started her morning routine.

When she was done, she felt more awake. She opened her purse and checked her gift card stash. She only had one left.

She had been avoiding cooking in the house. The kitchen was near Charlie's room and was *his* space. She didn't want to encroach on that.

One option was to use her renter's insurance money and continue going out to eat. But she was sick of fast food. One more burrito and she might lose it.

Another was to go downtown at rush hour to use Liv and Lewis's apartment. But that would easily add an hour to her drive.

By far the easiest option would be to use Charlie's kitchen. They had promised to be friends, after all. Friends asked each other to use their kitchens . . . right?

But Violet had no idea what a friendship with Charlie was going to look like. And even if it wasn't Charlie, who she had a complicated relationship with, she hated doing stuff like this. She hated asking for help, asking for permission.

And yet, she had to. Just the thought of getting in her car to get food from a fast-food restaurant made her want to barf.

She was going to ask Charlie for a favor.

She could only hope it went well.

Violet knew Charlie got up around the same time as she did. From the window in the guest room, she could see him leave for a jog each morning. She usually huddled in the room and snuck out while he was gone; but this morning she was going to try to wait.

She nervously waited next to the dining room table when Charlie got back. He was out of breath from his run and removed his earbuds without even noticing Violet was there.

He looked put together for someone who had just broken up with a long-time girlfriend. But then again, maybe he was hiding it. He turned to her after a moment, doing a double take when his eyes slid over her in the dining room.

"Hey," Charlie said. "You're not usually around this late in the morning."

"Um, not really. I usually leave to go get breakfast around this time."

"Are you skipping breakfast today or something?"

"More like I ran out of gift cards for places."

"What?" Charlie asked.

"My coworkers gave me a lot of gift cards when my apartment collapsed. I had been using them instead of cooking because I don't have a kitchen right now."

"But . . . you do have a kitchen. It's right in there."

"I didn't know if I could use it."

Charlie stared at her, and Violet internally cringed.

She needed permission to be able to do things. It started when her mother had gotten strict on money, and every cent counted. Violet was used to folding herself into a corner and melting into the background. Sometimes it worked, but this time, Charlie was looking at her with the same strange expression Liv always did.

Liv grew up with a loving family. She didn't get screamed at for wasting food or leaving a mess. To her, Violet worrying so much about being a burden was a weird quirk. She even joked about it a few times.

Violet didn't know where Charlie would land on it, and this was too sore of a subject for him to rib her on.

She silently begged for their delicate peace treaty to stay.

"Sorry," Violet said, laughing awkwardly. "I, uh, didn't want to assume."

Oh, he was *never* going to let her live this down.

"No!" Charlie said. "Don't blame yourself. I should have been clearer that you're welcome to use the kitchen, the dining room—whatever you need."

"Okay," Violet tried not to show the relief in her voice. "When I came to stay, you seemed pretty set on not seeing me, so I wanted to—"

"I never said I didn't want to see you."

"Well . . . Lewis said you liked your space, and you didn't exactly like me. So, I tried to make it like I wasn't here."

She could hear it now. *"Yeah, but you're here either way. I can't help but notice you when you constantly bother me,"* is what he'd say, and then the argument would start from there.

"I do like my space, but you're also allowed to exist. When I said you could stay here, I figured you would need the kitchen at least."

"It's still *your* kitchen."

"No, it's yours too. Seriously, use it for whatever you need."

"Okay, uh . . . I can get some stuff then. Maybe microwave meals? Those don't take up a lot of space, so—"

"Do you like microwave meals?" Charlie asked her pointedly.

Violet sighed. "No, I hate them."

"Okay," Charlie said. "I want you to use the kitchen for what you like. Not what takes up the least amount of space. You can take up whatever space you need. Take up more, if you want. Whatever makes you happy."

Violet's mouth shut so tight it hurt her jaw. She didn't know what to say to that. She didn't even know *how* to do that. But she was so, so tired of being invisible. It was way more tiring than she remembered it being in her teen years.

"Sorry," Violet said. "I know I'm reacting weirdly."

"There's nothing to apologize for. I've known for years you're better at helping others than getting help for yourself."

"How did you know that?"

"I'm not blind. You help Liv with *everything*. I've never heard it be returned though."

"She got me a bag of supplies when my apartment collapsed."

"I don't think that's the same as helping her plan the entire wedding."

"I didn't plan the *whole* thing."

"You did most of it."

"Okay . . . maybe you're right about all of it. Please don't make fun of it, okay?"

"I wasn't going to."

"Okay," Violet said, nodding. "Thank you. I guess I'm afraid you'll say something mean and we'll spiral."

"I'm working on that. I don't even want to after everything we've learned."

"I don't either."

"And about this kitchen thing, if I ever made you feel like you're a burden—"

"No, it wasn't you. At least not that I can remember. I feel like a burden every day of my life."

Charlie stared at her.

Oh, fuck.

"I . . . I mean—"

"Don't worry about it," Charlie said, his expression clearing. Violet felt her shoulders loosen. He wasn't going to pressure her on it. *Good.*

The last thing she wanted was for him to pity her.

Most people hated being pitied because it was shameful. She hated being pitied because it made what she went through real.

Sometimes it was easier to pretend it wasn't.

"I'm going to make breakfast," Charlie said, instead of pressing her on it any further. "Do you want anything? I'm making oatmeal."

She loved oatmeal.

"You eat oatmeal?" she croaked.

Charlie sighed, as if it was a question he heard before.

"It's an easy breakfast. I know it's boring."

"But it's the most nutrient-packed breakfast you can make in under ten minutes."

"That's . . . exactly why I make it."

"I used to make it too. Before my apartment collapsed. Since I've been eating fast food, I haven't had real oatmeal in forever. Only the sugary packets."

"I make it like an old man who's retired. Usually it's oats, milk, and then maybe fruit if I have some."

"That sounds so good," she said. "If I have to look at another breakfast fast-food wrapper, I'm going to lose my mind."

Charlie broke out into a smile, looking *relieved* she had admitted what she wanted. It lit up his entire face and dispelled her fears.

"So, oatmeal works?"

Violet still felt flustered from being on the receiving end of one of his smiles. "Yep, make it like an old, retired man."

"Come on, I'll show you where I keep everything so you can get familiar with the kitchen."

Violet nodded and followed. She watched him curiously. He showed her where he kept his food, where the pots were, and where the Tupperware lived. His kitchen was organized and clean. Violet could only imagine having so much space for storage.

"Is milk okay?" he asked after he had given her the quick tour. "I might have some oat milk, but I don't know if it's still good."

"Milk is fine."

"Are you not still avoiding dairy?"

God, that was more than six years ago, and she had mentioned she'd cut out milk in passing to him when they first met. Either this man had an incredible memory, or he knew more about her than he ever let on.

"No, I'm not. Turns out dairy wasn't the source of my problems."

It had been her mother, not that she'd tell Charlie. Stress had destroyed her body in high school. It was part of the reason she did yoga now.

Charlie didn't ask questions, though. He simply made the food as he did a million times before. Violet let her eyes roam over the kitchen, admiring all the original cabinets and tile work. The appliances were upgraded, but that was it. The green kitchen reminded her of being in nature, which she didn't get to do enough of until summer.

Violet didn't know anything about Charlie's family, but it seemed there were lots of good memories in this home. It had been kept through generations. One of the doorways had etched height lines for someone named Mara. Another had Charlie's name.

Violet didn't have things like that growing up. They never stayed in one place long enough to get attached. At first it was because they were poor, but then it was because her mother wanted the nicest of things and was constantly trying to upgrade their lives.

Violet had long since decided she liked places with history.

"Do you want any fruit or anything?" Charlie asked. "I've got blueberries, strawberries, and bananas."

"All of it. Or whatever you don't like."

Charlie rolled his eyes and put all three on her plate. "I sit at the dining room table to eat." He handed her a warm bowl. "Would you like to join me?"

"Sure. We can't argue if my mouth is full of food."

"I'll meet you in there. I'm going to grab some coffee."

Violet nodded but couldn't resist the wistful gaze at the coffee pot. Technically, she could go in and get some coffee at work, even if she was on break. Maybe she could even work on lesson plans while there.

"Do you drink coffee now?" he asked as he poured himself a cup.

"Uh, yeah. I have plenty at work though."

"How do you take it?" he asked.

"Don't worry about me, I'm fine."

Charlie gave her a deadpan look.

"Splash of milk and sugar."

"Thank you, I'll make you a cup."

Violet walked into the dining room, face aflame. How did he get past her barriers so easily? How did he make it feel so easy?

Maybe their new problem wasn't that they'd fight. Maybe her problem was that he knew her too fucking well.

Charlie set down the cup in front of her, and she stared at it. He'd even gotten the ratio of milk and sugar right, damn him.

"You didn't used to drink coffee in college," he said. "Sorry I didn't offer earlier."

"It's a habit I developed once I started my job," she admitted. "I did have about one hundred dollars in Starbucks gift cards, but that only lasted me about a week."

"Yeah, they aren't cheap."

"They do have a decent yogurt parfait though." Violet took a bite and almost groaned. He made good oatmeal.

"Is it okay?" he asked. "And you have to tell me the truth. No lying."

"It's actually really good. I'm happy to not be at a McDonald's right now. This is so much better."

"Do you even work today? Aren't schools out for the holidays?"

"They are. I need to get some work done while I'm on break. Plus, I need to call vendors for the festival. I'm going to be *busy*."

"Sounds like your break isn't much of one."

"They rarely are."

"You know, you could always go back to grad school," Charlie offered. "There's probably scholarships for returning students."

Violet had thought about it before, but the idea of going back to school didn't seem right for her. Violet's original degree was supposed to be in accounting, but then she secretly switched it to English one year in. Once her mom found out, Violet had come up with a bullshit plan for her to get her PhD and work for a prestigious university like Harvard or Yale.

Deep down, she knew that was never what she wanted. But it got her mom off her back.

Maybe teaching wasn't a glamorous job, and maybe she didn't have a lot of money to spare, but at least she knew she was making a difference.

"It's okay. I may not like every aspect of my job, but I do like most of it. Mainly the teaching."

"Even if they're sixth graders?"

"Especially when they are. I could have easily gone into high school curriculum by taking a few extra classes, but I felt like sixth graders were at the perfect place to learn. If they have a good teacher, it would prepare them for future classes. I've been doing this for six years, but my first set of kids are doing well in high school. It makes me happy I was able to do that."

Charlie paused in his eating and stared at her.

"I thought you hated it," Charlie said after a moment. "I mean . . . you always made it sound like you did, and Lauren did say for you to be a middle school teacher."

Hearing Lauren's name soured Violet's mood. She didn't realize how much resentment had grown overnight.

"I resent her for the comment, yes. I hate how low my salary is, and how I have to scramble to get by. I hate the standardized tests and the way people talk to me when I have an issue with their kid. But the rest? The actual teaching? I like that."

"Then I suppose that's one less thing I have to feel bad for."

"Why do you feel bad?" Violet asked. "Lauren made the comments, not you."

"I know, but . . . I shouldn't have deleted the document when Lauren told me to. I should have looked at it before I got rid of it. I knew something was wrong, but I didn't take the extra steps to find out what."

"I could have asked too. There were loads of things we did wrong, but we're trying to be better today than we were yesterday. That's all we can do."

It was one of the things she had learned to live with after moving out from her mother's household. She couldn't change the past. Only move forward.

"But if I had done something differently . . . maybe things would have been like this for the last six years." He gestured between the two of them.

"Like this?" Violet asked.

"I don't know," Charlie replied. "It's easier to talk with you than fight with you."

Violet blushed, knowing he was right. This was *far* easier.

"We have right now," she said. "So, let's focus on getting it right in this moment. Not what we did wrong."

"You're right."

"How are you, by the way? About Lauren, I mean. Still feeling relieved?"

"You ask like I'll change my mind at any moment."

Violet shrugged. "Maybe you will."

Charlie shook his head. "No. Not this time. I'm mad, I really am. Plus, we've gone months without talking before."

"Seriously?"

"Yeah. I could never stay with her for more than a year at a time. Near the end, maybe a month."

"That's awful. No wonder you don't believe in love."

Charlie shrugged. "It's not a huge deal."

"It kind of is. She sucks."

Charlie shrugged. "I thought it was the best it got. We knew each other for practically our whole lives."

"It's got to be better than that," Violet said, shaking her head. "There's no way that's what relationships are like."

"Maybe. Maybe not. It's not like either of us know though."

"I think Liv and Lewis are a good example."

Charlie paused, his face pensive. Violet almost asked what he was thinking, but she stopped herself because she didn't have a reason to know. Even though she wanted to.

"Maybe they are," Charlie said quietly. "Either way, I think I need a break from it all. I don't know if I'm ever going to date again after that fiasco."

"I felt like that after Elijah left. Liv keeps telling me I'd change my mind, but I haven't yet."

"Hm. Maybe I should resign myself to a life alone," Charlie said, leaning back in his chair.

"Oh, alone, huh? Do I need to leave?" Violet asked, raising her eyebrow.

"No," Charlie said, laughing. "You can stay. You're not half bad."

It wasn't praise, not really, but it warmed her cheeks regardless.

Even though it still sort of hurt to admit it, Charlie was right. Talking like this was much easier than fighting.

Charlie

Charlie was midway through his workday when he got an instant message from the front desk that he had a visitor. For a short, stupid moment, he hoped it was Violet. Then, he feared it was Lauren.

He got up quickly, wondering who was awaiting him. But when he rounded the corner to the front desk, he let out a sigh of relief when it was his mother.

It seemed like ages ago when they had talked about her coming to his work for lunch, but he was grateful that she had. It had been over four weeks since they had seen each other. Charlie had been busy trying to keep the peace at the house ever since Violet moved in, and his mother was on her work trip during the wedding.

"Hi, Charlie," Mara said, smiling. "Have you had lunch?"

"No, I haven't. Were you showing a place on this side of town?"

"I was in the neighborhood for something else, but I figured now was as good a time as any."

"Something else? Since when do you do anything not work related on this side of town?"

For a moment, his mother looked conflicted, as if she didn't know what to say. Charlie frowned at her. What was she doing over here that she couldn't tell him?

"Oh, I wanted to go shopping." Mara waved passively. "Do you want to get something to eat?"

"Sure. Is everything okay?"

"Yes, of course," she answered. "Let's go get food. Then we can talk more."

The grocery store near the office had a food bar he always enjoyed, and a small sitting area to eat in.

"How was the wedding?" she asked as they sat down with their trays.

"It was busy. I wished you were there, though. I can't believe they sent you on a trip right around Christmas," Charlie said.

The holiday was half the reason Lewis and Liv held their wedding. Usually, people were already off work at that time.

"Oh, it was nothing. I enjoyed it. Plus, I'm sure you had a great time."

"It was . . . something."

"Do you have any photos? Did you take Lauren?"

Charlie couldn't help the grimace that ripped through him. He was doing good not thinking of Lauren. He still felt raw and angry about everything that had happened, but it wasn't eating away at him.

Mara frowned.

"Did something happen?"

"Uh, yeah. Lauren and I are officially broken up. For good this time."

At first, she blinked in shock, and her eyebrows raised. Then she cleared her throat, obviously trying to appear unbothered by the new information, but the way her eyes crinkled combined with the slight upturn of her mouth told him she was relieved.

Charlie was sure Lewis was going to have the same reaction.

"What happened?"

"It's a long story," Charlie said.

"I have time if you do."

Charlie sighed, knowing he wasn't getting out of this. He told his mom everything, how Lauren had started a fight with a friend, and how that fight spanned six years. He said how awful he felt about his part in how the friend was treated, and he repeated some of the things he had said to Violet in anger. His heart raced as he saw his mother's displeasure at the words.

He had mentioned Violet in passing to her before, so she knew there was a woman he didn't like, but he never told her anything he had said. It hurt to say it because it made all of it real.

"Wow . . . that is a lot," Mara said when he was done. "So, she knows you never made the comments that started it all?"

"Yeah. We cleared it up. As far as I know, she believes me. But I want to make it right. I want us to be friends."

"I don't know if this is something you make right, Charlie. Obviously, she's listening and is choosing to believe you. That's good. But pain is a strong emotion. It may not be something she can get past, and there is nothing you can do to make her."

Charlie deflated because, as always, his mother got right to the crux of the problem. He didn't want to think too hard about it, but he couldn't help it. He'd liked Violet a lot when they met. They made the same jokes. They had similar interests. She had always been so *pretty*. But they now had six years of yelling at each other to add to it, and that made it so much harder.

Maybe he couldn't fix it. Violet may never be able to move past what happened, and that was her right not to. Charlie could only hope that didn't happen.

"I know," he said, sighing.

"I know you want to make it right, but what's done is done."

"I hate that it happened."

"But it did. You have peace, and that's good. If it's nothing more than that, then it's still better than where it started."

"And what if she hates me forever?"

"Then I guess it's good you don't see each other very much."

Charlie opened his mouth to correct her because they saw each other every day. They were practically roommates. He knew he should say something to his mother, but then again, he didn't really want to.

His mom knew how much he struggled having guests over, and there was something about his fights with and feelings for Violet he was *not* ready to get grilled on by his mom. He liked to share everything with her, and vice versa, but he wasn't ready to open up about this particular topic just yet. He had enough to deal with since Violet had decided to stay.

"Yeah," he said. "I guess I'll have to be happy with us not yelling at each other."

"Yeah, maybe. Sorry, kiddo," Mara said with a frown. Charlie could only nod, feeling disappointed.

"Is there anything else you wanted to talk about?" he asked, trying to keep a positive attitude.

His mother considered it for a moment, but then shook her head. "No, no. I wanted to catch up. Nothing important."

Charlie noticed her hesitation, and considered asking her about it, but then let it go, trusting that if it was something important, she would tell him.

He spent the rest of the lunch filling her in on the wedding and showing a few of the photos he took on his phone of the decor and Lewis and Liv. His mom seemed happy to talk about that.

He went back to work in a better mood than when he left. He was happy to see his mom and talk a few things out, but he also was a little worried about his future with Violet. Maybe she wouldn't be able to get past her feelings. Maybe they would always be stuck like this.

When he got home, he figured Violet would be upstairs, as far away from him as she could get. But the dining room light was on, and Violet was sitting at the table, hunched over pieces of construction paper. Roo sat on the corner of the table, batting at a piece of balled-up paper.

"Hey," Charlie said, wondering if he was dreaming. She was downstairs? Willingly?

She jumped. "Shit," she said, and she began gathering her pieces of paper. "Sorry, I can go upstairs. I lost track of time."

"You don't have to leave because I got back."

Violet turned a little red. "I figured you would want your space."

"No, you can stay. Whatever you're doing looks like . . . a lot." He eyed the pieces of paper, which had random bits of sentences on them.

"The desk upstairs wasn't big enough," she said. "I'll be done soon."

"What are you doing?"

"I'm making a word card game," she replied. "One of the focuses for the next few weeks is sentence structure, and I know kids often struggle with it, so when we get back, I'm going to play this a few times to see if it helps."

Holy shit. That was endearing.

Charlie opened his mouth to say something, but Violet was already back to writing. Her face was focused with her eyebrows pulled low on her forehead.

When she finished writing, she moved to cutting more paper, and he noticed a little touch of her tongue poking out of her mouth.

He darted his eyes away, trying not to make it weird.

Charlie wandered to the kitchen to make dinner before he sat in front of the TV to play a video game. He watched Violet out of the corner of his eye, remembering the last game night with Lewis, and how it had felt something like this.

He couldn't focus with her around. Charlie used to think it was because he was worried she would throw something at him, but now it felt like something else.

She was like a magnet in his home, pulling his eyes to her at any moment. He wanted to drink her in and memorize everything he could about her. He wondered if he could possibly know every inch of her personality, and if she would still find a way to surprise him.

Roo being adorable next to her also didn't help.

"Am I bothering you?" she asked, looking up. Charlie jumped, knowing he had been caught.

"W-what?"

"I feel like you can't focus because I'm down here." Violet frowned. "I'm not going to throw anything or make faces at you. I promise."

No, that wasn't what was on his mind at all.

"It's not you. Some of it is Roo going after that paper like it's a mouse." Right on cue, Roo threw the balled-up paper across the room and darted. Violet watched the small, white cat go with a smile on her face. "And I'm curious about what you're doing."

"Oh," she said. "Like I said, it's a silly game for my kids at school. It's nothing important."

"I'd say teaching the next generation of kids is pretty important."

"You'd be the first." She set down her scissors and rubbed her hand. "I think I'm done for the night. I've been at it most of the day, and I think I'm starting to see floating words."

As Violet gathered her things, he desperately reached for something to get her to stay, some conversation to root her with him.

"How is your apartment coming along?"

It wasn't the best conversation starter, but she paused for a moment.

"Um, I don't know. I've driven by but everything is sort of looking the same, and my landlord is dodging questions. Why? Do you want me to leave?"

"No! The whole point of you staying was to work on stuff. I'm trying to talk to you."

"Oh," she said. "Well, the roof is covered with a tarp, but it doesn't look like they've started working on it. My renter's insurance already sent me the payout from the damage, but I can't replace my furniture until I have a place to put it."

"Shouldn't this be more of an issue to them? Have you been withholding rent payments?"

"Of course," she said. "And I know the family who lived above me is too. They're even thinking of suing, but the guy who owns the building has always dragged his feet on repairing things. I knew when this happened it would be a while before I could get back in there."

"Why did you live there if it was so bad?"

Violet narrowed her eyes at him, and he rushed to explain.

"I know teachers aren't paid enough, but why not move out of county?"

"Because I didn't want to drive more than thirty minutes to the school every day. It's nice to be able to grab something from home if I need it, or if they need me to pull a late night or extra hours, I don't have to spend all my time driving. Plus, all my friends live here."

"Then hopefully he will get it fixed soon. But until that time comes, you're welcome to stay here. I've never wanted to admit that I need help maintaining my own house. Not after seeing Gigi Ruth do it by herself for so long, so I appreciate what you're doing for me."

"Don't worry about it. You inherited a gorgeous house, but not everyone finds repairs relaxing."

"I would say most people don't find that relaxing."

"Well, I never was a normal one." Violet smiled at him. "But I do worry that even though you're fine with it, I'm less of a guest and more of a roommate, and even if I go stay with Liv, I'd be doing the same there."

"It's not so bad. I never got to have roommates in college, and it could be worse."

"I know it could be, but it's still hard. No matter who I stay with, I don't have space of my own."

Charlie could fix that for her. He had an empty room he kept closed off. She could fill it with her things and make *this* house her home.

But as soon as the idea came to mind, he remembered his mother's words. Violet could easily decide not to be his friend, and she had the right to. So why the fuck would she want to stay in his house longer than she had to?

And besides, he never wanted anyone else in his space.

But he *wanted* her in it.

He needed to stop thinking about this, and fast. He didn't want to open doors he needed to keep shut.

"I bet you're stressed."

"I really am, and it's not like I'm even in the classroom right now to distract myself. Usually, I'd hang out with Liv, and go bowling or something."

"I like to bowl," Charlie offered. "I could go with you."

"Seriously?" Violet asked. "You're inviting me to go bowling? The last time we did we almost killed each other." She paused. "That was also when our friends figured out to stop inviting us to the same event."

She was right. But that was then, and he was eager to pave over the mistakes of their past.

"We have a good track record lately," he reminded her. "And this is a chance to see if we can hang out without problems when no one is there."

Violet considered it. "It probably would be good for me to do something fun before school is back in session."

"We made it through the wedding. Bowling can't be much worse."

"You know what?" Violet said. "Fuck it. Let's give it a try. How about tomorrow?"

Chapter Thirteen

Violet

As she was getting ready to go bowling the next night, Violet wondered if maybe this was a bad idea.

It was one thing to be in Charlie's home with him. Their arguments were confined to the same four walls. No one else could hear them, but being out in public meant if they lost it, people would know.

There was a reason Violet and Charlie never came to the same events. Their arguments drew eyes.

Violet was more nervous for this than she was for a date because she knew this would have huge implications. What if they were destined to be enemies forever? Could she have fun with Charlie in any capacity?

She stood in front of her measly collection of clothes for longer than she would admit. She was worried they would mess it up, and worried about what to wear.

All her current clothes fit into a cheap duffel bag she had bought at Ross. She had work dresses, a few pairs of leggings, and several things that had been in her car when her apartment collapsed.

And none of it was going to work for tonight.

Eventually, she settled on leggings and a light blue shirt that she sometimes wore under dresses. She also grabbed the one nice item she owned, a black peacoat. Her heart was racing, but she knew Charlie was getting ready, and she didn't want to piss him off by taking forever to get dressed.

They were also riding together. Charlie had made a good point that there was no reason for them both to drive, so he offered. But now, Violet was wondering if that had been a mistake too.

If they did fight, they would have to sit together in an awkwardly silent car for the ride back, which would feel a little like a time out reserved for naughty children.

Or Charlie could just abandon her at the bowling alley. Then how would she go about getting him to pay for it, since he would be saddling her with an expensive taxi bill that she couldn't afford? Would he fight her on that too? What if her pushing the issue made him change his mind and kick her out?

Biting her lip, Violet knew it was too easy to imagine the things that could go wrong.

But she was going to try to stay positive. Even now, when she looked at him, she didn't feel the anger she used to. Somehow, deep in her brain, she had accepted that he didn't make the comments. What once simmered below the surface was now... well, she wasn't sure what.

That's what tonight was for.

Violet took a deep breath and met Charlie in the living room. He was wearing a sweater and jeans, looking casual but nice at the same time.

He looked good. More than good. Maybe even hot.

Could she say that now?

"Are you ready?" she asked instead of thinking about it any further.

Charlie turned to her, and then did a double take. "You look nice."

Violet could feel her face heat up as she looked down. "Uh, do I? I'm just in leggings, but they're comfortable and I wanted to be able to move for bowling. Should I change?"

"No! I'm serious. You look nice. Beautiful even."

"Oh, thank you." Violet's face heated. She brushed her hands over her leggings, as if grabbing for cat hair that wasn't there. "Sometimes I want to look a little less like a dorky teacher and a little more like I'm in my twenties."

Charlie glanced at her again, his eyes lingering. She noticed him doing that more often over the last two days. What was he thinking? Was he still feeling bad about the comments? Was he thinking about when they were friends and didn't argue all the time? She didn't know, and she hated that she didn't.

Was he thinking she was beautiful again?

She hated that she liked being the center of his attention. Was she always like this?

And a deep, dark part of Violet had always loved getting Charlie's attention.

"Let's head out," he said, turning away.

Violet nodded, following Charlie out to his car. She expected to be jealous at how nice it was compared to her older vehicle, but all she felt was nervous excitement over actually being in the same car as Charlie.

There was something so intimate about an after-dark drive with someone. And this someone was Charlie.

She stole glances at him out of the corner of her eye, noticing how good he looked when he drove. The car was quiet, and traffic in the city was busy.

If this were a date, he'd be checking all her boxes.

But this was not a date. This was them salvaging the ruins of their friendship.

The bowling alley was packed when they walked in. This place didn't hold fond memories for either of them. They'd fought at this exact bowling alley before. Neither Violet nor Charlie had even shared a lane, and yet they somehow found a way to tease each other about their scores, which quickly devolved into a fight.

"Come on," Charlie said, grabbing her elbow. "There's one lane left in the corner, and I want to get it before anyone else does."

She nodded, trying to calm the mix of feelings rising within her. She was torn between being terrified that they would yell at each other again and being embarrassed by the way she had been thinking of Charlie in the car.

It wasn't a date, and she knew it wasn't. After everything, there was no way they could ever be more than friends, but she had spent six years not allowing herself to admit how handsome he was. Now that she didn't hate him, all those feelings were rushing back, pushing themselves to the forefront of her mind. She didn't know how to stop it.

"Two for the lane in the corner," Charlie told the disinterested teen at the counter.

"Do you need shoes?"

"Yep."

"Paying together?"

"No," Violet said forcefully before Charlie could. He looked alarmed for a moment before it melted away and he nodded.

Violet let out a breath of relief. She didn't want this to feel like a date or anything close to it. That was the last thing she needed.

After they paid, they sat down to lace up the shoes. Charlie seemed relaxed, as if this wasn't a huge thing for them to be doing.

"If I remember correctly," Charlie said with a smirk in the corner of his mouth, "you're pretty good."

"So are you," she replied, tossing him a matching smile.

It was their biggest issue. They were equally matched when it came to skill, and they both wanted to be the best.

"Well, what do you say, loser buys pizza?"

"Is that a good idea?" Violet asked. "Are you sure the competition won't devolve into us yelling at each other?"

Charlie paused to consider it.

"I think *friendly* competition is fine," he said eventually. "But maybe we'll keep personal insults out of it."

"And if we do insult each other personally, the one who did it has to buy a shitty, overpriced beer, and then chug it."

After she suggested it, her anxiety warned her this was a bad idea. But as she opened her mouth to take it back, Charlie laughed.

"Gross. That's truly evil, but it's a deal."

He held out his hand and Violet didn't hesitate to shake it. For them, shaking hands signified something. They had shaken on being fake friends, on Violet staying longer with Charlie, and now on this.

"You're on," she said.

Violet went first, hurling the ball down the lane with practiced ease. It was an easy strike.

"Ha!" she said, turning to him.

"Well, fuck," he said. "I see you haven't lost any of your skill."

"I wouldn't have brought you here if I was bad."

"Okay, my turn, Moore," Charlie said, walking around her to grab his ball.

"Oh, are we already back to last names?"

"Only during competition."

Usually, when he used her last name, she hated it. She hated that it was always said as an insult, like using *Violet* was beneath him.

But this . . . this felt like amicable rivalry. The smile he gave her was loose and relaxed. His shoulders weren't tight and he didn't have the frown on his face he always did when he looked at her.

Then he immediately bowled a strike, which shot all thoughts out of Violet's brain.

Damn it. He hadn't lost his skill either.

When he turned to smirk at her, she rolled her eyes.

"You know what, I'm glad to know I won't absolutely wipe the floor with you. That would be so boring for the both of us."

"I don't think it will be a sweep. I think I'm going to wipe the floor with you. You always mess up later."

"We've only been bowling together a few times."

"I notice patterns, and you mess up later in fights too."

"Okay, you win the arguments, yes. But you're not totally perfect at bowling. I remember you throwing a ball backwards one time."

"I remember you getting three gutter balls in a row."

"First off, that was an unbalanced ball, and second, I'd rather get it in a gutter instead of smashing Lewis's toe."

They were standing close, so close she could see his beard had grown out some. She liked the look of it. His face was rugged and hard like this, but he seemed so relaxed, so open. She decided she liked this method of arguing with Charlie. It had no heat to it, only pleasure.

"Your turn, Moore. Good luck following that up." Charlie stepped away from her, and she already missed the closeness.

"I don't need luck, Davis. I have skill."

Their strange competitive teasing went on for the entire game and Violet's worries over their teasing spiraling into something more were washed away by her desire to win. She was on autopilot, saying whatever came to mind, and Charlie never got offended.

If this were a date, the guy would have already left by now. But Violet wasn't worried about impressing Charlie or showing only the best sides of her. She was here to win, and Charlie seemed to enjoy it. They egged each other on, not taking it too far, but also not taking it easy on each other.

They probably were the most annoying people at the alley, hanging out in a corner hurling loud insults at each other, but it was easily the best game of bowling she had ever had.

"Ha!" she called on her final turn. "Three strikes on the last go. Beat that."

"I intend to," Charlie said, standing. He could easily do it too if he also got three strikes.

But on his extra throw, he only knocked down eight pins.

"Damn!" he yelled.

Violet pumped her fists into the air. "I don't have to buy pizza!"

"I want a rematch," Charlie said with his eyes squinting at her as he fumed. "There's no way you can do it again."

"I'm not starting another game until I have a pizza on the table," Violet told him.

"I regret making this deal."

"I don't," Violet said as she watched him trudge toward the concession stand, making sure he actually ordered her prize instead of weaseling out of it.

But as he walked, she found herself staring at *him* and not where he was going.

Charlie had always been attractive, but *damn*, he looked even better now. His jeans hugged his ass, and now that he had removed his sweater, she was treated to the sight of a white T-shirt underneath showing off his broad shoulders. She had spent all night staring at him as he bowled, but she was more focused on hoping he fucked up his form than actually checking him out.

And damn, was she missing out.

Violet tore her eyes away. She was *not* about to make it awkward by saying anything about how hot he was to his face. No. They were staying so far in the friend lane they might as well pay a toll.

"One pizza for the winner," Charlie said, returning after a few minutes of Violet reminding herself not to be an idiot. "And I got veggie, even though we live in a world with bacon and pepperoni as options for pizza toppings."

"You remembered that?"

"It's one of the things I'll support you in but never understand. Seriously, veggies?"

"I can't explain it," Violet said, grabbing a slice. "You didn't have to get vegetable though."

"Do you think I would get you a pizza you didn't like for your winning reward?"

"You could have been bitter that I won and got me a subpar pizza in a lame-ass attempt to stick it to me. But even that wouldn't have worked." She took a bite and through a mouthful, she added, "All pizza is delicious. Especially when it's free."

"Nope. You won. You get what you want."

Violet blushed. Admittedly, it was exactly what she wanted. After a moment, she asked, "Aren't you going to have some?"

"This is your win."

"Yeah, but you'll need all the energy you can get for the next game. I want to kick your ass fair and square. Unless you can't stomach a vegetable pizza."

Charlie laughed as he grabbed a slice.

Once they finished eating, they started a second game. They were neck and neck up until the very end, and Charlie barely edged her out of a victory by two points.

"Ha!" he said. "Redemption!"

"No, this is a tie!"

"But I won by two points instead of one."

"Only because you started loudly singing to the music on the last roll!" Violet argued back. There was no heat to either of their comments, and Violet felt more relaxed than she had in a long time. It was like they were back in college before any of the fighting had started. Charlie was a guy she had a lot in common with.

Violet didn't know she could feel this way.

"It was a well-earned win," Charlie said. "Want to play again?"

Violet flexed her wrist, wincing. "Can we do a raincheck? My wrist was already sore from having to make those sentence cards on top of this."

Charlie sobered immediately. "Wait, I didn't know your wrist hurt."

Violet smiled, unsure what to do with the attention.

"I'm fine. I promise."

"Still, if you weren't having fun . . ."

Violet rolled her eyes. "I had loads of fun. I need to give it a rest. It'll be fine! We can even go play the arcade games if you want."

"I do like a good arcade game," Charlie said, "though I think you owe me a pizza."

"Are you even hungry?" Violet asked. "We ate all of my pizza thirty minutes ago."

"Can I cash it in for ice cream?"

"I think I can make that work," she told him, smiling as they walked over to the food counter.

After he ate his scoop of ice cream, Violet dragged him to the arcade where they got a few coins to play with.

Charlie found a coin pusher game and got lost in it. Violet watched him with oddly focused interest. He took his time to come up with the perfect angles to get more coins out of the machine. She didn't know how he was managing to figure out all the moves he played, but she liked watching him do it.

She dragged him to play one of the shooting games with her, where they both made a pathetic attempt at beating the displayed high score.

By the end of the night, she was exhausted, but it had been one of the best nights she could remember. She didn't want it to end, but Charlie had work, and she needed to get to prepping for the winter festival. Neither of them could stay out any later.

But she knew something had shifted. The slate had been wiped clean. They both knew when to stop themselves, and they both had fun teasing each other without it getting serious.

When she looked at him, she no longer saw the guy that hurt her. She saw someone who was as blindsided as she had been. She saw a man who had still let her into his home despite their bad blood. She saw the person who she had once liked so many years ago.

Charlie could have been something more if things hadn't changed, if Lauren hadn't ruined it. Back then, when she had been asking for help with her essay, she had also been wondering whether she should ask him out. Especially since she was pretty sure they were on a break.

But then she saw the comments on her work, and she never let herself think of it again.

Now, though, she remembered why she liked him, which was a dangerous thought to have.

Charlie

Over the next week, things shifted. Violet ventured into the living room more often, and Charlie made peace with her magnetic power being around him at all times. It became normal for him to look up and see her sitting at the dining room table.

And he had one major problem with it.

Of course, it wasn't Violet. She hadn't done anything wrong. It was *him*.

He hardly recognized himself anymore.

Normally, when he was at home, he didn't socialize. He didn't look up and hope anyone else would be there. When he was within the four walls of his house, he wanted no one.

Until now.

Not only did he have Roo to hang out with, but Violet too.

Whenever Charlie would see her after work, he wanted to know how her day was. When she would cook, he couldn't wait to sit down with her and eat. When she would go up to the guest room, bitterness coiled deep within him because he wanted her to stay.

None of it made sense.

Charlie wasn't like this with friends, much less with a relationship. Usually, he would be tired of Lauren in a day or two, and he would need to go home to recharge. The same sometimes applied to Lewis.

Violet was the exception, and Charlie didn't understand why.

By now, he would be lonely. Lewis had been gone for over a week, and Charlie hadn't talked to him or Lauren in that time. Usually, he would be calling Lewis to hang out, or waiting by the door for Lauren to come back to him.

Instead, he was content.

And they didn't even have to talk. Having her in the same room as him was enough. Sometimes he would play with Roo and see her watching them from the dining room, and all he could feel was how *right* it felt.

It was terrifying.

Charlie had no idea if Violet had the same thoughts about him. She seemed to like being around him, enough to emerge from the guest room when he was home, but he didn't know anything else.

Violet always kept everything closely guarded. Beyond the night of the wedding, they hadn't talked about the essay. She said she wanted to work on their friendship, but he didn't know where she stood. Did she feel *anything* similar? Was she as terrified as he was?

Sometimes he would see her smile and hope she was feeling half of the things he was. But then he would lie awake at night, replaying every callous word he said to her. He hated how stupid he had been.

And if she was doing the same, he could only imagine what she thought of him.

She still rarely let him help her. Violet insisted she cook breakfast for herself, and then she started cooking for both of them. After breakfast, she would clean the kitchen without being asked.

After two days of being treated to breakfast, Charlie decided to start feeding her dinner in return. At first, she wouldn't accept. Then he made her favorite food—pasta and garlic bread—and she finally gave in.

They were falling into a rhythm, one so comfortable Charlie didn't even believe it was real. Sometimes he wondered if she was only playing along to humor him.

But she also seemed to be giving him more of a chance every single day. The dull look in her eyes had faded, and Charlie finally thought she might be seeing him for who he was, not the comments Lauren had made under his name.

That chance at redemption had changed him.

A week after their bowling night, Charlie and Violet were sitting down for breakfast. She was telling him all about her plans for the winter festival.

Charlie was a little bummed he wasn't going to be able to hang out with her that night. It made no sense because he should be used to lonely nights in his home, and yet, he could still feel his chest tighten as he thought about it.

Violet was interrupted by her phone ringing. She grabbed it out of her back pocket and frowned.

"It's a parent. I have to take this," she told him before answering it. Charlie kept an ear on the conversation, hearing something about the festival, and someone had canceled.

As soon as Violet hung up, Charlie asked, "What happened?"

"Oh, nothing big," she answered, but the frown on her face said otherwise. "One of the parents who usually helps for the winter festival had to cancel. I'll need to find a volunteer to replace them."

"I can do it."

Violet looked at him dubiously. "I highly doubt you want to spend your evening surrounded by sixth graders."

"I don't mind," he replied. He didn't dislike kids and had wanted to hang out with Violet anyway. "Really. What do you need help with?"

"Charlie, I wouldn't even ask Liv for this. It's fine."

"Violet," he said, leaning forward, "I wouldn't offer if I wasn't okay with helping."

"But—"

"Come on. Please? Let me do something for once."

"I'm staying in your house."

"Yes, to see if we can get along. And part of that is letting me help you. Friends help friends, remember?"

Violet stared. "I would need someone to help with serving food."

"Perfect, I can do that."

"Charlie, I know you feel like you need to make up for the past, but—"

"I'm offering because I like you and I want to help. Does it have to be anything more?"

Violet looked at him, exasperated. She must have seen he was being genuine because it faded.

"Okay, I can register you as a volunteer—"

"Yes!" Charlie said.

"You're not going to feel this excited when you're there."

"I'll feel how I want to. Honestly, I'm excited to see you in your element."

Violet's cheeks turned pink. "It's not that cool."

"I'll decide that for myself," he said, smiling at her. And it was true. Violet had been working her ass off for this festival. He was excited to see what came out of it.

The festival was one day away. It only took Violet a few hours to sign him up as a volunteer, and once she did, it all felt real.

The night of the festival was chilly and cloudy. Violet told him to meet her at the school at five, so he took off work early and arrived ten minutes till. When he walked in, he was greeted by a receptionist who was signing in the other volunteers.

She had dyed red hair piled high on top of her head. She wore thick reading glasses perched on her nose. A nameplate in front of her read, "Cathy."

"Hey," he greeted her. "I'm Charlie Davis."

"Oh yeah. Violet told me to expect you." She crossed his name off her list. "Are you the father of one of the kids?"

"Is that needed for signing me in?"

"I'm just curious."

"I'm a friend of hers."

"Wow, a friend helping out at a school event?" Cathy smiled. "You never hear of that."

Charlie didn't know what to say, and the sly smile on Cathy's face made him wonder what she was thinking.

"Cathy, are you harassing my volunteer?" Violet's voice came from behind them. He turned and saw Violet in her usual A-line dress and heels. Her dress was covered in different Einstein faces, which was both hilarious and beautiful.

"Volunteer? I thought he was your boyfriend."

Violet blushed but kept a straight face. Charlie felt his body tighten in reaction to being called Violet's *boyfriend*.

"You're only asking to see if you can get him for yourself." Violet strode to the counter and wrote Charlie's name on a volunteer sticker. She stuck it on his chest with a firm hand. "Come on, I'll show you around."

"Have fun!" Cathy called after them.

"Don't worry about her." Violet rolled her eyes as they walked. "She's a flirt. You should see her with the single dads."

"I don't think I want to," Charlie said. His chest was on fire from where Violet had touched him. "Where are we going?"

"My classroom. I have a student I watch after school. He's staying for the festival, and I want to see if I can get him to help set up."

When Charlie arrived at her classroom, he couldn't help but notice how it was the perfect embodiment of her. It was decorated with different quotes and sentence structures, with vibrant colors that made the area fun. A boy sat at a desk scribbling on his homework. He perked up when she entered the room.

"Can we go to the festival now, Ms. Moore?" he asked.

"Not yet," Violet replied, smiling. "We're about to start setting up."

"It's still not ready?" he moaned.

"Nope, but it may go faster if we have more hands to help. Why don't you join in?"

"That depends. Will you give me candy?"

"We'll see how good your work is," Violet answered. Charlie bit back a laugh at the kid's expression.

"Who's that?" the boy asked, looking at Charlie hesitantly.

"This is my friend. He's helping me work on the festival tonight."

The boy did eventually climbed out of his seat to help, and seemed to perk up when Violet thanked him. Charlie wondered why she came home so late some days. The boy must have been why.

Charlie was sent to the cafeteria to help set up the food. It was important, monotonous work, but he didn't mind it. Every now and then, he would look up and see Violet either talking to the boy from her class or another teacher. She walked through the halls like she owned them and seemed to be so caring about anything and everything within its walls—it was obvious she was good at any job she had. Watching her was like watching an artist paint, or a composer write a score.

Eventually, he was so busy he couldn't check on her. He talked to a ton of parents as he served food. He didn't expect it to be fun, but hearing the stories of a lot of the people in his own neighborhood was energizing.

Charlie didn't feel drained when he was done, in fact, he felt a little more alive.

"All right, Mr. Davis." Cathy had found him again. "Us school employees are going to clean up. You're free to go with the rest of the volunteers."

"I'll stay and help," he said, grabbing leftover food to put away in the teacher's lounge.

"Helpful *and* willing to stay late. Where did Violet find you?"

"College."

"She has herself a catch." Cathy winked at him. He opened his mouth to correct her, but she was gone before he could.

Ah, fuck it. He could say something later.

He carried the extra trays of food to the break room where the school employees were chatting. He introduced himself to a few of them and talked for a moment while he put things into the refrigerator.

They all seemed interested in seeing how Violet was doing, and since he was the only friend they had met, they asked him if her apartment was fixed.

He gave them an easy answer—that it was being worked on and she was staying with a friend. It was nice to see how much her coworkers cared about her.

As he left to get another tray, Violet found him.

She looked *exhausted*. There had been loads of fun science experiments and outreach activities set up by local vendors. He had heard her running around to make sure everything went well. She was wearing her usual light coating of makeup, but her eyes were dull, and her expression pained.

He also realized she probably hadn't eaten dinner.

"I am so sorry," she said, sounding out of breath. "I got so busy with everything, and I never had time to check in on you."

"I'm fine," Charlie said with a smile.

"Really? You weren't bored out of your mind?"

"No," he said. "I liked meeting a lot of the parents. A few of them are my neighbors."

"Oh, thank God. I know school stuff is super boring but—"

"It wasn't boring. I enjoyed helping tonight."

Violet blinked at him. "Really?"

"Yeah, it felt good to be a part of the community for a bit. Besides, I liked watching you do what you enjoy."

Violet's cheeks turned pink. "I didn't do much."

"Come on. You handled this whole thing." Charlie grabbed another tray of food. Violet followed him. "It was like the wedding but way cooler."

"It was not cool," Violet said, shaking her head. "And I need to do something for you to thank you. You're the one who helped tonight."

"Let's do dinner." He turned to her after setting down the food.

"W-what?"

"Dinner. You and me. We go get food. You can relax after a long night. I'm buying."

Violet stared at him. "Hang on. I'm supposed to treat *you*."

"I'm the one who's hungry, and I don't want to eat alone. So, you're actually doing me a favor by not fighting me on this and joining me."

Violet must have been exhausted because she struggled to come up with an answer for him.

"I-if I'm going, I'm paying," she settled on.

"I already offered first. You'll have to be faster next time."

"I'll seriously pay—"

"Nope. I'm buying."

"Charlie—"

"Oh my God, Violet," Cathy called from the corner of the break room. "Let the man take you out to eat! You're forgetting the first rule of being a teacher: you never turn down free food."

Charlie nodded along, glad for the backup.

"Okay, fine!" Violet said, rolling her eyes. "Let's go get food."

Charlie couldn't help the smirk that made its way across his face, and flashed it to Cathy to say thanks.

Cleanup didn't take much longer, and by nine, they were walking to the parking lot to discuss where to go.

"I'm not hungry," Violet said as they leaned against his car to pick out a restaurant. "I'm fine."

"But I'm hungry," Charlie reminded her. "And honestly, a giant waffle sounds good right about now."

Violet froze, and it looked like her icy wall of denial was melting. "How dare you mention waffles."

"You know who has good waffles? Waffle House."

"Are they actually good waffles?"

"Sometimes, but they're cheap, and I know how you are about people paying. You'll feel better if it's not expensive."

She glared at him. "That is exactly how I feel, and I hate you for saying it."

"Come on. I even checked their menu, and they have the blueberry waffle back."

"What?" Violet exclaimed. "That's been off the menu for years, and it's my favorite!"

"Exactly, which is why we need to go before they take it off the menu again."

"Okay, okay. You've convinced me."

"I'll drive."

"Hang on, you can't do *everything*—"

He opened the door for her, and gestured for her to get in. She glared at him, but he could see she was tired. Driving was probably the last thing she wanted to do, unless it was back to the house.

"I'm going to pay you back for all this," she muttered as she climbed into the passenger seat.

Charlie wouldn't allow her to, but he let her believe it.

The Waffle House was almost empty when they got there. There were only two employees, and one other occupied table.

"I know all Waffle Houses look the same, but I feel like we've been to this one before," Violet said when they walked in.

"We have. We came here a few days after we met." He pointed to the table in the corner. "We sat over there while Liv and Lewis made heart eyes at each other the whole time."

"Huh. You're right. How do you remember all this stuff from college? The sleep deprivation must have fried my memory."

Because you were there. Because, from the moment I met you, a part of me was always aware of everything you were. Even when I despised you, you occupied my mind in ways I could never comprehend, and now that we're here, I want you to take more of me.

The words came unbidden to his mind. For a moment, they terrified him. He had never felt this way about anyone.

But Violet wasn't just anyone.

"Good memory, I guess," he said with a shrug.

Violet looked like she wanted to ask what he was thinking, but thankfully, a waitress came and took their drink order. When she shuffled away, Violet turned to him.

"Are you okay? Are you sure you're not regretting coming to a Waffle House when there are other options?"

"I don't regret it. This is a nice reminder of college."

"Yeah, it kind of is. It's so bad it's good. Like ramen."

"Yeah," he said, trying to play it cool. "Cheap food is what I needed tonight."

More like what she needed.

"About that," Violet said. "I still feel bad I got busy and wasn't able to make sure you were okay."

"I had fun, I promise. Why are you so worried I didn't? I like being a part of the community."

"I don't know. My job is . . . my job isn't for everyone. And often it's forgotten about. I know what I do is important, but sometimes I feel like it's not enough."

"I think the kid you've been helping after class would disagree."

Violet turned a little red. "He's going through some things."

"And you're helping him. You job may not pay a lot, but it doesn't mean it's not important, Violet."

Violet smiled. "How did you know exactly what I needed to hear?"

"Lucky guess."

Because it's you.

"On the note of school, I think Cathy thinks we're dating. I should probably correct her."

"It's not a huge deal. I think it made it easier for people to understand why some young guy was there."

"Yeah, most people wouldn't volunteer at a school event. Even if they're dating a teacher."

"Maybe I'm not most people."

"Yeah, maybe." Violet bit her lip. Charlie was dying to know what she was thinking. "Anyway, you helped. I feel like I should be paying for dinner."

"Nope. You're here for me. As a treat."

"That doesn't make sense."

"It doesn't have to, but I did a fraction of the work you did, and I offered. So let me take care of you."

Violet blinked, and then leaned back in her seat. "Fine," she muttered. "But I'll get you back."

You already have.

Their drinks arrived, and the waitress took their food orders. Violet got two waffles, which Charlie didn't doubt she would wolf down.

He got the same.

"You know, I'm kind of glad I'm staying with you for the time being and not Liv and Lewis." Violet was stirring her soda, coming alive after finally consuming some calories.

"Yeah?"

"I love them, but after they get back from their honeymoon, I'd be staying with a couple. A *newlywed* couple." She shuttered. "It's my worst nightmare."

"And in that tiny apartment too."

"It's so small, and the bedroom has the only bathroom. What if I had to pee and they're in there for hours doing things? I'd have to pee in a bush!"

"I don't know what bush you're thinking of because their apartment building is all concrete."

"Exactly," she said. "It's so sad. I like visiting, but the charm would wear off in days. Plus, they're perfect together. Looking at them is like looking at the sun. It hurts after a while."

Charlie blinked. What did that mean? Was she hinting she was lonely? Or did she somehow have feelings for either of them?

"Don't look so weirded out," she explained after a moment. "I don't like either of them, but I want what they have. With someone else, of course. I know you don't believe in love, but I do."

"Right," he said, his chest loosening. "Yeah, staying with them wouldn't be good for you then."

"Yeah. I love them, don't get me wrong, but Lewis can't load a dishwasher to save his life, and Liv doesn't ever take out the trash. I think I'd wind up taking on everything out of frustration."

"You do like to clean. I'm happy I have a roommate I get along with."

The food came and Charlie said thank you to the waitress. When he turned, Violet was looking at him.

"What?" he asked.

"You said roommate," she said softly. "And I-I feel bad that we are. We're twenty-eight. We should be way past having roommates."

"There are lots of people who are twenty-eight with roommates."

"Maybe, but you own your house. You shouldn't have to deal with a roommate."

"It's not *a* roommate. It's you, and you're not a problem to live with."

"Yet." It was muttered, and he almost missed it.

"You say that like you're sure something will happen."

"Something always happens. I'm showing you my best side. I'll slip up at some point and show you the bad side of me."

Charlie laughed. "Violet, I *have* seen the bad. This is me, remember? We've insulted each other until both of us were kicked out of places."

"Well, yeah but that's—"

"It's not different. I've seen you. All of you, and I'm still here. It doesn't matter how long we're stuck together; I've already seen it."

Violet stared, as if realizing it for herself. Charlie wondered if she was going to run, or try to walk back what she said. She always wanted to do that when the conversation got real.

"You should eat your waffle," he said, instead of pushing her further. "You're too introspective when you're hungry."

Violet slowly nodded and took a bite. Their serious conversation was interrupted by her excitement over food.

"Holy shit, it's as good as I remember," she said with her mouth full. "Thank God it's back on the menu."

Charlie laughed, happy to see her so excited over where he decided to bring her.

"Some people like caviar and truffles, but I like waffles," she continued. "They're the perfect food."

"See why I brought you here?"

"Ugh, fine. You were right. I needed food, but I still feel bad about you paying."

"Violet, stop worrying about it. This is Waffle House, and I offered. It's not like I'm paying your rent for you. I don't mind doing this. Seriously. I wouldn't have offered if I wasn't happy to do it."

"I'm still going to do it." She rolled her eyes, but he could see a blush painting her cheeks. She went back for another bite.

They ate and joked about college, remembering all the times they had done stupid things in their group. They talked about Liv and Lewis and how obvious it was that they liked each other. They talked about Micah and how they all knew she was going to be incredibly successful in whatever career she chose. They talked about the few good memories they had before it all went downhill near graduation.

It was one of the best meals he ever had.

When they were done, Violet was in a good mood. She was laughing with him like they used to, and he could feel it wriggling under his skin, settling within him.

It was a dangerous feeling.

"Hey, we're near my apartment," Violet said as they drove back to the school. "Do you mind if we go see if they've started work on it?"

"I don't mind."

Violet told him where to turn, and they pulled up to an old-looking building with a tarp over one side of it. It looked poorly maintained, with overgrown trees and old, unpainted concrete. Trash was thrown in every visible crevice.

Seeing this awful place, and knowing Violet lived here, made him want to lock her in his home forever. He thought his old house was outdated, but this was simply negligent.

Violet abruptly leaned forward, and Charlie frowned, following her line of sight. Right on the front of the building was a red sign that said, "Sold."

And judging by the look on Violet's face, this was the first time she had seen it.

Chapter Fourteen

Violet

Violet was pissed. More than pissed—furious.

"You can't sell the building!" Violet yelled. She was standing outside of her old apartment, which had a sold sign on it. She had climbed out of the car and immediately called her landlord. She paced the vicinity, walking in circles as Charlie watched her from the distance.

"They gave me an offer I couldn't refuse." It was obvious he didn't care. She could hear his loud TV in the background. He hadn't even bothered to mute it.

"We have leases. Agreements!"

"And in those leases, it says I can break off anytime if I decided to sell. And I have. You don't have any legal ground here, honey."

Violet groaned. She had read the lease years ago when she moved in, and she had thought no investor would be dumb enough to buy a building on this side of town.

Obviously, she was wrong.

"Listen, if you leave me alone about it, I'll give your deposit back," he said. She pulled her phone from her ear to give it the finger. It didn't do anything, but it made her feel slightly better.

"I want last month's rent too," Violet added.

"Now why would I do that?"

"You want me to leave it alone? Then pay up. Otherwise, I'm going to the local media about it. I'll find these investors and make both of you look so bad they back out of the deal."

The landlord muttered something, and Violet didn't try too hard to make out what it was. She was mad enough. "Fine, but if I do, you keep your mouth shut."

"Deal. I better get that check within two weeks." She told him to send it to her school, and then hung up. There was only a second of silence before she screamed into the darkness of the night.

"That bad?" Charlie asked.

"I want to wring his fat neck until it's the size of his penis! I want to drag his sorry ass through the mud until we hit the fucking desert, and then I want to make him eat his own sorry excuse for a building brick by brick until it's sunk in that he sucks ass!"

Charlie didn't look perturbed by her rant. He had nodded along as if he had heard all this before, and he had. Usually directed at him, though.

"Fucking shitbag! I knew I shouldn't have signed that lease! I knew Nashville was doing well but I didn't think any investor would want this shithole!"

"It *is* a shithole."

"Ugh!" she yelled. Her anger faded, slowly being replaced by a blind panic. "Now I need a place to live, and I can't afford it. You know how fucking expensive this city is! I'll have to move out over an hour away."

She paused as the last of her anger left her.

"I should have gotten a higher-paying job," she muttered miserably. "My mom was right."

"Wait, what?" Charlie asked, pushing off from his car and walking in front of her. "This has nothing to do with your job."

"Yes, it does! I can't afford to live here on a teacher's salary. I can't afford anything!"

"But you like your job. Doesn't that matter?"

"It would if I had a home. But I don't. You see how bad this place looks, and it was the best I could do. And now it's sold and I'm really homeless!"

She resumed her pacing. Her frantic mind was struggling to come up with a solution.

"You have a home. You can stay with me." Charlie said it as if it were the simplest thing in the world.

"What? Charlie, I can't stay with you forever. You have a life, and I . . . I can't ask that of you. I'm talking *months*. Or potentially permanently."

"You're not asking. I'm offering."

Violet stared at him, and then shook her head in disbelief. "But . . . I'd want furniture of my own, and my own bed. I'd need a closet and—"

"I can make that work."

"I . . . Why are you offering this?"

"Because . . ." He paused for a moment. "Because I've lived alone for a long time, and I'm tired of it. And because you're my friend. Living together has been good for us. It doesn't have to change."

"But you have your family's furniture in the guest room."

"I have an empty room. You can have it."

"What if you have a date?"

Charlie shook his head. "You don't have to worry about that. I'm . . . not dating."

Violet sighed. "But—" She was struggling to come up with more reasons to say no.

"Violet," he said, grabbing her shoulders. "Do you want to leave my house? Is it uncomfortable or bad for you?"

"No," she said honestly.

"Then, don't leave."

"No," she said, shaking her head. "This is too much. I can't don't this to you."

Charlie sighed. "You need it to be even, don't you?"

"Of course, I do, I—"

"I need help with certain bills then." Charlie was blunt, but it stopped her mind. He needed help? "I need to save up for some bigger repairs, but the utilities are high, and it would be nice to have help."

"You mean like the roof?"

Charlie sighed. "You saw it?"

"Yeah, I did. It's going to need replacing sooner than later."

"I can't manage to save up because I'm spending all my money keeping the lights on. So how about you pay the utilities and help me keep up on repairs?"

It was a solid offer. The best she had, even. She was so close to her school. Plus, Charlie had Roo, who she had come to love. She knew where everything was in the house, and she *liked* looking at him every day.

"How much are the utilities?"

"Six hundred a month."

That was high for utilities, but still less than the rent she used to pay.

"Okay, I can pay that. I'd like to."

Violet expected him to look resigned when she agreed, like maybe he felt he had to offer but didn't really want her to accept. But instead, he looked *relieved*. Maybe he needed more help than she thought.

"So, you're staying?"

"I guess I am." She nodded. "I hope you're prepared."

"We can make it work." His hands on her shoulders squeezed, and Violet noticed how he was still touching her. She didn't mind it.

"We should get back. I'd like to see this room. Is it the one with the door always closed?"

"Yeah," Charlie said. "Let's go get your car. Then I'll show it to you."

Violet nodded and climbed back into his Mercedes. She was brimming with excitement when they arrived at the house. She was still nervous, but the idea that she got to stay in this beautiful home was overruling her nerves.

As promised, Charlie took her right to the empty room. It was the room on the right, the one he had told her not to go into. When he opened the door, she wondered if it was going to be grander than the rest of the rooms, but it was simply empty. It had a plain pink and green floral wallpaper, and the wooden floors that were throughout the house, but it was just a room.

"I'm not gonna lie, I expected a body," she joked.

"No, it's a room ... it's the one I would stay in when I was a kid."

"Oh." She looked at him, panic clawing its way to her throat. "You don't have to give me this room, not if it's special to you."

"I think it should be lived in," he said. "Not hidden away."

"Are you sure?" she asked once more.

"I am," he said, turning to her with a small smile on his face. "Feel free to get your own furniture. Do whatever you want."

Violet looked between the room and Charlie, honored that he trusted her. When he moved to turn away, she pulled him into a tight hug. It was hard to because he was so much bigger than her, but her arms wound around his middle, and his warm weight pressed into her. She could feel herself melting into him.

"Thanks for offering this, Charlie," she said, her voice muffled by his shirt.

"It's no problem." His voice sounded hesitant. Violet pulled away, realizing this was the first time she had hugged him. Usually, she kept her distance, but this seemed like a good first-hug occasion. He nodded at her, face red, and went back down to the first floor. Violet's eyes followed him the whole way down.

When she returned to her room, she pulled out her phone to message Liv about the change of plans. She bit her lip, deciding to check in before springing the news on her friend.

Violet: Hey! How are things?

Liv: So amazing! I NEEDED this break. I literally could not handle another thing to worry about.

Violet let out a long breath. She knew the moment that she said she was still staying with Charlie, her friend would panic.

Violet: I got a new place. Well, less of a place and more of a room.

Liv: With who?

Violet could practically feel her best friend's worry through the phone.

Violet: An old college friend. I'll tell you more when you get back. I'm super happy with it!

Liv: Okay . . . but now I'm curious. You better give me all the details!

Violet: Of course.

Oh, Liv was going to lose it when she found out where Violet was staying. But that was a problem for future Violet. Present Violet needed to order a bed.

Charlie

It took two days for Violet to get a mattress delivered. Charlie came home from work on a Thursday, and there it was. She had somehow gotten it up the stairs without help. The next day, she had a dresser, which she wanted to move herself, but Charlie helped her before she could even try it.

Violet only complained a few times.

The items matched the aesthetic of her room, and Charlie thought it looked nice when it was put together. Violet had been beaming when she showed him her bed, and any worries about her moving into his favorite room vanished when he saw her smile.

Charlie wasn't stupid; he knew what this was. He had known for a long time that Violet teetered between two dangerous options, but he couldn't let either one of them become reality. He didn't want everything to fall apart.

Sometimes not giving it a name was easier.

***

The morning was cold and foggy. Violet was up early as always, and by the time Charlie was done with his run, she was downstairs in the kitchen. She leaned over the counter, reading a cookbook with such focus she didn't even notice him come in.

"Hey," he said gently, but she jumped anyway.

"Hey," she replied, standing straighter. "How would you feel about trying this for breakfast?" She pointed to an oatmeal bar recipe in the book that did, in fact, look good. "If not, I can make it for myself. But it looks easy."

"It sounds great," Charlie replied. "Let me go shower and change. I'll be back."

Violet nodded, heading to the pantry to gather ingredients. Charlie smiled, glad she seemed so at home.

He made his shower quick, still enjoying the hot water knob that she had fixed a long time ago. He still didn't know how she did it.

When he finished, she was doing dishes as the oatmeal bars baked in the oven. Charlie watched her, glad living with her came so easily.

She did things without being asked to. She melted into his life as if she was always meant to be there, and he didn't know what to do about it. He should be struggling with this transition, and yet he wasn't.

There was a knock at the door Violet didn't seem to hear. Charlie frowned, knowing he didn't normally have people come by the house. He opened it and froze when he saw his mother.

Charlie wanted to curse everything he knew. Mara rarely came over unannounced, and when she did, he never had anyone over.

And now Violet was here.

"Hey, kiddo," his mom said. "Whose car is in the driveway?"

"Uh, what are you doing here, mom?" Charlie asked.

"I thought I'd check up on you since you were down the last time we talked. Do you have someone over?"

"Uh, kind of?"

"Who? Is Lewis back from his honeymoon?"

"Uh, no, not yet," Charlie replied, unsure of what to say. He hadn't told his mom Violet was staying with him. He hadn't even told her Violet's name. And now she was about to meet her.

Of course, it was that moment Violet came around the corner.

She was dressed in a loose and faded long sleeve T-shirt paired with the pants he had let her borrow when she first came to stay. She looked like . . . well, that she lived there.

This looked bad. Really bad.

"Hey, are we out of paper to—" She stopped when she saw his mother. "Oh, hi. I didn't know anyone was coming over."

Violet awkwardly rubbed her hands on her pants, and his mother's eyebrows rose. She gave Charlie a look that sent fear straight into his heart. "I'm Charlie's mother, Mara," she said to Violet.

"Oh," Violet said. "I . . . did not know you were coming over. I can make myself scarce."

"No!" Mara said. "It's that he rarely has overnight guests, is all. Are you in the middle of . . . breakfast?"

"Yeah, I was baking some oatmeal bars for us."

"Really? He let you into the kitchen?"

"With a little bit of force on his part," Violet joked. "Seriously though, I can leave if you two need to talk—"

"No, I'm not going to kick out Charlie's *friend* if you were here first. I didn't know he even had friends other than Lewis and his wife."

"Oh, I'm friends with his wife. That's how we know each other."

Charlie caught Violet's eyes and tried to communicate *not* to mention their past. He could only hope she got the message.

"Oh wow! Charlie's never mentioned you."

"That's because—"

"We only recently became closer," Charlie said. "It's not a big deal."

"Yeah, yeah," Violet said, catching on. "It's been super boring without Liv and Lewis here."

"Boring enough for a sleepover?"

Violet looked at him, panic in her eyes. *Shit.* She must have caught on to what his mother had been hinting at.

"Not like *that*. Violet's kind of, uh, a roommate?"

He glanced at Violet, who nodded slowly.

"A roommate?" Mara asked. "Since when do you want to share this house with anyone?"

"Since they raised electrical costs," Charlie answered.

"I've never known of you to even let anyone come here. She must be special."

"It was kind of an accident," Violet said, laughing awkwardly. She was totally unaware of how right his mother was. "My apartment collapsed, and he was the only one of our friends with space. Rent is high and I'm a teacher in town, so he's letting me live here more permanently. I've got the pink and green room upstairs."

His mother's gaze on him was sharp and piercing. He was *so* screwed. His mother knew better than anyone Charlie didn't let *anyone* in that room. That was where he spent his childhood.

"Wow," she said, her voice kind even though she was shooting daggers at him. "That's nice of him."

Thankfully, the oven timer went off.

"Oh, that's my cue," she said. "I'll be . . . getting those . . . and maybe disappearing while I'm at it."

Violet's exit was so quick, it was almost like she was never there. Charlie cringed as his mother rounded on him.

"She's staying here?"

"I don't think Gigi Ruth would mind," Charlie defended.

"Of course she wouldn't. She would help anyone. I'm talking about *you*. I've never seen you bring anyone over. You keep this house locked up like a secret."

"I love this house."

"I know you do, but you don't share it. So, I'm wondering why you did with her."

"It's like she said, she was in a tough spot."

"And she's still here? She's comfortable? You're letting her cook without hovering?"

"I mean, I sort of have to if she lives here."

"No, you don't. You would have never even let her live here if she wasn't someone special."

Charlie didn't have anything to say to that.

Because it was true.

"Who is she?" she asked.

"She's . . . I know her through Lewis and Liv."

"Sure, you say she's a friend, but it's more than that, isn't it?"

Charlie sighed and pinched the bridge of his nose. "Mom, she's in the other room."

Mara was silent for a long moment. "Okay. Sorry. I haven't seen you like this. Not with Lauren. It wasn't even close."

"I know."

"Are you dating?"

"No," Charlie said. "And I doubt we will."

"Why not?"

"You know how love works," he said with a nonchalant shrug. "It's fickle. It ends. Look at dad. Look at Lauren. It's not for me."

His mother frowned. "Where did you get that idea? Love isn't fickle."

"Of course it is. With Lauren I never felt . . . I never wanted to share a life with her. And even if Violet was somehow different, I know love ends, so I wouldn't put her through that."

His mother looked at him with wide eyes, looking more confused than he had ever seen her. "What are you even talking about? None of that is true."

"You stopped dating after dad. You said love ends."

She looked away, her face clouded, dark. Charlie blinked and wondered if this had anything to do with her showing up to his work a week ago, or why she had shown up now.

"Don't shut yourself away from it," she replied. "It's not like you think it is. Take it from me."

"What does that mean?"

"It's not a big deal. This isn't a conversation we should have now."

"What?" Charlie asked.

"We will talk about it later, but love doesn't end."

Before Charlie could think of what to say, she was giving him a hug and was out the door.

Mara's strange appearances, and her off mood, was all coming together. She said love didn't end, and to take it from her. Was she having a new experience with love? Was his mom seeing someone?

"Oh, she left?" Violet asked. "God, that was so awkward. She probably hated me."

"I think she's seeing someone," he said. "And she's keeping it a secret."

Violet blinked at the change of subject but seemed to follow along. "I'm . . . sorry? Is it a bad thing if she is?"

"No. I don't think so, as long as she's happy. But she isn't telling me."

"Maybe it's new."

"Maybe. But we don't usually keep secrets from each other."

"Really? I caught the vibe you didn't want me to tell her we hated each other for six years."

Charlie winced. "Yeah, I did hint that. But I know her. She would grill us."

"Maybe she's thinking the same about you." Violet said. "You've also had a lot going on. Has she tried talking to you before?"

Charlie sighed. "She came to my work not too long ago, but that was right when I broke up with Lauren."

"And this time you had a surprise roommate," Violet added. She put a warm, comforting hand on his shoulder. "Give her time, and if it takes too long, then ask her. She's obviously been trying to tell you, so I doubt she would lie."

Charlie took a deep breath. "Yeah, you're probably right."

"I usually am. Now, I'm about to be right about something else. You should try what I made." She held up an oatmeal bar. "I know you like your usual, but this might change your mind."

Charlie raised an eyebrow. "You seem pretty sure of yourself."

"I already ate one while hiding out in the kitchen. Trust me, it's good."

He took a small bite, and then sighed. "Fine, you're right about this too. This is amazing."

"Right? Now help me eat this tray of them," she instructed, looping her arm through his and dragging him to the kitchen. "You need a good distraction."

He did, but he wasn't sure how Violet knew so quickly. His mom's words repeated in his head.

This was more than a roommate.

And he was so screwed.

Chapter Fifteen

Violet

Violet was in her old apartment, which was odd.

Especially since it had been sold.

It looked like she had left it. The worn couch was sitting in the middle of the room, facing the old TV and dinged-up wall. Her tiny kitchen was to the left with her small appliances.

It was strange, being back. She hadn't thought of this place very much, trying to put its unfortunate end out of her mind. She didn't want to think about the terrifying night when things changed.

Violet walked into the kitchen, much like the night when the ceiling collapsed. She was planning on getting a glass of wine and relaxing after a long, hard day.

But then there was that cracking sound.

Violet would never forget the sounds of that night. The cracking of the plaster was unlike anything she had ever heard before, and the sound the building made before it collapsed was etched into her memory.

And now she was hearing it again.

But this time, she paid no mind to it. She went along with her business as if nothing was happening, even as the sounds got louder. In her mind, she knew what was coming. The cracks in her ceiling were getting larger, and it was going to give at any moment.

Yet her body did not move. When the ceiling finally gave way, and the loud, painful groaning shook through the room, she only looked up as the ceiling folded in and crushed her.

Violet jerked awake, her heart racing as she tried to make sense of her surroundings. She was in the pink room in Charlie's house, not in her old apartment. The ceiling was old, but stable, and yet, Violet checked it for cracks.

She slowly sat up, trying to blink tears out of her eyes.

She had been trying to forget about it.

Obviously, her dreams liked to remind her.

She could still feel everything if she let herself. She could feel the water splashing her, the smell of the broken building, and the site of all her belongings—crushed into nothing. She wanted to pretend it didn't bother her, but it did.

Violet sighed, knowing falling back to sleep wasn't going to be easy. She turned on the light in her room, checking once more for any cracks in the ceiling. Then she decided she needed a drink to try and calm down.

She crept down the stairs, going to the kitchen. Roo followed her, even though the kitty usually liked to stay in her room all night.

A while ago, she had purchased a box of chamomile tea to try and help her fall back sleep when dreams like this happened. She hadn't felt comfortable enough to make it just yet because she didn't want to wake up Charlie.

But this was the first time her dreams made her stay *in* her apartment as her ceiling caved in, so she was a bit more unnerved as usual.

She quietly heated up water in the microwave before dunking a tea bag into the warm liquid. She was proud of herself for being as quiet as possible, but then the door to Charlie's room opened, and she cursed.

"Violet?" He sounded sleepy. "What are you doing up?"

"I'm sorry," she said. "I wanted tea. I'll go back to my room now. I didn't mean to bother you."

"You didn't. I got up to use the bathroom and heard you."

Violet didn't know whether or not she believed him.

"Why are you awake?" he asked. "It's 2 a.m."

"No reason," she said, shaking her head. "I'm fine."

Charlie frowned at her. "You look freaked out. Kind of like the night your apartment collapsed."

Violet glanced away.

"You're thinking about that night, aren't you?"

"How do you know that?" she asked.

"Lucky guess."

"Well," she said, sighing, "you're not wrong."

"Do you need to talk about it?"

"It was a dream, Charlie. You don't have to worry."

"You dreamed about it?"

"Yes."

"Come on, Violet. Talk to me. I'm right here."

Violet bit her lip. "There's not much to say."

"Obviously there is if you're still up. We can go up to your room if you would be more comfortable."

Violet shook her head. "Can we go to yours? There's not an attic above it, right?"

"No, and it's pretty solid last I checked."

"Okay," Violet said. "I'm pretty wary of things being above me right now."

Charlie nodded, and she followed him into his room. Violet spent a moment checking the ceiling for any signs of wear and satisfactorily found none.

He sat on one end of his bed and gestured for Violet to follow him. She did carefully, not wanting to invade his space.

But knowing there was no attic or second floor above her helped.

Roo jumped up onto the bed as well, and Charlie looked at the cat. "So, she sleeps with you every night then?"

"Yes, even after I moved rooms." Violet watched as Roo found a comfortable spot next to Violet." She smiled. Having a kitty friend helped make it all easier.

Then her fears came flooding back.

"You're thinking about it again, aren't you?" Charlie asked.

"Sometimes I think I'm over what happened, and then sometimes I'm not," Violet said, sighing. "I try not to think about it too much, but it was terrifying."

"I couldn't imagine it."

"Neither could I," Violet said. "The building had its problems, but I figured they were at least making sure it was structurally sound. Of course, I could hear my neighbors all the time, but I figured it was normal for a bottom unit." Violet sighed and set her tea on Charlie's nightstand. "I can't believe I lost everything that night."

"Nothing could be salvaged?"

"No, it was a water leak above me from the sewer line. What wasn't crushed was contaminated. It sucks because all that stuff was mine. I built a life for myself, and it's gone."

"But it wasn't your fault."

"I should have seen the signs of how bad the landlord was. I should have moved."

"But that's expensive, and you thought they were at least doing the bare minimum."

"Yeah, but I should have realized—"

"No, you didn't have to do anything. They failed *you*."

She wanted to believe him, and yet she couldn't. She closed her eyes for a moment, only to see the dream behind her eyelids, and she opened them to stop from replaying it.

"What was your dream about?" Charlie asked, eying her worriedly.

"It was . . . it was me reliving that night. I can still remember the sounds the building made as it fell. I remember how *helpless* I felt as everything came down around me. And usually, I can ignore it. Except this time, I stayed in the apartment instead of going outside. So, when the building fell, it fell on me."

Charlie was silent for a moment. She glanced over at him and couldn't read the expression on his face. Whatever he was feeling, he kept it guarded.

"I'm glad you listened to your gut and got out of there," he said slowly. "And I'm sorry you're still remembering everything that happened."

"I want to stop thinking about it," she said, her voice thick with emotion. "I wish it never happened."

"But it did."

"I know," she replied softly.

"It's okay you're still bothered by it. What happened was awful. And over time, you'll come to accept it, but it's still okay you haven't yet."

"I don't want to bother anyone with it. Liv and Lewis got married and I know they haven't had time to think about it, but—"

"It would have been nice of them to check in?"

"Yeah. Is that selfish?"

"No, I don't think so. Even I've been feeling a little left out with all the wedding preparations. I'm glad it's over."

"I'm happy for them, I am. But so much happened over the last few weeks that it would have been nice to have things slow down—to be able to sit and talk."

"And they will slow down," Charlie said. "But for now, you have me. I don't mind listening."

How did he know how to get her to open up like this? It should have been impossible, but maybe Violet liked having someone to be herself with. Maybe she was so lonely that she had no other choice.

Or maybe it was him.

"Okay," Violet said. "As things come up, I'll talk about them."

Charlie smiled. "That's all I ask."

Violet yawned and leaned back on the bed. She doubted she could go back to sleep after seeing that night again, but it was nice to close her eyes for a moment.

"I could have this house inspected, if it would make you feel any better," Charlie offered.

"I couldn't ask you for that," Violet said quietly.

"I've been meaning to, actually. I had it inspected when I moved in, but it's been a few years, so maybe another wouldn't hurt."

"You don't have to do that for me."

"There's not much I wouldn't do to make you feel better."

Violet opened her eyes to roll them. "I seriously doubt that."

Charlie only shrugged.

"Besides, I know this house is stable. Most of the time I'm fine. It's when dreams like this happen." Violet shrugged. "I think it would happen anywhere."

"Even when we disliked each other," Charlie said. "I knew it was something terrifying."

"I thought you were more upset Liv asked for me to stay with you."

"I was nervous, sure. But I knew even then I was going to let you. There's no world where I would have said no."

"That's nice of you," she said. "And I'm glad I'm here. The idea of going back to another cheap apartment is a little scary. I'd rather be here."

Violet's eyes slipped closed again. Charlie's bed was unfairly comfortable. He had a nice, fluffy comforter and his room was pleasantly warm. She drifted off before she could even stop herself.

When she woke up the next morning, she was still in Charlie's room, but covered by his blanket. On his side table there was a note that read, *"Don't worry. I slept in the guest room. Glad you finally got some decent sleep."*

Violet blushed and looked around. Had she fallen asleep with him? In his room?

Shit. Maybe she was more comfortable with him than she thought.

Charlie

Violet came out of his room, looking a little like a deer in headlights. Roo followed along happily.

"I'm not going to shoot you, you know," Charlie said from where he was pouring coffee in the kitchen. He was a little jealous that Roo obviously loved to be around Violet more than him.

He could hardly blame her, though.

"I feel so bad for falling asleep in your room."

"Wasn't the whole point of us talking last night *to* fall asleep?"

"But still, this is your house, and that's your room."

"I have a feeling if it were me, you would have done the same thing."

"Okay," she admitted sullenly. "You have me there."

"Besides, it was good luck this happened on a weekend and not when we both had to work. You got to sleep in a little."

"Yeah, I guess that's one good thing about it," Violet said. "I still feel bad though."

"I promise I'm not mad," Charlie said. "Coffee?"

"Sure," Violet said, grabbing an empty cup. "So, anything fun planned for today?"

"Nope. I have to go pick up Lewis and Liv from the airport."

Violet looked shocked. "You're doing that?"

"They asked me to."

"Oh . . . they mentioned they had a ride, but I thought it was a cab or something."

"No, they asked me to weeks ago," Charlie said. At Violet's frown, he added, "I wouldn't take it personally. My car is a little bigger than yours, I think."

"Still," Violet said, pouting from the table. "I offered to do it, and I'd like to see them."

"Liv probably knew you were busy," Charlie said. "Besides, you said you needed to grade your students' tests."

Violet sighed. "I forgot about that. I need to have these test scores by Monday so I can know what my students are struggling with before the standardized tests."

"Sounds fun," Charlie said sarcastically.

"It's not."

"Just come on Tuesday when we do game night again. You can see them then."

"Okay, fine. But if they seem off or weird in any way, I want to know about it."

Charlie laughed. "It's cute you're so worried about them."

Violet blushed, and Charlie wondered if maybe he was pushing things a bit far by saying that—but he couldn't help it. It *was* cute.

"What time do you leave?"

"I should probably go now actually. I was hoping you would wake up before I left."

"Be safe," Violet said, sighing. "And avoid Charlotte Avenue. They're doing construction."

"Thanks," Charlie said. "I'll see you later."

He resisted the urge to walk over to her. He wasn't sure what he wanted to do, whether it was give her an awkward pat on the head, or something even more dangerous. But he walked out the door instead.

Traffic was awful, even on a Sunday morning. By the time he arrived at the airport, he was already in a bad mood. But he was happy to see his friends safe and sound.

Everything had been put on hold for the wedding, so he and Lewis hadn't gotten any time to hang out in over a month. Neither of them knew about Lauren or Violet, which felt weird considering he was used to telling Lewis everything.

"Taxicab for the Thompsons?" Charlie joked when he pulled up to them.

Lewis and Liv had matching smiles.

And holy shit, they looked radiant.

Of course they would, they had been on the beach for almost three weeks. Both of them had saved up for this honeymoon, and they looked like they had lived it up while they were gone.

Charlie surprised himself by being a little jealous. Maybe he needed a vacation soon.

He could save up for it now that he had help with the bills. Maybe he could even invite Violet. He bet she would enjoy it.

"Hey, man," Lewis said.

"Glad to see both of you are in one piece."

"Barely," Liv said. 'The flight back was rough; I knew I shouldn't have come back to America."

"Yeah, the honeymoon is always better than real life," Charlie said, opening his trunk.

After their suitcases were loaded into his car, they climbed into the backseat, instantly grabbing each other's hand as they sat. They looked so happy that even three weeks together didn't seem like enough.

Charlie didn't get it. They had to get tired of each other eventually, right? But no. They never did.

It was weirdly sort of like how he and Violet were now.

"So, how was it?" Charlie asked. "You guys look like you enjoyed yourselves."

"Oh, it was amazing," Liv gushed. "So perfect. I couldn't have imagined a better wedding and honeymoon."

"It *looked* amazing," Charlie said. "I'm glad it all turned out so well."

They described their honeymoon in more detail, talking about some of the other people they met and the things they did. It sounded idyllic. Charlie listened with rapt attention, happy to hear about what his friends had been up to while they were gone.

Usually, Lewis was always good about asking about Charlie's time too. And Charlie waited with bated breath to tell them he and Violet had finally worked things out, how she was still staying with him and making it work.

But the question never came.

There was one time where he even opened his mouth to mention Violet, only for Liv to abruptly change the subject to something else.

He let her out of habit.

Charlie knew Liv had to miss her, and he figured Violet would tell her who she was now staying with as soon as they caught up.

He knew it was going to be a big deal.

His and Violet's past hung heavy over everyone's heads. After all, only a few weeks ago, mentioning Violet would have made him tense up.

Charlie dropped them off at their apartment, knowing they needed time to get settled in.

As he drove home, he found himself excited to see Violet, anyway.

"Hey," he said to her as he walked in. "Still grading?"

"Nearly done," Violet said. "How are they?"

"Happy," he replied. "I think they needed that vacation."

Violet nodded, and her eyes fell back to her stack of papers.

"Something wrong?" he asked.

"No. Well, not anything huge," Violet sighed. "Jason didn't do so well on this test, and he's been quiet at school recently. I think on Monday I need to have a talk with his mom about how much what's going on at home is affecting him."

"Do those usually go well or are they terrible?"

"Depends on the parent. Some take it well. Others think I'm meddling," Violet said. "I've never had to talk to Jason's mom before, so we'll see. This is one of the parts of my job I hate. Parents get so defensive over their kids but it's not that I'm judging them. I want to help before things get worse."

"You're doing the right thing, though. Hopefully she'll see that."

Violet nodded, looking tired.

"Are you done with grading, then?"

"Yeah, basically. I could probably try to go through everything again to see if there's maybe another area I could work on, but my brain is melting a little, so maybe not."

"So, you have no plans at all for the day?"

"Not really. Why?"

"You want to play a video game with me?"

"Isn't that something you and Lewis do?"

"Yeah, but he needs to unpack."

"I get pretty competitive with video games, though."

"I think I can manage."

He stared at Violet, hoping she took the bait. Lewis was fun at video games, but he hated competition. Violet was the only one he knew who liked it.

"Okay, fine. But I get to pick. I want it to be something I have a slim chance of beating you at."

"I wouldn't want it any other way."

Chapter Sixteen

Violet

The next day was going to be a busy one. Violet had already set up a meeting with Jason's mom for later in the day. She was going to have to stay after five to meet with her, but she didn't mind. She only hoped Jason's mother would be understanding.

Plus, even though she was back in town, Liv hadn't texted yet. Violet figured she was getting settled in, though she wondered if somehow she'd pissed off her friend while on her honeymoon.

That morning, Violet was a bundle of nerves. She sat with Charlie, letting him make breakfast for a change. He had been eying her all morning, knowing something was wrong.

"So, did you tell Liv it's you that I'm staying with?" she asked as they sat down. Maybe Liv was mad about that.

"No, they didn't ask."

"They didn't ask?"

"They only talked about the honeymoon. I figured I didn't want to ruin their after-marriage glow."

"I'll need to tell her then. I'm surprised she's not already blowing up my phone trying to figure out who it is."

"They didn't mention you at all," Charlie said. "But then again, they probably were thinking about all that they needed to do when they got home."

She nodded absentmindedly. Her heart raced as she thought of her best friend's impending reaction to her and Charlie's change of heart.

"Hey," Charlie said, his voice gentle. "I'm sure whatever you're overthinking about won't be as bad as you think."

"But what if it *is*?" she asked, her voice becoming thick with emotion. "Ugh, I shouldn't even feel this way. I have too much to do today to be worrying about this."

"It's okay, Violet."

"I'm so scared they'll think we're dumb for doing this."

"Does it matter?"

"Yes."

"Why?"

"Because I want them to think I'm worth their time."

"What's the worst that could happen?"

"They could leave," she said, the words rushing out of her. She looked at her hands, which twisted in front of her.

"Is this a new feeling?" He asked.

"No," she muttered. "I've always worried about it. Especially when you and I fought. We were always causing problems."

"You must have always been stressed, then. But I doubt that's going to happen, and if it did, you'd have me."

"But you're friends with Lewis."

"If they suddenly drop you for no reason, I'll be on your side." Charlie said it like it was the simplest thing in the world. "And you'll always have Roo. I think she likes you more than me, and I'm the one that cleans her litter box."

Violet smiled. Hearing that had actually helped. Roo was at her feet, blinking up at her with innocent, bright eyes.

"Isn't it wild?" she said as her emotions faded. She leaned down to pet Roo. "We really went from enemies to this, huh?"

"We did. It feels like we've been friends forever though."

"It was like flipping a light switch once we talked it out."

Charlie smiled. "I'm glad you feel the same way."

"How do you think they'll react?"

"I bet they won't believe us," Charlie replied. "But they'll come around eventually."

"I still feel terrible that we argued for so long. I know it was hard on them."

"Yeah," Charlie said quietly. "We were idiots."

"Not idiots. More like emotionally constipated adults being played by an insecure monster with nothing better to do."

"That too," Charlie said. "But we were the ones that continued it. I wouldn't be surprised if they didn't mention you yesterday out of habit."

"Maybe that's exactly it," Violet replied. The thought made her feel better. "Honestly, I was so worried I had done something to Liv, but I bet she avoided it with you because as far as they know, we're still at each other's throats. The cease-fire was only good through the wedding, and they don't know any different."

"Maybe," Charlie said. "Does that make you feel better?"

"A little. I figure she'll call me once she's settled."

"They're going to lose it once they figure out you're still here."

"Hopefully they'll be happy. This'll be like old times again. Everything will be easier once they understand we can be in the same room."

"That'll be a fun conversation."

"I'll take Liv. You take Lewis."

"Maybe we should draft up something. Like a personal statement . . ."

Violet laughed. "You're bringing up jokes like that this soon after our six-year fight over my grad school application?"

"It got you to laugh. You're not that offended."

"I could curse you. I've been making friends with the spirit of your great-grandmother in the basement. One of these days, I'll know all of her secrets."

"Good luck with that. Gigi Ruth didn't speak much English."

"I can learn French."

"Gigi Ruth was German."

"But . . . the term 'Gigi' is usually from France, isn't it?"

"Yes," Charlie said. "She liked to be a woman of many mysteries. She'd be happy to know they continued in her afterlife."

Charlie

Charlie went to work and tried to function as usual, but his brain wouldn't stop rounding back to Violet. He wanted to find a way to tell all of this to Liv and Lewis so she didn't have to worry about it. He wanted to solve all of Violet's problems, but he also knew she would want to do that herself.

He loved seeing all sides of her. The fact she was so natural with him meant more than he could ever let her know. He felt special, knowing she was being herself rather than anyone else.

Charlie could see it all now. Violet was nothing but perfect around friends but had never been that way with him. He could see how it wore on her.

He was seeing a side of her no one else did.

It was terribly distracting.

He couldn't stop thinking about her. How was her day going? Was Jason acting out? Did she have any issues with other kids while she was teaching?

Would she be upset if he asked her?

His hand itched for his phone, but he managed to not make a fool of himself by reaching out.

He got off a little early but knew Violet would be talking to Jason's mother until late. He prepared himself for a night alone, coding until she got back, and then he'd ask about her day, hoping she'd open up to him.

Charlie knew he was beginning to get desperate.

However, his phone rang a few hours after he got home, and he answered it immediately, thinking it was Violet.

It was not.

"Liv is pissed at you."

"Micah? Why are you calling me?"

"Because Liv is coming over, and you should prepare yourself," she said, as if it should be obvious.

"For what?"

"An interrogation to find out who Violet is staying with."

"What?" he asked.

"I told her you couldn't care less. I bet you couldn't wait to get her out of your house."

"I . . . We're friends now, Micah."

"No one believed that. But what *you* should believe is that Liv is scary when it comes to Violet. She called four times today and Violet isn't answering. She's a little worried that this new roommate killed her."

"He . . . didn't kill her."

"He?" Micah asked.

"No, me. She's staying with me. As a roommate."

There was silence on the line, and then he heard Micah laugh harder than he thought possible. "Oh, this is perfect. I can't wait to hear Liv's reaction."

"I can," he muttered.

"Good luck with the interrogation. I look forward to hearing about it later."

Charlie groaned in frustration after she hung up, and of course, that's when the loud knocks on the door came. For a moment, he pinched the bridge of his nose. He didn't like unexpected visitors, and he liked interrogations even less.

While he wanted to be calm for this discussion, the second, more insistent knock reminded him he couldn't push this off forever, he couldn't ignore it.

"Do you know who Violet is staying with?" Liv asked, her face contorted in a way Charlie had never seen before. She came in without an invitation, which made Charlie's grip on the door tighten. Lewis trailed behind her, not meeting Charlie's eyes.

"This is a bad idea," Lewis hissed. "I told you he hates visitors."

"Seriously?" he asked. "Can you at least wait for an invitation?"

"There are more pressing matters at hand. Answer the question, Charlie."

As much as he would like to simply blurt it out, he also knew Violet would be pissed if she wasn't here for the reveal. Liv was her friend, after all.

But he also couldn't lie.

"She's safe."

"Then why isn't she answering her phone?"

"Liv," Lewis said, his voice firm. "I know you're upset, but you need to calm down. The last thing you need is to butt heads with Charlie. He does that with Violet enough."

Charlie turned to his friend. "Really? That's how you're mitigating the situation?"

"It's a fact," he said, holding up his hands in mock defense.

"Charlie," Liv cut in. "Where is Violet?"

"At work," Charlie said.

"I mean where is she *living*? Besides, it's after five. She doesn't work that late."

"She does when she has a parent meeting."

"How would *you* know if she had a parent meeting?" Liv shook her head incredulously.

Charlie heard a slamming door outside, and a car-locking beep.

Violet's car.

She was home, and judging by the sound of her footsteps, she was *not* happy.

"Motherfucker!" Violet cursed as she came in. "I fucking hate parents and I fucking hate traffic in this goddamn town! Charlie, you better have some wine because I'm about to—"

Violet barged into the living room and froze when she saw Liv and Lewis. He saw her take in a slow breath, but the flush of her cheeks from her previous anger remained. Charlie looked closer and could see unshed tears in her eyes.

"Is there a game night I wasn't made aware of?" Violet asked weakly.

"Violet!" Liv said, hugging her friend. "You're okay!"

Violet looked at Charlie with a bewildered expression, and he took a deep breath, trying to calm down.

"It's good to see you," Lewis said. "Liv was very worried about your new living situation."

Violet went a little pale, but the flush darkened. Whatever hold she had on her emotions wasn't going to last long.

"Listen," he started. He watched Violet closely to see if she would object to him telling the story. "Violet's landlord sold the building."

Liv looked at him with a sharp gaze, not letting go of Violet. "I think she can tell us what happened."

"N-no," Violet said. "he's telling the truth. My old apartment was sold instead of being repaired."

"That's terrible," Liv said. "But I want to know about your new place. Especially this mysterious roommate."

"I . . ." Violet looked at Charlie, baffled.

"It's all fine," Charlie added.

"Hang on, what is going on?" Lewis asked. "Violet, why did you come in here yelling at Charlie? Have we moved into instigating a fight in his home now?"

Liv glared at her husband and hurt flashed across Violet's face.

"Lewis," Charlie said, frustrated.

"What? I'm defending you, man. If she's coming to your house—"

"I'm not mad at Charlie," Violet said. "I was . . . I wanted to vent to him. I was in a god-awful parent meeting, and I had my phone off."

"I'm glad you're okay," Liv said. "But *who* are you living with? Not knowing is driving me up a wall."

Violet opened her mouth, only to close it. Charlie could practically see the gears in her head turning as she tried to figure out the best way to explain their newfound friendship.

"Why are you being so secretive about this person?" Liv asked, frowning. "Are you living with your mom again?"

"Of course not," Violet replied.

"Then why are you being so weird about this?"

"Because I *know* how you're going to react." Violet's eyes flashed to Charlie, then back to Liv.

"Hang on," Lewis said. "Why did you look at Charlie?"

"Lewis . . ." Liv said, irritated.

"No, I'm always reading you two when you're in the same place. Violet has looked over at him four times. Usually when that happens, you two fight."

"We're not going to fight," Charlie hissed.

"Yeah, I've heard that before."

"It's Charlie!" Violet snapped. "My roommate is Charlie."

Both Liv and Lewis turned to her. "What?" they yelled out in unison.

"It's the easiest solution, okay?" she said. "It's close to school and I can help him save up for things while I pay some of his bills. It's cheaper than rent anywhere in town."

Liv looked like she had been slapped.

Lewis shook his head. "I don't even have words to describe how bad of an idea this is."

"That was for us to decide," Charlie said. "And we could have come up with a more graceful way of telling you if you hadn't come here unannounced."

"You two can't even have a conversation."

"We're conversing right now," Violet reminded them.

"Guys, you don't have to do this to prove a point or anything," Lewis said. "You know that, right? The wedding is over, and now we're back to our usual schedule. You don't have to spend time together and we can all hang out separately."

"Wait," Liv said, slowly. "Hang on. You just said *Charlie*."

"Who?" Lewis asked.

"Violet, just now when she said who she was living with. Lewis, she used his first name."

Lewis blinked, and then turned to Charlie slowly. "Now that I think about it, you used Violet's at the reception."

"We have a lot to catch up on," Violet said softly.

"What the hell happened?" Liv asked.

Violet took in a shaky breath, opening her mouth to speak, but nothing came out. Her eyes still glistened, but her unshed tears teetered dangerously close to escape.

As Charlie was about to step in, she said, "I can't explain it right now."

"Why not?"

"She needs space," Charlie translated. "What happened was hard on us both, and I don't think either of us are in the place right now to talk about it."

Violet looked at him gratefully.

Both Liv and Lewis's eyes darted between them.

"Maybe we should do as he said," Lewis said. "If that's what Violet wants."

Violet slowly nodded.

"What is going on?" Liv asked. "Since when does Charlie speak for Violet?" She turned to her friend. "Seriously, are you okay?"

Since I started spending every second I could with her, he wanted to say, but he bit back the unhelpful remark.

"No, I'm really not!" Violet snapped. Liv turned to her. "I had a bad day and all I want to do is go sit in a bathtub with a gallon of wine and not look at anyone for twelve hours, okay? I know you want an explanation, but I am *so* tired. I can tell you more later, but please, can I be alone?"

For a moment, the entire house was silent. Charlie hoped Liv wasn't going to push anymore because he could tell Violet was close to completely unraveling.

"Okay," Liv said, quietly.

Lewis grabbed his wife by the arm. "We'll talk soon," he said.

Lewis waved awkwardly as he pulled Liv out the door. Charlie watched the door close, his anxiety leaving with them, now that they were alone. He took a deep breath, expelling the tension so he could be there for Violet. Once things were calm again, he turned to her, ready to listen, only to find she had sunk to the floor, head in her hands.

Violet

Violet could swear she was cursed.

On top of her already terrible day, she'd had to make Liv leave when Violet owed her an explanation. A lot had changed, and she knew it had to be baffling to someone on the outside, but she *couldn't*. Not yet.

Pretending to be fine was her standard, but she knew she couldn't hold it up forever. And now she couldn't deal with it anymore.

The moment they were gone, Violet's roughly constructed walls shattered, and she wanted to cry. She pressed her hands against her eyes, which made her head swim, and she slowly sat on the ground.

In that moment, hardwood was the greatest seat in the world.

"Violet," Charlie said after a moment. She could tell he was tense by the tightness in his jaw. And it had been Liv's worry about Violet that caused it. "Are you okay?"

"I'm sorry they came over," she said thickly. "I know you hate guests, and I should have communicated with Liv better."

Unhelpfully, the memory of Jason's mom yelling at her flashed through her mind. Her chest throbbed in emotional pain.

"No, I'm not mad at you. Besides, you can't control them."

"Then why are you mad?" Violet asked, looking at him.

"It's not anything you need to worry about. It's not anything you did."

"But—"

"No, we're not worrying about me. I'm more worried about you. What happened today? How did your meeting go?"

"Horribly, like everything else. Jason's mom was offended I brought it up. She said I was a terrible teacher for not fixing Jason's problems, and for insinuating his homelife could have anything to do with his behavior at school. I know she was being defensive, but I can't just *fix* a child by myself."

"I'm sorry, Violet. Some people think others should solve things for them. You're not a bad teacher."

"I know, but it still hurts to have that said to my face. Besides, it's not only my problem to fix. He's acting out for other teachers too, and he's spending most of his time in the principal's office. I don't want that."

"Maybe she needs time to get past her own defensiveness."

"I hope so," Violet said, sighing. "I wanted to vent and have a quiet night."

"I did too."

"I'm sorry," she repeated, the frown returning to her face.

"It's not your fault. Besides, if they had just called first, it would have been okay."

Violet frowned. "I know she worries, but I miss calls a lot, especially if I'm working."

"You were there late tonight."

She groaned. Maybe she should start leaving it on during meetings, but then again, Jason's mom could have found another reason to think she was a bad teacher if she had.

"It was a bad situation." Charlie's voice interrupted her thoughts. "But it's not your fault."

He was right.

"Okay," Violet said, voice shaking. She didn't even know why. Charlie was being nice to her, yet she could feel the tears, and she could feel herself losing the battle to keep them at bay. One fell out of her wet eyes; she wiped at it angrily.

It was one thing for her to have cried when her apartment flooded. That was bad, and none of it was her fault. She went to Liv and Lewis because she had no one else.

This time it was her job, the one she chose. She should be able to handle it. This was all usual teacher stuff.

Crying about it wasn't going to solve anything. She was being weak, and in her head, she could hear her mom scoffing, telling her she shouldn't be upset about her own misguided decisions. Especially not something as trivial as teaching.

But she couldn't help it. She was upset. The tears had started, and they wouldn't stop.

Violet wouldn't have been mad if Charlie walked away, or if he was silent while she cried. That's how Lewis was. He usually stood to the side whenever Violet had emotions. Violet didn't expect Charlie would be any different.

But Charlie's hand gently touched her arm and Violet looked over to find him slowly coming to sit next to her. Her lip wobbled, but Charlie met her gaze. He reached out, wiping away one of her tears. Violet couldn't help it. She leaned into the touch like a moth to a flame.

Charlie's other hand moved along her back, pulling her to him as if she weighed nothing.

He didn't hold her like she was nothing, though. His arms enveloped her, and it was then Violet remembered how much bigger he was than her. She fit into him like a key into a lock, and the physical contact was enough to break her.

She hadn't been hugged like this in a long time. So long that she felt like a failure for needing it, but so happy she wasn't alone.

She cried harder than she had in years. It was an ugly, hard cry, but his arms never wavered. He didn't push her away despite her tears soaking through his shirt. Instead, he held her tighter.

And as powerful as they were, the tears eventually ended, and her emotions faded into a dull throb. She didn't want to move, though. Charlie's heat was intoxicating. Now that she had it, she didn't want to let it go.

"Sorry," she said, once her emotions faded. "I-I needed that."

Charlie smiled and rubbed her cheek once more, and she hugged him tightly. It felt like the night he offered for her to move in with him, but so much more intimate. How had she done it all alone, without his support through everything? She couldn't imagine going back to how things were.

"It's okay to be upset." His voice was strong and warm, reverberating through his chest and into her core.

Violet could have stayed there forever, but embarrassment was quickly winning over her need for physical contact. She was in his lap, after all, and had hugged him for far longer than friends should.

Slowly, and painfully, she let him go.

"Do you want a bath?" Charlie offered. "I can get one started for you."

Fuck. That sounded like heaven.

Violet nodded, and Charlie helped her off the floor. She watched as he climbed the stairs and disappeared into the bathroom. Her whole body was cold now that he wasn't wrapped around her.

When she heard the faucet squeak on and the water running, she climbed the stairs after him.

"Hey, Charlie?" she called as she approached. She smiled softly at him. "Thank you."

"Any time," he replied so earnestly that she believed him.

Chapter Seventeen

Charlie

"This week has been terrible," Violet said, flopping on the couch after she had gotten home from work. Charlie was sitting on the opposite end, working on coding. He put his hand on her leg placatingly.

"It's fine."

"It's not." Violet pressed her hand to her eyes. "I keep meaning to text Liv and explain everything, but each day gets worse."

"Liv knows you're fine. Well, mostly."

"I should call her tomorrow. It's a weekend."

"No, you should sleep in and take some time for yourself."

Violet sighed. "I don't know how to do that."

"Hand me your phone."

Violet looked at him and raised an eyebrow.

"I'm turning your alarm off for one day. You need to rest, Violet."

"She's worried."

"I'll text Lewis and explain you had a bad week, okay? You can talk to her Monday."

Violet considered it for a long moment, so long that Charlie was worried she would say no. But then she fished her phone out of her pocket and handed it to him.

He did as he said. When her alarm was off, he tossed her phone back and then texted Lewis.

Charlie: Hey Lewis, I know Liv is worried about Violet and wants to talk. Violet isn't mad at her, but her week got progressively worse, and she needs to wait until Monday to talk.

Lewis typed for a long time. Eventually, he answered.

Lewis: Liv wants to know why Violet hasn't said that herself, and if you're somehow forcing her week to be worse.

Lewis: Sorry, man. It was either I said it, or she was going to take my phone.

Charlie kept his face passive so Violet wouldn't worry.

Charlie: That's fine. No, I haven't purposely made Violet's week worse, and Liv can ask her when they talk on Monday if she doesn't believe me.

Charlie: And as for why Violet didn't text. She's comatose on the couch, and if she did, she would force herself to explain and stress herself out further. I know neither of you believe that I have good intentions, and that's fine. But this is her way of taking the time she needs, and I ask that you guys let her.

It took a long time for Lewis to reply.

Lewis: Okay. I got Liv to agree to wait until Monday. But please don't let this be a joke. This is the closest you've ever been to actually caring about Violet.

Charlie sighed and decided not to respond.

"She wants me to message her, doesn't she?" Violet asked.

"She does, but I told her you need time. She'll ask on Monday."

"Ugh, I hate that my job was so hard this week. Jason snapped at me, and then we didn't have enough subs again, so I had double classes for two days. But I shouldn't leave her in the dark like this."

"Hey, you had no problems dealing with things yourself when she was on her honeymoon. Let her do the same for you when you need time."

Violet sighed but didn't argue. Charlie took that as a win.

She wound up falling asleep early, too tired to do anything. The next morning, she woke up after nine, which was late for her.

He had been up since seven, planning on spending the day trying to cheer her up. He knew how she worked. If she spent the day alone, she would wallow in her feelings the whole time and never feel any better.

Charlie had finished breakfast when she stumbled into the kitchen, looking out of it, but well rested. The whole house smelled like it did when he was a kid, when Gigi Ruth would wake up and cook him breakfast as a surprise. She would say something in her broken but useable English, and he would eat while she put on cartoons for him.

Charlie handed Violet coffee and a plate, and she blinked at him, confused.

"What's all this?" she asked quietly. Her hair was in a messy ponytail, and he couldn't help but smile at her.

"Breakfast," he replied. "Since this week has been so bad for you."

"But..."

"No buts. You deserve to have someone help you feel better."

She tilted her head to the side, a small smile on her face, and Charlie wondered if his heart was going to stop from seeing her look at him like this.

"Thank you," she said. "I mean it. No one has ever done all this for me before."

That was a shame. Violet deserved the world. "You're welcome. Now let's eat."

Violet nodded and followed him to the dining room. They ate across from each other, sometimes talking, but he could tell she was still feeling off.

"I was thinking about going downtown today," Charlie mentioned. "There're a few cool shops I wanted to check out. Do you want to come?"

"What kind of shops?"

"Some furniture and some tea and coffee places. It's a little bit of everything."

"Oh, I don't think you want me going to furniture shops. I might buy stuff."

"I wouldn't mind."

"I have everything for my room. I meant for other parts of the house."

"I wouldn't mind that, either."

"Are . . . are you sure?" Violet asked.

"Of course I am. It would be a nice break from grading for you and I could get out of the house for a bit. I think my eyes are burning from staring at my computer anyway."

Violet thought on it for a moment, but when she smiled, he knew it was a yes.

He let Violet drive, knowing she wanted to have some independence. Her car was older, but in good shape, and he felt fine with letting her take over. Unlike Lauren, she was a safe driver and didn't seem to be bothered by driving downtown.

There was something so easy about being with Violet. They didn't have to talk all the time, and the silence was comfortable. He didn't feel like he needed to entertain her or do anything to keep her attention. The more time he spent with her, the easier it got.

When they arrived downtown, they did lots of shopping. The tea shop was lovely, and they were able to sit down and try all the varieties they offered. The furniture store was packed, but Violet rambled about everything she saw, telling him what would look good in his house.

He loved how excited she was about his home.

Charlie was happy to let her do whatever she wanted because he trusted her. He knew she loved the history of the house and would never do anything to mess with it. When she mentioned she wanted new coffee and side tables, he got them. She was shocked, but he knew he needed to fill the space a little. He was done being protective and wanted to *live* in it.

The pieces were old and refurbished. They were the same wood stain as the dining room table and were going to match perfectly.

They had lunch at a small, local place. Violet excitedly talked about getting more furniture and wondered if she could refinish them herself. She seemed to be coming back into herself and opening up more after her tiring week.

Charlie felt a tightness in his chest loosen, one he hadn't felt before. When Lauren was upset, he'd tense up because he knew she was probably going to take it out on him. When it was Violet, he wanted to stop the world to protect her. It was an entirely different, dangerous feeling.

Even though it was chilly, the sun provided a pleasant warmth on them as they walked. He itched to reach out and grab her hand. It seemed so small compared to his. How warm was she? Would she reciprocate and curl her fingers against his, or would she jump away?

He knew it was a bad idea, but it was *so* tempting.

"There's a band playing," Violet said. "Perks of living in Nashville, I guess."

Charlie blinked out of his thoughts. He hadn't even noticed, but there was a small stage with a live band. It was bluegrass—not his favorite genre—but it was nice to hear. He glanced over at Violet and saw her wistfully look at the few couples dancing.

"Do you want to dance?"

"What?" Violet asked, a light pink dusting on her cheeks.

"You were looking at the couples dancing," he added. "I'd dance with you."

"I'm bad at it."

"You weren't too bad at the wedding."

Violet bit her lip, and then looked at him again, like she was gauging whether or not he was serious. Neither of them were good dancers, but it was fine. None of the other couples were perfect either.

Charlie held out his hand, trying to keep his expression open. He wanted this so bad, and if he let it show, he worried she would be scared off.

But then Violet accepted, and he could feel her skin ignite his in ways he didn't think possible. This didn't feel like something friends would do, but he didn't exactly care.

Their dancing was swaying and a few steps in circles, but it was one of the best dances of his life. She looked so happy, and her smile only grew when he twirled her. He could have stayed there forever, with one hand on the small of her back and the other holding hers. He didn't want to let her go.

Charlie loved feeling her small body against his.

He realized that, despite their fallout, Violet had never left his life.

Whether she was a friend or an enemy, she had always been under his skin. She was always on his mind, whether he wanted her to be or not. The pain and anger he felt when they didn't get along were only masks for the real feelings, but the real feelings were terrifying.

He had been trying to deny it, and maybe it would have been better if he could, but while dancing with her on a street corner, listening to music he didn't care for, having the time of his life, he knew one thing.

Charlie was in love with Violet. He was so in love with her it wasn't funny.

And he couldn't trace back to when it had begun. Maybe it had been the whole time. Maybe she had always owned a part of him from the moment he looked at her. Maybe he'd never exactly fallen out of love with her.

Lauren must have seen it from day one. That was why she was so hell-bent on keeping them apart, but it was always doomed to fail.

Because he'd always loved her.

But this was a feeling, not a fact. As much as he would have loved to kiss her, he didn't know how she felt, or how she would react. He didn't want to ignite a spark of pain and rekindle their arguments. He didn't want to ruin this.

Ignoring how much he loved her was futile, but he would try if it meant he kept her.

"Are you okay?" Violet asked, frowning. "You look deep in thought."

"I'm fine," Charlie said, trying to put it out of his mind.

"It's not the dancing, is it?"

"No, never," Charlie said, and he meant it. "I'd dance with you any day."

Violet

Liv: Can we talk after you get off work? I'm worried about you . . .

Her Monday was so much better. She and Charlie spent the entire weekend together, and it was hard to be worried when she was with him. When she finally got a message from Liv, on Monday morning, as promised, she felt ready for it.

Violet: Yeah, we can get coffee at five.
Liv: You're working that late?
Violet: Yes, I've had a lot to do.
Liv: Okay then. Five works.

Violet was excited to get coffee, but first, she was watching Jason for a few hours after school. He was quiet and spent the whole time reading. He looked like he didn't want to be bothered, so she left him alone. His mom showed up at 4:30, and Violet almost didn't want to look at her.

Jason's mom had been combative, almost as if she felt threatened by Violet. And Violet didn't want to overstep, she only wanted to help. But some people couldn't see the difference. After thinking about it for the last week, she decided to step back and try to help at school only. It was hard, but she needed to.

Violet watched as Jason climbed into her car, and for a moment, Violet wondered if Jason's mom was still angry. But she looked tired. Exhausted. Violet could only imagine what she was going through, so instead of holding on to hard feelings, she smiled and waved through her window. His mom returned the gesture.

Violet felt her chest loosen in relief.

As she drove to the coffee shop, she sent Charlie a text message letting him know where she'd be, and she'd bring him something if he wanted. He told her he had a big project from work, he didn't need anything, and wished her good luck.

The shop was warm and inviting. Liv was already there, sitting in the corner watching the door. When Violet entered, Liv immediately stood, looking worried. Violet smiled and got a drink before joining her.

"Hey," Liv said. "Since when do you work until five?"

"I sometimes watch a kid. His mom gets there late."

"You're not avoiding Charlie?" Liv asked.

"No. I'm not," she said, shaking her head. "I'm helping a student, that's all."

"I'm worried. Like, really worried. I never should have suggested you stay with him. You've been so distant this last week. You didn't even reach out."

"Didn't Charlie tell you I had a bad week?"

"I-I thought maybe it was a cover for him being the one that made your week bad."

"He said it wasn't." Violet tried not to get irritated. Liv hadn't seen the real him, after all. "Last week was a dumpster fire. No, a hot mess inside of a dumpster fire in hell, but none of it was Charlie's doing."

"What happened?"

"School, mostly. I have a student who's acting out. I've been trying to help him, but when I went to his mom about it, she told me I was bad a teacher for not fixing the problem myself. Then other teachers kept getting sick, so I was working with double the number of kids because of the lack of subs in the area." Violet cringed thinking about it. "I was barely a person last week."

"It must have been awful if it got *you* to admit it was bad."

"It wasn't great. The last few weeks have been a lot, and I wanted to be in the right state of mind when I told you. I'm sorry it took so long."

"Your job can be really hard, so I get it. But you have to see why I would think Charlie would be the problem. You've fought with him for so, so long. I know you guys were lying about being friends for the wedding, and I'm worried both of you have some weird bet going on to see who snaps first."

"It's not like that. I'm not acting. Charlie and I being in the same house made us *talk*. We had to work out our shit or else we were going to kill each other. It wasn't easy, but we did it."

"Why didn't you tell me who it was?"

"Would you have been able to enjoy your honeymoon if I did?"

"Okay . . . fair. But now I need to know what's going on. Please tell me what happened."

Violet took a deep breath. "It was rough at first, but we struck a deal that I'd fix parts of his house in exchange for him not using my staying there against me in the future, and it evened the playing field. We both agreed to keep the peace while I stayed."

"And it's worked?"

"The peacekeeping? Yeah, it mostly did. I mean, there was an incident with a cat on the roof. That was pretty bad, but we worked through it, and kept the cat."

"What? Charlie has a cat?" Liv asked, shocked.

"Yeah, she might have been hiding when you came in." Violet opened her phone and showed Liv one of the many photos of Roo.

Liv's face softened. "She's adorable."

"Right? And she only sleeps with me, which is an added bonus of staying with Charlie. But, that being said, maybe call first if you are coming over. Charlie is not a fan of unexpected guests."

"Yeah, that wasn't my best moment, but I hope he didn't take it out on you."

Memories of a tight hug flashed in Violet's mind. She pushed out the unhelpful memory.

"He didn't. He was very clear about being mad at the situation and not me."

"That's . . . very mature of him."

"Yeah." Violet blushed but kept her gaze firm on Liv. "I know it's a lot of change, but we're not messing with you."

Liv looked at her like she was an alien, but Violet didn't waver.

"This is so weird. If I knew sticking you two in a house together would fix things, I would have done it years ago. So, this friends thing is real, then? You don't hate each other?"

Violet opened her mouth to say yes, but something stopped her for a moment. She didn't have a doubt in her mind they were friends because they had said they were, and yet it didn't seem to fit. Her mind flashed back to the other night again, when he held her as she cried, when he took her out on Saturday because she was sad.

Did friends do those things? Maybe.

But boyfriends did too.

"Okay, maybe *friends* is the wrong word," Liv said, frowning.

"N-no, it's close. I'd say we're friends."

"Right . . . so you're barely admitting to being friends with him, and yet somehow you decided to stay with him permanently?

"Oh, it wasn't much of a decision, really. He offered."

"Really? Lewis always says he hates having people over."

"He does. But that's because his home belonged to his great-grandmother and Lauren was such a bitch about it. Once he figured out I wasn't going to shit on the place, he was fine with it."

"So, you're okay with having a roommate now?"

"As much as I can be."

"Wow," Liv murmured.

"You don't believe me."

"I do! I mean . . . I'm trying to. It's kind of hard to get the past out of my head. It feels like yesterday you were telling me how you wanted to kill him."

Violet shrugged. "We're working on it. That's all we can do."

"I still can't believe this," she said, shaking her head.

"Tomorrow is game night, right? Lewis and Charlie always hang out on Tuesdays. What if we all hung out?"

"Actually, I was hoping we could go see a movie tomorrow. I think I need some girl time after being gone for three weeks. Plus, I know Lewis is dying to talk to Charlie."

"Okay, then maybe after that? There's a fun sushi place I want to try."

"You know what? What the hell. I feel like risking a fight for sushi. Let's try it."

Violet winced at the mention of a fight between her and Charlie, but she had gotten Liv to agree. That was a good step.

Charlie

"Game night!" Lewis called as Charlie opened the door.

Charlie was glad his friend was back in town, but after the awkward confrontation with Liv on Friday, he dreaded game night. But Lewis had asked if he was still up for it, and he didn't want to miss out on the times he usually looked forward to.

Liv was in the background, about to leave. Charlie already knew she and Violet were hanging out again to see a movie, but he was hoping she'd be gone by the time he arrived.

He still wasn't happy with her.

"Charlie," she said when she saw him. "Hey, I'm sorry for coming over unannounced."

He was surprised at the apology. "Oh, uh . . . thanks for saying that. I know you and Violet are close, so if you do come over to see her, just give me a warning next time."

"Yeah, I will. It's so nice to hear you say her name without your usual grimace."

Lewis cleared his throat, as if trying to cut off the Violet talk. This was his usual deal. He tried to avoid mentioning Violet at any cost around Charlie.

"She's not good at asking for help," Charlie said instead. "I know it's easy to worry about someone like that, but things are fine. I promise. We're all good."

"For now," Lewis said under his breath. Charlie glanced at him. If this was how their conversation was going to go, then it didn't bode well for Charlie's patience.

"Anyway, I've gotta go. Violet and I are meeting for a movie."

"She left right when I did, so she's probably already waiting for you."

Liv nodded, her eyes a little wide at how much they'd dropped Violet's name without a hint of hostility from Charlie.

"I'm not even gonna ask what happened," Lewis said. "All I know is I'll believe it when I see you two not kill each other at a group function. Liv mentioned us all hanging out, so I'm reserving my judgment for then."

"Okay," Charlie replied. "But let's not worry about that right now—it's game night."

Charlie hated that his friends were so uncomfortable around them. He hated that it was half his fault for not talking sooner. But he was going to have to live with it. He and Violet had moved on, and maybe others would take even longer.

They played a few video games, but Charlie's heart wasn't in it. Everything felt awkward, as if Lewis was waiting for him to explode about Violet living with him.

They were walking on eggshells, and he hated it.

"So, uh . . . Liv wanted me to ask you how it is living with Violet," Lewis asked eventually. Every word sounded forced. "Like . . . from your perspective."

"It's fine," Charlie said, shrugging.

"Come on. You can tell me. I know you have issues with it. You never let people in your space."

Charlie shook his head. "There isn't anything to tell."

"But you aren't talking about it all."

"You two are still shocked when I say Violet's first name."

"Mostly because we don't understand why this happened."

Charlie heaved out a sigh. But he knew he didn't have much of a choice. "There isn't a lot to say. She came in, it was weird, and we worked it out. If you want proof, Violet offered for us all to hang out tomorrow night at a sushi bar."

"What? You hate sushi bars."

"Lauren hated sushi bars. I'm . . . hesitant, but apparently this one has a conveyor belt and is pretty good."

"What does Lauren think about this anyway? I'm assuming you told her after the rehearsal dinner."

Charlie froze. He had forgotten Lewis didn't know.

"Lauren and I are done," he said slowly. Hearing her name didn't feel like a stab in the chest anymore, but he still didn't like to think about the person he had been with her.

"Okay, so you definitely had a huge blowout with her about the rehearsal. Look, man, I'm sorry you're not with Lauren right now, but this usually is a phase that lasts a few weeks and then it's back to normal."

"Lewis, I'm not getting back together with her."

Lewis raised his eyebrows. "That's a first. You're the one that's mad this time?"

"I'm not mad. I'm done. She acted like a child at the rehearsal. She . . . egged things on with Violet and me. It's not worth it. She's blocked on everything, and I have no interest in undoing any of that."

"You're done this time?"

"Yes." Charlie paused the game and turned to his friend. "It's over."

"Okay." Lewis nodded, but Charlie wasn't sure he believed him. After all, Charlie had said they were done many times before. "So, you and Violet are getting along, and Lauren is out of the picture for now. Is there anything else I missed?"

"I got a cat."

"What?" Lewis said. "Why is *that* the most shocking thing I've heard so far?"

"Is it really? My mom had animals all the time growing up."

"Yeah it is, because you said you hated animals in college."

"Because Lauren did. Lauren doesn't matter now. It's what I wanted, and Violet found the cat on my roof, decided to *climb* on the roof to get her, and then I kept the cat. That's all that happened."

"Hang on, Violet climbed on your roof?"

"Yeah, she's not afraid of heights."

"You let her?"

"Have you ever told Violet not to do something?"

"Not me, but Liv has."

"And how did that go?"

"I've heard she's stubborn."

Charlie only nodded.

"But you hated how stubborn she was. You always complained about it."

Charlie thought about it, but then shook his head. "It's not a huge deal."

Lewis blinked. "I'm still thinking this is a prank."

"I know it's hard to believe, which is why we're both offering to show you guys at dinner tomorrow."

Lewis frowned. "You two could easily get us kicked out."

Charlie tried not to get annoyed. "We won't."

"But I am curious . . . fine. Let's try it. I'll have apologies ready if it goes downhill."

Charlie nodded, hoping this would be enough to show his friends they were better—that they truly got along.

After a long, awkward silence, Lewis asked, "Do you have photos of the cat?"

Charlie felt some of his tension ease.

Of course he had tons of photos of Roo. He would just have to scroll past all of the ones that had Violet in them too.

"Yeah," he said, finding a few good ones in a row without Violet either holding her or playing with her. "Here are a few."

Lewis was happy to talk about Roo after that, all conversation of Violet gone. Charlie was relieved. He didn't know how many more comments about their past he could take.

Chapter Eighteen

Violet

"Oh, shit," Violet said, looking through the window. "You can see the conveyer belt out here."

Violet was a little nervous to go to dinner with Liv and Lewis, but she also understood why they were hesitant. Things with Charlie had been good, so good she couldn't imagine fighting with him again.

But her friends didn't know any different.

She was planning on doing her best to make sure nothing was weird. She was going to be herself and try to show them that she and Charlie could be friends. Hopefully after tonight, they would understand.

But even with all the worry, she was excited to try this new place. It was a local sushi bar where everything was served on a conveyer belt. She hadn't been able to justify trying this place until now. Even with her paying for all of the utilities, her financial situation had gotten so much better.

Violet could see why people had roommates.

"Each table is right next to the conveyer belt," Charlie said. "We don't even have to get up."

"This is my kind of place."

"I'm a little worried about food poisoning."

"You shouldn't be," Violet said as she fished around in her purse to grab a baggy filled with white dust. "I brought your Gigi Ruth's bone dust from the house. It's good luck, right?"

Charlie turned, eyes comically wide. "Did you take that from home?"

Violet laughed. "No. It's confiscated Smarties from a student who was trying to pretend it was drugs."

"That's . . . worse."

"I confirmed it was candy. By seeing them crush it and by taste."

"I'm not entirely convinced you won't get arrested with that."

"I think I'd do well in prison. I could write people's letters to their loved ones."

Charlie let out his full-bodied, amazing laugh. It always came out when she was saying something ridiculous, and it filled Violet with a warmth she didn't know possible.

"You'd be popular—that's for sure," Charlie said.

"Yeah." Violet shoved the crushed candy into her purse. "Let's go. May Gigi Ruth protect us."

"I'll have you know," Charlie said, opening the door for her, "she was big on culturally accurate foods. She would have cursed you for being here."

"You don't think she would have been charmed by the sheer amount of food you could get from the buffet for twenty bucks?"

"Okay . . . maybe she would've been impressed."

"She was ninety-eight when she passed, right? She had to have an iron stomach to live that long."

"She did somehow never get sick to her stomach—even after an unfortunate family barbeque featuring rancid egg salad when I was a kid."

"Now that's a woman I can respect," Violet said.

"How many?" the hostess asked, breaking Violet out of her conversation with Charlie.

"Four, please," she said.

Charlie was looking around, his face pensive.

"What's wrong?" Violet asked. "You're not still thinking about food poisoning, are you?"

He was silent for a moment. "Lauren would have hated this."

"Oh." Violet deflated. "Are you missing her?"

"No," Charlie said, so confidently that Violet believed it. "If I hadn't ended it with her, I would have never tried anything new like this. It's freeing."

"So, what you're telling me is that you want to try every hole in the wall place in town?"

"I guess so. The shadier the better."

"What about a guy who sells burritos out of his shoe?"

Charlie looked at her with wide eyes.

"I'm kidding. It's out of the back of his truck."

"That's not any better."

They were led to a table, and Violet texted Liv and Lewis to let them know where they had been seated. She then put her phone away, focusing back on Charlie.

"You know this actually looks good," he said, glancing at the food as it passed by. It came on small saucer plates that followed a label describing what they were.

"I like that it has labels for everything, or else I'd be eating whatever and hoping I don't have a hidden allergy." Violet chose to sit next to Charlie, instead of across from him. After she slid in beside him, she wondered if he thought she was too close, but he only smiled at her.

Liv walked in with Lewis a few moments later and Violet's thoughts were chased away at the sight of their friends. Charlie was looking at the menu, trying to figure out how everything worked when they walked over.

"Hey," Liv said, looking between them. "Wow, I can't believe we're doing this."

"Me either."

Liv's eyes left them and trailed around the restaurant. "I'm loving the fact that every table is next to a belt. And they have little doors!"

"This is . . . Charlie, are you sure you're willing to eat here?" Lewis asked.

"No, but I'm willing to risk food poisoning in the name of peace."

Violet rolled her eyes. "No one's mentioned getting sick from here. Besides, live a little." She elbowed him.

Liv and Lewis watched them carefully. Usually, this would be where they would argue, but Violet knew that wasn't where this was going.

"I'm living. I'm living." Charlie looked at the menu. "Maybe not for much longer, but I am."

"I once ate a two-day old Taco Bell burrito that was in my car."

Charlie looked up at her. "What?"

"It was in college, and I was very broke, but I survived."

"How?"

"Sheer spite. Or maybe it was finals. Didn't have time to be sick."

"I remember that," Liv said. "It didn't even affect her."

"I am a human garbage can," Violet said. "I can eat anything and not die."

"I hope it didn't have meat," Charlie said weakly.

"It was in winter. My car didn't have heat, so it was a refrigerator."

"That's not how food safety works."

"It worked that time," Violet said. "And if you're worried about food poisoning, you don't have to be. The reviews of this place are stellar."

"I know," Charlie said, sighing. "I read them."

"So, you're good with eating conveyer belt sushi?" Lewis asked.

"As good as I can be."

"It's all-you-can-eat for twenty bucks. What can go wrong?" Violet said.

"Apparently they add a charge for uneaten food." Charlie said, his eyes on the menu.

"I will eat anything to avoid an extra charge. Garbage can, remember?"

"I don't know," Charlie said. "I feel like garbage is a little insulting. I'd say you're . . . recycling."

"You know in human terms we're all recyclers. We turn everything we eat into poop."

Charlie looked up. "How long did you spend in the presence of sixth graders today?"

"Too long. Sorry, the poop jokes rub off."

Charlie snickered but shook his head.

"I don't mean to break up the moment," Liv said. "But what the fuck?"

"We said we were friends," Violet replied.

"Yeah, but when you said friends, I thought you were meaning friends who fight but try to be low-key about it. You guys are actually getting along."

"We're fine," Violet said. "We're over the feud and we talked it out."

"You talked it out? You?"

"It may have taken some . . . time." Violet couldn't lie to them. "But yes. We're not going to fight."

"The jury's still out," Lewis muttered.

"We're fine," Violet repeated. "But if you're worried, we can easily say if either of us starts a fight, the instigator pays for the whole table's food."

"You want to throw money into this situation?" Lewis asked. "Because if either of you loses, you'll blame the other for making you lose and then fight over it."

"Come on," Liv muttered to Lewis. "They're trying."

"Lewis, we're serious," Charlie said firmly. "This is a normal dinner between four people."

"The last dinner we invited you both to, you said Violet only brought joy to people when she left the room."

Violet laughed. "That was actually a good one."

"Okay, but you followed it up by saying if I were the light at the end of the tunnel, you'd turn around and leave."

Violet laughed harder. "And it was *such* a good comeback."

"Yeah, you totally roasted me there. I should have known to never go up against a sixth-grade teacher because you people take no shit."

"Hey, we take shit in the form of bad salary and kids pretending to snort illegal drugs in the hallway."

"Wait, did that happen *again*?" Liv asked.

"This happened more than once?" Charlie added.

"It's a trend that comes and goes," Violet said. "My personal favorite is the floor is lava challenge, but for understandable reasons, the administration thinks it's best to stop that in its tracks."

"The things you see . . ." Charlie muttered.

The conversation died down when the waiter came to take their drink orders. Once they confirmed they were dining from the conveyor belt, they were free to start eating.

"Can you hand me that salmon roll?" Violet asked the moment the waiter was out of sight.

"Sure," Charlie said. He grabbed a plate, hesitated, and then grabbed one for himself. "Here goes nothing," he muttered as he took a bite at the same time Violet did.

It was a decent sushi roll. Nothing to write home about, but it was good enough to go for more.

"That's actually not bad," Charlie said.

"It's really not," Violet agreed.

"I did not eat enough for lunch," Charlie said, grabbing a second plate.

"Hunger breaks all fears of food poisoning."

"If I get sick from this," Charlie said after another bite, "you're making me soup while I recover."

"That's a fair deal," Violet said, shrugging.

Both of them realized at the same time they had an audience. Liv and Lewis wore the same baffled expression.

Great. The shock must not have worn off yet.

"So, enough about us," Charlie said after he had finished another plate. "I don't think you told Violet about your honeymoon."

She nodded, eager to get the attention off her. It was a perfect thing to talk about. Liv had been so busy apologizing that they didn't talk about anything else before the coffee shop closed, and it never was brought up during the night at the movies.

Their friends only stared, but Liv seemed to recover the fastest.

"It was good," Liv said. "Both of us needed a break after the wedding and all the stress. We mostly sat and enjoyed the beach."

"I got to swim with sharks," Lewis added, his voice still tense.

"I don't think what you did counted as swimming, honey."

"I *tried* to swim with sharks."

Violet listened as they continued telling her and Charlie about their three-week honeymoon. Every now and then, she'd tap Charlie's shoulder to signal she wanted something so he could dutifully get it for her.

When they were done, Liv grabbed a bite of food and said, "Tell me how your three weeks went."

"Yeah, what happened with all of this?" Lewis asked.

"We . . ." Violet glanced over at Charlie. "We got stuck together and neither of us exactly *like* fighting, I guess."

"No, we don't," Charlie added. "At first it was weird, but then it got easier over time."

"When you said it got easier, I expected stilted conversation and awkward pauses," Liv said. "I even brought flash cards in case it got awkward. But this? This is . . . this is way beyond what should be possible."

"We've been living together for over a month now. We wouldn't have survived if we didn't," Violet said.

"You did all of this while living on separate floors?" Lewis asked.

Violet and Charlie glanced at each other. How much did they want to reveal of the time they spent together? How many questions did they want to field?

Eventually, Charlie spoke. "We like the same foods, so we started eating breakfast together."

"I . . . started grading in the dining room because of how much space I need," Violet admitted.

"Willingly?" Liv asked.

"Yeah, so we're spending a lot of time together these days."

Liv looked between them, wide-eyed. "Okay, so you really needed to be trapped together."

"And my apartment ruined. It kind of helps I was literally homeless," Violet said.

"You were never homeless," Charlie said. "I wasn't going to kick you out."

"Yeah, I know that now. But the fear of being kicked out made me stop antagonizing you for five minutes so we could talk."

"You still antagonize me. I think dragging me to a sushi bar with a conveyer belt is the definition of antagonizing."

"Okay, but it's consensual antagonizing."

"Yeah, we'll go with that."

"I think I just witnessed a bomb timer hit zero with no explosion," Liv said. "This is . . . so cool! Like you guys are *friends*. Lewis, isn't this awesome!"

Lewis looked between the two of them. "Charlie, can I talk to you?"

"Me?" Charlie asked.

"Yeah, you. Let's go out to the lobby."

Charlie shot Violet a confused glance before he stood and walked away. Violet watched them go, worry filling her. Why did Lewis look confused? And why did she feel like they had done something wrong by being friends?

Charlie

"What is going on?" Lewis said, turning to Charlie.

"Why do you look so freaked out?" Charlie asked. They were out of eyesight of the table, and at his friend's panicked gaze, he almost wanted to try and escape back to it.

"Last time I saw you two, it pained you to agree with her. People don't change overnight, okay? What happened?"

"Nothing."

"Charlie," Lewis said firmly. "You can't pretend like this is normal. You hated each other for six years!"

"And then I dumped Lauren," Charlie said. "Lauren was . . . this weird cloud over my mind. She instigated most of it. She would talk down about Violet and tell me I was justified in being an asshole when I wasn't. So, when she was gone, Violet and I were able to talk. Really talk."

"Charlie, you know I believe you about Lauren. She's been off since we all went to college. I'm glad you're finally seeing her for who she really is, but what I don't get is how breaking it off with her led to this. Sure, maybe it's a truce between you two, but this is . . . this is better than *before* you fought."

"Because it's Violet. She's forgiving and understanding. She decided to stay with me because she wanted to work on it too."

"Yes, Violet is understanding, but she's held whatever it was you two fought about over your head for years."

"It was an . . . essay."

"An essay for what?"

"Just something for school. You remember how Lauren would borrow my laptop?"

"Because you had a Mac or something?"

"Yes, exactly. She wanted to look like she had more money than she did. She borrowed it and saw I was helping Violet with a rough draft of something that meant a lot to her . . . Lauren went into the document and left cruel comments on it. I sent it, thinking I had made a couple completely normal ones."

"What did she ask you for help with?" Lewis asked, frowning.

"She asked me not to tell anyone. I won't go back on that."

"Okay, fair. But that was it? That was the whole reason you fought? You said you never knew what caused it."

"I didn't because I only said she needed to have more conviction with some of her statements and that's it. But Lauren called her a waste of everyone's time and a disappointment that should go teach middle schoolers. Violet thought I said that and stuck with it for six years."

"And Lauren never said anything?"

"Only that Violet was too sensitive to take criticism."

"Holy *shit*, dude. That's . . . that's bad, but why didn't you ask Liv to talk to Violet?"

"Lauren said I didn't need to."

"Why didn't Violet tell Liv?"

"Because she was hurt by what I said. A lot. And it was for something that was important to her at the time, something she told no one she was doing."

"Yeah, Violet is really tight-lipped about certain things," Lewis said, sighing. "For the record, though, I told you Lauren was a bad influence."

"I know, and you can imagine how pissed I am at her," Charlie said. "Violet and I not talking was our fault, yes. But she still lied and egged it on for years. I wasn't going back to her after that."

"I hear you, Charlie, but she's literally a lawyer for a reason. She's done shitty things, but then she catches you alone and talks you out of your own feelings. How do you know that won't happen again?"

"She already tried. The night of your wedding. The night I broke it off."

"So, you didn't listen to her? Did that finally work?"

"Violet shut her down. She knows bullshit when she sees it. When Lauren tried to manipulate me, she called it out, and that was all I needed. Violet is . . . way smarter than I ever gave her credit for."

Lewis stared at him for a second.

"What?" he asked.

"You called her smart."

"What's wrong with that?"

"You have a . . . *thing* for smart woman. As in, you tend to fall in love with them."

Oh, fuck. Of course Lewis would call him out on that.

"Okay, maybe that's true."

"Is Violet included in that?"

Charlie winced

"No," Lewis said, horrified. "No, tell me I'm making stuff up and that you don't like her."

"Hey, quiet! She's not that far away."

Lewis was red in the face. "Charlie!" he hissed. "You *just* became friends with her!"

"Yes."

"And you've fought for six years!"

"I'm aware."

"You can't be serious."

"Of course I'm serious. Do you think I'd do something this self-destructive for fun?"

"Well . . . I'd mention Lauren, but I think this is worse."

"How is it worse? We're not fighting, are we?"

"What if she doesn't return the feelings, Charlie? What if your signals get crossed and you hate each other again?"

"That's not going to happen."

"Why not?"

"Because I'm not interested in hurting her any more than I already have."

"But what if she goes off on you?"

"For one, I'd have more of a reason to figure out why she did. Lauren isn't in my head telling me to not pursue the truth."

"What if you get back together with Lauren?"

"I'm not," he said firmly. "And if I did, I'm giving you permission to go off on me, to remind me why I'm angry at her. There's no more hiding what happened, no more running to anger when we need to talk. I plan on *talking* to Violet, not fighting, and she's in the same boat."

"Okay, I agree with all of this. But you're still new to communicating. Don't throw a relationship into this too."

"I'm not going to bring it up. And if she doesn't feel the same way, I'd be happy to stay her friend as long as she would have me."

"You would be fine if she found someone else?'

"Of course not. But a part of me would be okay knowing *she* was happy."

"Wait a second. This doesn't sound like a crush. This sounds like *love*."

Charlie sighed. "Yeah, I know what it is."

Lewis shook his head. He looked stressed as he paced around the lobby, staying out of sight of the table.

Charlie felt like a child being chastised.

Lewis eventually stopped and looked at Charlie with a firm gaze.

"Don't chase after her. I know you feel like you love her, but this situation doesn't need to be more complicated than it is."

For a moment, Charlie wanted to storm off. He wanted to tell Lewis to mind his own business, and he would do whatever he wanted with Violet.

But then he saw it from his friend's perspective. To them, Charlie and Violet were teetering over the edge, ready to jump back into fighting at any moment. They had been the ones to bear the brunt of the arguments over the last six years.

They were nervous.

"That was the plan anyway."

"I cannot believe that not only are you two friends but you're somehow in love with her."

"Yeah, I know it doesn't make sense."

"I don't even know how to feel. Liv and I have been between you guys for years keeping the peace. We had to literally make it our mission to ensure you were never around her."

"I know. I know we were hard to deal with for a while. I'm sorry."

A bit of Lewis's tension melted and he sighed. "I know. And I am glad you're working on this, but it's also a delicate situation."

"You're right." Charlie was sure of it. Just because he felt like it was over, it didn't mean it truly was.

"Six years of fighting can't be erased in a few weeks."

"I know it can't. I wish it never even happened."

"Well . . . that means you'll work hard to make sure it doesn't again," Lewis said. "And maybe down the line things will work out."

"Maybe. Maybe not. I'd understand it if she never saw me that way after the way we fought."

Lewis shook his head. "I don't know what she's feeling, but I know you. And I know it's hard to hold off, so thank you for being willing to."

"Yeah, it's no problem." Even though it definitely was.

Lewis nodded and took a deep breath.

"I know Liv is worried," he said. "We should get back."

Lewis moved to return to the table. Charlie stared for a few seconds, and then followed.

Violet

Violet glanced in the distance, mindlessly chewing her sushi.

"Are you worried or something?" Liv asked.

"No, but it's a little . . . suspicious to pull someone away during dinner, right?"

"They're best friends. Besides, Lewis is the one who pulled him away, so no need to be mad at Charlie."

Violet blinked in confusion. Then she realized Liv was trying to keep the peace and had automatically assumed she was upset at the wrong person.

"No, I'm not mad at Charlie. I'm not even mad. It's that this dinner was for all of us, and I figured we were *all* hanging out."

"I'm sure Lewis is making sure this all isn't some elaborate prank."

"Why would it be a prank?" Violet asked.

"Well, we did come back to you being two different people."

"We're not different people. We're just not fighting."

"Fighting with Charlie is in your DNA. Remember what I said at the engagement party?"

"But you were also the one who told me to stay with him."

"I did . . . but I didn't think this would happen. I figured I was lucky if the two of you survived the two weeks before the wedding. It really was the only option."

"I know we were bad for six years, but can you give us the benefit of the doubt?"

"I *am*. Lewis is the one who's struggling. You know how he is. He prepares for the worst. Always."

"I know, but it's getting tiresome to be looked at like a bomb ready to go off. I had enough of that when we fought. I'm more than tired of it now."

"It *was* pretty explosive."

Violet sighed. "Yeah, it was, but we haven't fought like that . . . well, since Charlie was mad at me for getting on his roof. But that didn't culminate in a huge fight. I apologized."

"Really? You?"

"I couldn't not. I was staying in his house for free."

Liv stared at her for a long moment. Then, realization dawned on her face.

"Oh, no. You've gone full grateful silent."

"I've gone what?"

"Grateful silent. It's when someone does something nice for you, so you never say what you need. You do it anytime you get help."

"I don't . . . I didn't—" Violet stuttered. Then she took a moment to collect herself. "Okay, fine. For a while, that's exactly what I did."

"It's what you *are* doing."

"No, I'm not. Charlie made it even the minute he realized what I was doing."

"'Made it even?'"

"He offered a way for me to break out of the cycle of misery I put myself in."

"And when did he realize you were grateful silent?"

"The day I apologized for the roof incident." Violet shrugged when Liv stared at her with wide eyes. "I don't know what to tell you. I think he studied me or something when we fought. He figures me out pretty easily, which is both annoying and great for communication."

"How did he make it even?"

"He asked me to help with some of the maintenance on his house."

"So . . . in exchange for the help on having a place to stay, you helped him with the house."

"Well, when we made it more permanent, I took on some of the bills."

"All of this is a totally even relationship and not at all based on him helping you out?"

"Yeah," Violet said.

"Well, shit. There goes my whole explanation for why you two were getting along."

"You thought I was getting along with him because I was being . . . grateful silent?"

"Is it that out of character?"

"No." Violet shook her head, annoyed she was figured out so easily. "The only explanation I have is that a lot of stuff happened at the right time to make it work."

Violet glanced over where Lewis and Charlie had gone off to talk and found them *finally* heading back to the table. Liv followed her line of sight.

"Just know, the next time it's the two of us, I need all the details." Her voice was almost menacing.

Lewis got back to the table first, and he still looked nervous. "So, what did we miss?"

"Nothing much. Just about how I act when people help me."

"You mean how you completely disregard all of your own personality and try to be extremely quiet?" Charlie asked.

"Yes, exactly."

"Wow," Liv said. "You got it right on the first try."

"Yeah, but it's not a big deal. We have a decent arrangement."

Violet glanced at Lewis and found him looking between them nervously. He looked tense after his and Charlie's discussion, and Charlie himself didn't look easygoing, either.

"Maybe we should head out," Charlie suggested. "It's getting busy, and people are waiting."

Lewis looked at Charlie, and Violet wondered what they had talked about.

"Yeah, let's get out of here before it gets too busy," she agreed. The sooner they left, the sooner she could ask Charlie what was going on.

They made quick work of their remaining food and paid their checks. They parted with Liv and Lewis outside. By the time their friends were out of sight, Violet realized the evening had been draining for her.

The car ride was silent, and Violet wondered if Charlie was feeling the same way she was. Then again, he'd been off ever since he had his conversation with Lewis.

"Did you and Lewis have a good talk?" she asked.

"It was . . . a talk."

"Are you okay?"

"Yeah, I'm fine. Just Lewis asking questions."

"Hard ones?"

Charlie nodded.

"What was it about?"

Charlie didn't answer, and in the darkness of the night, she couldn't get a read on him.

"You don't have to tell me," she added, though her curiosity was through the roof.

Charlie sighed. "It's awkward."

"Was it about me?"

"Yeah," Charlie said.

"What . . . what did you guys say?"

"Nothing bad," Charlie said. His voice was rushed, like he had it on the tip of his tongue, ready to fire the moment she asked about what happened at dinner.

"That's not convincing."

"He only wanted to know why we were suddenly getting along, so I told him."

"And it was awkward? Liv asked me something similar, but I would say it was uncomfortable, not awkward."

"Maybe mine was uncomfortable then."

"Then why say it was awkward?"

"Has anyone ever told you that you are way too perceptive?"

"You have. Multiple times."

Violet could feel him getting irritated. His grip on the steering wheel was tight. He was frowning at the road in front of him.

But she wasn't about to let it go for the sake of peace.

"We've been good at communicating. Let's not stop because our friends are back in town. Was it bad? Is that why you seem so secretive?"

"It wasn't anything bad."

"There isn't any other reason to hide it."

"Oh, there's one." It was more muttered than said.

"Okay." Violet turned to look ahead, watching the road with distant eyes. "If you're determined to keep this a secret, then you can. But I want to be clear I'm not happy about it."

The silence returned. Violet felt her annoyance build; she tried to let it go. He *did* have the right to keep it to himself, but she also had the right to not like it.

"Violet, I didn't say anything bad about you to Lewis."

"There's no other reason you would be purposely vague."

Charlie sighed. "Fine, I'll tell you, but this is not a joke, and I don't want it to turn into one."

"I wouldn't . . . but okay."

"I said good things. Only good things. And then Lewis might have assumed I had feelings for you."

"You mean murder feelings?"

"No."

It hit her then. He asked if Charlie had a *crush* on her.

"Oh," Violet said. "Okay, I get how it would be awkward now."

"You don't have to worry. I'm not going to act on it."

Violet's brain grinded to a halt. "Wait, you didn't even deny—"

"I do. Have feelings for you, I mean."

Violet froze. He admitted it? Just like that?

She was still embarrassed he had *hugged* her twice. Maybe she wondered if what they had was purely friendship, but she hadn't admitted it to herself yet.

And now, faced with the truth of his feelings, she had no choice.

She knew this was a bad idea. They had too much history. Too much negativity. But the idea of being something more with the man next to her lit her entire body on fire. She didn't know whether to jump into a bucket of ice water or let herself burn.

"I'm sorry I acted vague," he said, "but this wasn't something I planned on telling you. Our past is too complicated, and I know you don't feel the same."

"Hang on," Violet interrupted. "You can't know that."

"Why would you like someone you were enemies with just a month ago?"

"Why would you?"

"So . . . what are you saying?" Charlie's eyes flickered over to hers before he pulled them back to the road.

"I'm saying I . . . probably feel the same."

Charlie stubbornly stared ahead, but she wondered if he wanted to glance over at her. The eye contact would be too much. If her eyes met his, she might explode.

"How long?" Charlie asked, his voice rough.

Violet thought about it. "Honestly? I can't answer that. I think back to the last few weeks, and there's not a sudden moment where I started liking you. And if I go back to before, as painful as it is, there was some part of me that still wanted your attention. So, maybe it's been the whole time."

Charlie was silent, then he uttered a quiet, "Me too."

"Seriously? Since college?"

"Yeah." He took a deep breath and continued. "Lewis figured it out pretty quickly, but he said years of fighting can't be erased in a few weeks."

Violet sighed. Her heart screamed, telling her this was wrong, but her heart had led her down bad paths before.

"And you agree?"

"I think I do. You?"

"Yeah," Violet said softly. "This sucks. The first time a guy and I are on the same page and it's to not be together."

"Maybe someday. When we're more settled."

Her heart told her they were settled now. They had talked out their whole mix-up of feelings without so much as a raised voice. They had made so much progress; why not throw caution to the wind and say fuck it?

Pain, her head reminded her. Pain was why she needed to stay cautious. Elijah had hurt, but this was so much more than some guy she had seen for a few weeks. This was *Charlie Davis*. The man who had occupied her mind for six years. The man who she had fought with and screamed at, only for her soul to be longing for him with every word. If *this* went downhill, she didn't think she could recover.

"But we're friends, right?" Charlie asked. "Friends who hang out still and don't make something like this weird?"

"Yeah." Violet nodded, trying to push past the emotions she felt. "Nothing has changed, so it's not weird. I think it would be worse if neither of us felt it. We're in this dumpster fire together."

Charlie sighed, looking as miserable as she felt. Violet glanced out the window of the car, feeling her emotions still raging inside of her.

"You're going to Micah's party tomorrow, right?" she asked, changing the subject before she started crying. "It should be fun."

"Yeah, I am. We can ride together if you want," Charlie said. "Save on gas."

"I bet parking is going to be a nightmare. Micah has one of those fancy apartments with weird parking garages. We should save the stress and carpool. It's what friends do, right?"

"Right. Friends. What else would we be?"

So much more, her heart screamed. *You could be so much more.*

Chapter Nineteen

Charlie

It would have been easier if she had turned him down.

Now Charlie and Violet were friends. Only friends. And his body wanted to revolt. He wanted to feel her lips on his, know what it would be like to wake up next to her every day, to open his chest and let her make a home with him. Forever.

But he had said they were friends. *Only* friends.

He never realized how logic flew out the door when love got involved. This couldn't last forever. But how could he continue his existence feeling like this?

Charlie had never felt this before. Not with anyone. And now he understood why wars were fought over this feeling, why people wrote songs, and screamed about love at every moment.

But it would fade. It *had* to, or else he was about to make *so* many mistakes.

They didn't talk for the rest of the drive back to the house. Charlie had to bite down on words that threatened to escape him, and all he could do when in the comfort of his own home was lock the bedroom door so he wouldn't run to her.

Charlie didn't sleep much that night either. When he did, he was dreaming about what Violet had said in the car, what he could have had, but didn't.

It was torture.

His run the next morning didn't help. How did people go on without completely losing themselves to this god-awful emotion?

They didn't. And then they got hurt.

I like to believe love is a choice, Violet said. *You choose to love someone, even when you don't.*

He remembered her soft voice, and how confidently she had said it. What if he simply . . . chose to do this forever? What if he did throw caution to the wind and tried, *really tried*, to choose someone? He could choose to love her when she was cursing about a repair gone wrong, and when she shut down after getting help, and when she chewed loudly, and when she was mad about work and literally *every* moment she was there.

It seemed so fucking easy.

Charlie found himself back home. His heart hammered from his run, and his breaths were short and quick. Reality crept in, and he knew he was being an idiot. He told himself he would never *do* this. He would never put himself in a position where he would get hurt like his mom did.

What if he hurt Violet again?

He couldn't do that. He couldn't let her feel any more pain than he had. Part of love was the fun stuff. But the more important part was making sure *you* weren't the cause of their pain.

And he had already done that. He had done it for six fucking years.

He regretted every single day.

Charlie pushed everything down. He walked into the house, changed, showered, and made coffee.

"Good run?" Violet asked as she came into the living room. She looked stunning, no matter what she wore. Charlie allowed himself one second to drink her in before he tore away his eyes.

"Uh, yeah," Charlie said. "Good yoga?"

"It was fine," she said. "What's today's fruit in our oatmeal? We have strawberries, apples, cranberries, and I think some blueberries."

The last thing on his damn mind was *food*.

"Surprise me," he said.

She paused, and Charlie wondered if she would choose to surprise him with something other than fruit. His logic was hanging on by a thread, and he'd be happy to snip that string for her.

No. This feeling would fade. Give it time.

"The blueberries are about to go bad," she said after a moment. She handed him a bowl. "So, let's use those. I'll be at the table."

He nodded, watching her walk to the dining room. His eyes, of course, trailed down to her ass in her leggings.

No. No. You're not doing this.

But he wanted to.

"This is awkward, right?" Violet said, turning around.

Charlie blew out a breath. "Yeah, it is."

"What do we do? Do we distance ourselves?"

Charlie knew instantly he was *not* doing that.

"No-no, I think it would make it worse if we did. You remember what happened when we fought and distanced ourselves?"

"Yeah. Everything was concentrated."

"Yes, if we face it, then it'll fade. Feelings usually do."

Violet nodded, and then turned to head back into the kitchen. She paused, faced him, and bit her lip.

"Would it be easier to get it out of our systems?"

Charlie stared at her. Was she suggesting what he thought she was? His entire body wanted to say *yes*.

And he was about to, but then she shook her head.

"No, it's not realistic," she added.

"Probably not," he echoed, though it pained him to.

Violet sighed. "Then what do we do?"

Charlie closed his eyes, but then what Violet suggested played behind his eyelids. Just for one night he could kiss her and touch her the way he wanted to. What would that feel like?

Heat rushed through him.

"You know what? I need to get dressed for work," Violet said.

The idea was fresh in his mind, so that was to blame for what he did next.

He gently grabbed her by the arm, stopping her as she went past him.

"Listen, if this doesn't fade . . . then maybe we should look at hypotheticals. Maybe we should try getting it out of our systems."

Violet turned a gorgeous shade of pink, and she nodded absently. Her eyes flickered to his lips for a split-second, and then was out of his sight and going upstairs.

She left without another word, and Charlie stood for a long moment to collect his muddled thoughts. He cleaned up the table and left for his own job.

His workday went terribly. He was horny and distracted. And after work, when they rode together to Micah's party, he would have to be close to her and suffer through this painful awkwardness once more.

Violet was already getting ready when he got home from work. This was their first time seeing many of their friends since the wedding, and he could tell she was nervous about it. He could only hope it went well enough to alleviate their fears.

He changed into a dress shirt and nicer jeans. He met Violet in the living room, and couldn't help but stare.

Her hair was down, with waves. She had on a light touch of makeup. Her cheeks shimmered, and her lips were slightly pink. With that, she had on the damn emerald green dress from the rehearsal. But this time, his eyes lingered on her. And he didn't want to tear them away.

"Are you ready to go?" She turned to face him. Her face was carefully guarded, but her cheeks turned slightly red, and he had to avert his eyes.

"Yeah, I'm ready."

He was not. At least not emotionally.

They arrived with the party in full swing. Micah's new apartment was huge and spacious. It must have cost her a fortune, but she had a great job, so she could afford it.

People they knew were scattered around the open floor plan. Violet stepped a little closer to him and he realized neither of them knew everyone here. In fact, usually it was Liv and Lewis hosting things, but Micah had a lot of friends they didn't recognize.

He was glad Violet was here, even if he wanted to kiss her so badly, he could explode.

"I think I see Liv over in the corner," Violet said, grabbing his arm. He nodded, following her to Liv who was standing alone with a drink in hand.

"Hey," Liv said. "Did you arrive together?"

"Uh, yeah," Charlie said.

Internally, he was panicking. Did Liv know about his crush on Violet? Did she know about Violet's crush on him?

If she did, she didn't show it.

"Last night was fun. It almost felt like college again."

"Yeah, it did," Violet said. "Although truth be told, I don't remember much of college. It was mostly a blur of studying and trying to make sure I didn't lose my scholarships."

"It worked out. You literally had straight As."

Charlie remembered that. He remembered thinking she would get into any grad school she applied to, but she wanted something Ivy League.

"I'm glad it's over. That kind of pressure wasn't good for me. Not that teaching is any easier, but it's a different kind of stress."

Charlie nodded absentmindedly.

"Where's Micah?" she asked as the conversation died down. "We should probably say hello."

Violet turned to look through the people at the party. Most of them were folks Micah knew through work, but there were a few of their more distant friends in the crowd.

Without finding her, Violet turned to Charlie and Liv with a frown. "Everyone is looking over here," she muttered.

Charlie knew she was right. Most people had heard of them, or at least knew of their feud. People were waiting with bated breath to see if they would break.

Bitterness coiled within him.

"Yeah, maybe," Liv said. "But you're doing well. You guys haven't gotten on each other's nerves once."

"It would be pretty miserable if we were annoyed all the time," Violet said to her.

"Plenty of people do it," Liv said, shrugging.

"Where's Lewis?" Charlie asked, eager to change the subject.

"He's with Elijah and Damon," Liv said. "They're here too."

"Great," Violet muttered.

Charlie sighed. He didn't know Elijah would be here. He hadn't heard or thought of him since the wedding.

"I'm sure it'll be fine," Liv said to Violet. "Anyway, isn't this place amazing?"

"It is," she agreed.

"A little too . . . new for me though," Charlie added.

"Oh yeah, your house is historical," Liv said.

"The open floor plan makes me feel exposed," Violet said. "I think I'm in the minority there. Open floor plans are popular."

"They're actually pretty inefficient," Charlie said.

"Right?" Violet replied. "I mean, I know there's some appeal, but I can't imagine *your* poor heating system even trying to run in a place like this."

"There had been discussion on opening up the wall between the living and dining room, but the radiator there literally keeps the whole first floor warm. There's no way to fix that unless I redid the venting to the entire house."

"That sounds expensive."

"Old houses usually are."

"How's it going over here?" another voice asked. They all turned to see Lewis, who had Elijah in tow. Violet's expression turned icy. Charlie eyed Elijah, wondering if he would be stupid enough to try anything.

Elijah had been mad Charlie canceled the bachelor party, and was also mad at Violet for yelling at him. Eventually, the guy would snap back, and Charlie hoped it wouldn't be tonight.

Charlie didn't think he could stand to listen to it. Not when Elijah had gotten to be with someone as perfect as Violet and then fucked it up.

And Charlie himself had to wait.

"Actually, it's going well," Liv replied. "Elijah, good to see you."

"You too," Elijah said, but his eyes were on Violet. Charlie wasn't a jealous person, but he didn't like the way Elijah looked at her like she was a piece of meat. "Violet, have you gained a few pounds? I seem to recall that dress fitting much better a few weeks ago."

Violet's jaw fell open, and he could see a flash of hurt on her face.

"Dude," Lewis hissed. "What the hell?"

"What?" Elijah asked. "It's an observation. I doubt a girl like Violet would worry about something as silly as her weight."

"Okay, that's enough," Liv said, holding up her hand. "You can go if you have a problem."

"There's no problem here." Elijah shrugged. "Can't I be friends with an ex? Or are you worried she's a little too explosive to deal with anyone who hurt her feelings?"

"Seriously, Elijah?" Lewis snapped. "You're going to start stuff *now*? For once, everyone is getting along."

"And you might want to back off considering that's my best friend you're talking about," Liv said coldly.

Charlie hadn't felt this angry since the night he found out about Lauren, but he held his tongue. Barely.

"I'm sorry, but I refuse to be insulted by someone I lowered my standards for." Violet found her voice, and her expression was murderous.

"*You* lowered your standards for *me*?" Elijah laughed.

"Yeah, and you know it. That's why you're here like an immature child starting fights at a party."

"Oh honey, you don't get to come at me for starting fights. Look at you and Charlie."

"Yeah, you *should* look at us because you saw how fucking mean we got. Do you want me to dress you down in front of all our friends? How about I go into graphic details about the one night you managed to sleep with me? Do you want that?"

"Why are you even hanging around her, man?" Elijah said to Charlie. "She's a step down from that hot chick you were with. I mean come on, she's not that good of a lay."

"Don't fucking talk about her like that." Charlie's self-control flew out the window as pure anger overtook him. He was one move away from punching Elijah in the face. He had dealt with *enough* from him. It was bad enough he made little comments about everyone, that he disrespected Lewis's wish for a bachelor party, and that he always acted like he was above them.

But he didn't get to put down Violet. Not in the disgusting way even Charlie never stooped to. He was about to say something again, but Violet stepped in front of him.

"You couldn't get Lauren if you tried. If you can't get a word in with me, she would chew you up and spit you out, but you're welcome to try. I'm sure she'd be impressed with your lack of knowledge of female anatomy and your dick being your entire personality."

There was silence, only broken by the sound of Liv snickering.

Elijah went red in the face.

Violet continued on.

"Listen, I know you think you have something going on because you've got a trust fund and parents who never taught you how to work a day in your life, but let me tell you something: you are nothing to me. And if you think for one fucking second that I will let you walk all over me in front of my own friends, you have another thing coming. I told you not to fuck with me when you cornered me at the wedding venue weeks ago, and now you're doing it again to try and catch me off guard in front of everyone because it didn't work the first time."

"Hang on, what?" Liv asked. "This has happened before?"

"Oh yeah," Violet said, not looking away from Elijah. "I'd be happy to tell you *exactly* how I embarrassed him and why he thought he could come up to me and insult me. I'd also be happy to tell you how he antagonizes me because he told me he wanted a relationship and then bounced the minute he got what he wanted, and I'd really love to tell you why he's insecure."

"Oh, I definitely want to hear that."

Elijah was glaring, his face turning a darker shade of red. "S-so, this is what you do? Abuse men you don't like?"

"No, I only talk back to men who fuck with me. You started this, but I can end it."

"Fine. I'll wait for you to constantly embarrass yourself with Charlie like you always do."

"You're going to keep waiting," Charlie muttered.

"Oh, you'll get at it eventually."

"Don't be jealous that I give Charlie more attention than you, Elijah. It's not a good look." Violet rolled her eyes.

"I could never be jealous of *you*."

"Really?" Charlie asked. "Because it sure fucking sounds like it. You went at Violet before the wedding, and then you're trying it now in the hopes I'll jump on your side because I used to hate her. But I'm not on your level, Elijah. I never was and I never will be."

"You're making a mistake by being on her side," he replied. "She'll turn on you the minute you hurt her feelings."

"I only turn on people who deserve it," Violet said. "And right now, you're the one stirring the pot at an otherwise great party. Do everyone a favor and go run off before you make it any worse."

"No," Elijah said. "You're nothing, Violet. You're a girl who can't measure up to any of her friends because she works a dead-end, loser job and will never be able to find a date because she has a mouth that doesn't stay closed."

"What the—"

"Elijah!" Lewis snapped.

"No, I'm tired of all of you staying around her when she's nothing but a problem. She's beneath you and ruins everything she touches."

And that was the last straw for Charlie.

He didn't care people were around, or that he was going to make a scene once again at a party; this was for the right reason. Hearing Elijah go right for Violet in such a cruel way was too much.

He roughly grabbed Elijah's shirt, pulling him to meet Charlie in the eyes.

"I'm only going to say this one more time. You don't get to talk about her like that. You don't get to look at her, or even breathe the same *air* she does because she's better than you could ever hope to be."

Elijah went pale, which meant it was working.

"Charlie, you don't have to do this," Violet said, and Charlie looked at her questioningly. But she didn't look hurt. She didn't even look offended. "Let him go."

Charlie did so, and Elijah stepped back instantly.

"You—" Elijah began, but Violet cut him off.

"No," she said. "Stop. Elijah, I do not care what you think of me. You can think I am a loser, or that I ruin everything I touch. That's fine because you don't mean enough to me for me to even consider your opinion. You lost any respect from me when you made fun of me after sleeping with you."

"He did *what*?" Lewis asked.

"Get'em," Liv said, giving her best friend a thumbs-up.

"My opinion of myself doesn't come from a lowlife who wants me to feel like I'm less than him, because I'm not less than you, Elijah. And you know it. That's why you keep trying to hurt me. You want me on your level, but it's not going to work. You're a man who needs women to feel like nothing. It's why you blamed me for Charlie canceling the bachelor party. It's why you wanted me to feel bad after I slept with you. It's why you're here now. Stop. It's not going to work."

"And if you do it again," Charlie added, "I'm going to punch you in the face. You're a fucking bully, Elijah, and I spent my childhood getting rid of them. I did it for Lewis, and I'll do it for Violet too. Not that she needs any help."

Elijah's face was a deep, painful red. "I—You know what," he stammered, "I don't even need you people! Fuck all of you!" He stormed off, obviously making a scene. They stood in a thick silence for a moment before Lewis spoke.

"What the hell was that?"

"*That* was Elijah," Violet replied.

"I've never seen him act like that."

"I have," both Violet and Charlie said in tandem.

"Yeah, me too," Liv muttered.

"What? Why didn't you tell me?"

"I tried, honey." Liv shook her head. "You were determined he was misunderstood."

"Fuck that. He's an asshole. When you said he broke it off with Violet, I thought it was a misunderstanding, not *that*!"

"Yeah, well . . . that was Violet's story to tell."

Liv glanced over at Violet, who was chewing on her lip. She had done well in the face of Elijah's insults. She was good at dealing with drama in the moment, but Charlie knew it would hit her later.

"If you'll excuse me," Violet said. "I'll be in the bathroom."

Charlie watched Violet go and moved to follow her at the same time Liv did.

"Sorry," Charlie said. "You go."

Liv glanced between him and Lewis, who looked shocked he had just witnessed his friend's cruelty.

"Actually, maybe you should go. I think Lewis needs a gentler talk, and you still look like you're about to fight someone."

"If he comes back . . ."

Liv nodded. "You get the first punch. I want the second, though."

"That may be reserved by Violet."

"Fine. Then I get the third. You go. Good luck. She's hard to crack when she's hurt."

"Oh, I know," he replied. "I'll do my best."

"Yeah, I don't doubt it." Later, Charlie would remember there was a teasing edge to her voice, but in the moment, he needed to find Violet.

He made his way through the people who witnessed Elijah's meltdown. Their eyes were wide, and mouths open, ready to ask questions, but he was only worried about Violet.

He found the bathroom, which was the only closed door in the apartment.

Charlie knocked. "Violet, it's me."

"What do you want?" she asked, voice muffled.

"To be there for you. What can I do?"

There was a long moment of silence, and then the door swung open. Violet looked near tears, and Charlie stepped in, shutting the door behind him.

"I can't believe I can't make it through one party without fighting with someone."

"He started it." Charlie tried to keep the malice out of his voice. "You ended it."

"Ugh, I hate doing that."

"He deserved it. If you hadn't, I was about to punch him."

"I could tell. What was that about?"

"He's a bully, and I used to deal with Lewis's bullies all the time. It's not the most elegant solution, but I couldn't take him insulting you like that."

"Thanks, but I can handle myself."

"I know. I saw it. Honestly, it was kind of hot."

"Yeah right," she said, shaking her head. "It was embarrassing."

"Not from where I was standing."

"You weren't on the receiving end of it. Of course you'd think differently."

"I always thought you looked good when you were giving someone a piece of your mind. When we would fight, you would always take steps toward me, and even though you're tiny—"

"I'm not that tiny," Violet interjected.

"It was intimidating."

"And you thought intimidation was hot?"

"I mean, *it's you* . . . so yeah."

Violet blushed a beautiful color and laughed. Charlie stared at her, more than a little proud he had managed to cheer her up, even temporarily.

She pushed herself off the counter and walked toward him. She stopped right in front of him, her body mere inches away.

They didn't usually stand this close, and it was even more dangerous now.

"Remember what we said about hypotheticals?"

"What?" Charlie asked, confused.

"Fuck it," she said, and she grabbed his dress shirt, pulling him to her for a searing kiss. For a moment, he reveled in it, trying to memorize the feeling of her lips on his.

"Wait," he said, pulling away. "I can't believe I'm saying this, but we agreed this was a bad idea."

"Yeah, we did. And when has that ever stopped us before?"

Charlie knew he should tell her he couldn't do this. He knew he shouldn't give into what he was feeling and continue kissing her, but he was a weak man. He only nodded, and let Violet pull him back down to press his lips on hers.

Violet

Violet thought she could only hate Charlie Davis.

And she was wrong. In fact, there were a lot of things she could feel for him. Hate. Love.

Lust.

She didn't want to wait for the feelings to fade. She didn't want to hide from someone who liked her because she was scared.

She and Charlie were on the same page. They liked each other, and nothing else mattered.

Violet was going to enjoy this.

Charlie's scent surrounded her, all earth and wood, and it seared into her memory. She was reaching up to him on tiptoes, to fully press her lips to his. Something in her released. Violet finally knew exactly what his mouth felt like, tasted like, and she knew how perfect it was.

But that didn't compare to when Charlie's hands went to the small of her back, pulling her to him as if she weighed nothing. Their bodies forced together heated her down to her core, waking up parts of her that had long since been asleep. She felt like she would float away if he stopped now.

Charlie kissed like it was his last chance to, like she was going to change her mind any moment. But being kissed chased away any fears or doubts. All she could focus on was him.

Violet was direly out of practice, and yet the most empowered she had ever been. She wanted closer, impossibly closer, so she settled for swiping her tongue across his lip, unable to stop herself.

He instantly let her in, and she moaned at the taste of him. He pushed her against the sink to get her closer. It wasn't the most comfortable position, but she was too busy memorizing how Charlie felt against her to care.

His hands were roaming, and she regretted the fact there were any layers between them. Her body was afire in a way it hadn't been in a long time, and she wanted him. Desperately.

Violet hooked her leg around his ass, pushing her dress dangerously high, exposing her in ways she probably should have cared about.

"Wait," Charlie said, pulling away from her. Violet instantly stopped, wondering if she had gone too far.

Charlie looked *wrecked*. His hair was a mess, his eyes were wide, and his lips were smudged with the little bit of lip gloss she had on.

It was the hottest he had ever looked, but he had told her to stop. She gazed at him questioningly.

"This is the wrong place for this."

"What?" Violet asked. "No one's here."

His eyes slid to hers, and she had to stop herself from leaning in again. "I want to do *everything* with you, but not here."

Violet shivered. "Then where?"

"My bed. Yours. At home. Somewhere we can take our time."

Violet's desire grew.

"Let's go home."

"Violet," Charlie said. Her name sounded like a promise, like a desire she had never known. "I want to make sure you want this. That you don't feel like you owe me for defending you."

"I want this. I've been thinking about it ever since last night. I can't stop. And I know you've been thinking about it too."

Charlie leaned in again, and Violet thought he might caress her lips once more, but only their foreheads touched, their breaths intermingled for a moment. "I have."

"I want to go home," Violet said. "I want to do this. We're both on the same page, right?"

Charlie nodded. He painfully pulled away from her, and her brain cleared enough for her to notice how they both looked.

The last thing she needed was to look drenched in lust in front of all her friends. If Liv saw her, she would know what had happened in an instant.

Violet pulled down her dress, flattened her hair, and then turned to Charlie. She blushed when she saw her own lip gloss on his mouth and brushed it off. It shouldn't have been intimate, but it was. Just stepping close to him was enough to bring back the heat she had felt a few moments prior.

And Charlie returned the gaze. If she sat in it too long, she knew she wouldn't be able to leave the bathroom. Once they looked like they hadn't nearly had sex, she opened the door.

Violet pulled him by the arm, and she walked along the perimeter of Micah's apartment to get out. She saw Liv out of the corner of her eye talking to Lewis and thanked her lucky stars her friend didn't notice her.

She pulled Charlie out of the party. He was pliant with her, and she hoped whatever he had been feeling for her still burned bright.

When they were in his car, she pulled out her phone to tell Liv she was leaving.

Violet: I'm heading home. Too much happened and I need some quiet time.

Liv responded only a minute later.

Liv: We are too. Lewis feels bad about keeping Elijah around. I'm so sorry he insulted you, but you were a badass as always at handling it. Did Charlie help at all?

Violet blushed, remembering *exactly* how Charlie had helped.

Violet: Yes, he did. I'll be fine. Promise.

When Charlie pulled into the driveway, he leaned over to kiss her once more. Her desire came back to her in a wave. Thank God they were finally home.

They separated only to get into the house. The moment they were tucked inside, Charlie was kissing her against the door, and Violet wondered if he would take her right there.

"My room," Charlie said, pulling away from her. "It's closer."

She nodded, not caring where they ended up. All she cared about was getting more of him—his taste, his smell, *him*.

She wanted all of it.

Violet fell on the bed first, and Charlie pulled off his shirt to gaze at her hungrily for a second. Then, he was back on her.

If she thought kissing him was amazing, nothing compared to feeling his skin. She wanted more, and her dress was too much. Charlie's hand found the zipper at her back.

"Can I take this off of you?" he asked. She had never heard his voice sound like this. It was raspy and quiet, but so powerful it made her shiver.

"Yes," she answered, and he made quick work of the zipper.

Her dress came off, leaving her in her lace bra and underwear. For a moment, she realized he could easily ruin her with words, but when she gazed up at him, he was looking at her like she was art.

"God, Violet," he murmured. "I always imagined this, but nothing comes close to the real thing."

She didn't have time to think because he was kissing her jaw, her neck. Her body was on fire with something new, something she had never felt before, something that felt illicit. She was wet and empty, and all she wanted was for Charlie's pants to disappear so she could feel him filling her up.

He was pressing insistently on her hip, and she knew he wanted it just as much as she did. She was about to pull at his boxers when he started peppering more kisses on her jaw and down her neck, and then finally to her stomach.

"Can I?"

The last time a guy had gone down on her was right after graduation. He had *not* been good at it. Violet didn't think she could even come from it. "You don't have to."

"I want to," he assured her. "I really want to. Please?"

"I might not be able to finish from it."

"I want to make you feel good. I don't care about the finish line."

Well. She did have Charlie offering to go down on her. She might as well take the chance while she had it.

"Okay," she replied, biting her lip.

His first kiss felt odd. She wasn't used to anyone touching her there, but it didn't take long for him to find her clit, and once he did, she gasped and arched into him, desperate to get more contact.

In that moment, she realized he knew what he was doing.

He gently licked it, pushed his tongue against it. His other hand pressed on her stomach, keeping her grounded while she felt like she was floating.

Charlie gave her time. He made her feel good and never seemed to want to stop. When she grabbed his hair and told him to move a certain way, he kept doing it.

It was heaven. It didn't feel like a race toward an orgasm. Instead, Violet was able to lose herself in the feeling. This wasn't a performance; it was an experience—one she wanted to revisit a million times over.

She wasn't paying attention to anything but sensation, and she felt the pressure build insurmountably, culminating in the most intense wave of hot pleasure she could only moan into.

Charlie let up right when it all became too much, but the aftereffects took a minute to fade. Her body was lifeless, loose like she had never been before.

When Violet's mind finally began working again, she felt like she was on the other side of something. Could sex feel like this? Is this why people loved it so much?

She never wanted to leave this bed.

"You're so beautiful when you come," Charlie whispered. She glanced over at him and found him beside her.

Violet kissed him then, words escaping her. He responded enthusiastically, and rolled on top of her, pressing her into the mattress.

She could feel his desire throbbing against her leg, and after what he had done for her, it was her turn to make *him* feel good. When she reached down to touch

Charlie through his boxers, his breath hitched, and she tugged at the material until they finally came off.

And holy shit. If she had thought he had looked good naked the first time, it was nothing compared to this.

Charlie was all muscle and desire. His cock was hard and heavy in her hand. When she touched it, she felt a deep ache and only wanted him.

"Mm," Charlie said. "I want to fuck you."

"Fuck yes," she said. "Do you have condoms?"

She half expected him to frown at her and try to convince her not to use protection. That would have been the biggest turnoff in history. But he reached into his nightstand, pulling one out with no complaint.

Sometimes she wondered why she doubted him.

"Are you sure?" he asked her.

"God, yes," she replied. "For once, I'd like to get fucked literally instead of it being figuratively."

He laughed. "You can't resist literary banter, even in bed?"

"No," she replied.

He shook his head, but then kissed her again. Violet had waited long enough. She hooked her legs behind his ass and brought him right where she wanted him.

Charlie's cock pressed against her entrance, and as he gently pushed in, her body gave way slowly. It had been a while, but she was ready and he was able to push all the way in, filling her completely.

Violet had never felt like this before. She had never felt so full, so complete. They fit together perfectly.

"You feel amazing," Charlie muttered, his voice tight.

"You've got to start moving," she said breathlessly.

He started slowly, but then it quickly devolved into something fast and hard. She lost herself in the sensation of his movement, her body welcoming each thrust with its own wave of heat.

And *damn,* he had stamina. He went for what felt like hours, but she didn't mind the time. Her body needed this, and the longer he took, the more it felt like something was building. She was gripping his shoulders like a vice, begging him not to stop as she toppled over a mountain she didn't know she was climbing.

Violet had never come like this before, but when she did, the heat inside her turned into a fire, spreading all through her lower belly. She cried out, her body convulsing, and she was dimly aware of Charlie doing the same.

Her body glowed in pleasure, even after the sensation faded. She could feel Charlie panting, his cock twitching inside of her as his orgasm ebbed.

"Fuck," he panted. "Why weren't we doing this instead of fighting for six years?"

"I don't know," she said. "But it would have been a lot more fun."

"That was . . . It's never been like that for me."

"Me either."

He leaned down, putting his forehead on her shoulder as if exhausted. Violet didn't disagree with him.

"I need a shower," he muttered. "I should probably go do that."

Violet paused, trying not to let panic set in. Charlie had technically gotten what he wanted. Now he could easily make fun of her, or worse, dump her and say they were going to be friends. She desperately wanted to hope Charlie wasn't that kind of guy, but experience made her wary.

"Hey, why are you tensing up?" Charlie asked. She blinked back into awareness to see him looking at her worriedly.

"No reason," she said. In the back of her mind, she wondered how fast she could escape once he was in the shower. Maybe she could hide in her room forever and pretend this never happened.

"No. None of that," Charlie said softly. He gently kissed her cheek, and he caressed her cheek. "Did I do something wrong? Did you not like it?"

"No!" Violet exclaimed. "God, nothing like that. You . . . you slept with me."

"Yeah?" Charlie said. "Was that okay?"

"Yes, of course," she said softly. "But this is when people usually leave."

"I mean, I'd love to stay in bed with you forever, but I really do need a shower."

Meekly, she responded, "No, I meant leave *me*."

Charlie looked bewildered. "Why would I leave you?"

"You got what you wanted."

"That's not *all* I wanted," Charlie said. "I want to shower with you, and have you sleep here tonight, so I can wake up with you next to me in the morning. This was great, but there's so much more too."

Violet felt her cheeks grow hot. "I . . . I want all of that too, but I'm worried you'll change your mind."

"Then let me show you I won't leave," Charlie said. "Come on. Come shower with me."

"You sure?"

"I wouldn't offer if I wasn't. Do you want to join me?"

Violet could only nod and follow him.

She had never showered with someone, but it was as ridiculous and amazing as she imagined. Charlie's bathroom was inviting and comfortable. He offered to shampoo her hair, and it felt like one of the most intimate moments in her life.

Once they dried off and found themselves in comfortable clothes, Charlie lit the fireplace in his room and gently guided Violet to the bed. She blushed, wondering when his attention would fade, but she was happy to share a warm bed with him. Besides, she had always wanted to experience his fireplace.

Violet was pillowed on his firm shoulder, her leg slung over his. She didn't have a lot of experience sleeping in the same bed as someone, but his body was so cozy in the cold night, she couldn't imagine being anywhere else. They both laid in his bed, feeling the heat radiating off each other's body. Then, Violet drifted off into the safe embrace of sleep, cocooned in Charlie's arms.

Chapter Twenty

Charlie

When going back on promises, one should feel regret.

Charlie didn't feel it at all, which was odd, considering he was doing the exact opposite of what he told his best friend he would do.

He had never been the kind of guy to let lust cloud his vision. He always tried to think clearly, and he never understood why people lost their heads over something so primal.

But now he understood.

The connection combined with their understanding of one another intensified with every touch, every kiss, every moment, making their night . . . perfect. He had never felt anything as intense as the previous night was.

He'd never felt like this before.

Charlie and Lauren were together for many years, and while he had enjoyed some of it, there was nothing like *that*. The woman he fought with for six years shouldn't have held a candle to the woman he had been with since high school, but being with Violet was like the sun, not a candle. And he couldn't look away, even if he got burned.

He didn't know what the future held. Violet could wake up and tell him she didn't want to do this again, and they needed to stay friends. Maybe she was the one with sense, and she could tell him they needed to wait before they tried anything else.

But Charlie knew it would never be *him*.

He knew he couldn't let her go now that he had seen everything. His feelings on love be damned. Lewis be damned. He was going to go for this as long as she let him. Even if it meant getting his heart hurt.

That voice that had been urging him on, telling him to go for it, was pleasantly silent. He didn't regret it. He never could. The feeling he had now could sustain him forever.

He didn't care about the future, or his fears. When he was with her, he was only focused on her.

The next morning was a bright, sunny day. The sunlight broke through his curtains early, like it always did. Charlie rested comfortably in between sleep and consciousness, and when his alarm went off, he didn't want to move. He was pleasantly warm and held down by another weight on top of him.

Violet was still pillowed on his shoulder. The fire he had lit the night before lowly burned in the corner, and his room smelled of her scent. This was a perfect moment, something he wanted tattooed on his brain to return to.

This was peace.

Then he realized Roo was in the room with them too. As he had lit the fire the night before, he left the door open, just in case she wanted Violet in the night.

And of course, the little cat had wanted exactly that. There wasn't much room in the bed for her, but she was asleep near the fireplace, looking content.

Roo seemed to be just as enamored with Violet as he was.

Violet slowly woke right after he did. She sat up, her hair a mess, rubbing her eyes adorably.

His heart swelled as he watched her. Charlie sat up too, pulling her into his embrace, and pressed a kiss to her cheek.

"Mm, morning," she mumbled. "What time is it?"

"A little after when you usually get up."

"Oh, good. I still have time for yoga." She slowly moved to get out of bed, but then paused. "Would you like to join me?"

Normally, Charlie hated deviating from his schedule, but yoga was still exercise, and it sounded more fun than going out into the cold for a run.

"I'll try yoga. I think I have a mat somewhere."

She smiled and said she would get set up. They wound up doing the practice in front of the fire, which was a nice break from the cool air he ran in. His body slowly woke up, and he found yoga strangely challenging.

It also didn't help that Roo continuously distracted them. She would ask for pets or try to climb on them in downward dog.

It was hilarious, and they both had to stop multiple times to laugh.

As their morning unfolded, he waited for the awkwardness to kick in. He waited for Violet to look away or seem hesitant about their new relationship.

But it never came.

Once yoga was done, he pulled her into another kiss, which she responded to enthusiastically. He wanted to take it further, but the rumbling of his stomach told him that skipping breakfast, even for sex, was a bad idea.

Charlie pulled away slowly, eying the blush on her cheeks.

"Um, you did good. With yoga, I mean."

"Thanks. Not too bad for a runner, huh?"

"Yeah, your running helped you a lot. In more ways than one."

Images of the night before played in his head, and heat coiled within him.

Charlie was about to say *fuck it* and skip breakfast, but then he heard Violet's stomach growl too.

"We should eat," Violet said, rolling up the mat. "I've got to be at the school in an hour."

"I need to get heading out too. Do we have any leftover oatmeal bars?"

Violet nodded, and they got ready for the day together.

He went to work in a good mood. He was in the highs of love, but even so, he reminded himself this wouldn't last. One day he was going to fall back down again, and it was going to fucking hurt.

But he would enjoy this while he could.

His day was a mashup of people asking him questions and coding new updates. It was busy enough he didn't get much time to think, which he was grateful for.

His mind kept tracking back to Violet. He wondered how her day was going and couldn't wait to see her again. It was so bad, he wound up leaving work at three to grab dinner for them. He wanted to be there when she walked through the door.

Charlie went somewhere he didn't usually go—a fancy Italian place out of his way. He remembered it was one of the places he, Liv, Lewis, and Violet met up at before the fighting started. When he walked in to grab his to-go order, he glanced around the room curiously, checking out if this would be a good date spot.

That was when he saw his mother.

She was eating dinner with another woman who looked about her age. She had dyed black hair and bright eyes. They were smiling and laughing, as if nothing in the world could bother them.

Charlie glanced at them suspiciously and found himself particularly intrigued by his mother's expression. He knew that look. He had seen it in the mirror this morning.

Then his mom reached across the table and grabbed the other woman's hand, gripping it like a lifeline. The other woman laughed and kissed her.

It all fell together.

His mom was seeing someone, and judging by how comfortable she looked, she had been for a while.

Charlie was already feeling hurt that she hadn't told him directly, but seeing made it all the more real. He knew his mom had been reaching out, but probably couldn't find the right time to tell him the truth.

He'd found a comfort with only the idea of his mother seeing someone. Now that it was real, he didn't know how to feel.

Charlie felt the urge to go see her, but he knew his hurt would bubble to the surface, and it wouldn't be a good conversation. He turned to leave before he could do anything else, dinner now the last thing on his mind.

As he drove home, he thought back to how busy his mother had been, and saw it all in a new light. Had she really missed Liv and Lewis's wedding for a work trip? Or was it a romantic getaway? Was she really in strange parts of town for shopping, or was it for someone else? He may have kept some of the details on his and Violet's friendship secret, but he never outright lied about them. He didn't like being lied to, not after Lauren had done it for so long.

Hopefully, Violet would be home soon because she would know exactly what to say to make him understand the mixed feelings he had.

Which was why she meant so much to him.

Violet

Hello Violet,

We are reaching out to you for a new position in Phoenix, Arizona we think you would be a good fit for. It is a data-driven job monitoring the education of middle school students. The pay is $80,000 a year. You would work 40 hours a week. Please reach out if you're interested.

Violet couldn't stop re-reading the email. It was the first thing she had seen when she went to lunch, and she couldn't believe it.

$80,000? A better job without long hours? This was her dream come true.

Violet was on her lunch when she received it, and she had time to research the location. Phoenix was expensive, but she would be able to afford a nice place on her own with that salary.

This was what she had been waiting for, but she hadn't ever thought she would move across the country. Nashville wasn't the kind of city that offered a lot of education careers, and this was based out of a college in Phoenix.

She'd hate to leave her friends who she cared about so much. God, she'd hate to leave *Charlie*.

But in doing so, she would be able to live on her own. She needed to support herself without help, and this was her only option. It would be years of small raises until she could afford her own place, and who knew if she and Charlie would make it that long?

Sure, the sex had been great, and the morning after too. But they had thrown a wrench in their friendship. Charlie didn't believe in love. He had said this feeling didn't last.

So where would she be when it did finally end?

Violet took a deep breath and emailed the agent back. She had to interview for this. Even if the job wasn't going to be perfect, and she wouldn't be working with students, she knew she needed to try.

As Violet taught for the rest of the day, she couldn't get the possibility of a life upgrade out of her mind. She'd be away from her mom . . . but also away from Liv and Charlie.

But maybe that would be a good thing.

She had been left by her father, and then in a way, by her own mother. She was dealing with that pain since she was a little girl. Maybe it was time for *her* to run for once before she was the one screwed over again.

At the end of the day, when Jason was in her classroom doing homework, she browsed apartments in Phoenix. None of them spoke to her like Charlie's house—not that she expected them to.

She received a call from a recruiter to schedule an interview.

Violet panicked, not wanting Jason to know about her job lead. She set the details and tried to pretend nothing happened, but he had heard the whole exchange.

"What was that?" he asked.

"Nothing," she said, shaking her head.

"It sounded like a job," he replied. "Are you leaving?"

Violet sighed. She didn't want to have this conversation with him, but she didn't want to lie to him, either. "I don't know. It's only an interview, but maybe."

"I don't want you to leave. I like you here."

"I'm not sure, Jason. But I'll stay as long as I can, okay?"

"No!" Jason snapped. "I like you *here*."

"Nothing is set in stone. It may not happen."

"But you'll leave me! Just like everyone else does!"

Violet groaned, willing away her instinctive reaction. This was going to be hard to explain to a kid.

"I won't leave you," she told him. "I'll think about you every day, and once you're old enough, I'll be able to see you on social media. It's not *you* I'm leaving. And it's not like I want to, but I have to make choices sometimes, even if they're hard."

"Will you come back?"

"Yeah, my friends are here," she said, smiling. *Charlie is here.*

"But what about your boyfriend?" Jason asked. "Won't he be sad?"

"Who?"

"That guy from the winter festival."

"Charlie? He's not my boyfriend."

"Whatever, but he'll be sad too."

Violet paused. Maybe he would. Or maybe she was overestimating how much he cared about her. She tended to do that. If anything, she could come visit.

"Maybe for a bit, but I don't think he will. We aren't that close."

That was a lie, and she knew it. They were more than close. She trusted him far more than she should have. It was dangerous, actually.

More reason to run.

"But . . . but . . ."

"Hey, don't stress about it," she told Jason. "I don't know yet. But I'll let you know when I do. It's not like I'd be leaving tomorrow."

Jason frowned at her and didn't seem convinced. He went back to his homework, but she could feel him shutting down. She wanted to take it all back, and not even go for the job, but she knew she had to. She knew she needed to.

It didn't feel great. But then again, her mom had always said going for these kinds of things never did.

Would her mom be proud of her for finally doing what she always wanted? Would she finally be happy with Violet?

She wasn't sure it was worth it, but she wanted to try, so she would.

When Jason's mom arrived to pick him up, he gave her a sullen goodbye, acting as if he wouldn't ever see her again. She watched him go, feeling like a terrible person, but knew this was something she had to look into.

Once her classroom was empty, she left too. She still felt conflicted, and she hated it. Maybe she shouldn't be making such a big deal out of an interview—but *they* had reached out to *her*. She hadn't even applied.

Violet took a deep breath when she arrived home, hoping Charlie wasn't going to be pissed at her for considering it. The last thing she wanted was to hurt him too.

Charlie

Charlie was so shocked, his mind kept spinning in circles over what had happened, over what he had seen. He was sitting on the couch when Violet walked in, causing him to jump up to greet her. A little bit of the tension eased in his chest as the sight of her.

Violet raised her eyebrows at him.

"Is everything okay?" she asked.

"No. But maybe yes. I don't know."

"Something happened," she said, taking off her coat.

"Yeah, while I was getting dinner," Charlie said, he pointed to the table, where everything was set. He wasn't feeling hungry, but she had to be starving.

"Okay, let's sit and talk about it then," Violet said.

It was weird having someone who was so willing to talk to him about his problems. He was used to having his issues minimized by Lauren. Violet didn't do that. She was always there.

She sat at the table across from him. She glanced at him, as if asking if it was okay to eat while he talked, and he handed her a piece of garlic bread in response. She happily took it and looked at him expectantly.

He told her everything. How his mom had been a little off lately, and why she had missed the wedding. He talked about his childhood and how she never dated. He told her about the woman she was eating with and how happy she looked.

Violet listened intently, eyes focused only on him. When he was done, he said, "I know she needed time to tell me. She was with a woman, so maybe that's a factor, but what I'm more upset about is how she lied. She wasn't at Liv and Lewis's wedding and the more I think about it, the less I think she was on a work trip like she said. I know I didn't tell her everything about our past, but I didn't *lie*."

Violet swallowed, and said, "I think it's okay to be upset she lied, but she also is probably terrified to come out to you. This is a big change for both you and her. She could be working herself up to it."

"I mean, I'm happy for her. And this is a change. I thought she never dated because she was heartbroken over my dad. My views on love came from watching her do it all alone. She even told me love ends."

Violet seemed lost in thought, and he realized how callous he was being. Technically, after the night before, they weren't strictly friends.

"I'm not . . . I mean I'm not saying anything about *us*. I'm sorry if it—"

"No, you're fine," Violet replied. "I wasn't thinking about that. I was more trying to think of how to say something without it sounding bad."

"It's okay. Just say it."

Violet sighed. "Is it possible you misunderstood what your mom said to you?"

"What do you mean?"

"I mean . . . she said love ends, right? But maybe she was only describing her relationship with your dad. Did she ever say *all* love ends?"

Charlie opened his mouth to say *yes, of course she did*, but then he realized he never actually remembered her saying that. The thing about being a kid was that sometimes things got twisted. Sometimes someone said something, and it was heard in another way; just like playing a game of telephone.

"Oh, no," he said, the realization hitting him like bricks. "I don't know what she said."

"Maybe you need to ask her. But that aside, you can make your own beliefs at this point in your life. Even if she told you all love ends, you have loads of evidence it doesn't. Like Liv and Lewis. Or maybe this new love between your mom and this woman."

Or him and Violet.

If love truly ended, wouldn't he have never fallen for her? She had always had a hold on such a big part of him, even when they fought, he doubted he knew how to exist without some part of him belonging to her. He didn't know how deep her feelings went, but his struck down to his core and rooted within him. He didn't know if it would blossom or crumble, but she had always been integral to his life.

"Yeah . . . maybe I should evaluate where I stand on that," Charlie said slowly. "And I need to talk to her."

"That sounds like it's for the best," Violet replied. "But this is hard. I'm sorry you found out this way."

"It is, but she looked happy. And I've never seen her look like that."

"Then talk to her. Tell her what you saw and how you felt. I'm sure she'll listen to you. She seems levelheaded. Not like my mom."

"Am I ever going to meet your mom?" Charlie asked. He meant it as a friend, but he realized it came out a little more serious than it probably should have. Violet's eyes widened for a moment, and a dark blush settled over her cheeks.

"Um, probably not."

"You never talk about her."

"It's not a fun story," she said slowly. "My mom and I don't get along."

"I figured that. Can I ask why not?"

Violet sighed and was silent for a long moment. "After my dad left, she became obsessed with money. I would get yelled at for wasting food, or needing any money spent on me. And then she landed a high-paying job, but it was never enough. Suddenly everything was a way to get ahead. We constantly had to have the nicest house, or the nicest phones, and there was nothing else. I disappointed her by becoming a teacher, and she's always told me I need to be able to support myself. And now I'm not."

So much more made sense now. Charlie could see why she never wanted to accept help. Why she lived in a shitty apartment rather than get a roommate. How she felt she needed to contribute to everything rather than let someone take care of her.

"Anyway," Violet continued, "it's a sad story. I got out when I could and I'm fine now."

"Violet, that's terrible."

She shrugged. "She tells me I need to use my friends to get a job. In her eyes, people are stepping stones, and my friends aren't doing that for me."

"And she said all of this to you? Directly?"

Violet nodded. "Yes, all of it directly. I spent a lot of my college years trying to see it some other way and trying to make her words into something they weren't. But when my dad walked out, I think something in her snapped. All she cares about is money and status. And she's said that. I've given my mom a hundred chances to be anything but what she is, and she hasn't, so . . . I stopped trying. That's why she's never around. I've even started avoiding her calls. I mean, maybe getting a different job would fix things but . . ."

"Would it?"

"I don't know. I've never had an offer." There was something in her eyes, something distant. She sighed. "But I got an interview today."

"For a higher-paying job?"

"Yeah."

"Why don't you look happy about it?" Charlie asked.

"It's . . . it's across the country. I'd have to move."

Charlie blinked, something in him crumbling. Even before they'd buried the hatchet, Violet had always been near him. She was a constant force in his life. And imagining her leaving, especially now, would be like losing a limb.

"Are you . . . wanting to do that?" He asked, his throat dry.

"I don't know," she admitted. "But I know I don't make enough here. I won't get promoted soon, and . . ." She shrugged. "I don't want to move, but maybe it wouldn't be terrible."

Wouldn't be terrible? Well, it certainly would for him.

"Have you told Liv?"

She shook her head.

Charlie was torn between being proud he was the first to know, and terrified she was thinking about leaving.

"I'm sorry," Violet said. "You had a rough day. I shouldn't have sprung this on you."

"No," Charlie told her. "Thank you for telling me."

"Are you mad?"

"Not at all," he replied, and that was the truth. But it also wasn't. He had to clench his jaw to keep from begging her to stay, to not go after this job, whatever it was.

But then she could resent him, and that would be worse.

"It sounds promising. Let me know how the interview goes," he said, even though the words were hard to actually say.

"Are you sure?" she asked, eying him warily. He forced a smile on his face, but she didn't look convinced. He took a deep breath and then stood. He walked over to her chair, kneeling to plant his hands on her shoulders.

"I am," he told her. "You need to do whatever you think is right."

Violet looked him in the eyes, and he could have sworn her gaze was piercing into his soul. But he wouldn't tell her not to be independent, not to at least try to find a better job. It didn't matter how much he wanted her to stay.

She looked conflicted for a moment, and he could feel her eyes mirrored in his own. They hadn't talked about what they had done the night before, but he made sure not to let her feel like a one-night stand, not something to be used.

He stood, and pulled her up with him.

Violet leaned forward, resting her head on his chest. He took the weight gratefully, happy she wasn't pulling away when she easily could. Maybe this wouldn't last forever, and maybe it wouldn't even last another month, but he had it for now. And he didn't want to let it go.

"I'm sorry," she said, her voice muffled. "I don't even want to have to consider it."

"But I know you would regret it if you didn't."

Violet was silent, and it was all the confirmation he needed that he was right.

"Don't worry about it," he said. "You make your decision after you have an interview and if you like the new job. I'll be there for you either way."

"And if I do move?" she asked, pulling away to look him in the eye.

"Then . . . we'll figure that out too."

Violet blinked, her eyes looking dangerously wet. But then she reached up to kiss him, and he knew he had said the right thing. Even though this hurt, and it would kill him if she left, he couldn't bring himself to regret being there for her.

"It's freezing tonight," he said casually, pulling away. "I could start a fire if you wanted?"

Violet smiled at him and nodded. "That sounds great."

They didn't talk more about the job that night. Instead, Charlie focused on her, on spending time with her while he had her because it could easily end at any time. They went to his room, and he held her close while she fell asleep. Roo laid on his leg that night, as if she understood how conflicted he was.

He didn't know if he would have any answers by morning, but he was happy to have Violet now.

Chapter Twenty-One

Violet

Violet woke up in Charlie's room. She felt drained, dreading her interview later in the day. She shouldn't, since it looked like a perfect job on paper, but there was something about how Charlie looked at her that broke her heart.

She didn't get to talk to him much since she needed extra time to look nice for her virtual meeting after work. She only had time for a quick breakfast with him and then had to rush out the door to get to school.

Violet had a busy day planned. Her interview was at the end of the day, and she was planning on having lunch with Liv to catch up. This was her perfect opportunity to tell Liv about the job.

Her morning was a blur of teaching and helping students. By the time lunch rolled around, she managed to forget some of her anxieties.

Their plan was to meet at a small sandwich shop in walking distance of Violet's school. Since Liv had to drive, Violet arrived early. She waited out front until she saw Liv pull into the parking lot, and then her anxiety returned.

Violet had so much to catch Liv up on.

"Oh my God, why is traffic so bad?" Liv complained when she finally joined Violet.

"It's mainly the lack of public transportation."

Liv sighed. "You're right and I hate that you're right. How is your day going? Anything fun happening?"

Violet bit her lip as she joined the line. Her first thought was the fact she and Charlie had slept together. Then she figured she should go for the easier item first. "Um, someone reached out to me about a job."

"Wait, really? What kind of job?"

"It's sort of in education, but not on the front end. It's more of an office job, but it pays $80,000."

"Wow. That's almost double what you make now."

"I know."

Liv was beaming. "That's amazing!"

"I agree," Violet said. "But the only catch is that it's in Arizona."

Liv's smile faded as the shock of Violet's news washed over her. "That's . . . exciting?"

"It is, but I don't know if I would want to leave."

The conversation paused while both of them ordered their food.

"I know how trapped you've felt in this job," Liv said once they were done. "You love it, but your real dream is making enough money to be independent."

Was it? It should have been, but teaching had done something to her. It had shifted something to make her almost whole.

Except for the money aspect. She was still depending on Charlie, after all.

"Yeah, it is. And it's technically in education. Just more on the data side."

"That kind of stuff was what you were going for when you first started college. Maybe this is for the best."

"Yeah, maybe it is."

"I can't believe I'm asking this, but did you tell Charlie?" Liv asked. "You said you're helping him pay bills, right?"

"I did," Violet said. She tried not to think about the look on his face. "He was supportive about it."

"Wow," Liv said. "You already brought it up to him? This isn't like you. I almost want to get you a cake to celebrate your budding communication skills."

"Charlie and I like strawberry," Violet said, smiling ruefully.

"You two have even got cake flavors in common," Liv said with a shake of her head. "If it weren't for your history together, I'd say you should date him."

Violet stilled in her eating.

Liv caught it.

"I... shouldn't have said that," she said. "I know dating would be so weird with everything you guys went through. And it's good you guys get along. Ugh, I never want to be that person pushing my friends together. Forget I said that, okay?"

Violet felt her brain slowly come back online. Her first thought was about Charlie and how they had six years of fighting in their history. What the fuck were they doing sleeping together, even if it was mind-altering, amazing sex? Were they ruining this by taking it further?

No, her mind answered. *Because you both wanted this, and it's one of the best things you've ever gone for.*

But it could easily fall apart. He once said feelings could fade. When was that going to happen to them?

"Violet?" Liv said. "Did I ruin lunch with my dumb comment?"

"N-no." Violet put down her sandwich. "I have something to tell you, though."

Liv blinked and then carefully leaned back. "Okay. I might have a feeling where this is going."

"Where do you think this is going?"

"I think you're about to tell me you like Charlie."

"Oh, well..."

Liv sighed. "I saw it at dinner, and it's cute, but I think you may be confusing feelings for kindness. It has to be a complete turnaround from where you were before."

"Wait, hang on. You think I like him because he's being nice to me?"

"Honestly, yeah."

Oh, it was so beyond that.

"No, I know I have feelings for Charlie. That wasn't the problem."

"Oh, no, please don't tell me you asked him out."

"I didn't. I slept with him."

Liv's jaw dropped. "What?"

"Yeah."

"No, no. You're kidding. He has the redhead who acts like she's better than us, remember?"

"Charlie broke it off with her. I was there when he did it."

"When was this?"

"Your wedding night."

"What happened? Why did he break it off?"

"To make a long story short, Lauren was behind why Charlie and I were fighting, and when he found out, it was the last straw."

Liv threw down her sandwich, eating forgotten. "Wait, you guys finally talked about what happened? The school-related thing you refuse to go into detail about?"

"Yep . . ." Violet felt her face heat, but she ignored it. "And I know you're dying to know, so I can tell you why. It was an essay right before we graduated."

"An essay? You asked Charlie for help with something school related? You never asked anyone for help."

"This was important to me. I wanted to get it right, and I swore him to secrecy about it."

"So . . . an essay. Why would that cause you to fight for six years?"

"Lauren borrowed Charlie's laptop and left cruel feedback all over it, pretending to be him . . . like cyberbullying-level awful. And then I went off on him about it, but he thought he had only sent a couple polite comments."

"Why all the secrecy though? Why not tell me?"

"Because . . ." Violet sighed. It *still* hurt to bring up. Even now. "I was thinking about grad school. It was my statement of intent for my application. And the comments were too hard to read. I didn't want to tell you the truth and have to admit that I failed."

"Violet!" Liv said, reaching across the table to smack Violet's arm. "I totally would have supported you!"

"I know! But hearing I was only ever good enough to be a teacher, plus the fact I thought it was from someone that I trusted, made me unable to share it. I believed it. And it hurt."

"You really thought he said that?'

"Yes. And he thought he sent something else. So, when I asked him about it, he stood by what he said."

"That conniving bitch."

"I know, but we talked it out and we're okay now. Lauren came by to try to smooth things over with Charlie, but he was done with her after she lied to him for six years."

"Um, yeah. He'd better be. Hang on, when did you sleeping with him come into the equation?"

"The party."

"Micah's party? After Elijah exploded at you?"

"Yeah, but we both knew we liked each other at that point."

"When did that happen?"

"The night before. We agreed not to act on it, but . . . we went back on that. We're in this weird stage where we're kind of together, but with the job . . ."

"Wait, all of this is happening and he's still being supportive about it?"

"He said we'd figure it out."

"I've gotta reevaluate everything I know now."

"Is it that hard to believe we communicated?"

"I'm going from never being allowed to mention his name, to you being *with* him. It's a huge jump."

"I know. But it wasn't for us. Once Lauren was gone it was like flipping a light switch, like we were always meant to be friends."

"You used to be, before everything went downhill, but then it got worse and worse."

"I know," Violet said. "I was angry and hurt for what I thought he did, and he had Lauren telling him I was a terrible person. I had never told anyone my real reason for hating him, so I never got talked down from my own ledge. It exploded the rare times we saw each other. But then we *had* to see each other because of the apartment issue and then . . . it's like it is now."

"What you're telling me is I should have locked Lauren in a supply closet for a few weeks and it would have all worked out?"

Violet shrugged. "Maybe."

"So . . . you guys are almost dating, and you're still thinking about this job?"

Violet sighed, feeling her mood crash at the thought. "I think I have to. It doesn't feel great to have to live in someone else's house because I literally can't afford anything else. At the end of the day, he can afford a home with his salary, and I can't. That feels wrong."

Liv sighed. "I get it. I do. I couldn't imagine how you felt losing your apartment."

"I don't want that to happen again."

"Then I guess I have to agree with Charlie. We will support you no matter what you do."

Violet nodded, grateful for her friend's understanding. "Thank you," she replied. "It means a lot to me that you guys are willing to support me, even if I move."

"I love you, Violet. You're my best friend, and I want you to be happy."

Violet felt overwhelmed with emotion for her best friend.

"God," she said after a moment. "Enough about me. What else is going on? I need a distraction before I have this interview."

"I think Lewis is finally done with Elijah," Liv said.

"Really?"

"Yeah, he said he didn't like that Elijah started something when there was finally peace, and Elijah never truly apologized."

"He never does."

"The worst thing I heard was Elijah say you deserved it."

"I definitely didn't."

"No, you didn't, and usually Lewis isn't the type to argue with him, but he did. I think the smoke screen has finally cleared."

"Good," Violet said. "I don't want to see him again. Ever."

"Neither do I," Liv added. "But you did put him in his place."

"I guess I did. I hate that I was a part of another fight at a party."

"Psh, that wasn't a fight. It was a complete takedown."

"Still. Charlie and I earned a reputation, but I'm the one who can't keep a level head."

"Just because you didn't take shit doesn't mean you can't keep a level head. He came at you with comments about your body."

"That's what I hate about Elijah. He goes places not even Charlie did. At least with Charlie, it was petty shit that didn't mean anything."

"I don't know about that. It may have been petty, but all your fighting *did* have a certain tone to it."

"What kind of tone?"

"Micah said multiple times that you two should fuck and get over it already."

"She what?"

"You both subtly complimented each other without complimenting each other, and there was a line neither of you crossed."

"Ugh, that's embarrassing."

"Sorry, girl. I never said anything because I thought you would have killed me if I told you that you might have been attracted to him."

"Yeah, you're probably right."

"Besides, what you were fighting about was serious. I know you, and while it might have seemed petty, there had to be some real hurt under it. I didn't want to belittle it by making it a sexual thing."

"Yeah . . . even if it was Lauren's doing."

"She's a bitch," Liv said. "Let me see her in public. She can catch these hands."

Violet laughed, and they chatted for a while longer before Violet knew she had to get back to work.

When she was at her desk, Violet grew nervous for her interview. It was set for five, right after Jason left, and before she had to get home.

Her day flew by, and by the time five rolled around, her nerves had only multiplied.

It had been six years since she interviewed for any position. She was not ready for it.

Violet was interviewing with a woman named Lindsay Roberts on a Zoom call. She was older, with graying hair and heavy makeup.

"Hello, is this Violet Moore?" Lindsay asked the moment Violet got into the Zoom meeting.

Violet blinked, a little put off by the question. "Yes, I'm Violet. How are you today?"

"That's inconsequential," Lindsay replied. Violet blinked at the answer. "I'm here to talk about your experience. Are you ready?"

"Sure," Violet replied slowly, trying to keep calm. Was this seriously how this woman operated? Were there no pleasantries?

There wasn't much experience to talk about since she had only worked at the school for the length of her career, but Violet tried to connect it to the current position the best she could. A lot of online resources said to focus on results, and Violet had plenty of that.

She talked about how her average test scores were the highest in the district, how she connected with her work on a personal level. She spoke about how much she enjoyed education and was proud to make it better for kids.

Lindsay listened with a straight face. Violet wondered if she was doing well or terrible, and which would be worse.

"I think I've asked all I can," Lindsay said, bringing Violet out of her thoughts. "We'll be in touch."

"Wait," Violet asked. "I want to ask how you found me. I didn't even apply for this position."

"A mutual contact recommended you."

"Who?"

"My niece, Lauren Sheffield. I don't normally listen to recommendations from family members, but due to Lauren's impressive background and impeccable record, I thought it might be worth looking into you."

Violet barely heard the rest of her sentence "L-Lauren. Oh, I think I know a Lauren."

"Yes. She said she knows you through college and her boyfriend. If that answers your question, then we are done here."

Violet didn't even say goodbye. She was too shocked. The meeting ended, and she found herself staring at her desktop.

Lauren was behind this? The same woman who wanted Violet as far away from Charlie as possible? She felt like she was going to be sick.

Lindsay, her possible future boss, was *related* to Lauren.

She also seemed to have Lauren's pointed attitude, but in a biting, professional way. Violet didn't know how she would do working with someone like that.

She took a few deep breaths, knowing she was moments away from a panic attack. Her mother would say this was perfect. She was using her connection to someone to get ahead in life.

But she *hated* this. Lauren obviously wanted her out of the picture, and Lindsay wasn't a friendly boss. She would be miserable. Independent, with nothing to it. Besides, this interview made her look back on her career, on all the pain, tears, work, and reward.

And she had loved every second of it.

"Ms. Moore?" a voice asked. "Are you all right?"

She looked up to find Dr. Jones in her classroom.

"Hey," she said, her voice only slightly shaking. "Yeah, I'm fine."

"Why are you still here?" he asked, frowning. "Usually you leave by five."

Violet wasn't sure what to say, so she settled on the truth. "I . . . had a job interview. It's for somewhere out of state."

"I wasn't aware you were looking."

"Well, with inflation, I have to have a roommate now, and I want a job I can afford to live on my own with."

"Is that all? Is there anything I've done?"

"No, Dr. Jones. It's only the pay, and I know you don't control the yearly raises."

Dr. Jones sighed. "You're a great teacher, Violet. Losing you would be a step back for the school."

"Thank you, but I'm not even sure I'm going to take it. The thing is . . . I like teaching. I like the kids here, and I like you. But . . ."

"The pay isn't enough. I completely understand."

"I wish it was," and Violet wished it wasn't *Lauren* of all people helping her with it.

"Teaching is a forgotten profession, but a necessary one. I've gotten the school board to still offer pensions and good health benefits, but for so many, it's still not enough. I won't try to convince you out of it, but I will say we would be losing a top-notch teacher."

Violet gave him a wobbly smile. "Thank you. It means a lot to me."

Dr. Jones nodded. "Now, you go home. There's no good reason for you to be here this late."

Violet nodded, still unsure of what to do. But Dr. Jones was right. She needed to get home. She needed to tell Charlie about her interview.

Charlie

With Violet at work late for her interview, Charlie had a rare free night. His initial plan was to get a little work done. Maybe he could code a few things or work on emails, but he found himself unsure if he could even focus despite being in the office, where that usually wasn't a problem.

Something felt so off about Violet's opportunity, like there was a piece of it missing. He resisted the urge to look up the position and tried his best to focus on work.

It didn't seem to help.

He decided to research Phoenix. Was it a safe city? Would she be okay there? Everything he read indicated she would be, but he wanted a reason to get her to stay. He wanted something he could pull out of his back pocket to make her want to be with him.

But he couldn't find anything. He was almost grateful when his phone rang, and he saw it was Lewis calling him.

"Hey, man," he answered, closing his laptop.

"Why did I just get off of the phone with Liv who is excited you and Violet are dating?"

"What?" Charlie said ineloquently.

"Violet apparently told her you two were a thing, which is odd because you told me this wouldn't happen between you two."

"Liv found out from Violet? She told her?"

"At least try to deny it, Charlie."

"I didn't want to lie to you."

Lewis groaned. "What happened?"

"I don't know. It did. What I'm more surprised about is the fact Violet was willing to talk about it at all."

"You're playing a dangerous game here."

"I'll be fine. Besides, I don't know why you're not at least somewhat happy. This is the first time I'm with someone that's not Lauren."

"I'm worried you're with her because she hurt you like Lauren always did. Like you've become some kind of masochist."

"That's not why I'm with her," Charlie said firmly. "I'm with her because she's forgiving, and because she makes me a better person. She's not unnecessarily cruel, and she lets shit go, Lewis. You were there at dinner. We were fine."

Lewis sighed. "I *am* happy it's not Lauren this time. I am, Charlie. But I'm also worried."

"You always are."

"I know I am. I have a hard time looking on the bright side, and I want to, but I can't stop thinking about how mean you were to her, and vice versa."

"I'm not saying we've ignored that and moved on. I'm saying we remember and are trying to be better. That's all we can do."

"You know she's interviewing for a job out of state, right?"

"I do." How could he forget?

"And what do you think about that?"

"I think I want her to stay here, but I don't want to tell her because it's her decision. I know about her mom, and what she always said to Violet, and I get why she feels the need to try to not depend on me. So even if it hurts, I have to let her."

Lewis was silent.

"What?" Charlie asked. "I can feel you thinking through the phone."

"I never thought I would hear you sound so mature when talking about Violet. That's the *exact* right thing to do."

Charlie sighed. "And it's not fun."

Lewis was quiet for another moment.

"I'm sorry I'm being negative about this," Lewis finally said. "And I want it to work out, but if she moves . . ."

If she moves, it might be over. He couldn't even bear to think about it. The idea of losing her was something that would cut him to the bone.

"I don't know what she will choose. She's interviewing for the job today, so I'll hear about it tonight."

"If she stays, then I'll work on being better about all of this. I saw how you handled her with Elijah, and I hear you being better now."

"That's all I can ask." Charlie could feel the relief hitting him. Finally, Lewis was on his side.

"And about Elijah . . . was he always like this?"

Charlie sighed, trying to come up with the right words. "To people he sees as beneath him? Yeah. I canceled your bachelor party because he went behind your back to hire strippers. He completely used Violet . . ." Charlie closed his eyes as he felt the rage hit him over that particular fact. "But I think he liked feeling liked by you, so he put on his best face when you were around."

"Why did he snap then?"

"I think Violet pushed him over the edge. He came at her when she was setting up the venue for the wedding. Plus . . . the bachelor party thing, which he was pretty upset about. I think his need for revenge overrode his need to be liked."

"That asshole. I called him last night to try and hear his side. When he said Violet deserved it, I blocked him."

"Good," Charlie said. "I know you like to keep the peace between friends. You don't want to lose anyone, but he was not someone worth keeping."

"I know," Lewis said sadly. "I did the right thing."

"Thank you," Charlie said genuinely. "I fucking hate that guy."

"Apparently you weren't alone. You don't have to worry. He's gone."

Charlie nodded. At least one problem was solved.

"Hey," Lewis said. "Liv is calling me, probably to talk about dinner. I'll talk to you later?"

"Yeah, man," Charlie said. He gave Lewis his goodbyes and hung up. Once he did, he figured he could check his notifications while he was at it.

He paused when he saw a LinkedIn notification. It had been years since Charlie looked for a job, but he kept his profile up-to-date just in case of a layoff; they weren't uncommon in the tech world.

Charlie checked the notification and immediately saw the last person he wanted to see.

Lauren had invited him to connect.

Charlie glanced at her profile. He didn't even feel anything for her sharp features or red hair. He only felt pissed she was even reaching out to him. He immediately blocked her. He wondered if there were any more apps she would try.

But why was she trying now? She'd been leaving him alone for weeks.

Charlie shook his head and packed up his laptop to leave. He didn't need to be thinking about his ex, not when he had things going on with Violet.

He drove home, still perplexed and feeling a little guilty. Would Violet be mad if she found out Lauren contacted him? Had he done something to somehow invite this into his life?

When he arrived home, he headed straight for the couch to plop down and wait. Violet wasn't too far behind him, pulling into the driveway a few minutes later.

"How did it go?" Charlie asked the moment she walked in.

"Hello to you too," she said as she took off her coat. She leaned down to pet Roo as she always did after coming through the front door.

"Sorry, I guess I'm nervous for you." And for himself.

"It's okay. I think I did well. The manager was a little off-putting though. She was so . . . professional. Almost too professional."

"Do you think you would work well with her?"

Please say no.

Violet shrugged. "I can work with anyone."

She wasn't wrong about that. When Violet put her mind to it, she had even made it work with him while she still hated him.

"But will you like it?"

Violet stared out the window, eyes dull. She sighed. "There's something else I found out today. Something big."

"Okay," Charlie said. "Hit me with it."

Violet looked at him fully.

"Lauren recommended me for the job."

Chapter Twenty-Two

Violet

Charlie's demeanor changed quickly.

"What?" he asked, his voice hard.

"I found out in the interview that Lauren recommended me for the job."

"Have you been in contact with her?"

"God, no," Violet said, feeling sick even thinking about it. "I would never. I only found out today, I promise."

"So that's why she tracked down my LinkedIn."

"She *what*?" She was shocked.

"She requested to connect on LinkedIn. Obviously I blocked her, but if she was the one who recommended you for this job, then that would explain why she's reaching out to me now."

"She's trying to get me out of the picture . . ." The idea was disgusting, and it made her feel even worse that she *had* to consider it.

"This changes things. I guess this means you're not taking it?"

Violet paused. She opened her mouth, hoping she could find the words to explain everything to him, but they escaped her.

"Seriously, Violet?" Charlie's eyes went wide. "You're considering a job Lauren got for you?"

It was too close to how he used to talk to her.

"I don't know," Violet said, defensiveness creeping up her spine. "All I know is I can't afford anything with my job now and I'd like to be able to survive on my own."

"Come on, Violet. This isn't the way to do it."

"What other way is there? Am I supposed to depend on you forever?"

"But she's manipulating you!"

"I know!" Violet said. "I know, and it sucks. If I didn't hate how little I got paid then of course I wouldn't consider it."

"But is this a job you'd even like? Is this what you want?"

"I don't know. I don't know anything other than I'm scared about my living situation. I don't own this house. We never made an official lease. You could wake up one day and fucking kick me out!"

"Do you really think I'd do that to you?"

"Stranger things have happened to us, Charlie. You said it yourself: feelings aren't forever. They change. You like me now and then I'll screw up and we'll hate each other again."

Charlie glared at her. "I said that about love not . . . not . . ." He trailed off. "I won't change my mind."

"And I'm supposed to trust you? After you've said feelings change?"

"Yes! If you don't trust me, then why are even doing this?"

"It's not about trust—"

"But it is! You aren't seeing that I've changed. You've changed. We, as a couple, have changed."

"And we could change back!"

"How? We solved the problem that caused all of this. We don't fight anymore!"

"We're fighting now!" Violet yelled.

"Because you're letting my ex manipulate you."

"What other options do I have, Charlie?"

"You don't have to do this."

"You don't get it!"

"Violet, how could you be so *stupid*?" He slammed his hand on the coffee table. A nearby cup came dangerously close to tipping over, reminding Violet of the engagement party when a drink had gone flying.

She jumped back, chest heaving. She wanted to scream at him, to tell him to fuck off and to leave her to fuck up her own life, but then she remembered.

She wasn't at the engagement party, and they weren't *enemies*. They were supposed to be friends. Maybe something more.

Violet squeezed her eyes shut. Her heart was racing and she felt like this was the beginning of their descent back into hating each other. She turned away from him, loathing how afraid she was. Was this the end? Was he going to tell her they weren't friends anymore? Did he hate her again?

But there was no more yelling. Only silence. Violet turned, staring fearfully at Charlie, who looked as scared as she did.

"I . . ." he said, his voice shaky. "I'm sorry. I never should have insulted you like that."

Violet let the apology calm her. She took a moment to breathe before she answered.

"I'm sorry too," she replied, her voice as weak as his. "For even considering this."

"I don't want to fight," he said slowly. "This feels . . . *wrong* now."

"I know. It's too close to how it used to be."

Charlie let out a long sigh. "It's not how it used to be. I'm-I'm worried you're making a mistake."

"I understand," Violet said. "And I'm worried too. I'm not taking any of this lightly."

"Do you want me to let it go?" Charlie asked. "I can."

Violet thought about it, and then found herself shaking her head.

"It's just . . ." Charlie started, and then paused, trying to find the right words. "I know you feel like you need to be independent, but would leaving be better than staying here? With us?"

"Of course not," she replied. "And I know that, but I also know I feel like a failure for not even being able to afford an apartment and I-I'm so tired. I've always struggled to get by, and this is a chance for me not to."

"Violet, it's tough for us all. I make a decent amount of money, but I could barely afford my old place in the city. I got lucky I inherited this. Micah works her ass off and has nice things, but no free time. And Liv and Lewis have dual income. Hell, I need a dual income to even start working on this place. You're not alone, and it's okay to need someone."

"Yeah, but . . . that's usually when they leave."

The words hung in the air for a long time.

"I'm right here, Violet."

"I know all of this. I do," Violet said, "and I hate that I have such a hard time with it."

"I know it has to be miserable."

"I still need to think," she said, sighing. "And that doesn't mean I'm going to accept or anything, but I need to . . . I need to think."

Charlie took a deep breath. "Okay, but if you need anything . . ."

"I know," she said. "I know."

She headed upstairs where she could be alone. Her mind was a mess, and the traitorous part of it wanted to take the job if it was offered so she didn't have to deal with all the feelings staying could provide.

But she also didn't know if she wanted to move. She didn't know if it was the right thing to do. Plus, Lauren's involvement, Lauren who obviously pulled strings to get Violet the interview . . .

Evening turned into night, and Violet knew she needed to sleep on it. She went to bed, only to toss and turn as she kept thinking about Lauren. Even Roo avoided her after 2 a.m. once it was obvious she would never settle down.

The next day, Violet didn't know if she could even go to work. She opened her old laptop and looked up Lauren.

Violet read about Lauren's cases, how she went for the highest bid, and how she had recently won a case of a dog attacking a child.

She was on the dog's side.

Is this the kind of help she wanted? Is this the future she wanted? To be like her mother and only take jobs that took her soul?

Violet waited for Charlie to leave before she walked out the door herself. She didn't go to work. Instead, she went downtown to Lauren's office. She needed to see her, to be reminded of how terrible she truly was, to be reminded why this could potentially be a bad choice.

It was a high-rise; Violet doubted Lauren would settle for anything else. She was at the top of the building as a part of the law firm she owned. It should have been intimidating, but Violet was too focused to care.

Lauren's assistant glared when Violet approached. "Do you have an appointment?" she asked in a nasally, irritated voice.

"I'm Violet Moore. Lauren knows me."

"I seriously doubt that. She's busy and doesn't have time for—"

"She's gonna make time," Violet said.

"Ah, Violet," another familiar voice came. Violet felt herself tense as she turned. Lauren looked as beautiful and perfect as ever, but she tried not to focus on that. Underneath the flawless facade was nothing but spite. "What a surprise. Come in." The assistant turned red in the face. Violet gave her a fake smile before following Lauren.

Lauren sat at a huge glass desk that overlooked the city. It was far too showy and probably way too expensive. It matched her personality perfectly.

"You recommended me for a job."

"In Phoenix, right?" Lauren said, looking at her nails. "Probably hard to live with Charlie if you're all the way out there."

"So that's why you're doing this? To get me away from Charlie?"

"And out of the goodness of my heart, of course" Lauren added. Violet rolled her eyes. "Come on, even I know teachers don't get paid jack shit. You do deserve more."

"By more, you mean I'd be across the country?"

"Call it an added benefit."

"Why? Why do all of this?"

"Can I not do something for charity?"

"No, you can't. Everything has a reason with you."

Lauren stared and then leaned forward in her chair. "I don't owe you an explanation."

"No, you don't, but I figure you want to make it hurt as much as possible. I bet you let Lindsay tell me you recommended me. You want me to know what you're doing."

"Smart, as always, Violet. That's the thing about you. Charlie loves smart girls, but he also loves nice ones."

"I know you want me away from Charlie, but am I really worth all of this?"

"Let's just say you and I are alike in one way. You want to have money, and I can offer you that."

"How the hell would you know that?"

"Nancy Moore has a lot to say about you."

Violet laughed. "You found my mother? Seriously?"

"Charlie is mine, Violet. So yes, I will look into whoever is taking him away from me."

"But you've been at this for years! It started in college when we were only friends."

"You two were never *friends*," Lauren hissed out the last word.

"What does that mean?"

Lauren laughed humorlessly. "He met you and it was like he was looking at the stars themselves. All he could talk about was Violet this and Violet that, and he was *my* boyfriend."

"I . . ." Violet paused. She *knew* he had liked her since college, but it still made her heart race to think about.

Lauren huffed. "You act all embarrassed now, but I knew you were into him, just by the way you looked at him."

"So, you made us hate each other? Because it looked like we liked each other? And now you're trying to get me to move across the country because Charlie and I are friends? Are you out of your mind?"

"It's a win-win. He gets me back and you get to finally live your dreams with a mountain of cash out in the desert."

"I'd be alone."

"If I recall correctly, you like that."

Well . . . maybe she did. But she had also been lonely. Now? Now things were different.

"Let me give you some advice," Lauren started. "You like to appear to be a nice girl, but you want the money. Take it. Your problems with your mom and all your insecurities would be gone. I mean, look at me. I'm doing great."

"You're literally stalking someone your ex helped out of the goodness of his heart."

"I'm only taking what's mine."

"What's the point in doing this if you're happy with your life?" Violet asked, shaking her head. "And if I do what you want me to, I wouldn't be happy either. Money doesn't solve problems other than ones it can buy. My mother has no friends, only connections. If her house collapsed, she would have no one. But that wasn't what happened to me. I have *friends*. I don't have to manipulate them into caring for me; I don't have to buy friendship. They just do, and I'm not going to turn my back on that for any kind of money."

Violet was out of breath, but the decision settled within her, giving her a sense of peace she hadn't known since finding out about this job. She hadn't realized what she felt until she was looking at the embodiment of who her mother wanted her to be. Now it all seemed simple.

"Is it not enough then?" Lauren asked slowly. "Do you need more money?"

"I don't care about the money." Violet shook her head. "I care about having a life worth living. If I do this, I'm not sure I will have that."

Lauren opened her mouth to say something, but Violet decided she was done. She turned to walk away.

"Hey!" Lauren called. "I'm not done! I can give you what you want!"

"No, you can't," Violet said as she neared the door. She turned for one last smile in Lauren's direction. "Because I want to be myself, and I want to do that with Charlie. You could never give me that."

It was all so much clearer now. Money hadn't given her mother happiness, and it certainly didn't give it to Lauren, not if she was still chasing Charlie.

It was time to stop. Yes, she was broke. Yes, she had to depend on someone else. But she had a job she loved and excelled at and friends who cared.

And most of all, she would have Charlie.

Charlie

Charlie couldn't go to work. He tried. He even pulled into his office building's parking lot, but he knew his head wasn't in it. He was thinking about Violet, because of course he was. He was always thinking of her in some capacity, but now he was desperate to know what she was thinking.

He didn't know who to talk to about it. Lewis and Liv were out. They had spent enough time being in the middle of their issues. Damon hadn't said whether or not he was on Elijah's side after the incident at Micah's party, and there was no one else he trusted to know about this.

Well, except for his mother.

He needed to talk to her. Maybe fixing some of their problems would lead to clarity about him and Violet. Charlie made a U-turn in the parking lot and drove the hour to his mother's.

She lived in a newer house than his, but it was nice. This was the home he grew up in. He rarely got to visit since it was on the outskirts of town, but when he did, it was just as he remembered.

But as much as he would love to get lost in the small garden his mom kept, or check out the old treehouse in the backyard, he needed to talk to her about things. He needed to open up this uncomfortable secret between them, and he needed to talk about Violet.

The sun was hidden behind clouds in the dull winter sky, and it was chillier than usual. But Charlie was too nervous to care about any of that. Mara's car was in the driveway, and he knew she'd be there at this time since she worked from home.

He knocked firmly, stepping back to give her space to open the door.

"Charlie?" she said. "What are you doing here? Is everything okay?"

"Yes, mom. I'm fine, but I think we need to talk."

Mara frowned, but stepped aside to let him in. He entered, feeling the air grow warm. He shrugged off his jacket and took another deep breath.

"What's going on?" she asked nervously.

Charlie paused. He wanted to ask about Violet first, but he also needed to know if his mother had lied to him. And standing there, in his childhood home, looking his mother in the eye, he knew that was more important.

"Are you seeing someone?" he asked, giving her a chance to say it herself.

For a moment, he was worried she'd lie. Maybe she wasn't truly ready.

"I am," she replied. "How did you know?"

"You guys were having dinner the other day at that Italian place on the north side of town. I was picking up dinner when I saw you."

"The Italian place? But you never go there."

Charlie frowned. "You specifically picked somewhere I wouldn't go?"

His mother sighed and looked away guiltily. "I wasn't sure how to tell you."

"So, you hid it from me."

"I did. But you have to understand, Charlie. It's a big thing. Dating a woman is so—"

"You think that's what I'm worried about? I don't care who you date as long as you're happy."

"But... I never told you."

"Told me what?"

"That I'm-I'm interested in woman. Only women."

Charlie stared. His mom looked nervous, as if he was going to run off as she said it. Did his grandparents know? Charlie hadn't seen them in years—only his Gigi Ruth, up until she passed, but he remembered how his grandparents were old-fashioned, how they hated how new age Mara and Gigi Ruth had become.

Maybe they weren't accepting. Maybe his mother was afraid he wouldn't be accepting either.

"Mom, that's okay. I don't care at all."

Mara looked relieved. "I know I should have told you."

"Yeah. Maybe."

"I also didn't expect for it to happen so fast. I met her and suddenly everything was falling into place, like she was always meant to be here and I..."

His mother paused, but Charlie didn't mind. All he could think about was how that sounded familiar.

Too familiar.

"I want to know this part of you," he told her. "If you're happy, I'm happy."

Mara sighed deeply. "Thank you, Charlie. This means *so* much to me." She hugged him tightly, and he could feel how much of the tension was rolling off her.

"Are you in love with her?" Charlie asked, curiously.

"I am... yes," she replied. "Is that okay?"

"Of course it's okay. But when I was a kid, I thought I remembered you telling me that love falls apart, and it ends. Is that what you said?"

"Not entirely. Sometimes love ends, but not all the time. And with your father ... it was never real love. More like duty. It didn't end. It never started."

"Did you know that then?"

"No," Mara said grimly. "I didn't. And I can see how you'd think I meant it, but when love is real, you know it, Charlie. And you fight for it. You *choose* it. It's so different."

"Violet said something like that."

His mom smiled. "Violet, huh?"

"Mom . . . there's something you should know about Violet."

"What?"

"She's the woman I fought with for six years."

"The one you told me about at lunch? The same one in your house?"

"Yes."

"She seems special."

"She is. She's always been a part of my life, whether we got along or not."

"So then go for it," his mother said. "Take the risk. It's worth it."

Charlie shook his head. "She might be moving. She has a good job opportunity across the country." Charlie sighed. "I-I don't know if she should take it. Lauren is the one that pulled strings to get her the job."

"I wasn't aware Lauren liked to help people."

"She doesn't. She's doing it to get Violet out of the picture, but this job opportunity gives her a chance to be more independent, to finally make enough money to live on her own, and comfortably. She lost her apartment and had to start over, so I get why she's considering it."

"But you don't want her to go."

"What would you do in this situation, mom?"

"Charlie, what I would do is so different than what you would be willing to. For my love I'd . . . I'd follow her anywhere."

Charlie blinked. "You'd move? With her? Just like that?"

"I love her. I love her more than material possessions. She *is* my happiness. Now, she would never ask me *to* move, but I'd do it. I'd do it in a heartbeat."

"Even if I was here?"

"Oh, honey. I could fly back. I could call you on the phone. These days, the world doesn't stop because someone is across the country. But we only get one life, and we have to live it. I don't know your situation with Violet. I don't know if you feel the same deep love that—"

"But mom, I do," he said firmly. "I love her, and if I didn't have Gigi Ruth's house, I'd move."

His mother paused, lips pursed. "You don't have to keep the house, you know. Not if it comes between you and someone you love."

"But she left it to me."

"She was going to leave it to anyone who wanted it. Ruth had a huge family, and you were the one who she thought could use it, but so could your cousins, or your friends. The point of that house was to be loved, and if there is ever a day when you can't do that anymore, then it's okay to let it go."

Charlie blinked. "But I *do* love the house, I . . ."

"It's a house, Charlie. It's not a person, and in my experience, people mean more. If the house was burning, would you save it or Violet?"

"Violet." He didn't miss a beat.

"Exactly," she said. "And I'd feel the same way about you, or your cousins, or my girlfriend. Would I be wrong?"

"No."

"Ruth would be happy knowing it's with someone in the family. Even your chosen family. You've got amazing friends. Maybe they could use it. The point is, you don't have to be tied down to it if it means you're alone."

Could he leave his house for Violet?

He tried to imagine going back to it being empty, but he couldn't. That life wasn't his anymore.

The one with Violet was.

"My job could probably be remote," he said slowly.

"Probably. But I do have to ask something important. The only way this works is if you do with no conditions. Could you do it with without resenting her?"

Charlie thought about it.

Would he resent Violet?

She had not asked this of him. She would never. She fully expected him to stay, but without her, his life would be empty. Even when they hated each other, they always *had* each other. Moving would be odd; he'd never lived anywhere else. But he would have *her*. He could call Lewis, and she could call Liv. They could fly in whenever they wanted to.

But they would be together, and how could he ever resent that?

He didn't *want* to think about moving. But he *chose* to. And he chose her.

"Yeah, I could," he answered. "I really could. It would be hard, but I know we would have each other's backs."

His mother smiled. "That's love, kiddo. You choose it even when it's hard."

That sounded a lot like other advice he had heard on love—like what Violet had said.

"Oh, honey," his mother said. "I am so happy you finally found love. This is all I ever wanted for you."

"Even if I move? Even if it's with someone who was my enemy for six years?"

"Love doesn't have to be *logical*, Charlie. It just has to *be*. I support you when you're happy, and I saw the way you looked at her. I knew it even then."

"I-I think I need to go," he said. "I need to talk to her. I need to see if she if okay with this too."

His mother pulled him into a quick hug before letting him go.

"Go get her, kiddo. You've got this."

Chapter Twenty-Three

Violet

Violet hit send on the email saying she wasn't interested in the position. She was in her car outside Lauren's building, and she took a deep breath, trying and failing to calm her nerves.

It was the right move.

She was going to have to trust Charlie wouldn't screw her over, which was somehow harder than leaving, but she had to stop treating everyone like an enemy.

Lindsay's reply was immediate. Violet deleted the message without reading it. She didn't even care to know. After that, she went on a walk in the cool weather, trying to settle her racing mind. Charlie was going to be happy she said no, and Violet knew Liv would be too, but she had to fight the feeling she somehow failed.

Unlearning things wasn't linear. Sometimes you fell back into old habits and had to remind yourself what was right.

This was one of those moments.

Eventually, her emotions cleared and her feelings faded, so she knew she could go home. Violet was going to be alone for a while, considering it was midday and Charlie was at work.

But she wanted to be in the house. She wanted its familiar walls and warmth. She could tell Charlie the minute he got home, and hope he was okay with her decision to stay.

The drive was short. She had stayed closer to his side of town as the day went on, so she didn't have to go far to get back. She pulled into the driveway into her usual spot.

She didn't even notice Charlie's car until she got out. She stared at it for a moment, unsure if she was hallucinating or if this was real. Then worry hit her. Was he sick? Why wasn't he at work?

When she walked in, he was at the dining room table, working on something. He looked fine, wearing his black-rimmed glasses and a comfortable T-shirt. Violet let out a breath of relief.

"What are you doing here?" she asked.

He stared at her for a long moment, as if he was imagining her there. "I could ask you the same thing."

"I-I needed to think."

"I did too."

Violet stared at him. *Oh shit*, was she about to get dumped?

"Phoenix is a . . . decent city," Charlie said slowly.

Fuck. He was about to tell her she should move. She had already said no. She didn't want to go.

"I did some thinking and talked with my mom," he continued. "I could go with you to Phoenix . . . if you wanted that."

Hang on.

What?

"Wait, you're offering to move *with* me? Charlie . . ." She shook her head, confused. "You have this house. You'd sell it?"

"I have a cousin who's looking for a place. Gigi Ruth only wanted it to stay in the family, and my family is pretty big. If she doesn't want it, then I think Liv and Lewis could use it. They're family too."

Violet only stared. She had no fucking idea what to say. She never imagined he would sell his house.

Not for her, of all people.

"I . . . can't lose you, Violet," he added. "I've never considered moving, but I would be happy to if it meant we could give this a real shot. If you feel this is a good job, and you think you might like it, then I want to go with you."

Violet took in a shaky breath.

He was offering to sell his home . . . for *her*. This was beyond anything she imagined. This was more than she dreamt of—more than she deserved. She struggled to come up with words to describe it.

This was heartfelt. This was memorable.

This was Charlie Davis.

"Violet," he said slowly. "I love you. I love you even though every love I've seen and experienced has fallen apart. You mean more than any material possession I have. And I'm not letting you go because of something as simple as a job. I'll follow you anywhere if you let me."

Violet's heart raced. This was probably the most romantic thing she had ever witnessed, and she hadn't even said anything yet.

At her silence, he added, "And if you want to go alone, that's okay. But I wanted to offer this in case you wanted this too."

She was already planning to stay, but this . . . this was beyond her wildest dreams.

He was *choosing* her. Him—the man who didn't even believe in love, was offering to uproot his life for *her*.

She didn't deserve this. She didn't even know how to begin to express her feelings, or how to tell him she loved this house and she wanted to live in it forever with their roof cat and their weird, green cabinets and scratched table.

She couldn't find the words, so her body took over. She ran to him and kissed him.

And there, with her fingers in his hair, and her lips on his, her mind caught up to her. The feelings she'd ignored came to the surface and she was momentarily overwhelmed by how *right* this all felt.

When she pulled away, Violet was crying. Charlie looked so confused she almost laughed.

"Sorry," she said. "I'm . . . I'm so shocked. You'd move with me?"

"I would. We have a shot at this, and I want to take it."

"I want to take it too."

Charlie smiled. "So, are we doing this?"

"We're doing *part* of this." Violet laughed. "I'm not taking the job."

Charlie looked at her with wide, shocked eyes.

"Really? Why? I thought it was a chance for you to finally get better pay."

"I don't need better pay," Violet said. "I took today off work to confront Lauren about why she tried to get me this job."

"You saw Lauren? Today?"

"Yes, and I realized she's a carbon copy of my mother. She's only done things for money and has nothing else. If I took this job, then I'm trading away what I love for a paycheck. I wouldn't be experiencing a life worth living. I turned them down before I got home."

Charlie smiled softly at her. "That's an . . . incredibly smart way to look at it."

Violet laughed nervously. "It doesn't feel smart, but it was the right thing to do."

"It was, but I was serious about moving though. Now I feel like I overreacted."

"No," Violet said, her laugh turning genuine. "That was the sweetest, most romantic thing I've ever heard."

"Really? I wasn't going for romantic. I was going for committed."

"Well, it worked."

"And I mean it. I'd move if you wanted me to."

"But Lewis and your mom are here."

"I could call them, but calls wouldn't be enough for you."

"You'd resent me."

"I wouldn't because you didn't ask me. It came with no conditions."

Violet felt her eyes grow wet. *Shit.* She wasn't used to unconditional love.

"I-I feel the same. About all of it. I . . ." She was at a loss for words. *Again.* She had never not been able to come up with words in her life. Especially not to Charlie. "Just . . . Thank you," she said, her voice thick with emotion.

"You don't have to thank me for falling in love with you. I would have done that any day."

"Even if the bar is in hell and I'm playing limbo?"

Charlie laughed. "This is an emotional moment, and you bring up *that*?"

"Sorry, I had to break the tension somehow." She wiped at her eyes. "But I'm not leaving. Not ever. You get to have it all."

"I was going to have it all either way," he said, smiling. "As long as you said yes."

"I will *always* say yes. I love you too. Even though you're Charlie Davis."

Charlie laughed. "I'm torn between feeling lucky I have you and kind of insulted."

"Yeah, that's gonna be your future. We *were* enemies after all."

Charlie laughed and pulled her into another kiss. Feeling his warm body against hers cemented that this was real, he was real, and they were doing this.

And she had a good feeling about it too.

Chapter Twenty-Four

Violet

Two Months Later

When Violet woke up, Charlie was behind her with his arm slung over her waist.

She peered around at him, trying to see if he was awake, only to be met with a face full of Roo that left her coughing. She choked for a good minute before she finally was able to breathe again.

Charlie was awake and smiling at her, bemused.

"How did she weasel her way between us?" Violet asked as Roo hopped off the bed, presumably to go eat.

"She's stubborn," Charlie said as he leaned down to kiss her jaw gently. "Just like someone else I know."

A heat stirred in her and her eyes fluttered closed. Charlie's mouth on her jaw was always how he signaled he wanted to take things further, and lucky for him, she didn't have anywhere to be until the afternoon.

Violet slept in shorts and a tank top, and Charlie had on shorts and a shirt. Suddenly all of that felt like too much. She could feel an aching need for him to be able to touch more skin.

They moved at a slow pace. Charlie's hand trailed down to gently cup her breast. They kissed and touched, enjoying the slowness of a new morning.

Layers came off as they leisurely made out, and soon, Charlie was leaning back to ask permission, like he always did.

"You should get a condom," she said in between kisses.

Violet pushed him off her, only to coax him into rolling onto his back when he had put the condom on. She straddled him then, sinking down on him slowly.

Violet brought him up to kiss her again and she slowly moved her hips. This was a position she had only done with Charlie, and it felt good each time they did it. Gone were the days she was shy in bed. Charlie made her feel empowered.

Eventually, his hips moved with hers, finding a pleasurable rhythm that made heat pool in Violet's lower body. There was something about the pressure of the movement that always excited her, making her come without so much as a touch from Charlie.

She kissed him through her orgasm, her body twitching with pleasure. Charlie let her ride it out until he rolled them over and fucked her with the intensity she loved.

And his intensity *never* waned. It gave her enough time to feel herself build again, and as he thrust into her, she came again, which was getting severely addicting.

Charlie followed right after her, tensing as he came with her name on his lips.

"Now that is how you wake up on a Saturday," she said.

"It beats working in the garden," Charlie replied, kissing her cheek.

Violet rolled her eyes. Charlie had *not* found any joy in working in the front garden of the house. He was color-blind to proper mulch colors and hated weeding with a passion.

"If you think you can fuck me out of going outside today, you're mistaken," she said with a smirk.

Charlie laughed and rolled off her. She was covered in sweat, but it didn't matter. She did have a strange and rare Saturday meeting with Dr. Jones, but she could shower before then.

Since they had officially started dating, the only thing that changed was the bedroom Violet slept in. She had moved into Charlie's room, with its warm fireplace and built-in bathroom. Much like before, they split the responsibilities of cooking and cleaning, but now there was the added benefit of making out, snuggling, and phenomenal sex. Violet continued to work on the house while Charlie took on the cat cleanup duty that she hated.

As the weather warmed, Violet discovered gardening. She chatted with the neighbors during the weekend, and she made friends with all the morning walkers who passed by while she was working on the yard. Charlie would bring her coffee and sit with her when he got back from his morning run.

It was bliss.

Violet made true to her promise and went to work on the front garden after breakfast. Violet had strong-armed Charlie into picking black mulch over red at Home Depot, telling him how bad red would look against the white and black exterior. He had given up about thirty minutes into the fight.

It took an hour for Violet to lay it all out, and once she did, Charlie came outside with coffee, eying the new work with a frown.

"Okay, I'll admit it," Charlie said. "It was good we didn't go for red."

Violet stepped back, sweaty and tired from all the work she had done. But it looked amazing. The black mulch matched the newly painted shutters and brought out the bright white of the siding on the house.

"Thank you." Violet smiled at him. "I knew I was right."

"You always are," Charlie muttered, but he kissed her sweaty forehead. "Blegh, I shouldn't have done that."

"Aw, don't you want to give me a hug?"

"I mean, always . . . but maybe not now."

"Come here," Violet said.

Charlie backed away. "No, no. I just showered after my run."

"You can take another one!" Violet yelled, chasing after him. She grabbed him as he turned to open the door. Charlie groaned dramatically but his arms came to wrap around her like they always did.

"Are you happy now?" he muttered.

"Always," she replied. Her phone beeped and she sighed. "I need to get to the school for that meeting with Dr. Jones."

"Kind of stupid that you have to go back in on a Saturday."

"At least I'm not going in for long. It's just a meeting," she replied. "I'm going to shower."

"I guess I'm joining you."

After their shower, Violet arrived at work feeling refreshed. She had worked hard to remove the shame she used to feel when thinking of her job, even going so far as blatantly telling her mother she wasn't going to talk about it.

That conversation had been a difficult one. Her mom never apologized or admitted she was wrong. Violet knew she had no choice but to distance herself. Now, her mom didn't reach out much and Violet had to deal with it. She had been working up to formally introducing herself to Charlie's mom as his girlfriend, but after finding out his mother knew about their fights, she was nervous about it.

Dr. Jones was in his office, looking at something over his computer. He had been so thrilled when she announced she was staying that she almost regretted considering it. She could only hope this meeting wasn't bad news, but he hadn't given her much context.

"Ms. Moore, please sit down," Dr. Jones said.

Violet nodded and sat, her heart racing.

"I have some good news. A student of yours, Jason McMaren, spoke highly of you. His mother too. I forwarded the praise to the superintendent, who wants to offer you a summer position as the head of a new camp for disadvantaged students in the area."

"Wait . . . what?"

"You go above and beyond for your students, and the board recently received funding for a summer institution for those who need a place to go while their parents work. We were looking for someone caring and interested in students who may be having trouble at home. You are the perfect fit."

Violet blinked, trying to take in the words. "Me?"

"Of course," Dr. Jones said, a knowing smile on his face. "I am sorry it took me so long to get all this together, but I think you will love it. The camp would be set up here, and you'd oversee hiring the staff to work underneath you. Here is the offer letter."

Violet took it numbly. She saw she'd be getting extra pay for the three months, and it was a decent amount too. Probably enough to finance a new car. Or get the roof fixed at the house.

She read over the job description in shock. It was perfect— exactly what she wanted to do.

"I . . . I can't believe this. This is amazing," she said earnestly. "Thank you for recommending me for this."

This was incredibly rare. Not only had she not applied for it, but she didn't even interview. This was beyond luck.

"No, Ms. Moore. Thank you for being an amazing teacher," Dr. Jones said. "It may take some time, but good work always gets rewarded when I can help it."

Violet nodded at him, unable to speak without crying. She gave her boss a big, probably unprofessional hug, and headed home. She drove in total silence, still trying to process what all she had received.

She opened the door and shut it. Charlie came around the corner with his stupidly cute glasses on.

"You're back fast."

Violet could only nod.

"Oh no," Charlie said, frowning. "Was it bad news?"

Violet shook her head.

"Good?"

She silently handed him the offer letter.

"What? A summer camp program? You're *leading* it?"

"Dr. Jones offered it to me because of praise from Jason and his mother."

"Violet! This is great!" Charlie scooped her into a tight, almost crushing hug.

"I didn't even interview," Violet said after a moment. "This is *so* rare in teaching."

"But so deserved. The raise is huge, Violet."

"I can't believe it!" she said as the shock began to wear off. "With this we can fix the roof, or even *finally* upgrade the AC before summer gets here. This is great!"

"You want to spend the money on the house?" Charlie asked, looking perplexed.

"Of course," Violet said. "You said the house needs repairs, and I don't mind. I live here too."

"Right . . ." Charlie said. "We'll figure it out later. For now, we need to celebrate."

Violet had a feeling he was going to try to say the house could wait—that she should spend the money on herself, but she would gladly help him out. After all, she got to live here for basically nothing.

"We should definitely celebrate," Violet said instead of keeping the conversation going. That would be an argument for later. "What are you thinking? Maybe dinner somewhere?"

"How about a house party?"

"Are you sure?"

Charlie looked around the house. In the two months since he and Violet began dating, she had slowly made it feel more like home, hanging photos and getting decorations. These days it wasn't the empty shell of history. It was ready for new memories.

"I think so. Besides, I want people to see it. And I want people to see you."

"Okay," Violet said, feeling a blush rise to her cheeks. "Then let's have a party."

Charlie

It was Friday afternoon, and the office was done for the week. Charlie was ready to get home and back to Violet, who had already started preparing for the house party the next day. He was feeling nervous about it, a mix of good and bad. He could count on one hand the number of people he'd had over since inheriting the house.

People were filtering out of the office, and he was ready to go with them. He had gotten all he needed done for the day, and he was more than ready to start his weekend.

"I've never seen you so eager to leave," a voice said.

"Paula," Charlie replied. "You're here late."

"Oh, the bigwigs have us working on some project, but my computer's running slow. Can you help?"

Charlie sighed but figured he may as well look. The entire IT department was probably out for the weekend anyway.

"Sure," he replied. "But if it's not an easy fix, I might not be able to stay long."

"Got a hot date?"

"Kind of. More like a relaxing night before a busy weekend."

"Hm, with that girl of yours?"

"A different one, but yes, a girl."

"A new one? Wow, I never thought I'd see the day."

"What does that mean?" Charlie asked, following Paula to her office.

"Oh, just that usually when someone's not moving forward in a relationship, there's a reason."

"Plenty of people don't get married."

"Yeah, but they usually look a little less sad when they talk about their partners."

Charlie logged onto Paula's computer. "Yeah, maybe you're right."

"Well, what about this new girl?"

"Why so interested?" Charlie asked.

"Maybe I have a daughter I could set you up with. Or maybe I'm curious. Entertain an old woman."

Charlie shook his head, trying not to laugh. "She's a schoolteacher here in town. She just got offered a job as the head of a summer program for kids, so we're having a party to celebrate."

"At your place?"

"Yeah."

"Never thought I'd see the day."

"For what?" he asked as he rebooted Paula's computer.

"That you looked happy."

Charlie paused. He *was* happy these days. Violet was like a missing piece, slotting back into place within him. He had never felt so alive, so complete.

"Yeah, well . . . I am happier."

"Must be some girl."

Charlie laughed. "She is."

"I don't have a daughter by the way. I'm nosy, but I'm glad to see you look a little less sad when you talk about your girlfriend."

"It certainly feels better," Charlie replied. "Your computer is done, by the way."

"Thanks, Charlie. This is why you make the big bucks, huh?"

"Nice talking to you, Paula," he said. He smiled at her before leaving her office, more ready than ever to get home.

He hadn't stopped to think about how so much had changed. He knew it had but comparing this to how things had been six months ago was mind-boggling. He was so much happier, he was less lonely, and he felt like he truly had a life.

He used to pull into a cold and empty driveway. The lights were always off because no one was home. Now, they were on, and he could see Violet inside working on something. He could see the outlines of the new furniture they had gotten. The house was finally lived in.

"Hey," Violet said when Charlie walked into the house. "I was thinking—"

He cut her off with a kiss. Usually, he would wait for her to be done talking, but this time, it was urgent.

"What was that for?" she asked, sounding a little dazed.

"Everything you've done," Charlie said. "Forgiving me and giving me your patience. For loving my house and my life. I can't thank you enough."

"You don't have to *thank* me."

"I'm doing it anyway. You make my life better, Violet."

She blushed, and he kissed her again, savoring how she felt against him. When he finally pulled away, her eyes were half lidded.

"What were you saying?" he asked.

"Hang on, you can't come in here and kiss me like that and expect me to remember what I was saying."

"Yeah, maybe not,"

"But because I am amazing, I do remember. It was about the party tomorrow . . ."

Charlie laughed and listened, eager to help with what he could.

The next day, they finished the last-minute things for the party, and people started showing up at noon.

Charlie had never thought he would have so many people in his house.

He had never hated his home. It was the opposite. He loved it so much, and when Lauren talked it down, something in him broke, making him feel like it was something to be protected.

Now, he wanted to show it off.

The garden was finished. Violet was in one of her pink and green floral dresses, and she had cooked a ton of food for the event. She looked right at home, and Charlie wanted her to feel that way.

This was one of the first times his friends were going to see them both in their own home. Lewis still sometimes looked at them as if one of them was a land mine waiting to be triggered, but Liv had been dying to hang out with them both.

Micah was coming too, as well as Mara and her new girlfriend. Charlie tried not to be nervous, but Violet had done her best to assure him it would be okay. When people started arriving, he tried to stay calm and in a good mood.

"It looks good in here," Lewis said to him as he walked in with Liv. "It's like a totally different place."

"Wow, I can see a lot of Violet's taste in this furniture," Liv commented.

"Yeah," Charlie replied. "She picked out a lot of it, but we split who got what over time."

"I mean, I love it. I think this house is so . . . the both of you," Liv said. "It's a good thing. You guys mix well."

Charlie smiled at her, and that was when Violet came into the room holding a plate of snack foods. She set it down on the table and hugged Liv. "I'm so glad you guys made it!"

"Thank you. It looks great in here," Lewis said. "I was just telling Charlie it finally looks finished."

"It does!" Violet smiled. "I mean, it was great before, but I like how it's coming together."

"Me too," Charlie agreed with a nod.

Lewis returned the smile. "How are you two doing? Any big blowouts over . . . I don't know, curtains?"

"I don't actually have a strong opinion about curtains," Charlie said.

"I do, and that's why those are there." She pointed to the green curtains she had purchased a few weeks prior. She explained that the colors of the drapes tied together the whole room and she was unsurprisingly right.

"Those look nice," Lewis said, turning around. "I can't believe you're having a party. Charlie, are you sure you haven't been taken over by an alien?"

"Sometimes I think I have."

Violet rolled her eyes. "His house is amazing. He just needed someone to remind him."

Lewis looked at Violet and smiled. "Yeah, maybe he did need that."

"Hang on," Liv said. "We've been here too long and neither of us have said it. Violet, congrats on your promotion!"

Violet smiled and Liv brought her into a tight hug. Both talked excitedly about the future, and Charlie could only smile. He was so glad she chose him.

He glanced over at Lewis, who smiled softly at him.

"You look happy," he said.

Charlie glanced at Violet and nodded. He could only hope he would always feel this way.

Micah arrived next. She walked in and smiled at everything, telling them both it looked amazing, even if it wasn't her style. She told them how fantastic it was they were trying to move past their fighting and trying a relationship. She also mentioned she had always suspected they had a thing for each other.

Charlie could only agree because she was exactly right.

Mara arrived sometime later, her new girlfriend in tow. Violet quietly grabbed his arm and gestured to the door when they walked in.

"Hey, mom," Charlie said. His mother's jaw dropped, and she looked around in awe.

"Oh my God," his mom said, her voice wavering. "It looks so good in here."

"Hi, Ms. Davis," Violet greeted.

His mom turned to her. "Did you help him with this? Did you make this house look so lived-in?"

Violet blushed. "I mean, I wouldn't say it was *all* me, but—"

"It was all her," Charlie said without missing a beat.

"Thank you!" she exclaimed, hugging Violet tightly. "Oh, you don't know what it means to me to see this house so loved and lived-in again."

"It's a beautiful house. I just added a few things."

"Oh, she's modest too. Charlie, what were you thinking fighting with her for all those years? She's perfect!"

"I ask myself the same question every day," Charlie replied.

For the whole conversation, his mom's new girlfriend had been watching happily. She seemed interested but didn't overstep to insert herself into it.

"I'm Charlie," he said, holding out his hand. "It's really nice to meet you."

"I'm Brenda," the woman said. "Your mom is right. This place looks amazing. I can see all the love in it."

"Thank you, and I can see how much my mom cares about you too. Welcome to the family."

Brenda's eyes looked a little misty, but she smiled and stepped fully into the living room.

"Oh, honey, this is—" his mom began.

"Brenda," Charlie said, smiling. "I introduced myself while you were crying to Violet."

"I can't help it. I'm a good person to cry to," Violet said.

"Are you Violet Moore?" Brenda asked, looking curious. "The new director of the summer outreach program for the school system?"

"Yes, I am," Violet said, blushing. "Am I famous or something?"

"I wanted to talk to you about getting my grandson into your program."

Violet's eyes lit up. "Oh! I can help with that!"

While Violet talked to Brenda about the program, Charlie could only watch with a small smile on his face.

His mother elbowed him gently and said, "See? It's worth it, isn't it?"

"Yeah," was all Charlie could reply.

The party went without a hitch. Everyone got along and chatted. It was nice for Lewis and Mara to catch up. He saw Liv and Micah chatting away with Violet, and he really got to know Brenda.

He never thought this would happen, but now that it had, he was glad he took the risk.

After the party was over, it was late in the evening. Violet said goodbye to everyone on the porch, giving them all tight hugs and offering to do this again. Charlie leaned against the house, eyes fixated on her as she chatted.

Once people were finally gone, she turned and said, "That went well."

"It did."

"Did you ever think this would happen? A party at your house?"

"I never thought any of this would happen. Never in a million years."

"Me either," Violet said. "But you know what? I'm glad the ceiling caved in at my old place. I think I needed it."

Charlie reached for her and wrapped her tightly in his arms. "Yeah?"

"Yeah," she said, sounding content. "I mean, it was terrifying and I hated it, but a lot of good came from it."

"You never would have stayed here otherwise."

"You're not getting rid of me now."

Charlie stepped away from her nervously. She looked at him with a curious smile. "What?"

"I have something I want to give you." Charlie gestured for her to follow him, and walked away to their room. He had stashed the surprise in his nightstand drawer, where Violet wouldn't have seen it.

He took out the piece of paper with slightly shaky hands, not sure how Violet was going to react to what he was about to give her. He turned to her, taking a deep breath, and handed it over.

"What's this?" she asked before she even looked at it.

"It's a legal petition . . . to have you added onto the deed of the house."

Violet's eyes grew wide, and she looked down immediately.

"Charlie, this is . . ."

"You can think on it as long as you want. But think of it as a risk I'm taking with the intent of choosing you forever. This is permanent, and I'm offering this because I've seen how much you care about this place, and I want you to know you always have a home with me."

If she said yes, he could imagine their future. He'd ask her to marry him on some summer day when they're arguing about which flowers to plant, and they'd have a few kids to fill in the empty spaces of the house. He could see Violet building a treehouse in the back, and he'd read to them every single night and be the father he never had.

"Charlie, are you sure? What if we don't work out?"

"I've chosen you before, even when it's been hard, and when we've fought. This is me saying I'll always choose you."

Violet's eyes turned misty, and she nodded jerkily. "Okay . . ." she said. "I can't begin to tell you how much this means to me."

"You don't have to. You show me every day."

Violet pulled him into a hug, and he relished the feeling of her in his arms. It felt the same as the first time she had hugged him, when he had offered for her to move in. Every time she was with him, it felt like a new beginning, a new hope, making him grow and be there in every shape, form, and fashion.

It was so easy to choose her, and he always would.

Their lives started here—in the strange extension of a bedroom, with Roo running around the house, and he wouldn't have it any other way.

Acknowledgments

First, I'd like to thank my husband. You've been full of support for me, and I cannot thank you enough for taking care of the house while I worked on my dream of writing. Your support means the world.

Second, I'd like to thank Lizzie. You read an early version of this draft and helped me get motivated to edit it. I can't wait for you to read this version.

And last but certainly not least, I'd like to thank my amazing editor, Kasey. She did an incredible job of making this novel what it is. She took on an incredible challenge, and the end product was so worth it.

Every person who's taken a chance on me as an author means the world to me. Being able to write and share it with the world has always been my dream, so thank you for reading my words and making my dream come to light.

If You Liked This...

Check out Elle's other novels!

Forces of Nature

Ruth Murray thought she had seen the last of Knox Price when she walked away from him at their high school graduation.

After always coming in second place, she was ready to be done with their rivalry and make something of herself.

But then he went on to create PATH, a company that retrofitted cars to self-drive, cutting automobile accidents in half. His name was in everyone's mouths, especially her parents, who still compare her to him even ten years later. His success is a sore reminder of her own stagnant career.

When he mysteriously steps down as CEO of his company, she hopes this will be the reason he finally disappears from everyone's minds.

Until she walks into work and sees Knox is the newest executive of her company and, technically, her boss. All she can hope is that he doesn't remember their little rivalry, because he now has the power to make her life a living hell.

Knox Price should be on top of the world.

He's created an invention that saves lives, made his parents proud, shares his company with his best friend, and has more money than he knows what to do with.

And yet, he feels nothing.

He's a robot, pretending to be human but never actually feeling a thing. It's taken over his life, so much so, that his best friend suggests for him to step down and find passion in helping a different business build something great. When he returns to his hometown, he's content to spend extra time with his parents and work on a new app for a company he doesn't own.

That's when he sees the woman he could never forget.

Ruth Murray is as feisty and hardheaded as ever, and instead of feeling the emptiness he's grown used to, his heart starts beating again from the very moment he sees her.

The only problem? She hates him and he doesn't know why.

With the media clawing to get more information about him, and a ruthless boss out to fire Ruth for any reason, he should stay away from her. But the longer he's around her, the more he realizes he can't keep his distance.

Forces of Nature is a dual-POV, standalone book that will be part of an interconnected three-book series. It features the rivals to lovers, forced proximity, and only one bed trope. Spice and a HEA for the two leads is guaranteed!

Check out Elle's other novels!

Contractual Obligations

When Lily is offered a ticket out of the career and life she hates, she takes it. Even if it means signing a contract to marry the attractive but aloof Sebastian Miller for five years.

Her job is simple: play the happy house wife in person and on social media and she will get awarded a million dollars of her inheritance. That money is more than enough for her to start a life on her own and away from her controlling parents. It should be easy.

But four years in, she's more than ready to be done with this marriage. She's pretty sure her husband hates her, and she longs for the freedom the end of their contract will bring—a freedom that is threatened when she's called to meet Sebastian's father, the orchestrator of this whole sham. She worries he will try to extend their contractual marriage.

What he does is worse.

Forced to move across the country due to a promotion for Sebastian is her worst nightmare, but her only choice is to pretend to be fine.

She prepares for the last year of their marriage to be more cold indifference, but being stuck in a new city shows a sweeter side of Sebastian that Lily never thought possible. Gone is the indifferent man she knows and in his place is the kind and patient man of her dreams.

But their clock is ticking—only one year of their marriage remains. Will they find love or will contractual obligations get in the way?

Failure to Thrive

Riley Emerson is probably the last person anyone would expect to be a nanny. For starters, her life has fallen apart. Her boyfriend just cheated on her. She lives with her mom, and she might have a drinking problem.But Oliver Brian is desperate. His daughter, Zoe, has refused to go to sleep for anyone else in four years and with his career, Oliver can't always be there for her. Riley is only supposed to watch Zoe for one night, but somehow she gets Zoe to bed on her own. He's so shocked that he offers her a job on the spot.Riley needs the money, and Oliver needs the time for himself. It's a match made in Heaven... until feelings get involved.

Failure to Thrive is a full length romance novel with the nanny, single father, and friends to lovers trope. This version has three spicy scenes!

About the Author

Elle Rivers lives in Nashville, Tennessee with her husband, son, and seven cats. When not writing, she can be found at her day job, or out walking in nature. Her Twitter is Elleswrites, Tiktok is AuthorElleRivers or ElleRiversAuthor, and her Instagram is Elleswrites. If you would like more, please consider subscribing to Elle's mailing list for bonus content, including extra scenes and future announcements about novels. Subscribe at elleriversauthor.mailerlite.io/subscribe.